The Dark Clue

James Wilson read History at Oxford University. He has written plays, TV documentaries (including the award winning *Savagery and the American Indian* for the BBC) and a critically acclaimed history of Native Americans, *The Earth Shall Weep*, published by Picador and Grove/Atlantic. *The Dark Clue* is his first novel.

by the same author

THE EARTH SHALL WEEP: A History of Native America

The Dark Clue

JAMES WILSON

faber and faber

First published in 2001
by Faber and Faber Limited
3 Queen Square London WC1N 3AU
This open market edition published in 2001

Typeset by Faber and Faber Ltd
Printed by Mackays of Chatham plc, Chatham, Kent

© James Wilson, 2001

The right of James Wilson to be identified as author of this
work has been asserted in accordance with Section 77 of the
Copyright, Designs and Patents Act 1998

A CIP record for this book
is available from the British Library

ISBN 0-571-21043-0

2 4 6 8 10 9 7 5 3 1

For Paula
and for my mother, Tom and Kit
with love

Limmeridge, Cumberland,
21st January, 186—

This is a book begun, but not finished.

I could not finish it.

Many times I have come close to destroying it, thinking I should have no rest while it remained to reproach me.

I could not bring myself to do it.

I have therefore given instructions that it should be sealed in a box, which is to remain unopened until I, my wife, Laura, our sister, Marian Halcombe, and all our children are dead.

As I write these words, the man whose story I set out to tell has already answered for his life in the highest court of all. Before you read them, I shall have followed him there, and made answer for my own.

Remember, as you judge us, that you shall stand there too.

WH

Book One

I

Letter from Walter Hartright to Laura Hartright, 18th July, 185–

Brompton Grove,
Tuesday

My dearest love,

I hope you're sitting down as you read this, for I have strange news. (But don't be alarmed – *good* news, I think!) I've no time to confide it both to you and to my journal, so please keep this letter – as you'll see, I may have need of it later.

First, though, a coincidence. You are, in a way, responsible for it, for it arose from my mood yesterday, when you left. I was so melancholy at the sight of your dear faces drawing away from me that it was all I could do to stop myself jumping on to the train, and I must own that, afterwards, I cried. Feeling unequal to explaining my tears to a cabman, I decided to walk home.

As I started west along the New Road, I suddenly saw it, as I have never seen it before, as a scene from hell: the clatter of the horses; the stench of their ordure; a crossing-sweeper nearly knocked down by a brushmaker's wagon; a woman crying 'Stunning oranges!', yet so drearily you could tell she had lost all hope of selling her handful of pitifully wizened fruit, and so providing something for her child's supper; a boy turning carter-wheels, and the men on the roof of an omnibus tossing halfpennies and farthings at him, and then guffawing as he fell into the gutter. And everywhere a yellow, choking haze, so thick that, even in the middle of the morning, you could not see more than fifty paces. And all the while a stream of tilers' carts and brick merchants' drays rattling by with provisions for the armies of new houses which daily carry this new Babylon

3

still further into the lanes and meadows of Middlesex. Even as I rejoiced that you and the children would soon be breathing purer air and seeing lovelier sights, I felt myself alone and trapped inside some great engine from which all beauty, all joy and colour and mystery, had been banished.

This feeling so oppressed me that I quickly turned off and started to zig-zag through the maze of little streets and alleys to the west of Tottenham Court Road. My principle was simple enough: so long as I continued a certain distance west, and then a certain distance south, I must eventually come to Oxford Street, and avoid getting badly lost. And so it was that I crossed Portland Place (where, all those years ago, my journey to you so improbably began), entered a mean, dusty little court hung with dripping laundry that was already smudged with soot, and suddenly emerged into a street of handsome old-fashioned houses that seemed oddly familiar. But it was not the familiarity of everyday: rather the ghostly brilliance of some long-lost childish memory, or of something glimpsed once in a dream. I stood for perhaps two minutes, surveying the line of dark windows and blackened brickwork and heavy brass-handled doors. When and why had I seen them before? What was the original, of which they were such a plangent echo? Try as I might, I could not find it. All I noted was that my mind seemed somehow to associate it with feelings of powerlessness and smallness and a kind of awe.

Still musing, I set off again. After fifty yards or so I noticed a boy of eight or nine skulking in the area of one of the houses. His cap was too large for him and his jacket too small, and he wore an odd pair of boots, one black and one brown. As I turned towards him, he shrank back against the damp wall and looked up at me with the terrified stare of a cornered animal. As much to allay his fear as to satisfy my own curiosity, I called down to him:

'What street is this?'

'Queen Anne Street,' he replied.

I was none the wiser: I recognized the name, but could not recall anyone I knew ever having lived there. I took a penny from my pocket and held out my hand.

'Thank you,' I said.

He cowered like a dog, torn between hunger for a scrap of meat and dread of being kicked.

'It's all right,' I said. 'I won't hurt you.'

He hesitated a moment, before scuttling up the steps and taking the coin. Then, instead of running off as I had expected, he gazed wonderingly at me, as if even so small an act of kindness lay entirely beyond his knowledge and understanding of life. His eyes, I saw, were unhealthily large, and the pale skin was drawn into the hollows of his cheeks, as if age could not wait to put its mark upon him. And suddenly I thought of little Walter, and of the horror I should feel if I looked into *his* face and saw there such a world of want and pain and sickness. So I gave the boy six-pence more, and without a word he was gone, as if he feared that in another moment the spell would break, and the natural order of things would reassert itself, and I would change my mind and take the money back again.

And that is my coincidence. I already hear you saying: 'Walter! I see no coincidence'; but you shall, my love, I promise, if only you will be patient and read on.

I was in Brompton Grove again by three minutes to twelve. It was a sombre homecoming. The small things that spoke of our happy life here together looked already out of place, like a doll or a bonnet washed up on a beach. In the few brief hours since we'd left, the house had been occupied by an alien spirit, which now resented the return of the previous tenant. Whenever I entered a room, I seemed to feel its presence, like a silent wind, propelling me back towards the door.

5

Marian was still out, and only the distant murmur of the Davidsons' voices in the kitchen told me I was not entirely alone. I felt as lost and mopish as a child. I tried to draw, but could not settle to it. After ten minutes I laid aside my pencil and took up a book, only to set it down again ten minutes later. The lunch bell promised a welcome diversion, until I found myself sitting in solitary state in the dining room like an oriental despot, with Davidson hovering near as if I might need help raising the fork to my mouth. I sent him away, saying I could take care of myself and would ring if I needed anything, and then kept the poor fellow running up and down stairs with my demands for fresh water and more mustard.

When I had finished, I went into the garden, where the workmen were marking the foundations for the new studio, and solemnly reiterated all manner of things – that I must have a north light, that the entrance must be sheltered from the weather – that they knew perfectly well already from the plans. And it was here that Marian found me when she came home, and saved them from me, and me from myself.

'You cannot possibly come like that!' were her first words, delivered in such a forthright tone that the three workmen started. But she was smiling, and her black eyes shone. 'You look like a man who has walked across half London.'

'Come where?' I said.

'Why, to Lady Eastlake's,' she said, more quietly, drawing me towards the house. 'She was at the exhibition this morning, and afterwards I had lunch with her, and we talked of Laura's going away today, and my staying. And so, by a natural progression, of you.' She took my arm, and led me indoors. 'And she asked most particularly that I should bring you to meet her this afternoon.'

I was immediately struck by the notion that this might

6

have something to do with my painting: Sir Charles is, after all, Director of the National Gallery, and I confess that for a wild moment I imagined him emerging from behind a screen in his wife's drawing room and saying: 'Ah, Hartright, I much admired *The Artist's Wife and Children at Limmeridge, in Cumberland* at the Academy this year, and would like to buy it for the nation.' I soon recognized this pitiable fantasy for what it was, however, and concluded that Marian, as good and kind as ever, was merely hoping to distract me from my separation by introducing me to one of her blue-stocking friends.

As it turned out, neither explanation was remotely as strange as the truth.

Has Marian ever described the Eastlakes' house to you? It's too late now for me to ask her (after midnight, and she must be asleep) – so, if she has, simply pass over the next paragraph.

They live in one of those fine old stone houses in Fitzroy Square (here and there on the walls you can still see patches of the original honey gold peering through the grime), with lofty windows and a front door big enough to take a horse. As we arrived, a fashionably dressed woman in a fur-trimmed jacket and a tiny pill-box hat garnished with feathers flounced down the steps (in so far as you can flounce when you are imprisoned from the waist down in a giant birdcage) and into a waiting carriage. There were angry spots on her cheeks, and she barely acknowledged us as we passed.

The front door was opened by a tall footman with grey hair and thick dark eyebrows. Marian addressed him with a natural ease which surprised me.

'Good afternoon, Stokes. Is your mistress at home?'

'She is, ma'am.' He led us through a wide hall lined with marble busts and upstairs to a large drawing room. It was furnished in the modern style, with a heavy Turkey carpet, a set of carved oak chairs, and rows of watercolours jammed together on the green walls like carriages in Piccadilly. Above the picture-rail ran a line of Japanese plates (*really* made in Japan, I fancy, and not in Stafford!), and over the fireplace was a large classical landscape which, from its treaclish colouring, I took to be one of Sir Charles's own.

As we entered, a strikingly tall woman rose from a chaise longue in the window. For a moment she was held in silhouette by the evening light, and the only distinctive feature I could make out was her head, which tilted oddly to one side, like a bird's. As she came towards us, however, I saw that she was about fifty, wearing a soft green dress edged with braid, and with her still-dark hair pulled simply back into a net. She had a wide, uneven mouth that broke into a frank smile as she held out her hand.

'Marian,' she said. 'You must have winged feet.' Her voice was soft but clear, and I thought I detected a trace of a Scotch accent. She turned to the footman. 'Thank you, Stokes. If anyone else should call, I am not at home.' She touched Marian's hand and smiled sidelong at me. 'Did you have to rope him, and drag him to a cab, to make him come?'

Marian laughed. 'Lady Eastlake, this is my brother – well, my *half*-brother-in-law – Walter Hartright.'

'*Half* in-law,' said Lady Eastlake, laughing. 'How very complicated. I'm delighted to see you, Mr. Hartright. How do you do?' As we shook hands, she glanced about her, as if suddenly dissatisfied with where she was. 'I think we'll be more comfortable in my *boudoir*' – she gave the word an ironic inflection which made Marian laugh – 'if you will forgive the clutter.'

She walked to the back of the room and threw open a pair of folding doors. Beyond them lay a light, pleasant,

8

informal parlour, with a tall window overlooking the garden. The immediate impression was more that of an Oxford don's study than of a lady's sitting room. A range of bookcases, some crammed with books, others with what appeared simply to be stacks of papers, ran along the walls. In the corner was a bureau, the lid wedged half open by a cascade of notes and letters; on each side of the fireplace stood a large cabinet containing rocks, shells, pieces of broken pottery and half an Etruscan head; while in the centre (strangest of all) was a large mahogany table, entirely covered with more photographs than I have ever seen together in one place in my life. Despite myself, I could not stop my eyes straying across them in search of a unifying theme or a familiar image. In the first I failed, for the subjects seemed as various as life itself – portraits, a country cottage, a great mill veiled by the smoke from its own black chimney – but in the second I was successful, for there, between a haystack and a blurred carthorse, I quickly recognized a picture of Lady Eastlake herself.

She must have been watching me, for as I stooped to look at it more closely she said sharply:

'Well, Mr. Hartright, what do you think?'

'It is a fair likeness,' I said, equivocally; for I feared that, like so many people, she might resent the camera's merciless exposure of every blot and blemish, and feel it did her beauty less than justice.

'I mean', she said, 'about photography.'

'Well . . . ,' I began. I did not know how to go on, for, truth to tell, it is not something to which I have given much thought at all; but I did not wish to cause offence, either by seeming too cool, or by too warmly offering an opinion that might differ from her own. She spared me by continuing:

'Do you practise yourself?'

'No,' I replied. 'I still prefer pencil and brush.'

'And why is that, Mr. Hartright?'

This inquisition was so far from what I had expected that I was forced to consider for a moment. At length I said:

'Because it seems to me that photography can merely record facts.'

She gave me not an instant's respite. 'Whereas your pencil . . .?'

'Whereas a pencil should, I hope – in the right hands – be able to hint at the truth. Which is not perhaps the same thing.'

She fixed me with an inscrutable stare, from which I could not judge whether she thought me mad, dull, or fascinatingly original. Then she opened the bureau gingerly, to prevent the overflowing papers from spilling on to the floor, and took out a small notebook and pencil. 'Do you mind if I make a note of that?' she said, already writing. 'I am doing an article.'

'So,' said Marian, with a teasing familiarity, which again took me by surprise, 'prepare to see your words in the next issue of the *Quarterly Review*.'

Lady Eastlake laughed. 'Not unacknowledged,' she said. 'Whatever else I am, I am not a pickpocket. Besides, what makes you suppose I should want to claim Mr. Hartright's thoughts as my own?'

She put the notebook away and sat in an armchair by the fireplace, gesturing Marian to the seat next to her. She sighed, shut her eyes and sank back, in a dumbshow of tiredness. I wondered if this were some further comment on what I had said, and, despite myself, felt the heat rising to my cheeks.

'Forgive me,' said Lady Eastlake. 'I've just had to endure a duty call from Mrs. Madison. Did you see her as you came in?'

'There was a lady leaving,' said Marian.

'She can only have been here for a quarter of an hour, but it felt like three days. My stock of conversation on children's clothes is soon exhausted, I'm afraid. I did try venturing on to the weather, but even that turned out too mettlesome for her.'

Stokes entered, carrying a tea tray. He set it down on a low table by Lady Eastlake's chair. She watched warily, her head cocked, until he was out of sight again; then she went on, more quietly:

'She's one of those women who believe that a member of her own sex should have no views on anything. And certainly *never* read a book. In which, I must say, she sets a splendid example.'

Marian laughed. Lady Eastlake started to pour the tea, then put the pot down and touched Marian's arm. 'That's why I so enjoy your sister's company, Mr. Hartright. Someone to keep pace with me. She always has something fresh and interesting to say, no matter where my runaway mind has led me.'

'I know how deeply she values *your* friendship, Lady Eastlake,' I said. 'I'm afraid that in our house she must often feel the want of an intellectual companion.'

'Oh, that's not true, Walter!' burst in Marian.

'It is not what she tells me,' said Lady Eastlake. 'You write, do you not, Mr. Hartright?'

I had just handed Marian a cup and was leaning down to take one myself. Lady Eastlake's face was barely two feet from my own, and I felt the full power of her steady gaze. Again, it was impossible to avoid the sense that I was being interrogated – although to what purpose I could not begin to imagine.

'I have written a book,' I replied. 'But it is no more than the history of a conspiracy against my wife, which my own experience qualified me to narrate. Perhaps it would be truer to call me a chronicler than a writer.'

Lady Eastlake nodded.

'Or even an editor,' I went on. 'For, wherever possible, I

told the story through the words of those who were closest to the events described, and thus best able to give a true account of them. Including Marian, whose journal was an invaluable source of information.'

I glanced at Marian. I had expected her to gainsay me: *What nonsense, Walter: you are far too modest.* Instead, she was watching me intently, her dark complexion flushed with excitement. As I turned back to Lady Eastlake, I saw, out of the corner of my eye, the table laden with photographs.

'You could say', I continued, 'that I aspire to art in my painting. Whereas . . .'

'Whereas in writing,' said Lady Eastlake, 'you are a camera, perhaps?'

'Exactly,' I said. I was taken aback, both by her acuity and by her rudeness in interrupting me. I looked again at Marian: she was smiling at Lady Eastlake, as if to say: *There, I told you so.* The idea that there might be some secret understanding between them, of which I was the unwitting object, unsettled me.

'May I ask', I said (with, I own, a certain iciness), 'if this is tending towards some end?'

Lady Eastlake did not answer at once. She exchanged another furtive glance with Marian, then took a handkerchief from her sleeve and carefully smoothed it on her lap. At length she cleared her throat and said:

'Mr. Hartright, would you mind closing the doors?'

I did so. She went on:

'I would not, of course, expect you to keep anything from your wife; but I must begin by asking that you do not mention this conversation to anyone else.'

I felt I could not accept this condition without knowing more, but was hard put to find a delicate way of saying so. She must have seen what was in my mind; for she said:

'Och, you needn't worry about your honour, Mr.

Hartright. I'm not going to confess to a murder, or the theft of a child. Besides, your sister's presence in this room should give you assurance enough.'

I felt the justice of this, and nodded. She continued:

'My only concern is to protect my husband. His position – which God knows he never sought – is difficult enough already, and the last thing I want to do is stir up a hornets' nest around his poor head.'

'Very well,' I said.

'Thank you.' She looked warily towards the door, and when she spoke it was in little more than a whisper. 'Do you by any chance know a man called Thornbury?'

'No,' I replied. 'Who is he?'

'A journalist,' she said. 'And, I fear, an utter scoundrel.'

'That is not surprising,' I said. 'A cynic might say that, to be the one, it is almost a requirement to be the other.'

Lady Eastlake laughed. 'I have not myself met him,' she said, 'but, so far as I have been able to learn from my friends, he is intent – for no other reason than to sell the wretched book he is writing – on slandering a poor, misunderstood body who can no longer defend himself. And the result, I'm afraid, will be a serious injury, not only to the memory of one man, but to England herself, and to English art. For his subject was – in my view, and the view of many others – the foremost genius of our age.'

And it was then, with the force of a sprung trap, that the image of Queen Anne Street re-entered my mind, and, in the same instant, I knew why it was familiar. For a moment I was a boy of eight again, and sitting in a cab next to my poor father; the winter cold turned our breath to steam, and I huddled close to him, for in his thick coat he was an island of warmth and safety. As we jolted past a tall house with dirty windows and a heavy front door, he laid his gloved hand on mine and pointed out of the window. 'Look, Walter,' he said. 'That is 47 Queen Anne Street.

13

Where the foremost genius of our age lives.'

And now, in the space of six hours, I had walked down the same street and heard the same phrase again for the first time in thirty years. Without stopping to consider, I said to Lady Eastlake: 'Do you mean Turner?'

It was her turn to be astonished. She stared at me, her mouth half open, then looked at Marian. 'Have you . . .?'

Marian was equally perplexed. 'No,' she said. 'I said nothing. Walter, how did you . . .?'

I confess I was tempted to confound them further by pretending to some mysterious knowledge, but I merely said: 'Oh, it was just a guess.' And then, to forestall more questions (for both of them still looked puzzled), I went on: 'So is Mr. Thornbury writing Turner's biography?'

'That is what he claims.'

'But if you have never met him,' I said, 'how do you know it is defamatory?'

'I have been following his progress, Mr. Hartright – with, I have to say, a sinking heart. A few of those closest to Turner have, wisely, refused to speak to him at all. Of the rest, he appears to have given most credence to a gang of malicious gossips, most of whom scarcely knew the man. And they, as is the way with these things, have in turn referred him to more of their own kind.'

I must own that my first thought was the old adage: *There's no smoke without fire*. Perhaps she saw my scepticism, for she went on:

'No man as eminent as Turner could avoid making enemies among those less successful or less gifted than himself – particularly a man with such a thoroughgoing disdain of flattery and convention. You've probably heard all manner of stories about him yourself.'

Her raised eyebrow seemed to demand an answer, but I said nothing, for – beyond a few hoary old anecdotes about his meanness, and his garbled speech, that are common

14

currency at the Academy – in reality I was shamefully ignorant about him. She waited a moment, and then continued:

'He was, it cannot be denied, an odd, perverse, eccentric
little creature, but he was not a monster, and he deserves
better than to be commemorated by tittle-tattle.' She leaned
confidentially towards me. 'I came to know him well in his
last years. Indeed' – here her voice grew unsteady, and her
eyes glittered with tears – 'I am told that as he lay dying he
called my name. Which I cannot but feel as a charge upon
me. To try to protect his memory.' She hastily dried her
eyes, then clenched her handkerchief into a ball. 'Mr.
Hartright, what I am asking . . . what I am suggesting . . . is
that you might yourself consider undertaking to write a *Life
of J. M. W. Turner.*'

For perhaps three seconds I was, literally, speechless
with astonishment. A thousand questions crowded into my
head, and then flew off again before I could find words to
express them. I was conscious of Marian's gaze upon me –
watchful, anxious, almost pleading – and the sense that *her*
hopes and happiness were, in some way I could not yet
fathom, bound up with my reply, only confused me further. Perhaps Lady Eastlake mistook my perplexity for calculation, for she said:

'I have spoken to a publisher I know, and am assured
that there would be a ready market for such a book . . .'

'That is not my concern. I –'

'And I'm sure I speak for all of Turner's friends when I
say we should be happy to underwrite it . . .' She broke off,
suddenly noting that I was following another train of
thought. 'What?' she said. 'You think there must be others
better placed?'

I nodded. 'What about yourself, for instance?'

'As I explained, my connection to Sir Charles . . . Besides,
there are many doors closed to a woman that a man may
pass through easily and freely.'

'I cannot believe –' I began.

'What you must understand, Mr. Hartright, is that poor Turner died a recluse,' said Lady Eastlake. 'Most of those who knew him well are long dead. Of those who are still alive, Mr. Ruskin would seem to be the natural choice, but he' – here she smiled slightly – 'is too Olympian to contemplate it. My situation you already know. And as for my husband – well, it's entirely out of the question, I'm afraid.'

'Oh, I can quite see that,' I said. 'But –'

She appeared not to have heard me.

'Both Mrs. Booth, Turner's housekeeper, and his friend George Jones are good-hearted people, but . . .' She paused, and shook her head. 'Well, frankly, neither of them is equal to it. And Mr. Jones, I believe, in any case now spends most of his time dressing up as the Duke of Wellington. At best, they might both furnish you with useful memoirs.'

She paused, and again I found myself at a loss for words. It was Marian who broke the silence:

'There *is* no-one else, Walter. If you won't do it, Thornbury will carry the day unopposed.'

'And do not underestimate yourself, Mr. Hartright,' said Lady Eastlake. 'Unlike Thornbury, you are an artist, who will understand the painter in Turner . . .'

I cried – I could not stop myself – 'You cannot compare –!'

'He may have been a general, and you – forgive me – only a colonel,' replied Lady Eastlake. 'But all artists belong to the same regiment, and fight the same battles, and crave the same victory. And then', she went on, before I could protest further, 'you are also, by your own admission, a chronicler, who knows how to gather and evaluate and compile the accounts of different witnesses.'

'And a crusader, who has already proven his determination to right a great wrong,' said Marian.

Lady Eastlake nodded. 'Who could be more ideal?'

They were quiet then, leaving me to ponder what they

16

had said. I tried, again, to impose some order on my own jangled thoughts, but they all – save one, which rang through my head with the clarity of a bell – remained in turmoil. At length Marian said:

'This is all so unexpected for poor Walter that I think we must allow him some time to consider his response.'

'Yes, of course,' said Lady Eastlake.

And so we left it. No more mention of the idea was made, and, after exchanging the usual pleasantries for a few minutes, Marian and I rose to go. Only as Stokes ushered us from the room did Lady Eastlake say:

'I may expect to hear from you soon, I hope, Mr. Hartright?'

*

We barely spoke on the way home. I was still trying to marshal my own thoughts, which were all of you and the children, and of how our lives would change if I accepted Lady Eastlake's strange proposal; but I was constantly deflected by waves of wild emotion – dread, and a kind of dizzy exhilaration, in about equal measure – which I could not trace confidently to their source, but which seemed to gush unbidden from some hidden spring in my mind.

Marian, for her part, was uncharacteristically constrained. I thought little of it at the time, beyond merely remarking the fact; but now I think she must have taken my silence to mean that I was angry; for when we were back in our own drawing room, and had shut the door, she laid a hand lightly on my arm and said:

'I do hope, Walter, that you don't think I did wrong.'

'What,' I said, 'to invite me to Lady Eastlake's?'

'Not that,' she said. 'But to invite you without telling you the reason. She insisted that you should know nothing until she had met you, and could decide for herself whether you would be suitable. But when I saw you sitting there, so bewildered, it made me feel a traitor. Or, rather, made me

17

feel that *you* would think me a traitor.'

Poor Marian! 'I was taken aback, I must own,' I said. 'But I never suspected you of treachery, or doubted that you had my best interests at heart.'

'I'm glad.' She was silent for a moment, looking down at her bag and toying with the string. Then, as if she had decided at last to say something that had long been on her mind, she burst out: 'May we talk frankly, Walter?'

'Nothing I have ever known could prevent you talking frankly, once you were set on it,' I said. 'And I'm quite certain that it lies beyond *my* power to stop you.'

She laughed, and her voice had regained some of its old gaiety as she replied: 'I said "we", not "I".'

'Very well,' I said.

We sat together on the sofa. It was dusk, but neither of us suggested lighting the gas. Perhaps we both felt that it would be easier to open our hearts if our faces, at least, were veiled by the deepening gloom. At length she said:

'Many years ago I told you that we should always be friends, Walter, did I not?'

'Yes,' I said, taking her hand. 'And so we shall.'

'I hope so,' she said. 'At any rate, that is the spirit in which I now speak. You may think me impertinent; but please believe that I am prompted only by sisterly love for you and Laura.'

'Of course I believe it,' I said. 'I've never been surer of anything in my life.' And nor had I; but, notwithstanding, I waited with trepidation to hear what she would say next. A whole army of butterflies seemed to have taken up residence in my stomach, and my legs were so leaden that, if Davidson had rushed in at that moment shouting 'Fire! Fire!', I doubt whether they would have carried me to the door.

'Thank you,' said Marian. She breathed deeply, then went on: 'You know that, living as close together as we do, we cannot help noticing the smallest changes in each other's moods?'

'Yes,' I said.

'Well,' she said, 'recently I think I have noticed such a change in you. You have become restless, and distracted. You paint and draw less than you did. And, while you are still as loving a husband and father and brother as ever, I sometimes think it is with a greater effort than previously. As if . . . as if you have to bring yourself back from some other place in order to be with us.'

'It's difficult for me to paint here,' I said, 'until the studio is finished. And I have, as you know, been very taken up with planning it, and overseeing the work.'

'The want of a studio never stopped you painting before,' she said. 'And you may, I think, safely leave building it to the workmen. They do not require you to go out twenty times a day and tell them their job.'

I remembered where she had found me that afternoon, and was glad the darkness hid my blushes.

'No,' she went on, 'we must look for a deeper cause. And I think I know what it is.'

~~I need not burden you~~

I wish I could spare you what she said next; for it must inevitably hurt you, and make you think worse of me. But it is the truth, and you must know it – else you will cease to know *me*.

'Dear Walter,' she said, in a quieter, tenderer voice. 'You are the victim of your own sensitive nature. No-one else, knowing all the circumstances, could possibly accuse you of having benefited improperly from marrying Laura, and sharing the fortune which eventually became hers. Yet that, if I am right, is the charge with which you torment yourself. You know that your conduct has always been beyond reproach, and that you have brought her more happiness than she ever knew in her life. And yet, and yet, and yet . . .

19

You still harbour the faint suspicion that you have some-how become a pensioner, and it is an agony to you.'

I opened my mouth to speak; but, in truth, I could not find the strength to deny it. In a moment, she had cast a light into some dark corner of my being and found a canker to which, until now, I had been unable to give a name.

'Worse still,' she continued, 'you feel a certain vacancy at the centre of your life. You have everything that, in the eyes of the world, should make a man happy: a gentle and loving wife, two beautiful children, a fine estate, and the regard of your brother artists. Yet something is lacking: a *cause* capable of stirring your soul, and carrying you beyond the concerns of family and home.'

I nodded, and I think she must have seen me; for I felt her hand tightening on mine. 'It is nothing to be ashamed of,' she said. 'It is just that, like all noble natures, you know that family and home themselves are meaningless, unless they stand in relation to some greater purpose.'

Outside, a wagon squealed and rumbled across the cobbles. I clutched at the sound gratefully, and wrapped it about me like a cloak; for my eyes were full of tears.

'For months,' said Marian, 'I have been looking for some way to relieve you. And that is why my heart leapt when Lady Eastlake told me of her anguish over Turner's life, for here at last, it seemed, was a great purpose you were perfectly fitted to fulfil.' She paused, and then went on: 'You know, I hope, that I will gladly help you, as I did once before, when fate enlisted us in the same struggle. Dear Walter, please say you will do it!'

Once, many years ago – do you remember? – I called Marian our good angel; and so she is, for like an angel she seems to know what is best and truest in us better than we know it ourselves.

For some moments I could not speak; and when I did, all I could say was: 'Thank you.'

And so, my love, tomorrow I shall write to Lady
Eastlake, telling her that, on certain conditions, I accept.
And the upshot (if she agrees) is that you will have to get to
know me in yet another character. Drawing master, detective, husband, clerk of works – and now, of all things, biographer!

It is late here, and cold. I shall go to bed, and hold to myself
the pillow that still bears the smell of your skin and hair.

Good night,

Walter

II

Memorandum of a letter from Walter Hartright to
Lady Eastlake, 19th July, 185–

1. Thank you for your invitation; great pleasure finally
   to meet you.
2. After consideration, delighted to accept your proposal
   that I should write a *Life of J. M. W. Turner*.
3. Must, however, make one stipulation: respect your
   feelings towards Turner, but neither they, nor wish to
   thwart Thornbury, can be my guide. Shall do no
   more, and no less, than try to discover truth (which in
   biography *must*, I think, be same as facts!). Go where
   trail leads me, without fear or favour. Cannot
   promise, therefore, to paint portrait you wish.
4. Hope you will forgive bluntness, but important to be
   clear at outset in order to avoid misunderstanding
   later.

III

Letter from Lady Eastlake to Walter Hartright,
19th July, 185–

7 Fitzroy Square,
Wednesday

My dear Mr. Hartright,

Many thanks for your letter of this morning, and for so promptly putting an end to my unease.

I am very glad that you feel able to act on my suggestion, and will give you what assistance I can. And yes – of course I accept that Truth must be your only master. I would, indeed, expect no less; and, had I suspected for a moment that you would be deflected from your purpose by partisan considerations, I should not have asked you to undertake a task which so clearly requires the greatest integrity.

I hope, nonetheless, that you will not feel I am trying to influence you improperly if I recommend that – whomever else you may talk to – you should begin by approaching Mr. Ruskin, Mr. Jones and Mrs. Booth. I have given their addresses to Marian, with this letter, and I will write to Mr. Jones and Mrs. Booth myself this evening, telling them that they may expect to hear from you. Since I know that Mrs. Booth refused to speak to Mr. Thornbury, it occurs to me that – in the first instance, at least – Marian, as another woman, might have more success in winning her confidence and securing her co-operation. As to Mr. Ruskin – I fear a letter from me would not help your case, so you must take courage and disturb the great man yourself.

Yours most truly,

Eliz. Eastlake

IV

Letter from Walter Hartright to Laura Hartright, 20th July, 185–

The Reading Room, British Museum Library,
Thursday

My dearest love,

Thank you for your letter, and for Florrie's and Walter's drawings – they will soon outstrip their father if I do not look to my laurels!

Yesterday I wrote to Ruskin and to George Jones, R.A., but have received no reply from either of them. Not wishing to be idle, therefore, I have taken myself – as you can see from the address – to the new Reading Room at the British Museum Library. (It is, by the by, a prodigious building, which seems to me to belong almost to a new order of object; large and hushed and awe-inspiring enough to be a great cathedral, and yet erected not as a temple to God, but rather to our knowledge of His creation. Was such a thing ever attempted before? In Alexandria, perhaps; but what mankind then knew of the world was puny by comparison. Here, in London, for the first time, the Tree of the Knowledge of Good and Evil has been raised up in bricks and mortar; and who knows whether it will prove a blessing or a curse?)

My aim here has been to find out what I can of Turner – and, from what I have discovered so far, I think my life of him will be quick work indeed. He was born, in London, in 1775, on St. George's Day; he drew; he painted; he died. That, in essence – save for a few incidentals, such as his journeys in this country and in Europe – is more or less all we know, at the ordinary humdrum level. He never married; never fought a duel; never fomented a revolution; never declared his love for a princess – a million

23

Englishmen must have lived such lives, and none but their families and friends thought them worthy of a second glance. All that marks Turner out is his fanatical dedication to his art, which makes for sublime paintings, but leaves only meagre pickings for a biographer. I begin to feel sorry for poor Thornbury, who has perhaps resorted to slander in a desperate attempt to make the thin gruel of his narrative more palatable.

It is for this reason that, while I understand your anxiety, I believe it to be groundless. There will, of course, be unexpected difficulties, and I must not underestimate them, but I am sure that our separation need only be prolonged by two or three weeks – and if I thought otherwise I should, I promise you, write to Lady Eastlake this instant, telling her that I had changed my mind. Turner's close acquaintance was, it seems, pitifully small, and is now much depleted by death; and seeing the few friends who are left (assuming *they* will see *me*!) should take only a matter of days. After that, I shall have to seek out diaries, letters and so on to help me – particularly for the early years, for which there are presumably no living witnesses at all; but then I should be able to return to Limmeridge with my booty, and do most of the work there. Although I may have to come back once or twice in the interim, just for a few days, I'm sure I shall then be safe in Cumberland until we all return to London together next season.

So please, my dearest – don't worry! And let me end with a worry of my own: I was delighted to hear that you have been visiting our favourite haunts on the moor, but do you think, in your present condition, it is wise to walk so far, particularly when you have no companion to help you, should need arise? Please – be careful.

Your devoted husband,

Walter

V

Letter from Walter Hartright to Laura Hartright, 1st August, 185–

Brompton Grove,
Tuesday

My dearest love,

Your letter reached me this morning. Thank you! I confess I was hoping it might arrive in company, for over the last few days I have felt powerless to do more on the *Life* until I have heard from Jones and Ruskin (with the result that, to Davidson's evident annoyance, I have taken to anticipating the post by pacing about the house like a caged wolf awaiting the full moon).

But your words galvanized me into action; and as soon as I had finished reading them I at once resolved to go on the offensive, and try to find my own way into Turner's world. I confess I had no very clear idea of how, or where, I should begin (I think at the back of my mind was the notion that if all else failed I could end up at the Athenaeum, where I might happen upon someone who recollected him): my aim was merely to set out, and see where the day took me. And – although it may seem fanciful – I think my faith was rewarded.

Hyde Park was even more thronged than usual, but by avoiding the carriage-ways, and following the narrowest paths through clumps of bushes and over grassy rises, I was sometimes able, for a moment, to imagine myself not in the centre of the greatest city on earth but in some pleasant rural Eden. My way brought me at length through a fringe of trees and out by the Serpentine, which – as if pressed flat by the heavy sky – lay as still as a newly poured bath, glowing with the surly sheen of pewter.

Around the shore, as their nurses looked on, children played with hoops and sticks, or put dolls to sleep in their own perambulators, or chased after a silly dog (a bundle of white curls, with no discernible face) which had made off with a ball and chewed it half to pieces. One little boy was wailing inconsolably, and I stopped to ask him the matter.

'I've lost my duck,' he sobbed, pointing to a little wooden pintail, which had bobbed out of reach and seemed to be trying to join the real ducks in the middle of the lake.

It was here that fate first took a hand; for I went back to the trees, broke off a small branch, and (after a good deal of getting it, and losing it, and getting it again) managed to retrieve the toy, and return it to its owner. And had it not been for this small delay, I should not still have been there five minutes later, when a voice suddenly called out:

'Hartright!'

I turned, and could not for a moment identify the fashionably dressed young man who had broken from the crowd and was advancing smiling towards me. It was only when he pointed to the stick that still hung dripping from my hand, and said, laughing, 'What? Trying to catch dinner?' that I knew him by his voice.

'Travis!' I said.

It was no wonder that I had not recognized him, for he had grown a beard, and, instead of his usual get-up, was sporting a check waistcoat and a new soft felt hat. He carried a large portfolio, which he pinioned under his arm while he removed a flawless yellow glove and shook my hand.

'Where are you going?' we both said together, and laughed.

'Sir William Butteridge,' he said. He tried to sound nonchalant, but his face shone, and in struggling to suppress his smile he distorted his next words so much that all I could make out was '. . . discuss a . . .'

26

'A *what*?'

'A commission.'

'Really? That's wonderful!' I said. And I was, needless to say, truly delighted for him; but I cannot deny that I felt a pang of envy, too, swiftly followed by satisfaction at the recollection of my own commission, and as swiftly again by frustration that I was sworn to secrecy, and could not, therefore, counter 'Sir William Butteridge' with 'Lady Eastlake'.

'Is it in there?' I asked, nodding towards the portfolio.

'Just a few sketches. You want to see?'

He laid the portfolio on a bench and opened it. Inside were some rough drawings of a sickly-looking young woman with flowing hair clutching a broken column for support. 'She's swooning at the sight of her lover,' Travis explained, pointing at a vague blob on the left-hand side, 'who is returning, mortally wounded, after a seven-year absence. Faith and Purity, that's what Sir William wants. I think I've got it, don't you?'

'I'm sure he'll be very pleased.' It did occur to me that, since Sir William had made his fortune dispossessing widows and orphans from the path of railways, he might stand in greater need of faith and purity than most; but I said nothing.

'There's money in mediaevalism,' said Travis, perhaps feeling he had failed to impress me as an artist, and must therefore do so as a man of the world. 'Take my advice, Hartright. Find yourself a knight and a damsel, and set to work.'

'I haven't the time, just at the moment,' I said. I hesitated, giving him an opportunity to ask me why not; but he merely busied himself with putting his sketches away, so I went on: 'Tell me, what do you remember of Turner?'

'Turner? I barely met him,' he said, closing the portfolio. 'My first Academy dinner was his last. I did see him once or twice on Varnishing Days, but it would never have occurred to me to speak to him.' He turned towards me, and a spasm of silent laughter shook his heavy chestnut curls like blossom on a tree. 'Like sauntering up to the altar, and helping yourself to communion wine.'

'Was he really so extraordinary?' I said.

'Not to look at,' he said. 'Well, yes, *extraordinary*, but not in the way you mean. Not *impressive*. He was about so tall' – he held his hand out, below the level of his own shoulder – 'with a huge Jew nose, and beady grey eyes, and an enormous top hat with the nap brushed the wrong way, and an old-fashioned coat with tails that almost swept the ground (and couldn't have been much dirtier if they had), and long sleeves that entirely covered his filthy hands. Like this.' He hunched forward, miming the ridiculous little figure he had described. Several passers-by stopped to stare, and a small girl erupted in uncontrollable giggles. I could not help laughing myself – Travis always looks most beatific when he is being most malicious, and seeing his pale, noble face contort into this grotesque hobgoblin was irresistibly comical – but it made me uncomfortable, as if I had joined in the mockery of some poor unfortunate whose only fault was his unusual appearance.

'I meant,' I said, 'was he really so great a genius?'

'Certainly if you equate genius with industry,' said Travis. 'He never stopped. Rain, shine, awake, asleep, in the water closet . . . He's doubtless at it now, scraping sunsets on his coffin lid.'

'Oh, come now,' I said, laughing. 'What's your true opinion?'

He did not reply at once, but stared gravely at the ground, as if seeking an answer there. Finally, he said:

'We thought so then. Or, rather, we thought he was a genius who had lost his powers, and degenerated into madness.'

'How mad?' I said.

'Just look at his late pictures,' he replied. 'Colours entirely divorced from any object. Great splotches of paint that look like nothing at all, save – splotches of paint. *Pictures of nothing*, as the critic said, *and very like*.'

'And what do you think now?' I said.

He shrugged. 'Some of the early work. The Dutch sea pieces. The engravings.'

I waited for him to go on, but he didn't: he took a watch from his pocket, looked at it, then gathered up the portfolio.

'Can you suggest anyone else,' I said, 'who might have known him better?'

'Jones?'

'I've written to him.'

He shrugged again, and shook his head. It was only after we had shaken hands, and said goodbye, and gone a few paces on our separate ways, that he turned and called:

'Try Davenant. He's in retirement now, at Hampstead. But still has his memory, and likes to open it to the public sometimes, and display the contents.'

This slight encounter had given me, in truth, little enough; but for some reason – no more, maybe, than that I had at last taken the initiative – I came away from it filled with a new spirit. Or perhaps it would be truer to say an old spirit: for, like the face in a crowd which suddenly calls to mind a long-forgotten childhood playfellow, I knew it at once for something I had known before. My heart beat faster; my legs ached with a tremulous excitement; I filled my lungs, and found in the smoky air, which only an hour ago had tasted of drudgery and sickness, an intoxicating hint of romance – I felt, in short, like a young man again, newly released from dull routine and about to embark on some great adventure. Had you seen me striding through the

Regent's Park and up Avenue Road (it did not even occur to me to take a cab), you might have fancied you saw the ghost of that other Walter Hartright, who, fifteen years ago, his head full of simple purposes and grand hopes, used to walk from London to Hampstead three times a week, and think nothing of it. I seemed, indeed, to glimpse him myself sometimes, marching companionably at my side; and it was surely at his prompting that I broke my journey at a plain roadside inn, and sat with him over a plain luncheon of bread and cheese and ale – I the grave master of Limmeridge, and he the cheerful young drawing teacher, with neither the burden nor the privilege of fortune, and no prospect save the prospect of life itself.

Mr. Davenant (I learned at the post office) lived not half a mile from my mother's old cottage, in one of those quaint red-brick houses in Church Row. Its once-regular façade had started to sag and buckle with age, giving it the unsteady look of a child's drawing (Florrie, indeed, would have got the lines straighter!), as if it had tired of classical sobriety, and decided to get drunk. A big wood-clad bay window, jutting out pugnaciously from the first floor like the stern of an old man-of-war, added to the air of disorder.

The door was opened by a young manservant who still seemed pitifully uncertain of his duties. When I inquired if Mr. Davenant was at home he said: 'I'll go and ask him'; a moment later he came back, his cheeks flaming, to ask my name; and then, after a few steps, stopped, and turned again – presumably to find out my business. He was interrupted, however, by a man's voice booming down from upstairs:

'Who is that, Lawrence?'

'Mr. Hartright, sir,' called the boy.

'Who?'

'Mr. Hartright!'

'What does he want?' shouted the man, as if he were

commanding a company of troops.

'What do you want?' stammered the boy.

'To talk about Turner,' I said.

The boy relayed this to the man upstairs, who promptly roared:

'What the devil does that mean?'

'What the –?' began the boy, so thoroughly embarrassed now that you could have lit a cigar from his face. I stepped past him into the hall, to be met by a line of unsmiling family portraits and, at the foot of the stairs, a large oil-painting of what appeared to be the Battle of Waterloo. Staring down at me from the first-floor landing was a fine-looking man of seventy or so, with white whiskers, a noble nose and a heroic brow. He wore a paint-stained smock tied loosely at the neck, and was tapping the handle of a brush impatiently against the banister.

'I was told you knew Turner well,' I said.

'Oh, yes,' he said, 'and what of it?'

'I am hoping to write his biography.'

'Are you, by God?' He leant forward, peering closely at me. 'You're not that what-ye-call-him, been making such a damned nuisance of himself?'

'Do you mean Mr. Thornbury?' I said.

He grunted.

'No,' I said.

He pondered a moment, then said: 'Come up. Fifteen minutes.'

A moonlit seascape hung above the stairs, and another battle scene – showing a knot of red-coated soldiers clustered round a tattered union flag, while the shadowy enemy crept towards them through a fog of gunsmoke – dominated the landing. I stopped before it, and asked:

'Is that one of yours?'

He nodded abruptly. 'Can't get rid of 'em. No-one wants anything now except pretty little pictures of their families,

31

all scrubbed clean and dressed up like tailors' dummies. And those damned fainting women.' He shook his head. 'Madness.'

I could not help smiling – he had skewered both Travis and me with a single stroke – but fortunately he was too busy wiping his fingers on his smock to notice.

'It's very impressive,' I said.

He nodded again. 'There, I shan't smear you now,' he said, and grasped my hand. 'How d'ye do?'

As if that simple formality had qualified me to be admitted to his confidence, he turned and led me into a double room – divided in the middle by folding doors – which ran the entire depth of the house. At one end was the large bay, giving a distant view of the heath and washing the walls and floor with silvery light; at the other, a south-facing rear window, unshuttered, but screened with a sheet, presumably to mute the effect of the sun.

A huge unfinished canvas, held upright on a crude frame, stood in the bay, next to a table spread with brushes and an open paintbox. It was turned to catch the north light, and I could consequently only half-see the subject; but I made out enough – a woman on a horse, surrounded by armed men, and a line of sails on the horizon – to guess that the subject was Queen Elizabeth before the Spanish Armada. On a dais in the centre of the room, a woman in a blue velvet cloak and a tall hat sat for the central figure. Her 'horse' had been ingeniously constructed of three bolsters lashed together and laid between a pair of trestles; and she held before her a wooden sword, which – doubtless because she had been at it some time, and her arm was tired – wavered perilously.

'Very well,' said Davenant. 'You can have a break, Mrs. Holt.'

'It would be as well, sir,' she said, taking off her hat, 'if you're to get your dinner.'

'Never mind about my dinner,' he said. 'If I keep you here all afternoon, it's no matter: you can send out for a pie. A cup of tea in the kitchen, to restore you; and then back to singeing King Philip's beard.'

'Yes, sir,' she said, compliantly enough – but her eyes rolled with a comic exasperation that fell just short of out-right insolence.

'Begone with you, you besom,' said Davenant, raising his hand as if to strike her. 'And tell Lawrence to bring us some wine.'

'Yes, sir,' she said, laughing.

There was a moment's silence after she had gone. Davenant glanced out of the window, then turned and fixed me with a frank gaze. With a gravity I had not heard before, he said:

'Turner was my friend, Mr. Hartright. I'll not do any-thing to injure him. If you want scandal, or gossip, you won't get it here.'

'I give you my word,' I said, 'I am only interested in the truth.'

'I'll tell you that, and gladly,' he said. 'But mind – I speak only of what I know.' He paused; then, pulling two chairs from the wall, muttered: 'And I could earnestly wish others would the same. Will you sit down?'

'Thank you.'

'I sometimes think you could knock on any door in London, and find someone there whose acquaintance with Turner extends, at most, to having once seen him get out of a cab – and who will cheerfully swear on that basis that he was the most crabbed, suspicious, miserable skinflint in creation.'

I laughed; and he acknowledged it with a chuckle, and a curious little bounce of the head, as if I had complimented him on some soldierly skill. He went on:

'But I knew him for thirty years, and found him as kind

33

and sociable as any man I ever met. You certainly couldn't
have asked for a tenderer friend.' He sat down, tugging at
the knees of the old-fashioned breeches beneath his smock.
'I was sick as a dog, once – the doctors almost gave me up,
and most of my family, too – but Turner'd come every day,
to inquire after my health, and wish me better – even, I
afterwards discovered, when I was too weak to receive him
myself, and he got no more for his pains than two minutes'
conversation with my housekeeper.' He shook his head,
and his eyes sparkled with tears, which he made no effort
to hide.

'But what of his supposed moroseness, and meanness?' I
said.

'Why, as to that – you never saw such a fellow for merriment and hilarity, when he was easy, and among friends.
Get up any little social or professional party, and he'd gladly participate, and pay his share – and sometimes, to my
knowledge, he'd defray the whole expense himself, without others knowing it.'

'How then did he get such a reputation?' I asked. I was, I
confess, astonished: for this genial figure bore no relation to
Travis's crazed dwarf – or to the misanthropic miser I had
heard of at the Academy, or to Lady Eastlake's friendless
recluse.

'Oh, I won't deny there may have been reason enough,
for those who judge a man by his appearance, and never
trouble to look beneath the surface,' said Davenant. 'He
lived most of his life with his old father, and much of the
rest alone; and never learnt good domestic management –
and thus could not receive his friends at his own table, as
he told me on many occasions he would have liked. And he
could be gruff, sometimes, too – especially if he thought
you were trying improperly to find out his secrets, or interfere with his habits.'

But why (I immediately thought) should a man be at so

much pains to protect his privacy, unless he has something shameful to conceal? I kept the question to myself; but, as if he could look into my mind, Davenant said:

'I don't know if you've a wife, Mr. Hartright – and, if so, how you live with her, and, if not, how you do without one – but you might well feel that it was no damned business of mine, unless you chose to tell me, and I should heartily agree with you.'

The young manservant entered, carrying a tray with a decanter and two glasses. He stood trembling while Davenant made a space for it on his painting table, and then set it down without mishap.

'Thank you, Lawrence,' said Davenant, as the boy withdrew. 'That was Turner's view,' he went on, as if there had been no interruption. 'To hate humbug, and meddling, and condemnation, was almost a religious principle with him. I never heard him speak ill of a fellow-creature, or fail to put the best construction he could on another's behaviour. If he couldn't defend you, or approve your work, he'd hold his tongue. Will you take some wine, sir?'

'Thank you.'

'He wouldn't pry into your private affairs,' he said, busying himself with the decanter, 'and asked nothing more in return than that you shouldn't pry into his. And all I can say is: I wish to God there were more like him.' He handed me a glass, full to the brim with brown sherry; then raised his own, and, looking straight before him, as if he could see Turner's face etched upon the empty air, said: 'Here's honour to your memory, you old scamp.' He drank, and turned immediately towards me. 'Your very good health, Mr. Hartright.'

'And yours,' I said. And yet I did not drink; for, in some obscure way, it seemed that to do so would be to set a kind of seal on our conversation, implying that I accepted not only his hospitality, but also his account of Turner – which,

35

in truth, had left me more puzzled and unsatisfied than ever. I merely touched the glass to my lips, therefore, and tried feverishly to compose a question that would press him further without angering him.

Once again, he seemed to anticipate my thoughts.

'You may yet wonder', he said, sitting down again, 'how such a man could have been the butt of so much malice, and so many hateful anecdotes? And the only answer I can give you is: envy. Most people seem to conceive of artists as little less than angels, but they're not, by God! – in my experience, outside a schoolroom, you won't find a bigger pack of squabbling, jealous, backstabbing cheats and bullies anywhere on earth. They all try to make themselves into geniuses; and if they can't do that, they'll say anything, and believe anything, that seems to make the geniuses more like themselves.'

He hesitated; and for a moment I considered pointing out that I was an artist myself, of sorts; but quickly thought better of it.

'And Turner *was* a genius, Mr. Hartright,' he went on. 'He was *the* genius, I'd take my oath upon it. Varnishing Days at the Academy, before the Exhibition, the rest of us'd just be putting the finishing touches to our work; but he'd send in a more or less bare canvas, and you'd see the younger members looking at it, and laughing, and saying: 'What's he going to do with that?' And then he'd walk in, and open his little box of tricks, and get to work – never standing back, to look at what he was doing, for it was all in his head – and within a few hours he'd have conjured a picture out of nothing. If a savage had seen it, he'd have sworn it was magic. I remember, indeed, a young Scotch fellow watching it once, and going quite pale, and muttering something about sorcery.'

'But surely', I said, 'no painter could fail to admire . . .'

He gave a derisive splutter. 'Imagine, Mr. Hartright,' he

said, 'you have laboured for six months on a painting, and are mightily pleased with it, and think it will get you a knighthood; and along comes Turner, and in a single day produces its nemesis, so that you are utterly eclipsed . . .'

I laughed nervously, for his words had struck a hidden weakness in me; and I suddenly found that I *could* imagine it, all too easily; and for a moment felt the chill of some bottomless desolation fall upon me like a shadow.

'If you did a bright sun or a blue sky,' he said, 'he'd as like as not try to make a brighter or a bluer. Once, I recall, he'd done a beautiful grey picture of *Helvoetsluys*, without a hint of positive colour; and next to it was Constable's *Opening of Waterloo Bridge*, which seemed to have been painted in liquid gold and silver; and Turner looked several times from one to the other, and then fetched his palette, and put a daub of red lead on his grey sea, a little bigger than a shilling, and went away without a word.' He started to laugh. 'And poor Constable groaned: "Turner's been here, and fired a gun"; for, of course, his own picture now looked weak and insipid by comparison.'

'Perhaps, then,' I said, 'it's little wonder Turner was so much disliked.'

Davenant nodded. 'But what none of them understood was, he meant no harm by it. It was but a kind of friendly rivalry, a goad to make us all strive harder, to perfect our art. If you outdid him, he'd laugh about it, and clap you on the back, and tell you to enjoy your victory. And he'd as soon help you as fight you. No man had a truer eye for what was wrong with a picture, or for how to make it right.' He got up. 'Let me show you something.'

I followed him on to the landing and halfway down the stairs, where he stopped before the moonlit seascape I had passed, not a quarter of an hour since, on my way up. I now noticed, picked out in black lettering on the frame, the title: *Dover beach: night. By John Davenant, R.A. Exhibited 1837.*

'There,' he said.

It was a dramatic enough scene, with moonlight spilling out from behind a great bank of dark cloud, and then shattering into a hundred pieces on the inky sea. Just below the horizon was a heeling merchantman, its full sails almost black in the eerie light.

'It has great power,' I said, glad to be able to praise something wholeheartedly at last.

He nodded, colouring with pleasure. 'But the power is Turner's. My first conception was quite different – no cloud at all, and the moonlight falling straight on to the ship, and making the sails glow white – and that is what I painted. But when I saw it framed, and hung at the Academy, I knew it was wrong, and so did my friends – but could any of us say where the fault lay?' He shook his head. 'Not until Turner chanced by, clutching his palette, and looked at it for half a minute, and said: "It wants depth, and contrast. You should cover over the moon – make the mass of the cloud black, and the edges silver, so you've got the brightest and the darkest next to each other – put the sails in shadow, and a dab of light on the bow." Well, I felt the truth of this, but I was naturally rather cautious, and, try as I might, I could not get the effect he meant; and after coming back once or twice to see how I was getting on, he finally lost patience with me, and seized the brushes, and did it himself – two great strokes of black, two of white' – here he mimed the words, with large sweeping gestures – 'one, two, three, four. And of course we all saw at once that he was right.'

Davenant stood back to admire the painting, chuckling and shaking his head in wonderment; but I felt faintly disturbed – not merely by the high-handedness of Turner's intervention, but also by its result: for it had instantaneously transformed a scene of bland tranquillity into one of louring menace. My thoughts, however, were at that

38

instant disrupted by the sound of footsteps from below, and by Davenant's suddenly roaring, so loudly that I nearly leapt from my skin:

'Good God, Hartright, there's dedication for you!'

I turned, and saw Mrs. Holt coming upstairs towards us.

'She doesn't wait to be called, you note!' said Davenant. 'Can't wait to get back to harrying the dons!'

'We'll lose the light, sir, is all I was thinking,' said the cook.

'Very true, Mrs. Holt,' said Davenant. He turned to me. 'She's quite right, I fear, Mr. Hartright. You will, I hope, forgive me . . .?'

'Of course,' I said. 'It was very good of you to give me as much time as you have.'

'Nonsense,' he said. 'Delighted to help. If I have. Which I doubt . . .'

I started to speak, but he held up his hand, and went on:

'None of your damned flattery, now. Go on up, Mrs. Holt, and get on your regalia. I'll be with you in a moment.' Then he took my arm affably, and led me downstairs.

He had opened the door, and was about to shake my hand, when he stopped suddenly, and said:

'Will you wait a minute, Mr. Hartright? Something I think may assist you.'

He crossed the hall, and entered a room at the back of the house. I stood beneath his bay window, and looked about me. To the south, the smoke hung over London like a great mantle, so thick and black that just to see it was to feel the weight of it on your chest, and its woolly itch against your skin; but here a fresh breeze ruffled my hair, and there were chinks of blue between the grey-rimmed clouds that churned and tumbled above the heath. Something in their wild motion put me in mind of sporting sea creatures, and I watched, rapt, until his voice roused me from my reverie:

'Here,' he said, handing me a folded sheet of paper. 'Two

39

more people who knew him well. But neither of them painters; so you may be sure that what they tell you will be untainted by artistic rancour. Michael Gudgeon's an antiquary, who travelled with Turner years ago on a tour of Kent and Sussex. And Amelia Bennett is old Benjamin Waley's daughter . . .'

He paused, searching my face for some sign of recognition. I shook my head.

'You're too young, I suppose,' he said, with a sigh. 'He was quite a man in his day. A great amateur, who befriended Turner when he was little more than a boy.'

I thanked him warmly, and started for Kensington in high good spirits. I had trusted to fate, and fate had amply repaid me; and some almost superstitious conviction told me that it had not done with me yet, but would repay me further still when I got home.

And I was not mistaken; for there, in the hall, was the enclosed note from Ruskin!

My love as always, to you and to the children.

Walter

VI

Letter from John Ruskin to Walter Hartright, 1st August, 185–

163 Dennmark Hill,
1st August, 185–

Dear Mr. Hartright,

Thank you for your letter of 21st July. I should have replied sooner, had I been here to receive it, but I only returned yesterday from a long absence in Italy and France.

Yes, I shall be happy to talk to you about Turner – although I am not sure how far it lies within my power (or the power of any man or woman) to light your way. I fear, however, that I shall be unable to see you this week – for, as I am sure you know, it is the inevitable consequence of travel to come back and find one's garden choked with weeds, and, if I do not set to at once, some of my tenderest plants (a book, a lecture, and a thousand shy little shoots that seem to have sprung from my words, and to want only encouragement to flourish) will surely die. Would Thursday next, at three o'clock, be convenient?

Yours very truly,

John Ruskin

VII

From the diary of Marian Halcombe, 4th August, 185–

A small cottage, with but one window on each floor, and entirely unremarkable save for a curious iron railing on the parapet, that looked as if a balcony had decided to emigrate from its original home to the roof. On one side, a tavern; on the other a little shop, advertising 'ales', 'refreshments' and 'first-class ginger-beer'; next to that, a knock-kneed gateway bearing a weatherbeaten sign – all you could read was 'Ale anders Boat ard', so you had to fill in the ghosts of the missing 'x' and 'y' yourself – and leading to an untidy sprawl of spars and timbers and ropes. Facing the house, beyond the road, flowed the great river, hemmed in by a shallow embankment of rough stones, and approached by a flight of steps, which were crowded with lounging watermen smoking their pipes and waiting for custom. Further out, a desultory little army of mudlarks in ragged dress scoured the stinking mud for treasure.

'Are you sure this is the right address?' I asked the driver.

'Six Davis Place, Chelsea, miss?' he said, slowly, as if I were an idiot.

I got out. A knot of boys kicking a broken bottle stopped to stare at me, and two or three of the watermen stiffened and turned in my direction. They may simply have been bored, or hoping I would take a boat; but there seemed a kind of animal watchfulness in their unsmiling faces, as if, even at this time of day, a lone woman could have no rightful business here. I knew, though, that to show fear is to feed the monster that frightens us, so I paid the cabman and marched up the path without so much as a backward glance.

As I knocked on the door, however, I sensed a movement behind me, and, looking round, saw that the group of boys had followed me, and were pressing against the gate like a pack of wild dogs. Most of them instantly turned their heads to avoid my eyes, but one, a gangly beanpole of twelve or thirteen, held my gaze steadily.

'You want to know about Puggy?' he called.

I couldn't tell whether he was mocking me or trying to be helpful; but since I have found that, if you expect the best of people, they generally strive to live up to your expectations, I smiled and said:

'Booth. I'm looking for Mrs. Booth.'

'She won't tell you nothing about him,' said the boy.

There was no sound from within the house, so I knocked again.

The boy called: 'Ask Mr. Neave about him.'

The words were barely out of his mouth when I heard a man shouting: 'That's right, miss, I knew the Admiral!'

I turned, and saw one of the watermen (presumably Mr. Neave) crossing the road towards me. He seemed to have been drinking, for he staggered a little, and waved his arms wildly to attract my attention.

'I took them everywhere,' he said, gesturing across the

river towards Battersea. 'You come with me, I'll show you where they went.'

I had no idea what they were talking about, but did not want to show it, for fear that it might encourage them to take some advantage of me, so I said nothing, and knocked for a third time. But I was beginning to lose heart. What if – as now seemed probable – Mrs. Booth were out, and I had to walk down the path again, and through the throng? My cab had long since disappeared from view, and there was not another in sight. To add to my disquiet, three or four more men, apparently attracted by the commotion, now spilled out of the tavern. One was a most impressive figure, a black-bearded giant in a red flannel shirt and pleated black French trousers, who elbowed his way to the front and bellowed, in what sounded like a Russian or Polish accent:

'I tell you about the Admiral! The bottles! The ladies!'

'You lying foreign b–!' shouted Mr. Neave. Emboldened by drink, he clenched his fists and lurched forward, scattering boys on every side, although he could barely reach his opponent's shoulder.

'Please!' I shouted. 'I have no interest in any Admiral!'

I hoped this would calm them, but it appeared to have no effect. The men jostled themselves into two groups, while the boys lined up against the fence, either because they wanted to watch or because they could not escape. I quickly formulated a plan: I would appeal to the beanpole's chival-rous instincts and offer him and his friends a penny apiece to escort me safely to the nearest cab stand.

I had already started back towards them when, at last, I heard the door opening behind me. I turned and saw a handsome, dark-haired, sturdily built woman of sixty or so, wearing a plain grey dress and a white apron. Her eyes stared past me towards the crowd at the gate. Her sallow, heavy-featured face wore an expression of infinite, exasper-ated sadness, such as you might see on a nurse who discovers her charges, yet again, doing something they know is wrong. To my astonishment, that look alone was enough to restore order: the two opposing factions melted away without a word, and the boys, as if suddenly released from captivity, scampered at full tilt down the street.

'Mrs. Booth?' I said.

She turned towards me. She inclined her head slightly, but did not smile.

'I am Marian Halcombe,' I said. 'I believe Lady Eastlake wrote to you . . .?'

'Yes,' she said. There was a rural lilt to her voice, but its tone was perfectly neutral, neither friendly nor unfriendly. 'Will you please come in, Miss Halcombe?'

The hall was so poky and dark that I could see almost nothing, and had to rely on the bobbing beacon of Mrs. Booth's apron string to guide me. But the little parlour she led me into was pleasant enough, with a lively fire burning in the grate, and a strange-looking tailless cat stretched on the rug before it. A canary chirruped in its cage in the window, and a stout grandfather clock ticked soothingly by the door, as if Time, too, had been caught and tamed, and put in a corner to add his voice to the domestic chorus.

'Please sit down,' said Mrs. Booth, 'while I fetch the tea.' She was immediately gone again, and a moment later I heard her clumping down into the basement. I rose, and looked about me. The room was, for the most part, quite unexceptional, and such as you might expect to find in the housekeeper's quarters of any well-run large house: neat cupboards, with white-painted panelled doors, flanked the fireplace; a cavalcade of china milkmaids, led by a Macready toby jug, marched across the mantel-shelf; and on the chimney breast above hung a watercolour of a church and some miniatures in oval frames.

It was only when I turned back towards the hall that I noticed something unusual. Two oil-paintings, stacked one behind the other and half covered by a sheet, leant against the wall between door and window. Seeing the corner of a gilt frame, and a whirl of leaden colour, I was overcome with curiosity, and immediately bent down and lifted the cloth. The images that greeted me were so terrible, and yet so vague, that they seemed to have been conjured from a nightmare. The first showed a wild, grey-green sea stirred into an implacable fury; in the foreground, indistinct figures clung desperately to a queer, serpentine lump of wreckage which rose from the spume like a sea-monster, and, further off, a cutter sailed to their rescue. The second, behind it, was perhaps the same scene the following day: a crowd gathered on the shore, dumbstruck at the frightful proof of nature's destructive power littered all about them; while on the horizon, lit by an ulcerous, unforgiving yellow sun, a disabled ship with two masts gone was just visible through the haze. Their impact – at least on me – was almost physical, and somewhat as I imagine the effect of mesmerism to be; I lost all thought of where I was, or what I was doing there, and was still staring when Mrs. Booth re-entered.

'Ah, yes,' she said, colouring slightly. 'Those are his. He gave them to me.'

'What, Mr. Turner!' I exclaimed. I must have sounded, I fear, more amazed than I should have done – partly because the only Turner I could remember seeing was the stately engraving in the hall at Brompton Grove of *London from Greenwich Park*, showing a tranquil classical landscape with a distant view of the smoke-covered city and its river, which seemed to bear no relation to these desolate scenes at all; and partly because it had never occurred to me that Mrs. Booth might have any of his pictures in her possession.

'Yes,' she said, setting her tray down. I expected her to go on, but she busied herself instead with the tea, pouring two cups and then perching the pot at the edge of the fire basket

45

to keep warm. Hoping to revive the subject I said:

'That was very generous of him.'

I regretted the words even before they were out of my mouth. She coloured again, and said:

'What, you think I didn't deserve so much kindness?'

'No, of course not. I merely meant . . .' I could not, of course, say what I really meant: that few successful artists would have dealt so handsomely with a servant. To cover my confusion, I said:

'Why do you not hang them?'

'I had them upstairs, but I feared they might be stolen. My son is going to keep them safe for me.'

I confess I found myself wondering why she did not sell them, for they must surely be worth a great deal of money; and in doing so she could simultaneously remove the cause of her anxiety and ensure herself a comfortable old age. Perhaps she guessed what I was thinking, for she said:

'I could not bear to part with them.'

'They remind you of the sea?' I said.

She nodded.

'You have naval connections, perhaps?' I said. 'The boys outside mentioned –'

'The Admiral?'

'Yes.'

She nodded again, but wearily. 'That is what they called him.'

'Mr. Turner?' I said; for, though it seemed unlikely, we had talked of no-one else.

'Yes,' she said. 'They called him Admiral Booth.' She paused, and looked coolly at my astonished face; then, as if I should have divined it for myself, went on: 'They thought he was my husband.'

I felt quite lost, like a traveller who suddenly discovers he is without both map and compass. What could I ask that would not appear rude – the most obvious question, *Why?*, would certainly have fallen into this category – or, on the other hand, risk eliciting some new piece of startling information which would only bemuse me further? At length I said, cautiously:

'How long did you know Mr. Turner?'

'Twenty years,' she said. 'He first came to me when I had a boarding-house in Margate. Then, after Mr. Booth died, he wanted a retreat by the river; so he asked me to move to Chelsea, and keep house for him here.'

'He must have had great confidence in you,' I said.

She nodded, a proud woman briskly acknowledging her due. 'He used to call me the handmaiden of Art.'

'You helped him in his work, then?'

'Oh, yes, I'd set his palette every morning, and make sure everything was ready.' She said this with a certain warmth, as if she had begun to feel easier in my presence. A second or two later, the cat unexpectedly furthered my cause by getting up and jumping into my lap, where it stood lazily sinking its claws into my dress. For the first time since my arrival, Mrs. Booth smiled.

'Oh, you're very honoured,' she said. 'Jason generally only likes men. Mr. Turner, especially. He'd sit on his knee, his shoulder – even his head, sometimes.'

I laughed, and decided this would be a propitious moment to venture a little further.

'What kind of a man was Mr. Turner?'

'There were times', she said, 'when I thought he was a god.'

'A god!' I said. 'Why, did he resemble a Greek statue?'

Mrs. Booth laughed. 'Oh, I don't mean to look at!' she said. 'In his work.' She waved a hand towards the two oil-paintings. 'You or I could stand where he did, and see nothing but a rough old day, or a wintry sun. But he saw what ordinary mortal eyes can't see. He saw into the heart of things.'

47

I found myself thinking: *Dear Lord, I hope the heart of things doesn't look like that*. But I said:

'Yes, they are magnificent.'

That seemed to please her. She brightened, and – as if surprised by her own candour – said:

'Would you like to see the room where he died, Miss Halcombe?'

In truth, I should have preferred to stay where I was, and finish my tea, and ask her more questions; but I could not very well refuse, so I replied:

'Yes, I should. Very much.'

We went up the cramped staircase, which squeaked under our weight like a procession of complaining mice, and entered a small attic at the front of the house. The feeble sun seeped through a square, deep-set dormer, casting a watery pattern of light and shadow on the neighbouring wall. The left-hand side of the room was dominated by a simple brass bed, and a single wheelback chair stood before the window. The boards were bare, and there was no other furniture save a plain cupboard, a small table set with a bowl and ewer, and an iron ladder leading to a trapdoor in the ceiling. It looked like the kind of lodging where a struggling actor or a poor travelling salesman might seek refuge from the disappointments of the day.

'This was his room,' said Mrs. Booth. 'Every morning he would rise before dawn, and throw a blanket round him, and go up there' – here she indicated the ladder – 'on to the roof, and sketch the sunrise.'

'Ah,' I said. 'That's why the parapet's railed?'

She nodded. 'And then he'd come back to bed, and rest till breakfast time. And so he went on, right up until his last illness. He was indefatigable, Miss Halcombe. Even when I was nursing him, I had to make sure he always had pencils and paper to hand.'

'Was he still able to paint, then?' I asked.

'Not at the very end,' she said. 'But not to have the hope of it would have killed him that much sooner. So I always kept up the pretence: *Perhaps tomorrow, my dear.*'

How many housekeepers call their master 'my dear'?

'He was very lucky to have you, Mrs. Booth,' I said.

She did not answer, seemingly lost in her own thoughts. At length she said:

'I'll tell you a strange thing, Miss Halcombe. A few weeks before he died, the police dragged out of the river some poor girl, who had fallen into disgrace, and drowned herself.' She moved towards the window, and pointed down to the embankment steps, where the watermen were still idling the afternoon away. 'Just there. And Mr. Turner was very troubled by it, and kept waking me in the night, and saying he saw her face, and feared to sleep. "I must draw it," he said. "I must draw that face, or I shall have no rest." And so he drew it, and it was almost the last picture he ever made.'

'And was he still haunted by it?' I asked.

'He never spoke of it again,' she said. 'Leastways, not that I recall.'

She was quiet then, and I feared I had lost her to her own memories. I said:

'How did he come to see her, if he was in bed, and she outside?'

'It was a terrible winter,' she said. 'Nothing but fog and smoke for weeks on end. He'd say, "I wish I could see the sun again" – but he could barely more than whisper it by then, it'd break your heart to hear him. So he'd roll on to the floor, and try to crawl to the window to look for it.'

'I see,' I said. 'So he was there when the police found her?'

She nodded abstractedly, as if her mind were on something more important. 'Sometimes', she said, 'he was too weak even to go that far, and I'd find him here, by the chair, and have to help him back to bed.'

Again she was silent, and, though she faced the window, I

thought I saw a tear in the corner of her eye. Finally, she sighed, and said: 'But he did see it again. One morning, it suddenly broke through; and the doctor and I got him into the wheelchair, and pushed him here to the window, so that it could shine full on his face; and an hour later, as if he was satisfied at last, he died, without a murmur, with his head against my shoulder.'

Her voice did not quaver. And yet something in the way she spoke, bringing the thoughts from the depths of her own being, and then gently replacing them there, as if they were her most cherished possessions, told me, beyond doubt, that this was a woman who had not merely served Turner, but had loved him in every sense. And I knew – however hard it might be to believe – that the man described by Lady Eastlake as the foremost genius of the day had lived and died in this mean little house, under an assumed name, as his housekeeper's husband.

If I am honest, I have to say this realization prompted in me no other feeling for Mrs. Booth than deep pity, mingled with a genuine admiration. But what, I wondered, would Walter make of it? For the old widow, I was sure, he would share my sympathy and compassion; but would he view Turner himself in the same liberal spirit? Might the discovery of his subject's eccentricities (to put it as charitably as I can) make him lose interest in writing the *Life*, even before he has begun it?

It was therefore with some trepidation that I said:

'You have been very helpful, Mrs. Booth. Would it be possible for me to call again with my brother, who, I know, would like to talk to you himself?'

And it was with relief, as well as disappointment, that I heard her reply:

'I mean no offence, Miss Halcombe, but Mr. Turner's memory is sacred to me. I do not like to talk about him; and, to speak plain, I have already said more than I meant to. So, while I shall always be pleased to see you, if you pass this way, I must ask that you do not bring your brother here; for I could tell him nothing more than I have told you today.'

VIII

Letter from Walter Hartright to Laura Hartright, 11th August, 185–

Brompton Grove,
Friday

My dearest love,

Your letter is by me as I write – I glance over, and read 'I am so proud of you, Walter'; and the words sting me like a slap, for I am sure that had you seen me today you would have been anything but proud. I am just returned from Ruskin, you see, and know not what to make of him, or of what he told me – but I fear *he* has made a fool of me, and I of myself, and the result is that I am cast down, and quite confused.

The start of my perplexity is the man himself. Strange, is it not, how a famous name may produce an image in our minds, composed of who knows what scraps and trifles and odds and ends, yet strong enough, in the absence of personal experience, to *be* that person for us? Before today, without in the least reflecting on it, I saw Ruskin as a wild shaggy creature lurking in the dark somewhere (his natural abode has always seemed a cave, or a dungeon), waiting to rush out without warning and impale some poor unsuspecting painter. Perhaps this idea arises partly from my own dread, whenever I exhibit, that he will single out something of mine for particular scorn; and partly from – do you remember it? – that verse in *Punch*:

I paints and paints, and no complaints;
I sells before I'm dry;
Then savage Ruskin sticks his tusk in
And nobody will buy.

And just think – had I had no occasion to meet him, this fancy might, through sheer force of habit, have finally established itself in my mind as the truth; and so been passed on by our grandchildren to their grandchildren as a lifelike portrait of the great man!

At all events, they, and I, will be spared that; for the revolution of the last twelve hours has entirely deposed all my preconceptions, and despatched them to an exile from which they will never return.

My first surprise came even before I had met him, for 163 Dennmark Hill turns out to be a tall, rambling old house which – far from shrinking into the shadows – announces its presence with the beefy self-importance of a provincial lord mayor. It has its own porter's lodge (where I was obliged to state my business to a burly man with suspicious eyes and licorice breath, who said: 'That's Mr. *John* Ruskin, is it?' and then, before I was able to reply, peered at me through the window of the cab, and answered his own question: 'Yes, it'll be Mr. John'); and a carriage sweep; and walls furred with ivy; and a front door approached by railed steps, and almost hidden in the recesses of a heavy portico. From its size, in short, and its John Bull posture – feet splayed, elbows out – it looked more like the house of one of our fox-hunting neighbours in Cumberland than the home of the world's most celebrated art critic, on the fringes of the world's greatest city.

The footman who opened the door seemed ordinary enough; but for a fleeting moment I had the odd impression that the dim square hall behind him was filled with pale, elderly faces (it was difficult to be sure, for my eyes

52

had not yet adjusted to the gloom), which promptly scattered, as soon as they saw me, like rabbits startled by a walker.

'Is Mr. Ruskin at home?' I asked.

'Mr. *John* Ruskin?' replied the man, in a stiff parody of the lodge-keeper.

'Yes,' I said, wondering secretly how many others there might be, and whether they all had opinions on Art.

He went upstairs; and, as soon as he had gone, two of the rabbits (as I supposed) reappeared. One was an old woman in a bonnet and a black dress; the other, a stocky man with ragged white hair and thick whiskers, wearing a dark jacket and a speckled twill waistcoat. Neither looked exactly like a servant, and there was something proprietorial in their manner; yet they hovered at the margins of the hall, as if they feared to take full possession of it, smiling uneasily at me, and looking away again – like prosperous innkeepers, perhaps, whose house is their own, but who must defer to others within its walls.

'Mr. Hartright,' said a soft, gracious voice; and, looking up, I saw a man descending the stairs towards me. At first glance he seemed immensely tall; but as he reached the hall, and stood level with me, I saw that in fact he was merely extremely thin, with a long, close-fitting blue coat that hugged his slender frame and emphasized all the vertical lines in his appearance. He was about my own age, or a little older, with a bright complexion, thick yellow hair and whiskers, and beetling eyebrows. There was something almost foppish – even feminine – in the way he moved, and in the evident care he had taken in arranging his watch-chain and tying his cravat; but it was entirely contradicted by his sharp nose and deep-set blue eyes, which gave him the wary, petulant look of a beast disturbed in its lair.

'How very pleasant to meet you,' he said, taking both my

53

hands in his. His lower lip, I noticed, was slightly deformed; but his smile more than atoned for it, transforming his expression, in an instant, from bad temper to sweetness. He turned to the old people and said, with a courtly air:

'Papa, Mama, this is Mr. Hartright. He's here to talk about Turner.'

I had heard, of course, of the poor man's marital difficulties; but the idea that in his middle years, and at the height of his eminence, he should have abandoned the part of a husband only to resume that of a son was strange indeed. I thought of what Davenant had told me of Turner and his father, and Marian had learnt from Mrs. Booth; and wondered if it was a mark of genius to be incapable of normal domestic arrangements.

'How d'ye do?' said the old man; and, as he and his wife stepped forward awkwardly to shake my hand, I at last recognized their odd mixture of pride and diffidence and concern for what it was, and felt suddenly – and quite unexpectedly – like a schoolboy invited to the home of a gifted but over-sensitive friend.

'Will you indulge me, Mr. Hartright,' said Ruskin, 'and take a walk in the garden? I've been in the thick of it all morning, and can't see for the smoke, or think for the noise of the guns.'

Without waiting for a reply, he ushered me quickly out of the front door again, as if anxious to make good his escape before his parents had time to forbid it.

'In the thick of what, may I ask?' I said, as we turned on to the carriage sweep. 'A new piece of criticism?'

'I *am* struggling to finish the last volume of *Modern Painters*,' he said. 'But I'm afraid I've come to the wretched conclusion that all my critical and historical work up till now has been almost valueless.'

'Oh, come . . .!' I said.

'It *is* a sad thought,' he said. 'Especially when you've devoted your whole life to a thing, as I have. But when I look about me, and see the burden of dumb misery in the world, and calculate what an infinitesimally small fraction of it I have managed to lift with my ruminations on Turner or Veronese or the Gothic . . .' He shook his head.

'But *Modern Painters*', I said, 'has given delight – and instruction – to thousands. Millions.' I confess that I was slightly abashed, when I reflected how little of it *I* had read, and how long ago; but not sufficiently to prevent my adding: 'Myself included.'

'You are kind to try to console me, Mr. Hartright,' he said. He stopped, and turned on me a gaze of extraordinary candour. 'But – forgive me – you do not look miserable – at least, not in the way I mean. When I speak of misery, I am thinking of that great mass of suffering humanity which surrounds us, and which we see – and yet do not see – every day; and which we barely touch with all our ideals and concerns.'

He rounded the end of the house, and ducked his head to enter a dark tunnel, pungent with the scent of damp leaves, formed by a dense old laurel bush pressing against the wall.

'And that is why', he said, the words – suddenly muffled now – floating back to me in the close air, 'I have begun to turn my attention to the question of political economy.'

I was, I must admit, surprised that he should be so frank with me, and not a little flattered; yet mingled with my gratification, as I followed his stooping figure through the dimness, was a slight repugnance – although I could not, at the time, have told you the reason for it.

'You may, of course, feel I have little enough reason to complain myself,' he said with a laugh, as we emerged behind the house. He gestured languidly towards the lawn, dotted with trees and artfully laced with winding paths that stretched away below us; and at the kitchen gardens and orchards and a row of farm buildings beyond. 'Our own milk and pigs,' he said, 'and peaches from the hot-houses; and a meadow for the horses. Everything a mortal could desire, in fact, save a stream – and mountains.' I glanced towards him, and saw that he was smiling, and that he had the grace to blush.

'But enough of me, Mr. Hartright,' he said, suddenly setting off again. 'I have a lecture this evening, and fear I must leave at four o'clock. So, tell me, how fares your tremendous undertaking?'

'It's scarcely begun,' I said. 'But I have spoken to a few people who knew Turner.'

'Ah, yes,' he said. 'Who?'

I told him. He made no response of any kind; so I went on:

'And my sister has been to see his housekeeper.'

'Ah, the good Mrs. Booth,' he murmured. 'Did she elucidate the mystery, or add to it?'

From his sharp sidelong look I deduced that this was a test of some kind, and that his good opinion of me depended on my making the right answer; but since I had no idea what that might be, I said lamely:

'I don't know.'

He did not reply, but nodded; and, stopping by a green gate in a wall, opened it, and led me into one of the kitchen gardens. Around the perimeter ran a pleasant grassy walk, lined with fruit trees and rambling roses, and broken here and there by an arbour with a wooden seat.

'Peace,' he said, looking round. 'And the last blessed warmth of the sun.'

We sat on one of the benches, beneath a trailing rose that was still, even now, covered with flowers. Ruskin gazed silently at two apple trees near the opposite wall, as if gathering his thoughts. At length he said:

'You do know, do you not, that you are not alone, Mr. Hartright? There is already another labourer in the vineyard?'

'You mean Mr. Thornbury?' I said.

He nodded. 'What, if you will forgive my asking, makes you think that you are better qualified than he?'

This was delicate indeed, and I hesitated before answering:

'I was approached by a friend of Turner's, who expressed some confidence in me – and none whatever, I'm sorry to say, in Mr. Thornbury.'

'And may I inquire *which* friend?'

'That, I'm afraid, I cannot tell you.'

'I see.' He tapped his fingers and nodded, as if beating time to a tune in his own head.

I had chosen my words carefully, but I was forced to acknowledge that, even to my ears, they had sounded flimsy and unconvincing; and I was not entirely surprised when he went on:

'Sometimes, Mr. Hartright, we may deceive ourselves, or allow others to deceive us, into thinking we are capable of some great task which is beyond us. I speak here as a friend, and from my own experience. I regarded Turner as my earthly master. I venerated him. I knew him personally for the last ten years of his life, and for much of that time, and for long after his death, I thought of little but him and his work. And yet in many respects I feel I did not know him at all.'

Anxious not to appear still more foolish, I said nothing. He reached out to touch a white rose which drooped above his shoulder. A drop of moisture broke free from the petal where it had taken refuge, and rolled down his finger.

'Perhaps you know, Mr. Hartright, that the first volume of *Modern Painters* was intended as a defence of Turner against his critics. It was – as I am all too keenly aware – a

youthful effort, full of a young man's zeal and prejudices –
but it did enjoy a certain success. Yet it gave Turner, I
believe, not an ounce of pleasure. Cold and solitary though
he was, the flame of my approbation did not warm him. It
was a year and a half before he even mentioned the book to
me; and then, indeed, he did thank me, in his way – for he
invited me in, one night after dinner, and insisted that I
take a glass of sherry with him, in an under-room as chilly
as the tomb, and lit by a single tallow candle. Yet he always
made it plain that – though I regarded him, as I still regard
him, as the greatest landscape painter in the history of the
world – I had not grasped the meaning, or the purpose, of
his work. And I fear he was right.'

A wiry, grizzled man in a white shirt entered the kitchen
garden, pushing a wheelbarrow. He stopped when he saw
us, and tipped his moth-eaten felt hat.

'Good afternoon, Pearce,' called Ruskin.

'Good afternoon, sir.'

'Please, don't mind Mr. Hartright and me,' said Ruskin;
and the man continued on his way. Ruskin turned to me
again.

'But just how *little* I saw . . .' He shook his head. '*That* I
only discovered this past winter, when I undertook to catalogue and preserve his drawings and sketches – which, naturally enough, this being England, were gathering dust and
mildew in a basement at the South Kensington Museum.'

An electric tremor started in my stomach, and ran tingling to my fingertips.

'What did you find?' I asked.

He sighed. 'I found such pessimism, Mr. Hartright. And
such courage.' He turned suddenly, and pulled the rose
down so that it was close to my face. 'He saw the flower, in
all its beauty, with a truer eye than any man who ever
lived. And' – here he plunged his thumb deep into the
petals, prising them apart – 'he saw the canker within, just

58

as truly, and did not flinch from it. Look at any of his pictures with discernment enough, and at its heart you will find a dark clue.'

There was something in his manner as he said this – a portentous quiver in his voice, his eyes as mournful as a bloodhound's – that made me want to laugh. I mastered the impulse, however, and said:

'Clue to what?'

He did not reply; but raised a magisterial finger, and gave me a sternly pitying look – like a schoolmaster correcting a particularly obtuse pupil who has once again failed to understand some simple point.

I tried to keep the irritation from my voice. 'Are you speaking of any works in particular?'

'There are more than nineteen thousand of them,' he said. 'You must see them yourself. I can give you a note.'

'Thank you.'

'Indeed, the best advice I can offer you, if you would hope to know Turner, is: immerse yourself in his work.'

'But what of the man himself?' I said. 'His character? His tastes? His habits?'

He did not answer at once; but, raising his hand, called out to the gardener, who was passing with his newly filled barrow:

'Pearce!'

'Yes, sir?' said the man, stopping, and squinting towards us.

'Would you go to the house, and ask Crawley to fetch my Turner self-portrait, and . . .?'

'Beg pardon, sir, but fetch your *what*?'

'My Turner self-portrait,' said Ruskin (a trifle peevishly, I thought). 'And bring it here.'

'Yes, sir.'

'What were you saying?' said Ruskin, when the man had gone; and then, before I could speak, he went on: 'Ah, yes,

59

his character. Well, all I can do for you is what I did for Mr. Thornbury. And that is tell you what – in my view – were Turner's principal qualities.'

'That would be very helpful,' I said.

He breathed deeply; and then, looking ahead, as if the words were written on a bill on some invisible hoarding, said slowly:

'Uprightness. Generosity. Tenderness. Sensuality. Obstinacy. Irritability. Infidelity.' He turned towards me. 'And never forget: he lived and died alone and without hope, knowing that none could understand him or his power.'

And what, in heaven's name, I thought, *am I to make of that?*

'Forgive me,' said Ruskin earnestly. 'Have I been too cryptic? It's a perennial fault of mine, I'm afraid – and what makes it all the worse is that I'm equally guilty, on occasion, of its opposite' – here he suddenly laughed – 'and drive my friends mad with my discursiveness.'

Again, the same boyish ingenuousness showed in his face; and I reflected that I had never before heard a man speak so eloquently, or with such feeling, about his own failings. Yet as I looked into the limpid brilliance of his eyes, I knew suddenly why I was as much troubled as disarmed by it; for behind the patina of openness and warmth lay a kind of reptilian coldness, which put me strangely in mind of those Arctic regions where the surface thaws in summertime, but the earth beneath is permanently frozen.

'I must confess,' I said, 'I feel rather daunted.'

'I am truly sorry if that is my doing,' he said. 'I meant only to point out the deserts you must cross and the peaks you must climb on your great journey.'

'I fear', I said, smiling, and endeavouring to make light of it, 'that you think me unequal to it, and believe that I shall fall by the wayside.'

He did not (as I own I had expected) hasten to reassure

me; but rather looked off into the distance again, and resumed drumming on his knee. After a few seconds he leaned towards me and lightly touched my arm: 'I think perhaps it will be best', he said, 'if you continue your inquiries, and come to see me again at a later date. It may be then that what I have to say will seem less impenetrable.'

He spoke with such ineffable condescension that I bridled, and could not entirely keep the irritation from my voice as I replied:

'And how, in the meantime, do you suggest I proceed?'

'Proceed?' he said, as if his mind were already elsewhere, and he had to force it back again. He pondered a moment, and then went on:

'Few people, you will find, had even a faint inkling of Turner's true nature. But you might write to Colonel Wyndham at Petworth, whose father knew him well –'

'You mean the Third Earl of Egremont?' I said, anxious to show that I was not entirely ignorant, and remembering – from my researches at the library – that Turner had spent some time at Petworth in the Third Earl's day. Ruskin responded with a weary blink, which perfectly conveyed that he found my interruption tiresome, and resented having to pause, even for a second, to accommodate it.

'The colonel may yet preserve some family traditions about Turner,' he went on. 'As, too, may Hawkesworth Fawkes of Farnley, the son of another patron, and himself a true lover of art, and a true friend of Turner's.'

'May I mention your name?' I asked, with some trepidation.

'Of course,' he said. 'And go to Maiden Lane; for to know Turner you must see where he was born, and brought up.' He frowned, as if a new thought had struck him. 'Are you returning to London at once, Mr. Hartright? When we are finished here?'

'Yes.'

'Well, I can take you, if you wish; for I am going to Red Lion Square.'

'Thank you.'

He took his watch from his pocket, glanced at it, nodded, then hurriedly slipped it back again.

'But I must warn you that I have a great deal of preparation to do,' he said, rising, and brushing a petal from his sleeve. 'So I shall act as if you were not there; and you must promise not to be offended.'

We started together back towards the house, each occupied with his own thoughts, and had reached the lawn when we saw a manservant hurrying towards us, carrying a slim package wrapped in white muslin.

'Good heavens, Crawley!' cried Ruskin. 'Whatever is the matter?'

'Pearce said you wanted this, sir,' said the man gravely, holding out the package.

Ruskin stared at it for a moment, and then said: 'So I did, so I did. Put it in the carriage; and it can help Mr. Hartright to while away the time.'

He had not exaggerated: all the way there we sat as if in different worlds, he taking objects from a box – pieces of crystal, an apple, a ball on a chain – and consulting a notebook, or drawing (most beautifully, I have to say) a rose, on the margin of a page, as he thought; I, opposite him, at first looking out of the window, as we made our way up Vauxhall Road, and across the bridge; and then taking up the Turner picture, and unwrapping it.

To my surprise, it showed not a man, but a boy, with intense eyes looking out directly – and with something approaching insolence – from beneath dark eyebrows. The nose was long and fleshy, and there was a hint of wantonness in the full, unsmiling mouth. He was fashionably

dressed in the style of sixty or seventy years ago, in a
brown coat, with a white stock carefully tied at his throat,
and his hair neatly parted in an inverted 'V'. On the back
was a handwritten label which read: 'Turner, *aet* c. 24 years,
by himself. Given by Hannah Danby.'

'Who was Hannah Danby?' I said.

'His housekeeper. At Queen Anne Street,' murmured
Ruskin, without looking up.

I turned the picture over again. As I stared at it, I found
myself – already unnerved by my conversation with
Ruskin – thrown into turmoil; for, yet again, instead of
deepening my knowledge of Turner, I seemed merely to
have discovered a different version of him. This was not a
portrait of Travis's buffoon, or Davenant's good fellow, or
Ruskin's misunderstood martyr: it seemed to be of someone else entirely – and someone who, in the enigmatic
image he had left of himself, challenged me to find him out,
and declared that I should fail. For a moment, I felt something akin to panic; and only finally succeeded in bringing
myself under control by reasoning that, in view of the
young age at which he had drawn it, it was perhaps not
surprising that it bore no resemblance to the man remembered from later life.

As we drew up in Red Lion Square, Ruskin at last looked
up from his work, and closed his box, and said:

'Well, Mr. Hartright, here, I fear, we must say goodbye.'

I wrapped the picture up again, and handed it to him.

'I shall show it to my working men,' he said. 'To inspire
them.'

The coachman held the door; and, as I followed Ruskin
out, I said:

'Are there any other portraits of him?'

'Very few,' said Ruskin. 'He hated being painted. I
believe he went several times to Mayall's photographic studio in Regent Street. You could ask there.'

And so we parted, he already nine-tenths in his lecture, and I so distracted that I barely remembered to thank him.

And all the way home my mind churned; and I found myself asking, again and again:

What is it you have undertaken to do? Where will it lead you? What if you cannot do it?

And I am still no nearer a resolution now; but it is nearly one in the morning, and, though sleep feels an impossibility, I know that if I do not go to bed I shall never think straight again.

So let me end with a kiss, and that which I *do* know:
I love you.

Walter

IX

Letter from George Jones, R.A., to Walter Hartright, 14th August, 185–

The Royal Academy, Trafalgar Square,
14th August

Dear Sir,

I write in answer to yours of July 24th. I have already communicated a brief memoir of Turner to another gentleman, whose subsequent conduct – to speak plain – has resolved me to hold my tongue in future. I fear, therefore, that I shall be unable to accommodate you with a meeting.

Yours truly,

George Jones

X

Memorandum of a letter from Walter Hartright to
J. Ruskin, Esq., 14th August, 185–

1. Thank you for seeing me – very helpful.
2. Have written to Lord Egremont and Mr. Fawkes.
3. This afternoon will go to Covent Garden as you suggested (if the rain eases!)
4. If – as I feel sure it will – it would be helpful to talk further at a later date, may I accept kind offer to see me again?

XI

Letter from Walter Hartright to Laura Hartright, 15th August, 185–

Brompton Grove,
Tuesday

My dearest love,

Lord! The rain today! – it continued without let, from dawn until the middle of the afternoon. And not just a downpour, but a biblical deluge, so that you might suppose God had tired of the filth and squalor to which we have reduced His world, and sent a second Flood to wash it away. Indeed, the spectacle filled me, for an instant, with a superstitious awe; for the violence of the weather seemed of a piece with my discouraging letter from Jones (which, though it had been provoked by Thornbury, yet I could not help taking as a personal rebuff) and my pained recollections of the day before – and it was easy enough to imagine that all three had been ordained by some great force with the express purpose of thwarting me!

I soon put such unworthy thoughts behind me, however

(and it was not just the fear of Marian's mockery that made me do so!), and resolved that, rather than seeing these setbacks as a deterrent, I would take them as a spur to further action. I therefore busied myself with reading and correspondence until, a little after four o'clock, the rain relented sufficiently for me to venture out of doors without being immediately soaked to the skin.

Perhaps, as it turned out, it would have been better if I had been more credulous, and stayed at home all day after all.

Maiden Lane is a narrow little street lying between Covent Garden and the Strand. I must have passed it a hundred times, on my way to and from the theatre; yet I am ashamed to own that, before today, I scarcely knew of its existence. It is, in truth, a mean, poor, dingy kind of a place – yet not entirely abject, for two or three of the houses still have vestiges of respectability, which cling to them like the shreds of some finery passed on by one of their richer neighbours in Buckingham Street or Villiers Street. This afternoon, however, it looked desolate enough: for the rain seemed to have swept down all the detritus from Covent Garden market, and knots of children squatted in the gutters, patiently making little mountains of mud and old cabbage leaves and broken fruit. They turned and looked at me as I approached; and then, as I passed, returned without a word to their game.

Turner's father, I knew, had kept a barber's shop on the corner of Hand Court; but whether Hand Court still existed, and, if so, which of the half-dozen or so gloomy little entrances (crammed here and there between the houses at odd angles, as if a giant dentist had prised the bricks apart to accommodate them) might lead to it, I had no idea. As I looked about for someone to ask, my eye fell on a girl of twelve or thirteen, standing a little apart from the rest.

'Good afternoon,' I said.

She stared at me, but said nothing. Her large eyes, I noticed, were brown, and flecked with amber. Her dark hair was matted, and there was a grey smudge on one cheek; but had you washed her, and dressed her in new clothes, and placed her in any drawing room in Harley Street or Berkeley Square, she would have been counted very striking, and made much of by the ladies.

'Can you tell me', I said, 'which is Hand Court?'

Again, she did not speak; but continued to stare, as if trying to find some meaning in my face that she had not heard in my words. At length she wiped her hand on her grubby pinafore, and jerked her cracked thumb towards a gloomy passage on the other side of the street. It was barred by an iron gate, beyond which nothing was visible save a line of discoloured wooden slats that seemed to dissolve, after a few yards, into pitch-blackness.

'Is that a barber's shop?' I asked, pointing at the corner building.

She hesitated a moment, then at last broke her silence. 'No, sir,' she said, in a flat, weary voice. 'It belongs to Parkin.'

'Parkin?'

'The grocer, sir. 'E keeps it for a warehouse.'

I walked to the window, wiped a film of soot from one of the little panes, and peered in. All I could see to start with was a heavy metal grille, but as my eyes adjusted to the meagre grey light I at length made out a row of shadowy tea chests stacked against the far wall. So much for my hope of finding the shop unchanged, and perhaps even occupied by a member of the same family.

'Does anyone live in the court?' I said, turning back to the girl.

She looked at me as if I had asked her whether the sun was warm, or water wet. 'Why, yes, sir.' She started to laugh. ''Unnerds of 'em!'

For the life of me I could not imagine where hundreds of people would fit, unless the court were a mile long; but I contented myself with asking:

'Anyone called Turner?'

'Turner? No, sir, not as I knows.'

'Any old people, who might remember how it was years ago?'

'Well, sir . . .' She frowned, and her gaze flickered towards the gate. 'There's old Jenny Watts, as I've 'eard tell is ninety . . .'

There was a sudden eagerness in her tone; and I could not help noticing that her eyes followed my hand as it reached into my pocket and drew out a shilling.

'Will you take me to her?' I said.

For answer, she glanced at the pawnbroker's across the street, then trotted to her charges playing in the gutter, and said something to the eldest girl. Then she ran back and took the money, before looking round furtively again, and muttering:

'Only I mustn't be long.'

She opened the gate easily enough, but as we passed through, a boy of perhaps fifteen suddenly emerged from the shadows and blocked our way. Without taking his eyes from us he half-turned his head and shouted a word – I could not make it out, but it sounded like 'khulim' – into the court behind him. All at once, in the darkness beyond, I saw figures hurrying about, and there was a frantic chink and scraping of metal, which led me to suppose that they had been gambling, and were gathering up the evidence.

'All's well,' said the girl. ''E's not' – and again I could not discern the word, but it might have been 'esclop', or possibly ''Islop'. The boy seemed no more inclined to let us pass; for he spread his feet, and folded his arms, and started, slowly and insolently, to whistle.

'Come on, Sam,' said the girl. 'We're just going to Jenny

Watts'.'

The boy widened his eyes and grinned; and then, glancing behind him again, to see that his companions had finished their business, lazily stepped aside.

Perhaps it was their slang which put the idea in my head (for there seemed a distinctly Arabic ring to it), but my first thought as we entered the court was that I had been transported to some city of the East. The buildings, four or five storeys high, faced each other across a space so narrow that – as, supposedly, in Damascus or Baghdad – a woman on the top floor could shake hands with her neighbour opposite without fear of mishap. The eight or nine boys who stood about, watching me silently, only added to the impression; for, if there was nothing exotic about their clothes or their complexions, yet their blank sullen faces made it all too easy to imagine that they belonged to a different race entirely. Only when you looked up, and saw a strip of foul grey tinged with brown – made fouler and browner every second by smoke from the fires of those who could afford them – did you realize that this was not a cool refuge from the Mediterranean sun, but a part of our own city, which we have condemned to perpetual twilight.

'In 'ere, sir,' said the girl, stopping by a green door that had wrenched its hinge from the frame. She pushed it open with her shoulder, and led me into a kind of lobby which gave access to a scuffed and dirty wooden staircase. The air was cool but close, and so foetid that I had to press my handkerchief to my nose.

'Are you not well, sir?' said the girl, clearly unaccustomed to such faint-heartedness. 'It's a bit of a way; and 'ard if you ain't got your wind.'

The cause of her concern was soon apparent. Treading gingerly (for the steps were bowed and shiny with use, and I feared my boots might go through them altogether), I followed her up three flights of stairs to the top of the building, where she succumbed to a terrible fit of coughing so violent that I found myself looking for blood on the hand she held to her mouth.

It was almost a minute before she had recovered enough to knock on the door. A frail voice answered (though too faintly for me to understand what it said), and the girl pushed her face to the wood and wheezed:

'Sarah Bateman. With a gentleman to see you.'

And this time I heard, distinctly enough:

'Oh! Come in!'

The girl opened the door, and – how to describe what met my eyes? First, the light: a pearly grey haze, diffused through a grimy skylight, which almost dazzled me for a moment, after the gloom of the lower storeys; then an impression of space, which I soon saw came not from the great size of the room, but from its bareness. The floor was uncovered, and there was nothing on the walls, save – on the chimney-piece – an engraving of a sportsman and his dog. A single iron cooking pot, its bottom smeared with ash, hung above the lifeless fire. A small table, a crate which had been pressed into service as a dresser, and a crude bed in an alcove completed the domestic arrangements.

But what struck me most was the figure sitting in the small attic window. She was probably, in truth, little bigger than the girl; but her upright bearing, and her old-fashioned sea-green silk dress, gave her a kind of stateliness that made her appear too large for the Lilliput in which she found herself. Heaps of clothes were piled against the wall behind her; and she held before her a pair of black breeches, which she seemed to have just finished mending. Her face was the colour of cork, and wrinkled like a monkey's; and, as we entered, she turned and looked at me with light, curious eyes and an ingratiating smile.

I expected the girl to say something more, by way of introduction, but she merely stood aside; and, after a few seconds, I realized I must speak for myself.

'Mrs. Watts?' I began.

The woman made no response, and I wondered whether she might be deaf; but the girl said:

'Go on, she can 'ear well enough.'

'I believe', I said, 'that you remember this place as it was, many years ago?'

Again she said nothing; but cocked her head, and shifted in her chair – like Florrie preparing to hear her favourite story.

'I am interested in a family called Turner,' I continued.

She frowned; and then, after a few seconds, said: 'Toorner?' Her voice was strong and clear; but having no teeth, she seemed to hold the word in her lips, almost squeezing the life out of it.

'They kept a barber's shop,' I said. 'On the corner of the court.'

'Oh, the *barber's*.' She nodded. 'Yes. Where Captain Wyatt went.'

'Captain Wyatt?' I asked.

'To 'ave 'is 'air dressed, o' course!' she said, as if I must as well know who Captain Wyatt was as why he would go to a barber.

'Did you know them?' I said. 'William Turner? And Mary? And their son?'

She nodded again. And then, to my surprise, she winked at me, as if she knew something remarkable about them, and was acknowledging my shrewdness in guessing it.

Even though I knew it to be foolish, the thought that I might be the first person to discover some secret about Turner's childhood (for I could not imagine Thornbury coming here, and I fancied that she would have been less conspiratorial with me if he had) set my heart beating

71

faster.

'Can you tell me something of them?' I said.

The woman reached down beside her chair, and brought out a little stool, which she gave to me. I sat down, and – since she said nothing more – coaxed her by going on:

'I should especially like to hear about the boy.'

'Ah!' She grimaced knowingly. ''E was a slippy one.'

'Slippy?'

'Up and down, sir. In and out.'

'Up and down the court, you mean?'

She nodded. 'Reg'lar little fish.'

The girl giggled; and, after eyeing her uncertainly for a moment, Mrs. Watts joined in – as though she thought she had made a joke, but needed confirmation to be sure.

'And what about the Strand?' I asked. 'Did he go there much, to see the river?'

'Oh, yes, sir.'

'That's well enough, for a fish,' said the girl; and they both laughed again.

I pressed ahead doggedly, anxious lest the whole interview dissolve in merriment:

'What, he liked the ships, did he?'

'Ah, yes,' said Mrs. Watts. 'The ships. They was much thicker then, before they built the new docks.'

'And did he paint them at all, or draw them, that you remember?'

'Ay, sir,' she said; yet I doubted that she did, for her tone was quite mechanical, and she immediately went on:

'My father was a purlman, and plied all the vessels 'ere-abouts; but them docks pretty much ruined him, for after they was made 'e couldn't get near the boats, and when a seaman's ashore 'e don't want purl, do 'e, sir?'

'No –' I began; but before I could say more she continued:

'For nothing'll please 'im but to sit in a tavern, with 'is mates, and them women.' She laughed, and looked past

72

me, towards the girl. 'In't Jenny right, pet?'

'Do you recall anything of the mother?' I said, hoping that a different approach might nudge her back to the subject.

'Why, yes, sir,' she said, with sudden animation, 'that I do.' She shook her head. 'She, sir – oh, my, she was a very gale –'

'A what?' I asked, thinking I had misheard her, or that this was her form of 'girl'.

'A gale, sir. You'd think the end of the world 'ad come.' She looked about her; and, her eye lighting on the little casement, seized the handle, and shook it, and then drummed her fingers on the glass. 'Like that. Captain Wyatt heard 'er once, 'owlin' up from the basement; and 'e said 'e never 'eard nothing like it, no, not in the Indies, where 'e saw a ship go down once, in a 'urricane.'

'A fish,' said Sarah, 'and 'is ma's a gale.' She giggled; and after a few seconds the woman joined in again, and soon they were whinnying and spluttering like a pair of infants, until the exertion proved too much, and sent the girl into another paroxysm of coughing. Even this Mrs. Watts seemed to take only as evidence that the child had reached some new pitch of hilarity; for she continued to watch her with streaming eyes, laughing herself, until I said:

'Can't you see the poor girl is ill?'

I sounded, perhaps, unduly harsh; for I was beginning to suspect that this had been an entirely wasted journey, and that the old woman was either too deranged or too simple to tell me anything of value. I decided, however, to make one final attempt.

'Do you recollect', I said more gently, 'any particular stories about them?'

She looked perplexed for a moment, as if she had not understood me; and then pressed her hands together and said:

73

'The frost fair! 'Ard to credit now, sir, what with them takin' down the bridge, but them days the river was all-over ice, 'ere to Southwark, and there was fireworks, and puppets, I even seed a 'orse-race; and after, the Captain walked me down the City Road, and stopped before a stall; and 'e said, "You're nothing but skin and bone, girl, you need a bit of meat on you." And 'e bought me a pudding.'

'How old would you have been then?' I asked.

'Ooh, let's see.' She sucked in her cheeks, and counted on her fingers. 'Sixteen, I'd say, sir, pretty near.'

And that settled the matter; for I had vivid memories of my father telling me about the last frost fair – *there was a great mall in the middle, Walter, where the ladies and gentlemen promenaded; and they called it 'City Road'* – which, I knew, had been held in the winter of 1813. If she had been sixteen at the time, she must have been born in 1797, when Turner was already a successful artist, and only two years before he had moved from Hand Court to Harley Street. There might be the remnant of some genuine anecdote or local tradition about the family in what she had told me; but, if so, it was inextricably jumbled with the recollections of her own life, like the image in a splintered looking-glass.

I rose to leave, thanked her, gave her sixpence (which she left lying on her open palm, as if I might add to it), and beckoned to the child. We had barely reached the door, however, when, from below, came the sound of hurried footsteps on the stairs, and a woman's voice calling: 'Sarah! Sarah!' The girl gasped, and stopped quite dead; then, crying, 'My ma, she'll flay me!' she ran back into the alcove, and hid herself, as best she could, behind the blanket that served as a curtain.

'Come,' I began, 'why should she be angry –?'; but before I could say more a woman rushed into the room. She was about thirty, poorly but respectably dressed, and must have been handsome once; but fatigue and disappointment, like a victorious army, had traced their advance in the lines upon her face. She looked frantically about her, and then, not immediately seeing her daughter, pointed accusingly at me.

'Where's my girl?' she said, panting heavily. Her voice was quiet, but some emotion she could barely master made it squeak and waver, and her eyes – remarkably like the child's, I now saw – were feverish with anger.

Not wishing to betray the girl, but equally unwilling to tell a lie, and a useless one at that, I said nothing. I must, though, have given her away unwittingly; for my gaze strayed towards the alcove, and the woman at once read its meaning, and pushed past me towards the bed. I managed to bar her way, but not before the child had revealed herself by whimpering, and then promptly abandoned her flimsy sanctuary to take refuge behind me.

'What 'ave you done, you little cat?' said the woman, lunging towards her, and raising her hand as if to strike her.

The girl made no reply, only pressing herself further into the narrow space between me and the wall; but Jenny Watts clapped her hands, and started to laugh again, as if this were a kind of Punch-and-Judy show, put on especially to entertain her.

'She's done no harm,' I said, laying a hand on the mother's arm to restrain her.

'I shouldn't 'ave known, save for Sam Telfer,' said the woman, ignoring me entirely, and addressing the girl. 'I'm gone ten minutes, just to get the tightner, and when I'm back 'e says 'e sees a gentleman givin' you brownies, and you takin' 'im in 'ere.'

'I only asked her to bring me to Mrs. Watts,' I said.

'Oh, so that's what you calls it now, is it?' said the woman, suddenly rounding on me.

I braced myself, for she was now swaying and trembling

75

so violently that I thought her rage would not be contained; but, having been denied the girl, must vent itself on me instead. After a second or two, however, she brought herself under control, and merely clenched her fists, and said with scalding contempt:

"'Bringin' you to Mrs. Watts!'"

I longed to cry out: *For God's sake, woman, what do you take me for? I have a daughter myself!* and yet I knew that to do so would be useless. Looking at the man before her, she saw not me but someone else entirely; for all her experience had taught her that a gentleman talks to a girl in Maiden Lane, and gives her money, with but one purpose; and nothing I could say or do would persuade her that I should have sooner died than violate her child.

'I didn't do nothin'! 'E didn't do nothin'!' screamed the girl, suddenly darting out from behind me, and lifting up her dress. ''Ere, 'ave a look if you don't believe me!'

And, without a word, the woman did so, barely pausing long enough to tug the blanket a few inches across the gap, and so afford her daughter a scrap of modesty.

At length, she grunted and stepped back. She said nothing, but looked at me; and for the first time I saw a doubt in her eyes, and she seemed somehow smaller, like a kite that has lost the wind, and begun to sag. For a moment, I felt, I had the advantage, and at once determined to make the best of it.

'I will not insult you by offering you more money,' I said, 'but Sarah has a shilling, which she earned fairly, by bringing me here; and I think you would do well to spend it on the doctor; for that is a bad cough, and should be treated.'

And before she had time to reply, or to tell the girl to give the shilling back again, I left, shutting the door behind me, and made my way back through the court, exciting no more than some whispering, and a derisive laugh, from the boys. A few moments later I was in the Strand – which,

with its street-vendors, and gas-lamps, and crowds of
cheerful theatre-goers, seemed like the waking world after
an oppressive dream.

Forgive me, my darling, if what I have described distresses
you; but – as you may imagine – it troubled me, and we
have agreed that we must have no secrets from each other.
I am haunted not merely by the thought of that poor child
and her mother, and the knowledge that, quite unintention-
ally, I have brought more care into their already over-bur-
dened lives, but also by the nagging question of why
Ruskin should have suggested I go to Maiden Lane at all.
Surely he must have known – as I know myself, if I pause
to reflect upon it – that after almost sixty years it is almost
inconceivable I should find someone who remembers the
Turners? Yet what, otherwise (save only malice; and I hesitate to believe he would be so cruel to a man who has done
him no harm) could have prompted him to send me to a
stinking slum, from which all traces of the family have been
long since obliterated?
　My one hope is that I shall find the answer when I see
Turner's pictures – in which case, I shall know it soon
enough, for Marian and I go to Marlborough House on
Monday.
　My love to you always,

　Walter

XII

Letter from Michael Gudgeon to Walter Hartright, 15th August, 185–

Box Cottage, Storry, East Sussex,
August

Dear Mr. Hartright,

   Lord, yes! – I remember Turner, though the journey I took with him must have been almost forty years ago now. If I were to draw up an inventory of my memories, I should list them under the following chief heads:

1. Being very cold.
2. Being very wet.
3. Being sick in a boat.
4. Being footsore and saddle-sore in about equal measure.
5. Being ill-housed and ill-fed.
6. Being well housed and well fed.
7. Not giving a damn about any of the above; for my companion was a Great Genius, and I a lusty, impudent, carefree young fellow.
8. Turner very silent when sober.
9. Turner very boisterous when drunk.

   I fear I cannot furnish you with a long memoir, for my hand is rheumatic (my poor long-suffering wife, indeed, is taking this letter down to my dictation); and nowadays I do not go about much. My friends, however, are good enough to call upon me here; and if you think it worth the time and expense to do likewise, I should be delighted to welcome you as one of them, and to tell you all I can recall.

Yours very truly,
Michael Gudgeon

XIII

From the diary of Marian Halcombe, 16th August, 185–

Marlborough House is not, I am sure, the most magnificent palace in the world: a long, plain red-brick building in the Palladian style, it hangs back a little from Pall Mall, as if ashamed to show its dowdy façade in such distinguished company. And the crowds that throng it – now that the ground floor has become a temporary art gallery – make it feel more like a railway station hotel than a private residence. But palace it is, and the first I have ever entered; and as we walked down a long covered passage into the lofty hall (so vast that Jenny Lind has sung here, before an audience of hundreds), and paid our shilling for a guidebook, I could not but reflect on how different it was from the house in which Turner had spent his last years, and in which I had first seen one of his paintings.

Perhaps Walter was preoccupied by a similar idea; for he was unusually silent all the way there; and, when we arrived, looked about him with an almost incredulous air, as if comparing it with the scene of *his* last adventure – for surely the filthy little street where Turner had been born, though nearer in miles, must have presented an even starker contrast to this place than the cottage in which he had died?

But then we turned, and all such thoughts and calculations instantly evaporated. We had both seen individual Turners before, of course; but never – for this is the first public exhibition since his death – more than thirty of them displayed together. All at once our eyes were assailed by the most brilliant radiance I have ever seen in paintings – and far more, I have to say, than I should have conceived possible. Reds, oranges and yellows, as hot and tumultuous as burning coals, erupted from the walls, making even the brightest objects about them – a woman's gaudy green dress, a huge picture of the Battle of Blenheim above the chimney-piece – appear suddenly drab and lifeless. They seemed, indeed, more intensely real than the press of people staring at them, or the building itself – as if we were trapped in Plato's cave, and the pictures, rather than merely flat pieces of canvas hanging *inside*, were in fact holes in the rock, through which we could glimpse the unimagined world beyond.

The effect on Walter was immediate; and so dramatic that I wish I could have found some means to record it, for it would have convinced even the dourest sceptic of the power of art. He stopped dead, and drew himself up, as if someone had suddenly lifted a great weight from his back; his mouth set in a small, surprised smile, and the skin appeared to tighten across his forehead, raising his eyebrows into an expression of wonderment and pleasure. His gaze was fixed on a square picture on the opposite wall, which showed an indistinct white figure apparently emerging from the smoke and flames of a raging fire. From where we were standing it was impossible to make out more; but, rather than going closer (which, indeed, would have been difficult, so dense was the press of people), Walter remained there, seemingly uninterested in the subject, content merely to bask in the radiance of the colour, like a cat stretching itself in the sun. I waited for him a moment, and then, since he still showed no inclination to move, set off on my own to explore further.

The impressions of the next half an hour were so forceful and so contradictory that I must try to set them down here in some detail, before they disintegrate into brilliant confusion. There were more than thirty pictures in the exhibition, and what you noticed about them first was simply their enormous variety. The view I had always associated with Turner, *London from Greenwich Park*, was there – although the original had a grandeur and richness you could not have guessed from our engraving of it; and a terrifying picture of a puny cottage caught in a mountain avalanche, and crushed by a deluge of broken ice and uprooted trees and a giant rock (so ferociously painted that the pigment was as thick and ridged as mortar), recalled some of the dread and horror the pictures in Mrs. Booth's house had inspired in me. Almost everything else, however, took me by surprise. Here was a magnificent sea piece, showing distant ships heeling in a stiff breeze, which (save for the waves, which gathered menacingly in the bottom right-hand corner and threatened to spill over the frame and wet your feet) might have been by a Dutch master; there a gorgeous classical landscape saturated with honey light, or a sublime mountain darkened by angry clouds. Most striking of all were those wild swirls of paint – like those which had so captivated Walter – in which the pure colour seemed to strive for freedom, detaching itself from form like the soul leaving the body, so that you could not clearly discern a subject at all.

I think most people, confronted by such splendid profusion, would find it hard to believe that it could all have sprung from one hand. Certainly, as I embarked on my tour, that was the uppermost thought in my mind. It was only after I had examined three or four of the pictures more closely that I recognized – with that sudden dawning that comes when you at last become conscious of some insistent sound, like a dog barking in the distance – that there was, indeed, a family relationship, suggested not by obvious similarities of style, but by certain recurrent quirks and oddities. What they mean, or whether they mean anything at all, I still do not know; but they have left me with the nagging idea that they are a kind of message in code, and that I need but the right key in order to decipher it.

81

The first painting I looked at (for no other reason than that it was the closest) was a luminous, gold-tinged historical scene which, at a casual glance, I should have taken to be by Claude. I failed, in my eagerness, to note the exact title, but the subject was the decline of Carthage. You are standing, as it were, in the bottom left-hand corner of the picture – in the entrance, perhaps, of a great palace, for the foreground is in shadow. Immediately before you, like flotsam on the shore, lies a clutter of objects: a pile of fruit; a standard bearing a shield and a wreath of withered flowers; discarded cloaks and weapons; and a strange, bulbous brown blob with a pro- tuberance at the top, which might be a buoy with a chain but which also – you realize after a few seconds – has a fleshly quality about it, like a giant squid, or the internal organ of a beast. Beyond that is a narrow quay, and then a dazzling strip of water, fringed in the distance by lines of hazy masts, which stretches to the horizon. Above it – almost in the cen- tre of the canvas, but a little to the left – hangs a burning sun, filling the sky with an incandescence so bright that it stings your eyes to look at it.

On either side of the harbour, like the jaws of a vice, are clusters of classical buildings, their steps crowded with little doll-like figures. Those on the left are floridly baroque, and covered with ornate carvings, but those on the right – to which, because of the diagonal perspective, your gaze is nat- urally drawn – are more restrained: passing an odd little tower that looks like a dwarf lighthouse, you enter them by a narrow flight of steps (so narrow, indeed, you feel the walls will squeeze the breath from your body), and then ascend gradually until, at length, you reach a temple of Parthenon-like simplicity on the summit of a distant hill.

I could remember little about the fall of Carthage, save that she had been reduced to surrendering her arms and children to Rome, but the import of the picture seemed clear enough. It was, in effect, a moral tale, told (unlike a written

82

narrative) from top right to bottom left: once, the Carthaginians had had the vigour and discipline to climb the straight and narrow path; but, as their wealth and power grew, they had abandoned the austere and lofty heights of greatness, neglecting their industry and defences, and descending into the flyblown city on the left, where they had dissipated their strength in idleness and luxury.

The picture was dated '1817', a mere two years after the defeat of Napoleon, and it suddenly occurred to me that Turner must have intended it as a warning to England – which, with her great trading empire, must surely be the Carthage of the modern age – against lowering her guard and sinking into complacency. Convinced (but how foolishly, I think now, looking back) that I had correctly divined his meaning, I turned to a second Claudian scene, *The Bay of Baiae, with Apollo and the Sibyl*, to see if my great perspicacity could unlock *its* secrets, too.

A simpler and more tranquil piece, this, with soft light and sweet curves in place of the other's fierce sun and harsh architectural planes. You are standing (again, a little to the left of centre) on a wide sandy path that draws you enticingly to a golden beach. A stone pier lined with boats reaches diagonally into the sea – which is no more than a long finger of blue, really, laid across the middle of the canvas, and yet enough to give you a pang of longing, and make you think you feel the warm breeze on your face, and smell its cargo of salt and the scent of wild flowers. The bay is ringed by gentle hills of a pale yellowy-green, which fades into grey on the horizon and differentiates itself into darker shrubs and bushes and leaves as it reaches the near-distance. It is only when you look closely that you see that among the rocks and foliage there are also ruined buildings: broken stone walls crumbling back into the sand, or a pair of subterranean archways – two great eyes separated by a brick nose, like the top of a buried skull – half hidden under a tangle of scrub. As if to heighten the air of menace, a barely visible serpent, almost the same colour as the earth, lurks in the bottom right-hand corner, waiting for its prey.

The picture is dominated by a V-shaped pair of trees on the right, which start close to the bottom of the canvas and reach almost to the top, spreading a band of shadow nearly to the left-hand edge. It is here that the only creatures – apart from the snake – appear: first, immediately under the trees themselves, a tiny white rabbit (soon to be the reptile's victim?); and then, on the other side of the path, the figures of Apollo and the Sibyl. He, dressed in a wreath and a red robe, is holding his hand towards her; while she, naked from the waist up, kneels on a rock, arms outstretched, inclined slightly towards *him*. Both of them seem somehow flat, and too small, giving the odd impression that they have been cut from another picture and pasted on. And the Sibyl, in particular, has the same doll-like appearance as the figures in *The Decline of Carthage*, as if she were the work of a gifted child rather than of the genius who painted the rest of the picture. There is something strange, too, in her hands and feet, which have the blunt shape of flippers rather than the complex geometry of human limbs. You might almost think that Turner had conceived her as a mermaid rather than a woman – an impression accentuated by her dress, which has a sort of scaly brightness, and clings to her legs like a skin.

Walter has several times reproached me for being too practical, and preferring dry facts to the sweeter but less substantial world of myth and fancy; and now, for once, I felt the justice of his criticism; for if I had ever known the story of Apollo and the Sibyl, I had quite forgotten it, and was forced to seek him out, and ask him to explain it to me. I found him gravitating – as if drawn by magnetic attraction – towards another of those bolts of colour that had so struck us upon entering: a square canvas, cut in half by a horizontal blood-red bar so vivid that you could have seen it from half a mile away. Falling into step beside him, I said:

'What did Apollo do to the Sibyl? Or can you not tell me in such august company?'

'Sad,' he said, 'but perfectly respectable. He granted that she should have as many years of life as she held grains of sand.'

That at least explained what she was doing with those fin-like hands. 'And what happened?'

'He was as good as his word; but she failed to ask for perpetual youth, and gradually wasted away until only her voice was left.'

I felt I now understood the subject; but I was still left with the faint consciousness – which remains with me still – of an unanswered question. It was put out of my mind at the time, however, by the square picture, which, as we approached it, imperiously claimed our attention with mysteries of its own. The red strip, I now saw, was a flaming sunset, spreading, it seemed (the painting was so indistinct it was difficult to be sure) across some desolate seashore. Before it stood Napoleon, his arms folded, his eyes cast pensively down, entirely alone save for a lone British sentry standing behind him, and his own elongated reflection in the wet sand. He was staring at a tiny triangular object on the ground, which I could only identify by looking at the title: *The Exile and the Rock Limpet, 1842*. To the right was a pile of debris that might have been a wrecked ship, and above that the smoking ruins of a war-torn city.

We stood looking at it in silence for a few seconds, and then Walter sighed and said:

'"And the light shineth in darkness."'

He paused, and seemed to be waiting for me to go on; so I said:

'"And the darkness comprehended it not."?'

He nodded, but said nothing more. I am not sure what he meant – unless, as a painter himself, he was merely admiring the ability to create colour so radiant that it seems to burn from within – but his words nonetheless helped to galvanize something in *my* mind; for they startled me almost as if he had uttered a profanity. After a moment's reflection I realized why: Turner had, without question, captured the beauty of the sun more gloriously than any artist I knew; but in the paintings I had seen there was always something terrible about it, too – a cruelty, a heedless power to destroy, that made it seem a fitter symbol for the bloodthirsty deity of the Aztecs than for the pure love of our Lord, expressed in that lovely passage from St. John.

I said nothing of this to Walter, for I did not wish to disturb him, at least until I had had a chance to see more, and discover if my impression was justified. I did not, however, scruple to point out another idiosyncrasy I had come to recognize; for, although the technique was entirely different from Turner's earlier works – the paint so coarse and mixed that it looked as if it had been applied by a madman in a frenzy – yet Napoleon and his guard had the familiar toylike quality, making them look more like tin soldiers than men, and I felt I could safely generalize about his figures.

'At least your people are better than his,' I said, laughing.

I thought this compliment would please Walter, but he barely even acknowledged it; and after a moment I left him again to his reverie, to continue my researches on my own. Rather than examining another picture in detail, I decided to test my theory by merely glancing at them all; and flitting rapidly from one to the next I soon persuaded myself that I was right. I cannot remember every painting now, but enough to prove the point: a gory sunset lights the last journey of an heroic old warship, *The Fighting Téméraire*, towards its destiny in a breaker's yard; terrified people flee the wrathful *Angel Standing in the Sun*, the flesh burned from their bones by his all-engulfing fire; even a sun-soaked picture of Venice, which at first sight seems like a cheerful Canaletto seen through a heat-haze, at length reveals its own tragic secret – for its subject, you realize on closer inspection, is the Bridge of Sighs, which carried condemned criminals to their death.

My exploration also yielded another discovery. As I was hurrying past a dark picture – which I had already dismissed in advance as unsuitable for my purpose, since there seemed no sunlight in it at all – my eye was caught by a glint of gold, and the hint of a familiar form, in the middle of the canvas. Stopping to examine it, I saw that it was the coil of a giant serpent, emerging from a low, dark cave half hidden by brush, which immediately put me in mind of the snake and the ruins in the *Bay of Baiae*. There was more to come; for confronting the beast, in the foreground, is a man – presumably Jason, for the piece is called *Jason in Search of the Golden Fleece* – kneeling on a split and twisted fallen tree – which, when you look at it, seems to turn into a writhing monster, or two monsters, like the buoy in *The Decline of Carthage*. Less than two minutes later I happened upon *The Goddess of Discord in the Garden of the Hesperides*, where the effect is inverted: beyond a gently wooded valley, peopled with nymphs and goddesses, stand two mountainous walls of stone, leaning ominously towards each other˙ (like the sides of a half-formed arch) across a narrow pass. In one place, the top of the rock has an odd serrated shape; which – when you examine it closely – turns out not to be rock at all, but the back of a terrifying monster guarding the entrance, with stone-coloured wings and crocodile jaws that might almost have been hollowed from the granite by wind and rain.

I had, and still have, no idea what to make of these connections, but I must confess that finding them excited me, and made me think, for a moment, that I should turn critic, and go into competition with Mr. Ruskin. At the same time, they troubled me (for they are undeniably disturbing), and put me in a quandary which I have still not resolved as I write this: should I point them out to Walter? To do so would have been to risk casting him back into gloom just at the moment when his delight in Turner's work seemed to have lifted his spirits; but to keep silent would have been to leave him in ignorance of something that might be important – and also (I must be honest!) to deny myself the chance of demonstrating my own insight.

Fate, however, spared me from having to make an immediate decision, for when I looked about for Walter I could not at first see him; and no sooner had I eventually found him again – standing in front of another lustrous canvas, in a corner I had missed – than I heard a voice behind me calling 'Marian!'

I turned, and saw Elizabeth Eastlake – her head towering above all the other women, and most of the men – making her way towards me. She was not, it seemed, alone; for as the crowd parted before her I noticed a little cavalcade in her wake: a middle-aged couple (as I supposed) and their daughter, and an old woman in a bath chair pushed by a manservant.

'Marian!' she repeated, as she drew near; and then, seeing Walter: 'Oh! And Mr. Hartright too! What a pleasant surprise!' After shaking our hands she turned towards the old woman in the bath chair, and, raising her voice, said:

'Lady Meesden, may I introduce Miss Halcombe?'

I bowed, and for a moment had the extraordinary idea that I was meeting one of Turner's doll-people; for the woman's face was chalk-white with powder, save for a dab of rouge on each cheek, and the skin seemed to have folded in about her eyes, reducing them to no more than a pair of black shining buttons. She stared at me, unsmiling, for a moment, and then bobbed her head, like a bird pecking water from a pool.

'And her brother-in-law, Mr. Hartright,' said Lady Eastlake. Walter can usually extort a smile from the stoniest misanthrope, but the old woman was as frosty with him as she had been with me; and it was, I thought, with some relief that Lady Eastlake turned away from her to present us to the other members of her party: Lady Meesden's daughter, Mrs. Kingsett; her husband (who appeared, among his other misfortunes, to be called Mauritius); and their own daughter, Florence, an awkward, coltish seventeen-year-old who blushed when you looked at her.

'Marian is a particular friend of mine, Lydia,' said Lady Eastlake.

'Indeed?' said Mrs. Kingsett. She was about fifty, with plaited greying hair coiled neatly behind her head, and wearing a loose-fitting walking dress in a fine red-and-white check that looked wonderfully free and comfortable. She was too square and craggy to be considered beautiful; but there was a certain vivacious charm to her voice when she smiled and said:

'Well, there can't be a better recommendation than that.'

'Perhaps "By Appointment to the Queen"?' said Lady Eastlake.

Mrs. Kingsett laughed; and – as if trying to make up for her mother's coldness – shook my hand in the most easy and affable manner imaginable.

'Sir Charles and I are away on our autumn visit to Italy next week,' Lady Eastlake went on. 'And I have come to remind myself what great *English* art can be.'

'What do *you* think, Miss Halcombe?' said Mrs. Kingsett, casting her eyes about her in a way that seemed to include the whole exhibition. 'Are you quite overwhelmed?'

'Quite,' I said.

'I, too.'

At this, her husband, who was standing at her elbow, gave a derisive 'tk' – which she studiedly ignored – and looked away with a long-suffering smile. Nature had not dealt kindly with him; for he had a turned-up nose like a pig, and a pulled-down mouth, with too many teeth, like a wolf; and whiskers so curled that you'd think they'd been singed by his hot and florid complexion; and in his little gesture of defiance, and his wife's pointed refusal to acknowledge it, I suddenly fancied that (as sometimes happens) I could read the whole history of their connection. Here were a plain man and a plain woman, who had married – as they thought – for mutual advantage: he for the respectability that came with her station, and her mother's title; she, poor thing, for fear that a shy and ungainly girl like herself might have no husband at all if she refused him. But over the years, both had come to realize that she was his intellectual, as well as his social, superior; and as she had grown in confidence, and blossomed into maturity, so he had dwindled into sourness and disappointment. Any true feelings they might have had for each other had been eaten away by the acid of his resentment and her contempt – leaving the marriage an empty shell, into which she had steadily expanded, by developing as independent a life as was consistent with respectability, and he had been reduced to sulking in a corner.

You could not help but feel sorry for both of them, but I must own that the balance of my sympathy lay with her – if only because her fate, or something like it, might all too easily have been my own. Perhaps Mr. Kingsett sensed this; for, though he shook my hand (he really could not do otherwise, when his wife had already done so), his grip was as slack and uninterested as a dead fish, and he immediately turned away with an inaudible mumble, and fixed his watery gaze on the fireplace. To my surprise, as I moved myself, I noticed that Lady Meesden was scowling at us, with a ferocity that suggested she had witnessed the whole episode.

Certainly, Mr. Kingsett's hostility cannot have arisen from any consciousness of social distinction, for he received

Walter as one greets an old friend – or, perhaps it would be truer to say, as a drowning man greets a log, for here was a promise of rescue from the ocean of females in which the poor man found himself, and he clung to it for dear life. Within less than a minute he had manoeuvred Walter away from me and established a small gentlemen's club, with a membership of two, in the corner. A moment later I heard him opening the proceedings with: 'I think a picture should be *of* something, and you should be able to see what it is.'

Not wanting to add to Walter's embarrassment by eavesdropping on his reply, I turned back towards Mrs. Kingsett; but she – doggedly pursuing her policy of disregarding her husband altogether – was already deep in conversation with Lady Eastlake again, and I felt I could not intrude. Rather than brave the bellicose Lady Meesden or her tongue-tied granddaughter, therefore, I decided to study the picture before us.

It was another classical subject: *Ulysses Deriding Polyphemus*. Again, we are close to the bottom left-hand corner, looking diagonally across the canvas to a brilliant sunrise on the low horizon, which casts its rays into the sky, burnishing the underside of the clouds and veining them with bloodshot streaks. The foreground is dominated by Ulysses' ship, its gilded hull trimmed with stripes of black and red, moving from left to right into the centre of the canvas as it makes for the open sea. The water is soporifically calm, with tiny lapping waves that seem barely to have the energy to reach the shore, but on board everything is bustle: the decks are crowded, the oars are out, and sailors swarm up the mast and yards, frantically setting the ornately decorated sails or raising their red flags. Behind them, almost in darkness, is the dark mass of Polyphemus's island.

I knew, I think, even before I had consciously noted any of the details, that this picture was unlike the others – or, rather, that it somehow *fulfilled* the others; for, like a song, of which, up until now, you have only a few notes and half the chorus, it seemed to bring together all those peculiarities which I had glimpsed elsewhere, and miraculously fuse them into a glorious whole. Here was the beautiful but merciless sun; here the entrance to the underworld – the mouth of Polyphemus's cave, its blackness broken this time not by the gleam of a serpent, but by a single smear of reddish gold, which could be the glow of a fire within, or of the sun without; here, above all, those weird hybrid objects that seemed to be two things at once, or one thing in the process of turning into another. The prow of Ulysses' ship was a gaping fish-jaw, its shape echoed by two great arch-like rocks in the sea beyond, while about it, in the foam, played silvery figures – nymphs? spirits? – which gradually faded into transparency, until they were one with the water, and disappeared. Saluting it, on the right edge of the canvas, was the figurehead of another ship, which rose up like a clenched fist – or one of those odd flipper-limbs: fish, and flesh, and wood, all at once – before a cluster of clouds that turned out, on closer inspection, to be the horses of Apollo's chariot, drawing the sun into the sky. And the wounded giant himself, rearing in agony above his island, was so vague that he, too, might be a cloud, or the mist-covered peak of a mountain.

Each of these effects taken on its own could have been merely disturbing, but in their totality they seemed to achieve a kind of dreamlike enchantment which made me think for a moment that I had at last glimpsed (though I could not put it into words) Turner's purpose. The subject was sombre enough, and its treatment strange to the point of insanity: yet (in this picture, at least) the beauty seemed finally to outweigh the horror and the madness – and to be, indeed, all the greater for having absorbed the base elements of our experience, and transmuted them into gold. Exhilarated, I opened my notebook and wrote: 'Magician. Alchemist.'

I had barely finished when I was startled (the 't' of 'Alchemist' has a long squiggling tail to prove it) by someone speaking at my elbow:

'I sing the cave of Polypheme,
Ulysses made him cry out . . .'

Astonished, I looked round. There was Lady Meesden – one hand raised, to signal to the manservant that he should stop – gliding into place at my side. Without pausing, she continued:

'For he ate his mutton, drank his wine,
And then he poked his eye out.'

Her voice was rather faint, but there was something commanding about it – not the imperious tone you might imagine from a woman in her position, but rather a kind of operatic flourish that made you think you were listening to a performance rather than a conversation. I noticed several other people glancing at her as if they expected her to break into song; and, in truth, I half-expected it myself, for I had no idea what she was talking about, and it seemed as likely as anything else that she was mad, and merely reliving some entertainment from her youth – like Walter's old woman in Hand Court.

'Tom Dibdin,' she said, as if by way of explanation.

The name was familiar – it somehow conjured in my mind a world of stage-coaches and sailing-ships and breezy spring mornings, before railways and factories turned England into a great machine, and swaddled it in smoke – but I could not for a moment place it.

'*Melodrame Mad*. 1819.'

And then I remembered: Thomas Dibdin's *Reminiscences* had been a great favourite of my father's when I was a child –

although, fearful that it might corrupt me, and make me run away, and become a travelling player like its author, he forbade me to read it. (This interdiction, of course, only increased its romance for me, prompting me to sneak into the library whenever I could, and stealthily devour two or three pages of an anecdote about a theatre manager or an actress, before approaching footsteps forced me to make my escape.) I still could not see the relevance to Turner's work, however; and the perplexity must have shown on my face, for, pointing a wavering finger at the picture, Lady Meesden said:

'His inspiration for that. Or so he claimed.'

'Turner, you mean?' I said.

'Of course Turner,' she snapped; but then softened it by (for a marvel) smiling at me, and saying more gently: 'But he might not have meant it.'

'Why should he say it, then?'

'Why, to shock,' she said, as if nothing could be more natural, and I must be an idiot to ask. 'It was some damned silly woman, as I recall, whispering to a clergyman. *So misty, so spiritual, so ethereal, Mr. Whatever-his-name-was. Upon my word, I don't know how Turner does it. He must be a magician.* Or some such nonsense.'

I confess I felt myself blushing, but had the grace to smile.

'And he told her he'd got the idea not from *The Odyssey*, as we'd all supposed, but from a ditty in a comic spectacle.' She shook her head, and started to laugh, almost silently. 'I bet she never dared offer another opinion in her life.'

'Were you there yourself?' I asked.

'He told me of it afterwards.'

'Oh, so you knew him personally?'

'Oh, yes, I knew Turner,' she replied, with a knowing emphasis on the 'I' and the 'Tur' that immediately made me wonder if their acquaintance had been more than mere friendship. The same thought, I fancy, must have struck the little audience that had gathered around us; for a stout woman who had been listening (and pretending not to) from the beginning, shot Lady Meesden a stern glance, and turned her back; and a man behind us took his wife by the arm and hurried her away.

'He was a great lover of the theatre,' Lady Meesden went on, entirely heedless of the stir she had created. There was something proprietorial in her tone which suggested that the theatre was *her* world, and she would therefore naturally know anyone who frequented it; and for the first time it occurred to me that – improbable as it might seem – she might, from her appearance and the way she spoke, have once been an actress.

'Did you appear there yourself?' I said – with just enough levity to be able to pretend, if necessary, that I was merely joking.

'Lord, yes,' she said, laughing; and then, to save me from the need for a further question (which I was already trying to devise): 'I'm Kitty Driver.'

'*Mrs.* Driver?'

She nodded. 'Or was, until Meesden plucked me from the green room, and set me down in the drawing room.' The phrase had a worn, over-rehearsed air, and I wondered how many times she must have resorted to it over the last fifty years, hoping that a show of wit in discussing her origins might disarm disapproval of them.

'I was never fortunate enough to see you –' I began.

'Of course, you're too young.'

'But Walter's mother still speaks of your Lady Wurzel.'

She shook her head, but the faintest glow of pleasure appeared beneath the white mask.

'That was the end of my career. My Mrs. Mandible, 1810, now, there was a thing. Or Lucy Lovelorn in *All in a Day*. Meesden saw it thirty-nine times.'

'Really?'

She nodded again. 'He wrote to me every night; and at the

95

end he met me at the stage door and said: "There's no denying it, by God, you've got my heart, fair and square, Mrs. D.
And if you give it back again, I'll go straight into the street
and offer it to the first woman I meet there, damn me if I
won't – for, if you won't have me, I don't care what happens
to me."'

There was another ripple in the crowd about us, which,
again, Lady Meesden seemed not to notice; for she guffawed
and went on: 'What could I do but marry the dog?'

I laughed. 'And what of Turner?' I said – a trifle clumsily,
for I could think of no other way to guide the conversation
back to its original subject. 'Was he also an admirer?'

She did not answer directly, but rested her chin on her
hand and stared at the floor for a moment, as if the idea surprised her. At length she said. 'He was a sly, secretive fellow,
Miss . . . Miss . . . Miss . . .'

'Halcombe.'

'Miss Halcombe. He felt a hurt more keenly, I think, than
any man I ever knew – and, as a consequence, was morbidly
careful to avoid any risk of public humiliation. Few of us
knew anything of his private affairs – save that he lived with
his father, and had a mad housekeeper. There were *les on-
dits*, of course, about a woman, but . . .' She paused, and
shook her head.

'An actress?' I said, with some trepidation.

'A pretty widow, so the story went. Who gave him a bastard or two. But you can't credit everything you hear.'

A gentleman at my shoulder – of whom I was only aware
because of the strong smell of cigar smoke – cleared his
throat noisily, and clumped off; and I must have looked discomfited myself, for Lady Meesden said:

'Lord, woman! – what's the matter with that? It ain't natural for a man to be alone, nor yet a woman, neither.' She suddenly fixed me with her gimlet eyes, discomfiting me
further. 'Sooner one warm bed than two cold.'

How foolish to feel embarrassed and confused, yet I did; and, for fear of hearing more such confidences (or rather, if I am honest, of being *seen* to hear them in that place), I started towards Walter, saying:

'My brother is writing a biography of Turner, did you know that?'

And I wish now that I hadn't; for, had I been less delicate, I might have learned more.

'Don't fetch the men,' said Lady Meesden plaintively. 'They're all such infernal prigs nowadays – like lawyers and schoolmasters.'

I paused, but it was too late. I heard Walter say, 'I, too, have a daughter called Florence' – as if all topics of conversation, beyond the coincidence of their children sharing a name, had already been exhausted – and then he caught my eye, and gave me an imploring look that would have melted an iceberg, and made it impossible for me to withdraw.

'I'm beginning to think we should have called 'em "Venice",' said Mr. Kingsett, with a snorting laugh, and a wave towards *The Bridge of Sighs*.

Walter edged in my direction, his face frankly saying what his lips could not: *Save me!*

'Lady Meesden was a friend of Turner's,' I said. 'Did you know that, Walter?'

'Oh, no,' he said, moving towards her. 'How interesting.'

But Mr. Kingsett, with a nimbleness I would not have suspected, was there before him; and a moment later, as if some signal had passed between them (though I own, if it did, I saw nothing), his wife had joined him, and was saying:

'Now, Mama, we mustn't detain Miss Halcombe and Mr. Hartright any longer. If we don't continue on our way, we shall be here all night, and most of tomorrow.'

I was, for a moment, quite furious; and then I remembered my own response to the old woman, and was forced to reflect that, had she been *my* mother, and I had heard her chattering indiscreetly to a stranger, I should probably have acted in the same way.

It was when I had shaken hands with them all, and Walter was exchanging a few polite words with Lady Eastlake on the subject of his researches, that I suddenly thought – like a sailor with time enough to snatch only one treasure from a sinking ship – of a final question for Lady Meesden. Leaning down, I said:

'Which painting here do you think is truest of Turner the man?'

And without a moment's hesitation she replied: '*Calais Pier.*'

After they had gone, Walter and I sought it out. It is another marine picture, with a marbled grey sea churning and breaking beneath a stormy sky. On the right-hand side, a ramshackle wooden pier lined with disorderly knots of figures juts out towards the horizon – where two distant ships appear in silhouette, and a crack in the clouds lays a pencil-stroke of sunlight on the water. Closer at hand, in the centre of the picture, is a chaos of boats trying to put into, or set out from, the harbour. In the nearest – which an oarsman with only one oar is frantically trying to keep from being dashed against the wooden piles – a man in the stern, far from helping, is angrily shaking a bottle of cognac at his wife on the pier above. Only the approaching English packet, its sails confidently set, appears to be under control.

The bluff, John-Bullish air – a crowd of drunken, cowardly, disorganized French people being shown up by English seamanship – is echoed by the full title: *Calais Pier, with French Poissards Preparing for Sea: An English Packet Arriving*; for, according to my dictionary, *poissard* means not (as one might suppose) 'fisherman', but 'base' or 'vulgar'.

We stood before that picture for perhaps fifteen minutes, and I must have thought of it every hour since; for although it was easy enough to imagine the author of this jaunty, humorous, patriotic satire quoting Tom Dibdin, I could find not the slightest evidence to suggest that the same artist could also have painted *Ulysses Deriding Polyphemus*.

XIV

Letter from Colonel George Wyndham to
Walter Hartright, 29th August, 185–

Petworth,
29th Augt, 185–

Dear Sir,

I have received yours of 17th August, and will be glad to
see you here if you are near Petworth. I fear, however, that
you may find it a wasted journey, for there is very little I
can tell you about Turner, or my father's dealings with him.

Yours truly,

George Wyndham

XV

Letter from Walter Hartright to Laura Hartright,
19th September, 185–

Brompton Grove,
Tuesday

My dearest love,

I fear you may have begun to grow anxious about me, so
long is it since I last wrote; but the truth – which I hope you
guessed – is that what with being rattled about in coaches
and railway carriages, and twice nearly thrown from a fly,
and having to make so early a start (on the one morning
when I thought I should have leisure to write) that I was
still half asleep as I left, I have scarce had thirty minutes
together in which to put pen to paper. But here I am, home
again at last, with nothing worse to show for my adventures than a bruise or two, and a pair of boots scuffed white

by the downland chalk.

The new railway to Brighton is a marvel of speed and convenience (as you will see; for I am resolved that when we are next in town together, we shall astonish the children by taking them to the seaside, and bringing them back again, all in the same day!); but for this very reason I found that it depressed my spirits. Every mile seemed to be putting a greater distance not merely between me and London, but also between me and Turner; for *his* journey to Michael Gudgeon, all those years before, must have been an entirely different affair – a jolting, jostling, day-long lurch from one inn to the next, by dusty roads where the only sound was the clop of hooves and the squeak and rumble of wheels, and the only steam the vapour from the horses' flanks. Just at the moment when I felt I had finally glimpsed his elusive figure, in those extraordinary pictures at Marlborough House, I now seemed to be losing sight of it again, in the smoke and bustle of the modern world.

But matters soon mended after we arrived. I took a fly at the station, and within ten minutes we were driving through streets of white stuccoed boarding-houses, with square, cheerful faces, that must have been there in Turner's day; and after ten minutes more we had begun to climb into the downs – which it was hard to imagine had changed greatly since Caesar first saw them, or for a thousand years before that. On every side stretched a rolling, billowing ocean of grass; and when I looked behind, I saw, in the distance, a broadening ribbon of silver-gilt sea.

After perhaps three miles, at the entrance to a small village, we bore left down a narrow lane lined with bramble hedges. It soon dwindled into no more than a cart-track, and it was here that the first near-accident occurred; for, while the driver was momentarily distracted, the horse trotted blithely ahead on to the rough surface, where it missed its footing, and – twisting violently to right itself –

dropped one of our wheels into a deep ruck with a tremendous bang that almost overturned the fly. The driver had to hurl himself across his seat to avoid being flung out. The next moment he pulled up abruptly.

'I'm sorry, sir,' he said. 'I can't go no further. Another knock like that, and I shall want a new axle.'

'Is it far?' I said.

'Not half a mile,' he said, pointing to a smoking chimney just beyond the next brow.

So I paid him, and picked up my valise, and set off on foot, picking my way carefully between the ruts. The soft wind stroked my face; and for a moment everything that connected me to the humdrum world seemed to be vanishing with the retreating fly, and I was left with nothing but the cuff and slither of my own boots, and the cry of the larks urging me back to some great task, or reminding me of some great grief, that I had somehow forgotten in the noise and distraction of everyday.

As I came over the brow I saw below me what appeared to be a small farm, with a muddy yard, bounded on two sides by ranges of ramshackle outbuildings, and on the third by a long, low house of whitewashed stone, protected to the rear by a line of trees. It was so unlike the snug cottage I had expected that I immediately supposed the driver must have brought me to the wrong place, and by the time I reached the gate I had quite persuaded myself that I should have to retrace my steps to the village, or even go back to Brighton and start afresh.

A gaunt black-and-white dog signalled my approach by springing up and barking furiously, jerking on the end of its chain like a child's toy, and scattering a troupe of chickens which were strutting across the yard. Moments later, a red-faced woman of perhaps sixty-five, with her sleeves rolled up to the elbows, appeared from one of the outbuildings and started rapidly towards me. She moved with the

rolling, exaggerated gait of the comic widow in a pan-
tomime, which at first made me think she might be drunk;
but then I noticed that she was merely working on to her
feet a pair of stout wooden clogs to lift her above the mire.

'Good morning,' I called. 'I'm looking for Mr. Gudgeon.'

The cacophony of squawks and barks must have
drowned my words; for she frowned and shook her head,
and then – shooing the last of the hens on its way, and
shouting to the dog to be quiet – cupped a hand behind her
ear, and raised her eyebrows, and opened her mouth, in a
charade of "I beg your pardon?"

'Mr. Gudgeon?' I said again.

'Are you Mr. Hartright?' she asked, in a gentle Sussex
brogue; and, when I nodded, she held out her hand in a
forthright manner, and said: 'I'm Alice Gudgeon.'

'How do you do?' I said.

'The man's in his study. Will you forgive me if I take you
through the back?'

She led me across the yard and into a warm kitchen filled
with steam and the tang of boiling bacon and the sweet
smoky fumes of meat roasting on a spit. From the low
beamed ceiling, and the black range cluttered with pots,
and the brace of hares just visible through a half-open
pantry door, you would have supposed – again – that this
was the home of a prosperous yeoman. Only the table
seemed out of place; for, beneath the old sheet which
entirely covered its surface, you could just see four finely
turned mahogany legs, which suggested that it might have
once adorned a dining room, but had fallen on hard times.

We entered a cool hall, floored with polished flagstones,
where Mrs. Gudgeon stopped. 'Will you leave your bag
here,' she said, pointing to the foot of the stairs, 'and we'll
show you to your room after?' Something in the way she
spoke – slowly and loudly, and with an eye on a door
opposite – made me suppose that this was as much for her

husband's benefit as for mine. Having thus alerted him to my arrival, she huffed and fussed and muttered over my valise for a few seconds, before standing back with her hands on her hips and saying: 'There, no-one'll break their necks on that now.' Then, without knocking, she opened the door.

What I noticed first was the paper – single sheets, and rough heaps tied loosely together with ribbons, and old notebooks piled into rickety columns that looked as if they would collapse if you breathed on them – which seemed to cover almost every square inch of floor and furniture. The air was heavy with the smell of mildew and old leather, and the dust so thick that you could see a great funnel of it floating before the window like a muslin curtain. Here, I immediately decided, was something I had never thought to see: a room even more disorderly than Lady Eastlake's boudoir.

But this impression was immediately dispelled when I turned to Gudgeon himself. He was a slight, dapper little man, with amber eyes and a shock of white hair sweeping up from his forehead, wearing a snowy cravat (as white and plump as a swan's breast) and a well-cut brown worsted coat which made him look fastidiously neat. As he came to greet me, he picked his way carefully between the papers like a general anxious not to disturb the disposition of his troops.

'Mr. Hartright?' he said, looking at his wife. She nodded; and he extended his left hand towards me. 'How kind of you to come, sir.'

'The kindness is yours –' I began, surprised at his tone; but he stopped me with a shake of the head.

'You're an angel,' he said. 'Sent from heaven to save me.' He swept his hand about him, like a sower broadcasting seed. 'You see what I am reduced to.' He shook his head sorrowfully, and broke into a rueful smile – from which I took courage to ask:

'Why – what is all this?'

'The work of forty years,' he said. 'And it will take me forty more to organize it, if I do not make haste.'

I looked at the stack nearest to me. It was bound with a piece of twine, and beneath the knot someone (presumably Gudgeon himself, or his wife) had slipped a small card, marked with an alpha, and the number '7'. Above it, in faint pencil, was written 'Chap. 1? Chap. 3? Chap. 4?'

'You are planning to write a book?' I asked.

At this, his wife – who stood still in the doorway, watching him fondly with bright indulgent eyes – began to laugh; and, after glancing sharply at her for a moment, he joined in himself, with a deep, self-mocking chuckle.

'When I was younger, Mr. Hartright,' he said, 'I was elected to the Beef-steak Club in Brighton; where, at the monthly dinner, you might be required, at the whim of the chairman, to compose an *extempore* epitaph – either for yourself, or for another member. And Jack Marwell, of the Theatre Royal, who was a humorous fellow, wrote this on me:

> Here lyeth, friend, a gentle wight
> Who did no wrong, but could not write
> Each day he'd plan – but plan in vain –
> A book – and then he'd plan again;
> Until at last his soul was took –
> Yet, though his life hath left no book,
> Pray, with his grieving friends and wife
> His name be in the Book of Life.

There were tears in his eyes when he had finished – though whether from merriment, or the recollection of his friends, or merely the melancholy that the thought of our own death must arouse in us all, I could not tell. At length, however, he chuckled again, and said: 'But I took my revenge the following month; for the chairman demanded I should compose one on Marwell, and I said, "I'm still planning it"; and was excused for my wit.'

I laughed; and, looking about me, said: 'It seems to me you were slandered; for you must have the makings of at least half a dozen books here –'

'Oh, the makings!' he said. 'The makings! But how to make 'em? – that's the question! Here are graves' – pointing to one pile – 'and Roman fortifications' – indicating another – 'and a giant's thigh-bone, and druidical stones, and a thousand other curiosities; and between them they would amount to a very respectable *Guide to the Natural Wonders and Ancient Remains of the County of Sussex*, which is what I always intended them to be.' He paused a moment, perhaps because he had suddenly recalled the reason for my visit; for he went on: 'That was, indeed, part of my original object in travelling with Turner – I hoped he might furnish me with engravings.'

'And did he refuse?' I asked.

'I did not ask him outright, but I think perhaps he guessed my intention, for he told me plainly that all the pictures were destined for a publisher, who wished to make his own book. Later, I heard that failed, and I could have approached him then; but felt I was still not sufficiently advanced.' He shook his head in a sudden frenzy of frustration. 'Try as I may, I can never find a way to arrange my material; and just at the point when I seem about to manage it, damn me if something new doesn't turn up, and throw the whole thing off the road, horses and all.' He began jabbing the air, as vigorously as the conductor of an orchestra. 'If I order everything according to place, I must jumble together temples to Diana and mediaeval coins and batteries from the late war; if I do it chronologically, I make myself and my reader giddy by flying from one side of the county to the other – and back again – in a single after-noon.' He shook his head. 'It will end by making me mad.'

'Perhaps I might help?' I suggested; for I could not but feel for the poor man, and yearn to cut him free from the net in which he had enmeshed himself. 'I do have some small experience – and, indeed, am beginning to face simi-lar problems in my *Life of Turner*.'

'Lord bless you!' said Gudgeon. 'It's uncommon good of you to offer; but God knows I mustn't waste your life, as well as my own. Besides' – here he smiled at his wife, who coloured and smiled back, as though they had some secret understanding – 'the woman's depending on you to restore me to sanity – if only for an instant – by taking me away from the whole sorry business.' He laid a finger on my arm. 'Come, we'll go to the museum. And there, I swear, I'll talk nothing but Turner.'

From our preparations – he insisted I put on my coat again, and borrow a muffler; and he himself donned an old redingote, and seized a shepherd's crook – you'd have thought the 'museum' must be a day's journey away, and up a mountain. It turned out, however, to be no further than the corner of the yard, squeezed into an old cattle-shed between the end of the house and a tack room and stable – from which, as Gudgeon fiddled with the latch, a brown pony with a shaggy white mane watched us, tossing its head and twitching impatiently. Inside, the room (if room it may be called) was cold and damp, smelling of wet earth and old hay, and lit only by a row of small dirty windows set high in the wall, which gave it something of the feel of a gloomy church. I could see nothing clearly, but was aware of being surrounded by indistinct shapes – which nonetheless some-how conveyed a sense of bulk and presence, for they seemed to press in upon me as palpably as a crowd of people.

Gudgeon took down a lantern from the back of the door; lit it with surprising adroitness (considering that his right hand could do no more than hold the box of matches), and then slung it on to the crook.

'Would you be so good as to hold this?' he said. 'I think we shall get on better if I can point.'

I raised the staff like a bishop's crosier, spilling light on to a broken black stone slab that leant against the wall immediately before me (so immediately, indeed, that, had I taken one step more in the darkness, I should indubitably have tripped on it). There were uneven letters scratched into the surface; and, bending down to read them, I saw:

> *Gaius Ter*
> *Et sua coniunx caris*
> *HSE*

'From a Roman cemetery near Lewes,' said Gudgeon. '*Gaius Tertius*, I imagine. *Et sua coniunx carissima.*' He ran his fingers gently along the top, and nodded, as if in approval; and I fancy he was thinking of *his* beloved wife – as I, most assuredly, was of mine. '*Hic Situs Est* – so he died before she did, and her name was added later.'

'I find it rather touching,' I said.

He nodded again. 'But Turner would have none of it. Said that a true painter could be married only to his art. An idea for which he gave, as I recall, no less an authority than Sir Joshua Reynolds.' He smiled, and said: 'See, I'm as good as my word! Nothing but Turner!' – and then turned abruptly, and marched off into the void.

I followed him, bearing the lantern aloft, and watching the shadows dissolve in its yellow glow. My first thought was that I had stumbled upon the cave of some demented Aladdin; for the walls were lined with rough shelves – divided into rectangular compartments, something like the berths in a ship's cabin – which appeared to overflow with the biggest hotch-potch of rubbish I have ever seen: broken pots; a horn knife-handle without a blade; the sole of an old shoe, dotted with rusty studs; half a black, fibrous wooden box (the other half, presumably having rotted clean away); a tray of flint chips that might have been crude arrowheads, but so frayed about the edges that they looked as if they had been nibbled into shape by a teething dog rather than formed by a human hand. Surely, I thought, this must be the product of some disease of the mind (had not the study, indeed, already afforded me a glimpse of it?) which renders its victim incapable of discarding anything, however small or useless, and hence of ever imposing any kind of pattern on his life?

But if this was madness there was certainly some method in it; for each section bore a neat handwritten label, stating a place and a date – 'Braysted, 1845', or (the ink here faded with age) 'Tamberlode, 1816'.

'Are these all finds that *you* made?' I asked.

He nodded curtly, and muttered something I could not hear. I could not but feel awed by his industry (if not by his discrimination!), but he seemed to think it scarcely worthy of comment, for he continued on his way without altering his pace or turning his head, and said nothing more until he had reached the end of the room, and slapped a shelf with his hand, sending up a plume of dust.

'Here's Turner for you,' he announced proudly. 'He loved this spot.'

There were, I saw, objects from four different excavations here – the earliest dated 1811, the last 1825 – yet they all appeared to come from a single place, identified by a large sign in the centre of the wall: 'Sturdy Down'.

'He never said so, for he was taciturn about such matters, but I think he liked it for its layers,' said Gudgeon.

'*Layers*?' I said, not sure if I had heard him correctly.

Gudgeon nodded. 'Stand on the top of Sturdy Down, and within two miles – if you have eyes to see – you'll find evidence of almost every stage in our island's past.' He lifted a pitted iron axe-head, and weighed it in his hand. 'Anglo-Saxon, from some princeling's grave.' Before I had had time to examine it, he set it down again, and picked up a shiny fragment of orange tile, which he dropped into my palm. 'Roman. From the hypocaust of a villa in the valley.' As quickly again, he pointed to an intricate brooch, gracefully curved like an elongated snail's shell. 'Bronze Age. Buried with some priestess or chieftain's daughter, to allow her to appear in the next world with proper dignity.' He was jabbing his finger so rapidly now that I had barely even glimpsed one treasure before he was on to the next. 'A stone from the mediaeval priory, most of which has been plundered to build that damned folly up there. A flint spear-point, which might have killed a mammoth.'

'But why was Turner so fascinated?' I asked – partly to slow him down, but partly out of genuine puzzlement – for while, in the pictures at Marlborough House, there had been abundant evidence of a taste for mythological subjects, and even more of a passion for the moods and effects of nature, I could remember none suggesting a deep interest in British history.

'He was a man of the people,' said Gudgeon. 'A man of the *labouring* people. Many times I have seen him stop to sketch a fisherman, or a shepherd – not as a curiosity, or as some fanciful figure in a classical scene, but as a fellow-man, with the sympathy born of common experience. A great part of his purpose, indeed, was to present the mass of British men and women – those who would never enter a gallery, or have the means to buy a painting – with views of their country.'

'But still –' I began.

'For he, too, you see,' said Gudgeon, interrupting me (yet with a little nod, that seemed to say that he noted my objection, and would answer it in due course) 'knew what

110

it was to be poor, and footsore, and storm-lashed, and to work hard all the day long, and go to bed hungry.' He paused, and then went on more quietly. 'There were tears in his eyes as he stood there. Almost as if could see them, marching across the landscape – all those generations who had lived and toiled and died in that one place.' Emotion, or the raw air, had thickened Gudgeon's voice, and he had to clear his throat before continuing: 'I confess I did not truly understand it myself at the time. I was too young. It's easier for me now; for I find, as I get older, I feel closer to the people who made these things' – here he looked about him and nodded, as if he were greeting a party of old friends – 'and used them, and at length died, and left them behind for me to find.' He was silent for a few seconds; and then – perhaps in an effort to master his feelings, for he seemed close to tears himself now – turned away abruptly, and seized another object from the shelf. 'Here's something will interest you, Mr. Hartright.'

At first I could not identify it at all, but as he brought it into the light I saw that it was the lower jaw of some great animal, long and lined with jagged teeth like a crocodile's. But it was so huge that – if the rest of the body were in proportion – the brute must have been at least five or six times bigger than even the largest crocodile you have seen in the Zoological Gardens; and I confess that when I took it in my hands I let out an involuntary gasp of amazement.

'Part of an extinct dragon,' said Gudgeon, with the practised chuckle of a man who has seen the same response many times before. 'What I believe Owen now calls a *dinosaur.*'

'Owen?' I said.

'William. *Sir* William, I should say.' (You would have supposed from his emphasis that no man ever deserved a knighthood less.) 'Superintendent of the British Museum. And so, naturally, to be deferred to on every point of classification.'

He glowered round at his collection, his mouth working, like a rumbling volcano about to erupt; and I prepared myself for the long catalogue of his differences with Sir William. At length, however – perhaps again recalling his undertaking to talk of nothing but Turner – he nodded at the jawbone and said:

'At all events, Turner and I saw it being dug out of the chalk, and he stood there, quite mesmerized for a moment, his face all aglow like a schoolboy's; and then he started to sketch, like this' – making wild thrusts with his hand – 'as if his life depended on it. Later, I believe, he clothed it in flesh, and put it in one of his pictures.'

'Yes,' I said; for, as he spoke, the monster in *The Goddess of Discord in the Garden of the Hesperides* suddenly slithered before my mind's eye, and I recognized it for this creature as surely as you may recognize a face that you have seen before only in a photograph. 'I know it.'

'And here', said Gudgeon, laughing, 'is a paintbrush, left on the down by the greatest artist of our age.' He handed me a worn wooden handle.

'You mean this was his?' I said; and, when he nodded, felt a tremor pass across my skin like a crackle of lightning, for (save, perhaps, for Mr. Ruskin's self-portrait) I had never yet held anything that Turner had held; and for a fanciful moment I imagined that his power might still reside in this slender shaft of wood, and communicate itself to me, so that I might paint as he did. Then I lifted it to the lantern-light, and saw that only one bristle remained.

Gudgeon must have noticed my amazement; for he laughed again, and said: 'He was happy to keep working with only three hairs left, he told me, and content with two; but when he was reduced to one even he had to admit defeat.'

'But why?' I said, thinking with a prick of guilt how easily *I* will condemn a brush for the slightest fault. 'Surely he

112

could have afforded to replace it sooner?'

Gudgeon nodded. 'Yes, he was already a rich man when I knew him. But he chose to live simply.'

'Surely,' I said, suddenly remembering some of the rumours I had heard. 'To call such behaviour "simple living", when there is no occasion for it, might seem . . .?'

'Yes,' said Gudgeon, 'I know that he was considered mean. But that is not how I should describe him. Frugal, yes. Careful – and quick to anger, undoubtedly, if he feared he was being cheated, or imposed upon. But I have seen him give five shillings to a young widow with a crying child at her breast, and tell her to buy something for it, and make sure it went to church, and learnt right from wrong.'

'Was it bravado, then?' I said, recalling Turner's delight in displaying his skill on Varnishing Days.

'In part, perhaps. He certainly took a great pride in being able to *make do*. And partly, too, that he feared losing his independence; for he told me once, when we had both drunk too much, that he detested above everything being subject to the whim of patrons.' He paused; and when he went on again, it was with a doubtful tone, as if he was giving voice to some question that had just struck him, and that he had not yet resolved. 'But there was, I think, something else, too. Something akin to a *superstition*.'

'You mean,' I said – and I don't know why, save that it seemed, of a sudden, to fit with all those recurrent images of luxury and ruin and destruction at Marlborough House – 'that he believed that if he was wasteful it might provoke some sort of a catastrophe?'

For some reason Gudgeon coloured slightly, as if I had confounded him; and then he nodded and said: 'That is very astute of you, Mr. Hartright. And not just a catastrophe for himself. But for the country. Or even for the world.' He smiled, and laid a finger impulsively on my arm. 'I think you will do very well, sir. Very well indeed.' And then, nodding towards the brush. 'Keep it, please. I should like you to have it.'

'Really?'

He nodded again.

'I shall carry it with me always,' I said, slipping it into my pocket. 'As a talisman.'

It was a small enough thing, of course, and yet I could not help feeling delighted by it; for this was the first real encouragement I had received from anyone but Lady Eastlake – Mr. Ruskin's comments, for all their ineffable condescension, having had much the same effect on my spirits as a bucket of cold water over the head. And it seemed to confirm what I had increasingly begun to feel (though still scarcely dared to hope) since seeing Turner's paintings: that I was, at last, starting to get the measure of the man. It was, in consequence, in the highest good humour that – when Gudgeon took a watch from his pocket, and looked at it, and said: 'The woman'll have dinner ready, I fancy; best not to keep her waiting; shall we go in?' – I replied, 'Gladly, sir,' and followed him back into the house.

It was a hearty, old-fashioned meal, in an old-fashioned dining room with heavy beams and a huge open fire that must have consumed a whole tree in the time it took *us* to eat a boiled fowl, a pudding, and half a leg of mutton. Since Gudgeon could not carve, I thought his wife might ask me to do it in his stead; but she took the burden on herself, and I soon saw why: when she came to her husband's portion, she discreetly cut it into little pieces, so he should not be humiliated either by his own incapacity to hold a knife, or by having to ask, like a child, to have it done for him on his own plate. Another man, perhaps, understandably reluctant to draw attention to his disability, might have chosen not to acknowledge this kindness; but Gudgeon touched

114

the back of her hand, and thanked her with a smile of a great sweetness. I must have seen, as we sat together, twenty such instances of their mutual affection and regard. Let us hope, my love, when we are their ages, that we make such a picture!

When we had finished, Mrs. Gudgeon cleared away the dishes, and then left her husband and me alone with the wine. We talked a little of his family; and then, without my having to prompt him, he started to tell me more of his adventures with Turner: of how Turner loved storms – 'the fouler the weather, the better' – of how they took a boat once at Brighton, and a gale came up, and the sea broke over the gunwales with a sound like thunder, and all were ill, save Turner, who merely stared intently at the water, remarking its movement and colour, and muttering 'Fine! Fine!'; of how they walked twenty or thirty miles a day, in rain, shine or deluge, and put up sometimes at the meanest inns, where Turner would be content with a piece of bread and cheese, and a glass of porter, and a table to rest his head on, if there was no bed to be had. 'Those were wonderful evenings for a young man,' said Gudgeon at last, shaking his head in wonderment at the memory, 'for there was Turner, who would show you nothing of his work, and barely say a word, during the day; but when the ale had freed his tongue would sing, and make jokes (though you could hardly understand them), and boast of his success, and how he meant to be the greatest painter in the world.'

He was silent a long while after this, and I think must have fallen asleep, for he nodded, and then jerked his head up again, and stared at me for a moment, as if he did not know who I was. And then he smiled, yet still said nothing, as if our sitting there companionably were conversation enough. There was no sound save the plaintive stammering of distant sheep, and the whisper of the fire – which, like us, seemed to have grown sated and sleepy; for, though

115

Gudgeon had thrown another log on when he had last filled our glasses, the flames had scarcely even charred it. The candles had burned low, and through the window I could see the first stars appearing in the sky; and I thought of those far-off days (yet not so far off, in truth) when young Gudgeon and not-yet-old Turner had sat together, just like this; and of how – in no more than one flickering iota of a second in a star's life – Time creeps up on us all, and overtakes us. And so at length must have fallen asleep; for the next I knew was that Mrs. Gudgeon was shaking my shoulder, and laughing, and offering to light me upstairs with a lamp.

The following day I rose late, and made a leisurely break-fast in the kitchen – at that hour, thanks to the fire, the only warm room in the house. Afterwards, I sat a while with Gudgeon in his study, and we exchanged 'Thank you's and 'It's been a great pleasure's until, at length, his wife entered, and told me that it was time to leave if I wished to be sure of the train. He came out into the yard with me – where the resourceful woman had already harnessed the trap to the brown pony, which waited, stamping its feet, as if anxious to be off. Then, sheltering in the doorway against the sharp east wind, Gudgeon unwound the cravat from his neck and stood waving it, like a scarf, in his good hand, as his wife drove me away.

In the event, she deposited me at Brighton station in ample time for the train to Chichester, by which I was to start my journey to Petworth, and I –

But no – if I embark on that now, I shall be another day in the writing. So, let Petworth be the matter of my next let-ter, and this one delay no longer its most important busi-ness – telling you that I am well, and that I love you. Walter

XVI

From the journal of Walter Hartright, 19th September, 185–

Michael Gudgeon told me one thing more about Turner, which I set down here (as nearly as I can remember) exactly as he said it:

'One day, I recall, everything pleased him: a gothic ruin, a view of the sea, an effect of the light he especially loved, where the sun breaks through at a slant, and grains the cloud like a piece of slate. Late in the afternoon we stopped at an ale-house, and then rolled back to the Royal Oak at Poynings, singing "I am a Friar of Orders Grey".

'Do you know the Royal Oak, Mr. Hartright? No? Well, I dare say you'd think it a simple enough house – I dare say *I* should, now – but it seemed a very palace then, after what we'd been accustomed to, for the beds were comfortable, and we had a room apiece, for a marvel.' [*A pause. A laugh.*] 'That night, as we sat drinking after supper, we fell into conversation with two big village girls, and Turner, I remember, told them his name was "Jenkinson" – with a twinkle in his eye, that told me not to gainsay him – and that made me laugh; and the girls laughed too, though I am sure they didn't know why; and the upshot, by and by, was that I took the one with the brown ringlets to my room, and he took the other to his.'

[*I confess I do not know what I did to provoke this next comment; certainly I said nothing.*]

'Lord! You young people are such prudes, Mr. Hartright. Do you mean to say you've never had resort to a jolly girl?' [*Another pause, another laugh.*] 'I must say, though, Turner's didn't look so jolly the next day. Her eyes were red, and her skin was all chafed.'

XVII

Letter from Mrs. Tobias Bennett to Marian Halcombe, 21st September, 185–

Brentford,
21st September

Dear Miss Halcombe,

Thank you for your letter of 17th September. I should be delighted to see you – and your brother, if he is returned from his travels – any day next week. Thereafter we shall not be here, for the doctor orders us to the coast for my husband's health, and we may be gone some months.

Mention Turner, and my first thought always is of the Thames, and boats, and picnics. I know this time of year is famously wild and wayward, but if we should be blessed with a fine day, would you care to undertake a modest expedition with us on the river (we keep a small skiff, just big enough for four), and see some of the haunts I most fondly associate with him?

Please be so good as to let me know what day would suit best, and whether my little proposal is agreeable.

Yours very truly,

Amelia Bennett

XVIII

Letter from Walter Hartright to Laura Hartright, 22nd September, 185–

Brompton Grove,
Friday

My dearest love,

It is past three o'clock, and here I am, at last, setting about the letter I promised you yesterday. I should have started this morning; but, having woken early, I decided to take myself to the park, and try to paint the dawn. The result – as I should have foreseen – is dreadful: an over-boiled egg squashed on a bed of cinders. How did the man get such colours from his palette?

So – where did I leave you? Entering the train at Brighton railway station, I think; which proceeded to hurtle me at breakneck speed through Shoreham and Worthing, Angmering and Littlehampton, and at length – little more than an hour after I had left – delivered me, like a well-cared-for parcel, at Chichester. I was then obliged to continue my journey to Petworth by walking to the Ship Inn and taking the London coach – which, needless to say, contrived to cover only half the distance in twice the time, and lurched and bumped so much that I soon boasted a fine pair of bruises on my shoulder and forehead, and was starting to feel like a very *badly*-cared-for parcel.

Yet although I did not realize it at the time – indeed, I was inwardly cursing my ill-fortune, in terms you would have been shocked to hear! – fate was smiling on me; for among my fellow-passengers (who also included two elderly widowed sisters; and a young draughtsman with a case full of drawings, which he tried manfully to review, until a jolt sent them on to the floor; and a party of drunken students outside, who whooped and jeered with every swerve) was a pleasant-looking woman of about forty, who sat opposite me – and, as it turned out, was to play a material part in my adventure. She was well but not fashionably dressed – from her appearance, you might have supposed her to be the wife of a country doctor or attorney – and, as we bounced this way and that, smiled at me, with the conspiratorial air of a fellow-sufferer. At length (when I had received my knock on the head), she grimaced, gave a solicitous 'ooh', and said:

'Jabez Bristow.'

'I beg your pardon?' I said.

'Jabez Bristow.' I must have still looked blank, for she went on: 'You're not from these parts, then?'

'No.'

'Jabez is famous. Or infamous, rather. Can't drive unless he has a pint of brandy inside him to keep him warm. And who cares for anything after a pint of brandy?'

I smiled. I could not place her voice; it was not that of a lady, but it had a kind of confidence that spoke of prosperity, and a practised ease in conversing with people of all sorts and conditions.

'How far do you go?' she said.

'Petworth.'

She nodded. Her eyes flickered towards the two widows, and then she leant towards me and said, more softly: 'Pity the poor souls who are going all the way to London. At least we shan't have to endure this much longer.'

We felt the horses slow, and then strain forward, as if their load had suddenly become heavier. Looking out of the window, I saw a little farm bounded with knobbly flint walls, and, beyond it, our road rising sharply up into the downs.

'In a year or two,' said my companion, 'we shan't have to endure it at all.'

'Why?' I said. 'Are they building a railway?'

She nodded. 'Though you'll still have to walk when you get the other end,' she said, with a smile. 'Or take a gig; for the station will be a clear two miles from the town.'

'Good Lord!' I said. 'Is it impossible to build it closer?'

She shook her head. 'The colonel won't have it near his park.'

'Colonel Wyndham?' I asked.

She nodded; and then, after a moment, said: 'Why, do you know him?' Her tone was neutral, but she studied my face intently as she spoke, as if the question was prompted by something more than mere common politeness.

'No,' I replied. 'But I am hoping to meet him.'

'Indeed?' she said non-committally, still watching me closely.

I had the strong impression that she knew something about the colonel, which might prove helpful to me, but that – like a card-player unwilling to disclose her hand until she has seen her opponent's – she would only confide it to me once she had satisfied herself as to my own purpose in visiting him, and established that it was of a purely professional nature, and that I was an entirely disinterested party, who posed no threat to her. I therefore said:

'I am writing a life of Turner.' She did not reply at once, so I added: 'The artist?'

'Oh, yes, I knew Turner,' she said. 'I knew all of them, in the Third Earl's time. Chantrey, Carew, Phillips, Haste, Constable . . .'

This was more than I had dared to hope; and, scarce able to believe my luck, I began: 'What was . . .?' At that exact moment, however – to my extreme annoyance – one of the two widows leaned towards me, scowling; and in a stern tone – as if she had caught me red-handed trying to make off with something that was rightfully hers – said:

'Are you talking about Turner?'

'Yes,' I said. I held her gaze for what seemed the minimum demanded by good manners, and then turned back decisively to the woman opposite. 'What was he like?'

'Oh,' she said – and I suppose, by now, I should have come to expect her next words – 'he was a funny little man. Ruddy face' – she paddled her fingers against her own cheek – 'and always carried a big umbrella. You'd never have thought he was an artist, to look at him. More like . . . more like a . . .'

She pondered a moment, and the hesitation was fatal; for it allowed Widow A to recharge her conversational guns, and – at the very instant my companion concluded, '*like a sea captain*' – to boom:

'We saw *The Fighting Téméraire*, at the Academy, in 'thirty-nine'; and then, as if I might be disinclined to believe this startling intelligence on the strength of her word alone, she turned to her sister and shouted: 'Didn't we?'

'What?' yelled Widow B.

'See *The Fighting Téméraire*!'

'What!?' repeated her poor sister, who must have been completely deaf; for even the students on the roof heard the commotion, and one of them banged on the door with a mittened hand and bellowed: 'Hoi! Less noise there below!' His fellows promptly erupted into stifled laughter, and I confess that I was suddenly possessed by a kind of desperate hilarity myself, and had to avoid catching the eye of my new friend opposite, for fear I might join them.

Widow A finally gave up on her sister, and fixed me with a gimlet eye. 'It was of particular interest to us,' she said, in the same accusing tone (which I was beginning to realize was her normal manner of address), 'for our father served with Nelson, in just such a ship as that.'

'Really?' I said. 'How fascinating.' And so, indeed, it might have been, in other circumstances; but at that instant, and in that place, it seemed nothing but a monstrous imposition, and I felt my temper rising. Once again, though, fate came to my assistance; for the young draughtsman – with a discreet wink in my direction, which said, as clearly as if he had spoken the words, *Leave this to me* – removed his hat, and held out his hand to Widow A, and said:

'Well, now, *there's* a thing – I'm in the ship-building business myself, in a small way; and it's an honour to make your acquaintance.'

In less than a minute, he had charmed both the sisters into submission – though one could not have heard what he said, and the other could barely have understood it, since the ships *he* talked of had nothing to do with the romantic old man-of-war in Turner's painting, and everything to do with the modern steamboat tugging it to its doom. And my companion, too, was touched by his spell, if only obliquely – for, seeing our fellow-passengers engrossed in a conversation of their own, she seemed visibly to relax a little, and to be more willing to talk frankly to me.

'Yes, it was altogether different, in those days,' she said, settling back in her seat.

'Petworth House, you mean?'

She nodded. 'Liberty Hall. People would come and go as they pleased, and there'd always be a bed for them, and a meal, and a room for them to work in, if they wished.'

'Were they all artists, then?'

'Many of them. *The greatest patron in England*, the Third Earl, that's what I heard say. And with the finest collection. I wouldn't know, myself, though I liked to creep into the gallery, and look at the statues. It was quite a thing, for a fourteen-year-old girl, to see a marble man with no clothes on.'

I glanced at the widows, but they showed no sign of having heard. I wanted to ask her how she came to be there, at such an age; but since it was clear that she was not a member of the family (and to assume that she was would have been a kind of mirror-image condescension, as bad as the thing it reflected), and the only other probable explanation was that she had been a servant, I could not think of a way to frame the question without the risk of insulting her. Instead, I said:

'And was Turner there a great deal?'

'Oh, yes; his lordship gave him the use of the Old Library, as his studio; and Turner' – it suddenly struck me that she said 'Turner', rather than 'Mr. Turner', which seemed curious, when the man she was talking of was a guest in her master's house – 'Turner shut himself away there, all morning sometimes; and no-one was allowed to disturb him, save his lordship himself.' She smiled, and laughed softly. 'One time, I heard, Sir Francis –'

'Sir Francis?'

'Chantrey. The sculptor?'

'Oh, yes,' I said.

'Well, he decided to play a trick on Turner; and he imitated his lordship's footsteps in the corridor, and his special knock on the door, and did it so wonderfully well that Turner was deceived, and admitted him.'

'And what happened?' I said, impatiently. It was galling to find that even now, when I had supposed I was beginning to understand Turner, I could not guess the answer for myself. It all depended *which* Turner you believed in – the suspicious recluse, jealous of his privacy, or the hearty good fellow described by Gudgeon? The one would surely have resented such a prank; the other, equally surely, would have slapped his thigh, and made light of it.

'Oh, he took it in good part, and laughed when he saw his mistake,' said my companion. 'He and Sir Francis were old friends, so I believe, and liked to tease each other. There was much merriment about it that evening at dinner, you may be sure.'

A point, I thought, *to Gudgeon*. I smiled and said: 'That's an illuminating story. Do you suppose the colonel will remember more, and be able to tell me?'

'He might.' She hesitated, and clenched and unclenched her jaw before going on grimly: 'But he's not like his father.'

'In what way?'

'He's very shy. And has a terrible temper on him.' She paused, as if her own words had surprised her. 'Well, so did his father, come to that. But . . . but the colonel doesn't *love* like his father. That's the difference.'

'Love what, or whom?' I said.

'Everything,' she muttered, flushing slightly; and then, more confidently: 'His people.'

'Why, you make him sound like a monarch!' I said, laughing.

'And so he was!' she cried. 'Wasn't there a French king once, they called the Sun King?'

'Yes,' I said. 'Louis XIV.'

'That is how the Third Earl was,' she said. 'He was our Sun.'

We had reached the top of the hill now, and could feel the horses gaining speed, and hear the harness jingling freely again, as it eased about their shoulders. My companion glanced out of the window, but I kept my eyes on her face, in the hope that she would return to her subject. She seemed to think she had said enough, however, and after a long silence I decided I must prompt her, or risk losing her attention altogether.

'Louis was a despot,' I said.

'Hm?' She turned sharply, like a straying animal suddenly recalled by a tug on its rope.

'A tyrant,' I said. 'He ruled by fear. Hundreds died building his palace. I take it you don't mean –'

'Oh, no!' she said. She seemed genuinely shocked, and frowned, and looked this way and that, casting about for a way to explain what she meant. At length she said: 'All I meant was, the sun *shines* on you, don't it? That's what his lordship did, he shone on us all. Even the animals; for he doted on his dogs and horses and cattle, and loved to have them about him, and you could fall over a sow on your way to the kitchen garden, or even see her galloping through one of the rooms, and all her little ones behind her.' She smiled, and her eyes hazed with recollection, and she lowered her heavy eyelids to brush the moisture from them. 'And the people, too. They'd play cricket on his lawn, and walk in his park as if it were their own – Lord! you should have seen them, sometimes – the boys'd scratch their names on his walls and windows, and he'd say nothing about it.'

'Truly?' I said; for I could not conceive of any landowner *I* know willingly suffering such behaviour – and, indeed, would not tolerate it myself, at Limmeridge.

She nodded. 'And every year he'd mark his birthday with a great feast for the poor. Once, when he was past eighty, it could not be held at the usual time, because he was ill; and so he arranged a fête in the park the next May. Four thousand tickets were given, but many more came; and the old man could not bear that any should go hungry outside his gates, and went himself, and ordered the barriers taken down, so that all could enter. I've heard six thousand were fed that day – think of it! six thousand! – even our Saviour did not feed so many. I was there, and I know I shall never see such a sight again – a great half-circle of tables spread before the house, and carts full of plum puddings and loaves, piled like ammunition, and an endless army of men marching back and forth, carrying sides of mutton and beef on hurdles. And his lordship forever slipping in and out of his room, for the pleasure of looking upon it all, and reflecting what he had done.'

'Magnificent,' I began, 'but –'

'Yes, magnificent,' she said, so swept up now in the torrent of memory and feeling that she could not contain herself, but must rush on. 'And he provided houses for the
poor, and a doctor; and brought gas to the town, twenty
years before they had it in Midhurst . . .'

'Like the sun, indeed,' I murmured.

'What?' she said, almost snappishly. Then, as if she had
just caught my meaning, she laughed, and said: 'Oh, yes, I
had not thought of that!'

'But a hard example', I said, returning to my theme, 'for
an ordinary mortal to follow.'

'What, his son, you mean?'

I nodded; and, in truth, I did feel sorry for the colonel; for
only an angel could avoid being unfavourably compared
with such a splendid figure, and only a saint bear it without
rancour. Before I could speak, however, the woman shook
her head fiercely, and said:

'Oh, I shouldn't waste your sympathy on him.'

'Why?' I said. 'What has he done?'

'He began as he meant to go on,' she said, 'by putting me
out of my place, and scores with me. For no worse offence
than that we were employed by his lordship. Truly, you
wouldn't think they were of the same race, let alone the
same family.'

And suddenly, a question which had only been fluttering
at the edge of my mind until now, like a half-seen moth,
sprang into consciousness.

'Why is he only a colonel, if his father was an earl?'

'Because he is a bastard,' she said venomously.

I tried to press her further, but she evaded my every
inquiry, and at length lapsed into silence. Only once, when
we had stopped some time later at a lonely little tollhouse
(much like the cottage in a fairy tale, with diamond-paned
windows, and a tall chimney) by a country bridge, did she
venture another remark; pointing to a deep scar in the val-

ley, where a team of navvies was at work, she said:

'There! That's where Petworth station is going to be. That's how well Colonel Wyndham likes humanity!'

The guidebook mentioned three hotels in Petworth; and I had decided in advance, out of a childish fancy, that I should put up in the first of them that I saw. This proved to be the Swan Commercial Inn, a long, white, nondescript building of uncertain age – distinguished only by a great picture of its namesake fixed over the central first-floor window – which overlooked the little market square where the coach set us down. It was not, I had to own, the romantic hostelry I had envisaged – even as I looked at it, I felt I could see within, to the too-bright dining room, and the smoking room full of stale air and stale travelling salesmen; but I kept to my resolve, and having bade a grateful farewell to the draughtsman, and a fond one to my companion, I crossed the street, and went inside.

It was, if anything, drearier than I had imagined, with a dingy hall smelling of sour beer, and I approached the girl behind the desk, to ask for a room, with a sinking heart. Once again, however, luck was on my side; for she told me that all their beds were taken, and directed me to the Angel, where she was sure I should be accommodated to my satisfaction.

She was right, for the Angel turned out to be an ancient, lopsided, timber-framed inn, with arthritic joints and drooping eaves, yet clean and well kept within, with bright scrubbed floor-tiles, and a welcoming fire in the hall. I was greeted by an old man in a stiff leather apron, who gravely took down from the rack behind him a key big enough to secure the Tower of London, and led me upstairs to a neat little room, with coals ready-laid in the fireplace, and a casement overlooking a row of quaint houses. And when he had gone, I sat on the bed, and listened to the breathy stir and thud of a herd of cattle being driven through the street below, and thanked my own good angel for bringing me here, and wondered how many travellers over the years had had the same thought, and thanked their own.

I soon had another reason to be grateful that I had ended up at the Angel; but I was not to discover that for an hour or two more, and shall come to it in its rightful place.

Nothing prepares you for Petworth House. You leave the market square by a dingy cobbled alley, lined with small shops and taverns that offer no hint of what is to come, and all at once – there it is! a mass of roofs and chimneys, of kitchens and stables and coach-houses, coiled around the northern edge of the town like a giant serpent that, having set out to crush the whole place in its embrace, has tired and fallen asleep before it could accomplish its aim.

A gate, with a small lodge beside it, stood open, from which it was apparent that in one respect, at least, Colonel Wyndham still continued the traditions of the Third Earl's day; for even now, on a cold September afternoon, a stream of people seemed to be passing through it, on their way to or from the park, as freely as if they had been strolling by the Serpentine – and, while I should have been startled indeed to see any of those respectable matrons or sober-suited shopkeepers scrawling their names on the walls, they might, had they chosen, have done so with ease, since their path took them close to the side of the house for a hundred yards or more. By screwing up my eyes, and so blurring the details of their clothes, I could fancy myself back thirty years, and Turner yet in his studio – an illusion aided by the fading light, and the wistful autumn smells of fallen leaves and distant bonfires, which always seem to raise the ghost of other times so palpably that you feel its presence in a tightening of the throat and a prickling of the skin. In that hazy, magical moment, I allowed myself to

129

hope that my companion on the coach had been exaggerating, and that I should, after all, find the son as welcoming as the father.

To enter Petworth House is to repeat, after a fashion, your experience of approaching it from the outside. The lodge-keeper directed me to a door so unassuming that I should have missed it entirely if he had not pointed it out – it stood in an odd angle of the wall, with none of the clues (steps, or columns, or a pediment) that normally suggest the entrance to a great house – and for a dizzying second or two I wondered if Petworth were so magnificent that even the tradesmen dressed as I did, and he had mistaken me for a butcher or a grocer, and sent me to the kitchens. At length, however, the most immaculate footman I have ever seen – wearing a livery of dark blue coat, yellow-and-blue striped waistcoat and moleskin breeches which would not have disgraced an ambassador – answered the bell; and, on being told that I had come to see Colonel Wyndham, nodded and ushered me inside.

I recall walking along an unremarkable passage, which would have seemed too plain for the hall of a simple country parsonage, let alone one of the grandest mansions in England. And then, without warning, we passed through another door, and all at once I found myself in a world conceived on an entirely different scale, and built on entirely different principles. We entered it beneath the first flight of a vast staircase, which rises (you see, as you emerge into the light) round three walls of a cavernous hall, until at length it reaches a great balustraded landing extending the full width of the fourth side. Above the middle section are two huge windows, each as tall as three men; but almost every other square inch of space seems cluttered with ornament: swags and festoons; medallions and urns; laughing *putti* holding shields; painted figures, in togas and laurel crowns, standing in painted niches; and marble busts, in flowing marble wigs, haughtily surveying the world from real ones. And, dominating everything, a series of enormous wall- and ceiling-paintings in the Baroque style – a gaunt Prometheus fashioning mankind from clay, Jupiter forcing Pandora to open her box, a woman (perhaps some ancestral Wyndham) drawn in state on a chariot, accompanied by earthly and celestial attendants, and a black-and-white dog. It was hard, indeed, to find a surface that someone had not somehow contrived to cover (even the underside of the stairs was panelled and painted), save only for one doorway, which – yielding to the practical necessity of allowing people to enter and escape this odd dream-state – has been cut straight through a woman's figure, leaving a great notch in the middle of her.

The effect, I have to say, is rather like being swaddled in a giant tapestry; but, for all that I found it oppressive, I should have liked to look a while longer – partly to feast my own eyes on this great dragon's hoard, and partly to try to see it through the eyes of a man brought up in Hand Court, to whom it must surely have seemed even more alien than it did to me. The footman, however – determined to prove himself a man of the world, by affecting a complete indifference to his surroundings, and clearly expecting me to do the same – marched ahead, and stood waiting for me by a door at the other end of the hall, with a bored expression that plainly said: *The master will not be kept waiting.*

When I had caught up with him, he led me quickly through two smaller rooms – which might have furnished the text for some moralist's sermon on the dangers of excess; for they were crammed with treasures, each of which individually would have repaid an hour's attention, but which seen together simply stupefied the senses, as a surfeit of fine food jades the palate – and knocked on the door of a third. After a moment, we heard a faint 'Come in!'; and, entering before me, the man announced, 'Mr.

131

Hartright, sir,' and stood aside to admit me with the jerky grace of a mechanical toy.

After my strange introduction to the house, it was, I have to say, with some surprise (and not a little relief) that I found myself in a pleasant library, not much larger than our drawing room at Limmeridge, to which one might almost have applied the term *ordinary*. The immediate impression was of warmth – warmth from the bright coal fire in the marble fireplace; warmth from the fading sun creeping in through the windows, and giving its last lustre to the yellow-gold carpet; warmth from the ranks of leather-bound books lining the red-painted walls, and from the two hissing gas-chandeliers, hanging in the entrance to an alcove at the far end of the room, that made the polished hide and the gilt lettering sparkle. A cream-coloured cat preened itself on a large round table in the middle of the floor; and all about were thickset sofas and chairs, covered in a pretty white fabric patterned with flowers, that seemed to beg you to sit down, and take your rest.

Colonel Wyndham, however, was clearly not of the same mind. He was a broadly built man of about seventy, with sallow skin and a mane of white hair; and, from the moment he saw me walk in, he made it perfectly obvious that he would not be easy until he had seen me walk out again. He did, it is true, come forward to shake my hand; but as soon as he had done so he sprang away again – like a magnet forced close to another of the same polarity, and then suddenly released – and paced about the room, rubbing his fingers on his well-cut grey coat.

I waited for him to speak; but he remained stubbornly silent, and after a minute or so I saw that, if we were to have a conversation at all, I must initiate it.

'You may remember', I said, 'that I wrote to you. About Turner?'

He nodded.

'I was wondering if –'

'I barely remember him,' he mumbled, without looking at me (and, indeed, the whole time I was there, his eyes never met mine directly, but kept straying behind me or above me or at my feet, as if, even for him, the room had not yet revealed all its secrets, and he was constantly finding new objects of interest to distract him).

'But surely', I said, 'Turner must've been here a great deal when you were younger?'

'A soldier's away a lot, Mr. . . . Mr. . . . Mr. . . .'

'Hartright.'

'And this is a big house. People don't necessarily see each other.'

I waited for him to go on, but he turned towards the fire, pressed his hands together, and then spread them before the heat, as if the subject were closed.

'What about servants?' I said. 'Would any of them –?'

'Most of the staff came with us,' he said, shaking his head. 'From the previous house. Don't think any still here would've known him.'

Again I waited – there must, after all, be scores of servants at Petworth, and surely a moment's thought would yield the name of at least one who had been here in the Third Earl's day? – but again in vain. He continued to stare morosely at the fire; and at length I was once more forced to break the silence myself.

'Would it be possible for me to see some of the paintings your father commissioned from him?'

'Afraid not,' he said, shaking his head again. 'All the pictures are being cleaned and catalogued at the moment.'

'Or the room where he worked?' I went on, nothing daunted.

'Shut up for the winter.'

'His bedroom, even?'

'The whole end of the house,' he said, flapping his hand impatiently.

This was, I suppose, a plausible answer – all those cavernous apartments, whose only purpose was to be filled with people and laughter and music, must have been a constant reproach to a solitary man like himself, reminding him only of his own puniness and isolation; and it would be natural enough to keep most of them sealed off. I could not, however, avoid the suspicion that he was lying, for he flushed slightly, and, fixing a marble bust on top of the bookcase with a trance-like gaze, set about tweaking the end of his nose between thumb and forefinger, as if it were the most absorbing occupation in the world.

But I could not, of course, challenge him; and, after waiting a few seconds, in the futile hope that his conscience might do so on my behalf, and prompt a change of heart, I saw that – as, to be fair, he had suggested – I was merely wasting my time.

'Well,' I said. 'Thank you.'

He appeared not to notice my tone – which would have turned another man to ice – but simply nodded, as if he were at last able to agree with something I had said, and gratefully seized the bell-pull. Then, as we waited, he said nothing more to me, but paced fretfully up and down the room, twining and untwining his fingers; while I, anxious to preserve my dignity, gazed out of the window at the park – which was as cunning a piece of artifice as I have seen, with a Grecian temple on a little knoll, and graceful slopes dotted with deer, and planted with copses and broad sweeps of trees. As I watched, the last few drops of crimson were seeping out of the dying sun and soaking into the horizon – making, for a moment, the sky redder, and the earth blacker, than any paint could make them; and I knew why Turner had loved this view, and returned to it again and again.

'Where is the damned fellow?' muttered Colonel Wyndham, under his breath; and, as if in response, the door opened, and the footman reappeared. A few minutes later – less than a quarter of an hour after I had passed it on my way in – I found myself once more at the porter's lodge; and distinctly saw the lodge-keeper smirking out of the window at me, as much as to say: *I thought I should see you again, soon enough.*

It was, as you may imagine, in a thunderous mood that I retraced my steps to the Angel. It sprang, in part, from my natural disappointment at finding that my journey had been fruitless; but I was also nagged by an obscure sense of grievance, such as you might feel if you suspected that you had been cheated at cards, but had no way of proving it. A faint taint of dishonour seemed to cling to me, and I could not go down to dinner until I had washed, and put on a fresh shirt.

Once installed at a small table close to the fire, with a girl spreading a clean cloth before me, and cheerful guests all about, and the old man who had shown me to my room – now in the character of a waiter – hurrying to do my bidding, I found my spirits somewhat recovered; but I knew that this comfort was only temporary. It would keep me company as far as my bed, but forsake me in the small hours of the night, leaving me to wake all alone, and lie there in the darkness and the cold, agonizing over my humiliation.

But then, the good fortune that had aided me so often that day – call it fate, or chance, or providence, or what you will; though for myself, I cannot but see some benign power at work in it – took a hand once again. I had finished my soup, and was just making the first inroads into my steak pudding, when a woman's voice close to my shoulder suddenly said: 'Why, Mr. Hartright!' and, turning, I saw my companion on the coach, her eyes wide with surprise and pleasure, with a bearded man next to her. I was, of course, delighted to see her; but also astonished – for I could not recall telling her my name, and I certainly did not know hers. She must have seen my confusion; for she laughed, and picked up the key to my room, which I had laid next to my plate.

'There's no mystery to it,' she said. 'Giles told me a Mr. Hartright had taken room 7. Though I own I never supposed it might be you.'

'Giles?' I said.

She jerked her chin towards the porter/waiter, who was just emerging from the kitchen with a tray laden with dishes.

It took me a moment to grasp the import of what she had said; and while I did so she stood there smiling at me, like a child who has baffled you with a riddle.

'Oh,' I said, at last, 'so you're . . .?'

'Yes,' she said. 'We keep the Angel.' She gestured towards the bearded man, drawing him into our conversation. 'My dear, this is Mr. Hartright, the gentleman I was telling you about.'

'How d'ye do, sir?' he said. His voice was strong and businesslike, but he flushed slightly, and briefly inclined his head.

'Mr. Hartright, my husband, Mr. Whitaker.'

I rose to shake his hand. 'Would you both sit down, and take a glass of wine with me?' I said.

'No, sir – please – do us the honour of taking one with *us*, in our own house,' said Mrs. Whitaker.

I started to protest; but she insisted, and I soon saw that I should only cause offence if I continued to refuse.

'Well, then,' I said. 'Thank you.'

'Giles!' she called. 'If you please!'

They drew chairs to my table; and, as soon as a fresh bottle of wine was before us, and the glasses poured, she leant towards me and said quietly:

'So. How was the colonel?'

'Very much as you described him,' I said. 'Only perhaps more so.'

She laughed – the delighted, mischievous laugh of one who expects to hear a piece of illicit gossip, and intends to enjoy it.

'Tell us!' she said, confidentially – as if, instead of hotel-keepers and guest, we were three friends who had chanced upon one another at their club.

And, strange as it may seem, I did; for I felt I owed Colonel Wyndham no debt of loyalty, and had nothing to lose by being frank about him, since there seemed no possibility now that he would ever help me. And it was a relief, truth to tell, to unburden myself to an attentive audience – particularly one that seemed so ready to take my part.

'Bless me!' cried Mrs. Whitaker gleefully, when I had finished. 'That's surly enough, even for him!'

Her husband chuckled, and looked into his glass – like a man embarrassed by his wife's forthrightness (for it must be perilous for a tradesman in Petworth to be heard criticizing the colonel) but powerless to stop her.

'And you must wonder', she went on, 'why you troubled to come here at all, if that was all you were going to get for your pains?'

'Yes,' I said, surprised at her perspicacity (though it shames me to admit it – for she was an intelligent woman, and why should an innkeeper know less of disappointment than we do?).

She bent towards her husband, and whispered something in his ear. He gave a startled grimace, and then, almost immediately – with such practised rapidity that you could only suppose this was not the first time he had been taken aback by one of his wife's suggestions, and subsequently forced to accede to it – nodded, and muttered something I could not hear.

'Mr. Hartright,' she said, facing me again. 'Are you game for an adventure?'

'I hope so,' I said. 'When some good may come of it.'

'Why, then,' she said, leaning closer, and dropping her voice. 'Whitaker's nephew, Paul, is a footman up at the house. And a good boy, who'd do anything to oblige us.'

'That's because he hopes to follow us here one day,' said Whitaker. 'And is conseckently more eager to please his uncle than his master.' He nodded at his wineglass, and gave a knowing little smile that seemed to say: *I may be under my wife's thumb, but don't imagine I'm a sentimental fool*.

'Oh!' said Mrs. Whitaker, mock-chidingly, tapping him playfully. She turned back to me. 'We'll get word to him that you want to see Turner's studio, and arrange for him to meet you in the cowyard.' The wine had heightened her colour and brightened her eyes, and given her voice a kind of reckless animation.

'But surely', I said, 'it would be dangerous for him. If he was found out –'

She shook her head. 'We'll say you're a relative, visiting from London.'

'That's right,' said her husband, with a grim little laugh. 'From the *gentry* side of the family. Come to pass a pleasant evening in the servants' hall.'

'Ssh!' said Mrs. Whitaker. She pulled back her head, and squinted at me appraisingly, like an archer taking aim. 'In one of your hats, my dear, and one of your coats, he'll look well enough.' She stared a moment longer; and then, evidently satisfied, nodded. 'Well, sir, what do you say?'

I still don't know exactly why – did I truly think I should learn something of value, or was I simply attracted by the chance to outwit the man who had humiliated me? – but I did not hesitate.

'Yes,' I said.

And so it was, an hour-and-a-half later, that I set out for my second appearance at Petworth House, wearing a curly-brimmed bowler hat, and an old muffler, and a heavy worsted coat that was too tight at the shoulders, and too baggy at the waist, and left six inches of wrist showing below the cuffs. Had you been in Petworth that night, and seen me walking towards you along one of those narrow little streets, you would not, I am certain, have known me for your husband, but thought me a different sort of man altogether, and crossed the road to avoid me.

The cowyard gate, it transpired, was on the London road, a little away from the centre of the town – which was just as well, for I had to wait there twenty minutes or more, and had I been in view of the porter's lodge, or of curious passers-by, I might have been challenged, and asked to explain what I was doing. As it was, though I managed to keep myself out of sight, I could not feel entirely easy, for I was tormented by the thought, which had not struck me before, that the Whitakers' nephew might be the footman who had admitted me that morning. It did not seem likely, for they had spoken of him as a boy; but I could not feel entirely convinced until I saw a tall young man in a blue cape hurrying out of the blackness towards me. It was, of course, quite dark now, and he kept his head lowered; but I caught a glimpse of a fresh-faced complexion, and almost-white golden hair, that told me, beyond doubt, that I had never seen him before in my life.

He glanced up and down the street, and then said, in a quiet voice:

'Good evening, sir. I'm Paul Whitaker. I'm sorry you was kept so long.'

'Not at all,' I said. 'It's good of you to help me.'

'I should have been here punctual,' he said. 'Only Mrs.

Smith said to see her; and I couldn't say no, her being the housekeeper.'

'No, of course not.'

'It was only a small matter,' he said – just in case, doubtless, I should imagine he had stolen the plate, or murdered the under-butler.

He conducted me quickly across a dank, gloomy courtyard stinking of dung and wet straw, and then, through an archway, into a second, as different from the first as light from day – for it was full of the noise and smells of the kitchen, and paved with light from its windows. His policy (which I could only applaud, for I should have done the same myself) was to tread softly, and to keep as far as possible to the shadows, in order to avoid drawing unnecessary attention to himself – yet not to appear so surreptitious as to suggest, if anyone did stop him, any consciousness of wrongdoing.

Looking round sharply, to see if we were observed, he opened a door to the side of the kitchens, and led me into a broad, well-lit passage – which, save for the dingy yellow paintwork, and the pervasive fumes of pickles and jams and boiled cabbage, was not unlike that by which I had entered the house earlier in the day. An old man with no teeth and a moth-eaten white beard, who was just coming out as we went in, stopped dead when he saw us, and watched open-mouthed as we passed. I feared that he suspected something amiss, and would instantly report us when we had gone; but as soon as we were out of earshot, young Whitaker whispered:

'Don't mind him, he's only an old man, and won't say anything; and no-one will believe him if he does, for he's half mad.'

At that moment, however, he clearly sensed a greater danger; for he took my elbow, and pushed me ahead of him, just as a door to our right opened, and a surge of laughter and conversation and the heavy, drowsy scent of wine spilled into the corridor. I had time only to glimpse a stout man in a black coat, and the gracefully tapering legs of an old-fashioned mahogany sideboard, before we had turned a corner, and were descending a flight of stone steps.

'Upper servants' dining room,' muttered Whitaker. 'Best avoided if we can.'

We were now in a long, low underground tunnel, with a curved ceiling and worn flags on the floor. It was lined with pipes, and lit by gas-lamps, although there were little niches set at regular intervals in the clammy walls where, presumably, lanterns had once stood. To the right, about halfway along, was a brick arch, barred by an iron gate, which seemed to lead into the void. Whitaker jabbed his thumb towards it:

'The well,' he said; and then, as if divulging this titbit had reminded him of my ignorance, and made him feel he should explain more: 'This is the way into the main house.'

When we finally emerged, we did not continue straight ahead, but turned into a small courtyard, like one of the older and pokier quads at an Oxford college, which – from the crude construction of the surrounding walls, and the shape and alignment of the plain square windows – was clearly of an earlier date than the rest of the mansion. To my surprise, however, I felt no change in the air, such as you normally experience when you go outside; and when I looked up, instead of the stars I expected to find there, I saw a pattern of rough roof beams, and, beyond them, a blackness more profound than even the darkest sky. And in an instant I realized that this sprawling monster must have been built about an entire other house, which still stood within its walls, invisible to the outside world – like the ghostly leg-bone that, according to anatomists, lies trapped beneath the skin of a seal.

'Turner's studio's up there,' said Whitaker, nodding to a dark upper window. He opened a narrow door, and, reaching into the gloom, brought out a lantern – further evidence of his intelligence and forethought, for he must have placed it there earlier, to avoid rousing suspicion – and quickly lit it. Then, lifting it high, he led me stealthily up an old spiral stone staircase, so rank with the stench of dust and mildew that it seemed to cling to the roof of my mouth like grease – and, indeed, the taste of it lingers there still, even as I write. And I was suddenly, forcefully, reminded of another place – although it was so unexpected that it hovered for a few seconds at the edge of my mind, like a powerful but half-forgotten image from a dream, before I could put a name to it: Hand Court.

'Just a moment, sir,' whispered Whitaker, when we reached the top. He appeared far more nervous now, and peered out gingerly, to ensure that the coast was clear. And when he did at length stride on to the landing, beckoning me to follow, he moved so fast that my next distinct memory is of being in a large dark space, and of Whitaker closing the door and then leaning against it, half panting and half laughing softly with relief.

'Pardon me, sir, if I don't light the gas-lamps,' he said, when he had got his breath back, 'but I fear we might be seen.'

It might not have been strictly true to say that the room had been shut up for the winter, but it certainly had an unused air about it. The atmosphere was chilly and damp, and the only evidence of a fire was the fusty smell of long-dead coals. In the centre of the end wall was a huge arched window, unshuttered and uncurtained, and against its weak grey light I could see the silhouettes of a sofa and two or three chairs, and the outline of a convoluted statue – rising from its pedestal in the form of an enormous ragged cone, like a drunken witches' hat – which seemed to show some mythic mortal combat between man and man or man and beast. It was difficult to make out much else – for Whitaker's lantern, swinging in his hand, illuminated no more than a few square feet of carpet – but as my eyes grew more accustomed to the dimness I noticed that the walls were lined with bookshelves, and realized that this must be another library. (How many books can Colonel Wyndham own, in heaven's name?! How many of them has he read?) There was no evidence of it ever having been used as a studio – no obvious connection with painting at all, in fact, save for a few pictures hung over the fireplace.

And yet, for all that, I could not help but feel Turner's presence strongly – so strongly, indeed, that for a fleeting moment I almost fancied I saw his shadowy little figure standing before an easel in the window, a brush clenched between his teeth, another in his hand, a gleam of furious pleasure in his eye. It may be that I really am starting to know him, or perhaps I was merely following the train of thought that had begun on the staircase, but I seemed, in an instant, to understand why he was easy here: it was a kind of ideal Maiden Lane, giving him, on a far grander scale, and with unimaginably greater comfort, the same relation between society and seclusion that he would have known when painting in his bedroom as a boy. The great door that so effectively protected him from the prying eyes of the world could, quite as easily, re-admit him to its company; for beyond this private island stretched a giant warren, teeming with servants and children and fellow-artists, all presided over by his kindly patron – just as, years before, Hand Court, too, must have teemed with familiar faces.

Conceive, my love, my feelings when, in the midst of these ruminations, without warning, I heard, not a dozen yards away, the stifled giggling of a girl. I defy any man, however brave – unless he be a turnip, with no imagination whatever – to deny that he, like me, would have gasped, and felt his scalp tighten with fear, and the sweat break out on his back.

'Nancy!' said Whitaker. He sounded almost as startled as I was, and his lantern shook visibly, slopping splashes of yellow light on the floor and walls. In its palsied glow I saw the girl rear up behind the sofa, patting the dust from her print skirt. She was still laughing, but it was the uncertain laughter of one who hopes to escape censure by making light of what she has done.

'I thought you wasn't here yet!' said Whitaker.

'I waited ten minutes on the stairs,' she replied, in a wronged tone. 'But when you didn't come and didn't come, I thought I'd bestest hide in here.'

He clearly felt he could not reproach her further; but could not keep his anger at being taken by surprise, and made to seem frightened, from his voice. 'Well,' he snapped. 'Have you got it?'

'Course,' she said, starting round the sofa towards us. She was walking with small, awkward steps, and as she came into the light I could see why: she was clutching something beneath her apron.

'Nancy,' said Whitaker, more gently. 'This is my cousin from London. Mr. . . . Mr. . . .'

I was, I must confess, momentarily at a loss; for if – as seemed apparent – Nancy was a fellow-conspirator, why should he not introduce me as myself? Almost in the same instant, however, I guessed the answer: he was (again with admirable prudence) trying to protect both her and us. If we were discovered, she would be less likely to betray us, and would herself appear less culpable, if she was ignorant of my true identity, but really thought that she was merely helping to entertain a visiting relative of Whitaker's.

'Jenkinson,' I said – and, had you heard me, I'm sure you would have said: *There's a man born in Covent Garden, who went on to better things.*

144

'How do you do, Mr. Jenkinson?' She was young – only fifteen or sixteen – with a strong, fine-featured face and an almost gypsy-brown complexion; and there was a kind of modest attentiveness in the way she took my hand that made me think she was anxious to win my good opinion, perhaps as a suitable wife for my supposed cousin.

'Let's see it, then,' said Whitaker.

Nancy crouched down, slipped an old oilskin pouch from behind her apron and laid it in the pool of lamplight on the floor. 'He gave this to my ma,' she said, drawing out a flat package covered in tissue-paper, and starting to unwrap it.

'Turner?' I said.

I don't know whether she replied or not, for at that moment I saw, beneath her fingers, the first patch of that familiar burning orange-red, and then a dark strip of fore-ground, and then a brilliant button of sun, furious as a raw wound, leaking its radiance into a sky ribbed with cloud.

'Here,' she said.

It was, I saw, as I took it, a little watercolour of the park, which might perhaps have served as a sketch for a larger oil. The brushwork was so rough and indistinct – some-times an object would be suggested by no more than a line, or a single speck of paint – that it was difficult to make out anything clearly, but I was able to identify the Grecian tem-ple; and a herd of deer (no more than a cluster of dots, real-ly) roaming across the hillside; and something that looked like an empty chair in the bottom left-hand corner, on what must be the terrace in front of the house.

'Did your mother know him well?' I said.

'She saw him often enough, I believe,' said Nancy. 'She was a housemaid here, like me.'

'And why'd he give it to her?' I said, with a leer that made me cringe inwardly.

'I don't know, Mr. Jenkinson,' she said. 'She never said.

145

Why do you suppose?' She looked me straight in the eye, and gave a little smile, but I noticed she was blushing.

I felt I could not ask more without seeming to act out of character; so I chuckled, and gave her the picture back, and said – with the air of a man whose limited curiosity has been satisfied – 'That's very interesting, gel. Thank you.'

This encounter, you may think, afforded me little enough; and yet it gave my visit to Petworth some point and purpose, which it would have otherwise lacked, and left me feeling – whether rightly or wrongly, I still cannot tell – that I had learnt something of value about Turner, and gained an insight into his character.

I should, indeed, have come away quite satisfied, had it not been for an incident on the way back, when – just as we had emerged once more from the tunnel into the service wing, and I was starting to breathe more easily – I saw, coming towards me, with a tray laden with glasses and a decanter for the house, the man in all the world I most, at that moment, dreaded meeting: the footman who had taken me to Colonel Wyndham that morning. There was no point in turning around, or pulling up my collar to hide my face, for he was already watching me, with a little frown of puzzlement, and would have undoubtedly seen any hesitation or evasion on my part as a confirmation of guilt. My only hope, I realized, was to make him doubt the evidence of his own eyes; and when he slowed his pace, therefore, and made to waylay us, I stopped, and gave him a frank smile, and said:

'Who's this, Paul?'

'Mr. Bond,' said Whitaker. 'Mr. Bond, Mr. Jenkinson. My cousin from London.'

'It's a pleasure to meet you, Mr. Bond,' I said. I did not offer my hand, for he could not take it; but bobbed my head respectfully. 'Paul's a good boy, and writes often, and never fails to say what a help you are to him, in learning his duties.'

Bond made no response, save to look deep into my eyes, and then at Whitaker, and then back again. At length he said:

'And where do you put up, Mr. Jenkinson?'

Before I could reply, Whitaker – anxious, no doubt, to show that he had not flouted the rules by inviting me to stay at the house – said:

'At the Angel, Mr. Bond.'

Bond said nothing more, and, after a moment, nodded and moved on. As he turned into the tunnel, however, he looked back at me with a cool gaze that plainly said he was not convinced; and I knew that he might tell the house-keeper what he had seen; and that she might tell Colonel Wyndham; and that the colonel might send to the Angel to make enquiries after me. I resolved, therefore, that to avoid the risk of embarrassment for my kind hosts, and of dis-grace – or perhaps even dismissal – for their nephew, I must quit Petworth within the hour.

And so it was that I thanked Paul Whitaker at the cow-yard gate, and gave him a sovereign for his pains, and five shillings for Nancy, and made my way back to the hotel, and ordered a fly to drive me to Horsham, where I sup-posed (correctly, as it turned out) that I should be able to take an early train to London. Mr. and Mrs. Whitaker implored me to stay, saying they were sure no harm would come to them or to Paul; but I would not be swayed. Then they refused payment for my room, since I should not have slept in it; but I insisted, and at length they relented, and we parted with many professions of thanks and good will on both sides.

I was so exhausted that even the cold air could not keep me fully awake on that journey through the night, and I slipped between sleep and consciousness, and half-dreamed that I was fleeing some dark confinement with Turner, who chuckled gleefully at our escape – or, rather, that I *was* Turner, and the chuckle was mine.

But now – you will be relieved to hear! – I am fully restored to myself.

Your loving husband

Walter

XIX

From the diary of Marian Halcombe,
29th September, 185–

I have been on my knees, giving thanks. I shall, I know, meet grief and pain and weariness of heart again, as surely as I have met them before; but today – let me joyfully acknowledge it – I have been truly happy. *Thank you, Lord*.

The morning, it must be said, gave little enough hint of what was to come; for I had slept poorly, and gave myself a momentary fright when I peered into the glass and saw there, instead of the lively, cheerful face I had expected, a haggard, half-familiar woman in middle life, with dark rings beneath her eyes and the first silver threads in her tangled black hair. By energetically plying the hair-brush, and smiling brightly (as you do on being introduced to a stranger), and murmuring silly little phrases of encouragement – 'You'll do very well, Marian, indeed you will' – I soon banished her; but the baleful image lingered in my memory, like an awful vision of the future.

Matters were not greatly improved when, leaving the house a little later, we suddenly found ourselves in the middle of a dense fog, as still and chilly as the tomb, which stung our eyes, and clogged our mouths and noses, and speckled our hands and faces with sharp little crystals of soot. I had – I now realized – been looking forward to our boating expedition with unreasonable, childish pleasure, and the certainty that I should be deprived of it cast me down as palpably as a physical burden, bowing my shoulders and slowing my step. I tried, however, to conceal my disappointment; and, taking Walter's arm, laughed, and said with as much bravado as I could muster:

'We shall be fortunate to find the river at this rate, let alone see anything from it.'

The journey to Brentford seemed endless, for the cabman – unable to see further than his horse's ears, and fearful, presumably, of colliding with another vehicle, or running down a child – crawled along at a snail's pace (and a cautious snail at that); and when we looked out of the window we could make out nothing to tell us where we were, or how far we had come – so that, for all we knew, we might have been travelling very slowly in a circle, and still only a hundred yards from our own front door. But then, all of a sudden, the fog thinned to reveal a line of black battlements (belonging, alas, not to the romantic old castle I at first imagined, but to a row of hideous brick villas, which seemed to think they might disguise their newness with a show of trumped-up antiquity); and then it had dwindled to a few wisps of mist; and by the time we neared Brentford, ten minutes later, you could see, through a dazzling chalky gauze, the unmistakable brilliance of a cloudless sky.

We turned into a broad, tree-lined road, and pulled up, about halfway along, in front of a modest gate crammed between a coach-house and a tall boundary wall. The house itself – which stood back a little way, behind a worn carriage sweep mottled with weeds – seemed, from the street, entirely characterless: neither large nor small, neither old nor new; quite indescribable, in fact, save as a catalogue of angles and dimensions. As soon as you walked through the door, however, you found yourself in a charming, well-proportioned hall, hung with delicately drawn portrait sketches, and

freshly painted in pale, old-fashioned colours that accentuated the impression of light and space.

A stocky manservant of about thirty, with a florid complexion and a sweet smile (that peculiarity alone, surely,
must make the household remarkable, for how many footmen are encouraged to *smile* at visitors?), led us to a large
parlour at the rear of the building. For an instant, I had the
illusion that I was entering Elizabeth Eastlake's boudoir; for
this room occupied the corresponding corner of the house,
and exerted, as it were, the same architectural force: you felt
the shadowy bulk of hall and staircase bearing down on
you, pressing you forward as insistently as a hand on the
neck, and the big french window drawing you towards it,
with its promise of freedom and fresh air. It took but a
moment, however, to see that the presiding spirits of the two
places were entirely different; for where Fitzroy Square is all
oak and varnish and titanic chaos, this was brightness and
elegance and classical order. The books were ranged with
military discipline along their shelves, without a single
mutineer on chair or table; there were no curiosities to be
seen (unless you count a pair of graceful porcelain figures on
the chimney-piece); and in place of the bulging bureau was
a little writing desk, with fluted Grecian legs, and a drawer
barely deep enough to accommodate a small family of
envelopes, that looked as if it might have been used by the
Empress Josephine to compose billets-doux to her husband.

A slender woman of perhaps sixty-five – who contrived,
somehow, to appear fashionable in a straight powder-blue
dress that would have been considered *démodé* twenty years
ago – rose from a scrolled chaise longue to greet us.

'Miss Halcombe! Mr. Hartright!' she said, advancing
towards us with arms outstretched. 'You've brought the
sun!' Her voice was soft and melodic, with none of the
roughness of age – so that if you had heard it without seeing
her, you would have imagined that it belonged to a woman

thirty years younger. She glanced at the window, flung up her hands in a kind of priestly invocation, and then – in a single sweeping movement, as gracious as a dancer's – extended them towards us, taking Walter's hand in one and mine in the other, so that we stood like a chain of children preparing to play ring-a-ring-o'-roses.

'If we stop to be polite,' she said, 'the day will be gone. So shall we agree, this very minute, we'll take our chances, and venture out, now?'

'Yes,' said Walter and I together, without a moment's hesitation.

She coloured and nodded with evident pleasure. 'I confess I didn't entirely despair when I saw the fog,' she said, moving towards the door, 'but my poor husband was quite determined we were doomed. He'll be more than glad to hear that matters have mended.' She paused, and added, as if as an afterthought: 'You will not, I hope, object to taking the oars, Mr. Hartright? There will not be room for our man as well.'

'No, not at all.'

'Good.' She hunched her shoulders and rubbed her hands with excitement; and then – with a little 'Oh!' that was as much a cry of joy as a word – disappeared into the hall.

Sometimes, when their little one has done something especially charming, you may see parents give each other a conspiratorial smile compounded of fondness and indulgence and shared delight; and it was just such a smile that Walter and I exchanged now. Then, without a word (for why speak, when your meaning has already been so perfectly conveyed?), we gravitated to the window, and gazed out on an artful confection of paths and lawns and rose-bushes – still dotted here and there with flowers, and with the last vapours of mist clinging to them like fleece snagged on a bramble – surrounded by formal little hedges. We had been standing there, in companionable silence, for a minute or more, when Walter suddenly startled me by saying:

'He must be blind.'

'What!'

'Her husband. Look.' He gestured towards the french window; and then, realizing he might make his point more strongly, opened it. 'No. Smell.'

I did so. The air was hard and cold, and thick with the smoky residue of fog; but mingled with it, like the last echoes of a forgotten world, were the pungency of thyme, the narcotic sweetness of rosemary, and the dying breath of the roses.

'The garden is planted for scent, not sight.'

'That's a small enough foundation for a great edifice,' I said. 'Perhaps they both just prefer sweet smells to brilliant spectacle.'

Walter shook his head. 'If he could see, he would have known without being told.'

'Known what?' I said, half-laughing (and, it must be said, entirely lost).

He raised his face to the clearing sky. 'That the weather was better.'

'How do you know he didn't?'

'Because she said: "He'll be delighted to *hear* that matters have mended."'

I considered a moment. He was right, of course: Mrs. Bennett *had* said that, and it did seem curious, now I came to reflect on it, though I had paid no attention to it at the time.

'Very good,' I said. 'We shall lose you to the detective police.'

It was at that instant, I think, that I first became aware of the change in Walter – a change I should, perhaps, have noticed before, for the signs must have been there since his return from Sussex, and, once I was conscious of it, I found myself remarking it again and again. Instead of laughing, and replying in kind – as, assuredly, he would have done only a few weeks ago – he made no response at all, but continued looking out of the window, his brow slightly creased with the effort of pursuing some train of thought I could not even guess at. It was not that he was cold or distant, exactly – only that our friendship, with its teasing and its affection, its rituals of mockery and self-deprecation – had been supplanted in his mind, at least for the time being, by something larger. For a few seconds, it is true (I could not help it then, and cannot deny it now), I felt wounded and bereft, like a child whose boon companion has entered the adult world, and left her behind; but, almost at once, this tincture of bitterness was swept away by a flood of joy – for had I not hoped and prayed that my dear brother would recover himself, and grow to manhood again? And was he not doing so, before my very eyes? And should we not then be truer, deeper friends yet?

'Now, I think we are quite ready,' said Mrs. Bennett's voice behind us. We turned and saw her standing in the doorway, next to a stout old man in a thick black redingote. He was almost bald, but with heavy white whiskers – as if his hair had decided to migrate, like Mrs. Booth's balcony, but in the opposite direction, from the top of his head to his cheeks – which gave the odd impression that his face was wider than it was tall.

'My dear, this is Miss Halcombe, and her brother, Mr. Hartright,' she went on. 'But time enough for proper introductions later.'

She had already started back into the hall; but her husband stayed where he was, and held out his hand, and mumbled 'How do you do?', staring at a point exactly midway between Walter and me with the dull milky eyes of a blind man.

Quite a spectacle we must have made, as we processed to the river: Mrs. Bennett, in a brilliant red cloak and carrying a small guitar, talking to Walter in the vanguard; then me, talking to no-one, but simply glorying in the sun that shone more brightly on us with every step; and finally the manservant, with Mr. Bennett hanging on to his elbow, and a basket of provisions and a stack of railway rugs in his arms. At length we entered a small untidy boatyard littered with planks and wood-shavings and coils of rope brittle with dried tar, where the servant vanished without a word. Mrs. Bennett was talking animatedly to Walter about cutters and skiffs and dories, her hand darting about like a frantic wren as she illustrated her argument with a mast here and a thwart there; and her husband, though he stood a little apart, as immobile as a Buddha, and could presumably see nothing, seemed to be listening with keen interest; so I ventured by myself on to a rickety wharf to admire the view.

Even this far upstream the Thames was strewn with filth, which the current had thrown against the piles of the jetty and formed into little islands – with plains made from fallen leaves and waterlogged paper, and mountains from the necks of half-submerged bottles, and, in one instance, an entire hinterland created from a drowned cat, its sodden fur as sleek as a rat's. But the far shore was another world; for there, rearing up like an exotic temple, was the new Palm House at Kew Gardens, its billowing glass roof shot through with light, and the gorgeous red leaves of an American maple flaming beside it; and beyond that, towards Richmond, the tree-fringed slopes and hollows of the Old Deer Park, rising and falling and rising again with the sweet regularity of a calm sea, or of some gentle pastoral melody. The associations with Turner were not hard to see: indeed, this whole scene was a kind of mirror image of *London from Greenwich Park*, with the foreground dominated by the mighty Thames, the father of our greatness, now reduced to little more than a stinking cesspool by the greed and venality of the modern age; while, in the distance, an Elysian landscape, restored to glorious life by the unclouded sun, seemed to show us a vision of a happier time. Less explicably, I also found myself thinking of another painting I had seen at Marlborough House. There was no sea, and no figure that might remind me of Apollo or the Sibyl; there were no ruins; and – while its character was undoubtedly classical – this vista of beech and chestnut, of copse and meadow, had none of the parched brilliance of the Mediterranean, but seemed to glow with that deep-hued, temperate lushness you see only in England. Why, then, was I so forcefully put in mind of *The Bay of Baiae*, and of the vague, troubling sense of mystery that still seemed to hang about it in my recollection? The answer must be there before me; but, try as I might, I could not find it, and was still vainly searching when the manservant returned to announce that our boat was ready.

'Thank you, Jonathan,' said Mrs. Bennett. She led the way through the yard (to my surprise, she seemed to know all the workmen personally, and greeted them by name, receiving in return a grimy thumb and forefinger raised to a frayed cap, or a muttered 'Good afternoon, ma'am') and down a flight of stone steps. At the bottom, a broad little skiff, neatly furnished with rugs and cushions, with the basket set squarely amidships and a pair of oars resting in the rowlocks, bobbed and shivered at the end of its rope. She held it steady while Jonathan handed her husband in, and settled him in the bows; then she climbed nimbly into the stern herself, helped me to the seat beside her, and smiling up at Walter said:

'Very well, Mr. Hartright, if you please.'

And so began six wonderful hours. Walter took his place amidships; and then Jonathan cast us off, and stood watching and waving from the steps (truly, he seemed more like the Bennett's son than their servant) as we glided into midstream and turned to go upriver. There was no space for a tiller, but steering expertly with a piece of ribbon attached to the rudder, and calling instructions to Walter – 'A little harder with your left, Mr. Hartright,' or 'We should not, I fear, come well out of a fight with *that*. Why don't you take a well-earned rest for a moment, and let it go?' – Mrs. Bennett brought us safely past a string of barges, and astern of a clanking collier that set us bouncing and rocking in its wake. For a moment we seemed lost in the pall of black smoke that gushed from its funnel and hung threateningly over the water, blotting out the sky and dimming the sun to no more than a pallid silver disc; but then it was gone, as miraculously as the morning's fog, and we emerged into that sunlit other world I had seen from the boatyard.

We could not, of course, entirely put the ugliness of modern life behind us: it was there in the ceaseless traffic of the river, and the broken cigar-box that slapped against the side of the boat, and the streets of mean, anonymous little houses sprawling along the north bank. But it ceased, from that moment, I think, to be the dominant reality. Lulled by the rhythmic dip and groan of the oars, delighted by the sight of a wild tangle of roots here, or the gothic ruin of some old coots' nest there, we drifted along in a kind of enchantment – saying nothing, and each of us thinking his own thoughts, of which the only outward sign was the dreamy smile on every face. I think, indeed, I must have really fallen asleep, though I have no idea for how long; for one moment I was watching Mr. Bennett put his hand over the side of the boat, with a look of beatific pleasure, as if by trailing his fingers in the water he might *feel* the colours that he could not see; and the next we had stopped with a jolt, and Walter was making us fast to an overhanging branch; and Mrs. Bennett was opening the basket, and saying:

'I hope you care for cold veal pie, Miss Halcombe?'

'Yes,' I mumbled. 'Yes, indeed.'

She took out a white cloth, and laid it, still folded (for

there was not space to spread it out) in a narrow strip at our feet. 'I have chosen the bill of fare on purpose, Mr. Hartright,' she said. 'If you cannot share a picnic with Turner, you shall at least know what it would have tasted like. A pie' – here she started removing the dishes as she named them, and setting them before us – 'Beef. A chicken. A lettuce, cut this morning, if you will believe me, from our own glasshouse. Pull-bread. A cranberry tart. *Then* it would have been *strawberry* tart, but, alas, the autumn is upon us.' There was a gravity and wistfulness in her voice, as she said this, which I had not heard before, and which made me suppose she was thinking: *And not merely the autumn of the year, but the autumn of life, too.*

'I like cranberry just as well,' said Walter.

She made no response, save a shake of the head; and realizing that he would not coax her from her melancholy by making light of it, he took another approach, and tried to distract her with a simple, direct question:

'How was it that you came to know Turner?'

'Oh, his uncle was a butcher at New Brentford,' she said – and I knew instantly that Walter had judged right, for there was a renewed liveliness in her voice that told you this was a subject close to her heart, and that it was a relief to her to speak about it. 'Mr. Marshall.' She shook her head and smiled. 'I still remember him. Turner stayed with him as a child, I believe, and later continued to visit him. We lived nearby – my father was a clergyman' – here she nodded and smiled at Mr. Bennett, who, as if he mysteriously sensed it (or perhaps merely because he anticipated her next words), nodded also – 'like my husband; and a fine amateur artist. He met Turner one day when they were both sketching by the river, and saw immediately that he had genius, but that he stood in need of friends.'

'Because he was poor, you mean?' said Walter.

'Yes.' She hesitated. 'Well, I don't know about *poor*, exactly.

He was, I believe, quite successful, even then. But –'

'Forgive me,' said Walter, 'but when was this?

'Oh, I don't know exactly. Some time in the middle or late 'nineties, I suppose.'

Walter nodded encouragingly; and, drawing a notebook from his pocket, started to write. 'So Turner was still a young man?'

'Yes. Little more than twenty, I should say. But he had started exhibiting at the Royal Academy by then – just watercolours, you know, but still . . . And working for Dr. Monro, and . . .' She smiled at some sudden recollection, and paused to grasp it before it vanished back into the abyss. 'I remember him telling me once,' she went on, 'the doctor had a great collection of pictures, and employed him and Thomas Girtin to make copies of them, for two-and-sixpence or three-and-sixpence an evening, and a bowl of oysters.'

I laughed. 'I'm sorry to seem so ignorant, but who was Thomas Girtin?'

'You would have heard of him had he lived,' said Walter quickly, without taking his eyes from Mrs. Bennett. 'Another young artist, as gifted as Turner himself, supposedly. But Dr. Monro . . .?'

'Oh, he was a famous mad-doctor,' said Mrs. Bennett, with an edge of pride in her voice, as if Monro's professional eminence somehow redounded to Turner's credit. 'He helped to treat the late king.'

I could not help smiling, for there had been two 'late kings' since the one who had required the services of a mad-doctor. The strange petrifying process that had arrested her idea of fashion, and fixed it for ever about 1830, had clearly had the same effect on her notion of history.

'And he was already travelling a good deal, as well,' she went on.

'Travelling where?'

'Oh, I don't know. He couldn't go to the continent, of

course, for we were still at war. But all about England and
Wales – wherever there were picturesque views to be found
of lakes and mountains, or ruined abbeys, or old castles.' She
laughed. 'Places where you might imagine a skeleton in a
crumbling tower, or a maiden locked in a dungeon beneath
the black waters of a moat. Those sorts of subjects were very
popular at the time. He did not want for commissions.'

'Why then did your father think he needed friends?' said
Walter. 'If he was already so successful?'

She did not answer at once, but suddenly busied herself
with taking plates and glasses from the basket, as if she had
only just remembered that they were there, and must attend
to them at once. At length she muttered, 'I believe there were
domestic difficulties'; and then, before Walter had time to
reply, handed him a wine bottle and a corkscrew, and said:
'Come, Mr. Hartright, we mustn't let your sister starve.
Would you be so good as to open this?'

'Of course,' said Walter. But if she had hoped thus to deter
him, she must have been disappointed, for as he set to work
he went on: 'What sort of domestic difficulties?'

She seemed entirely absorbed in cutting a loaf of bread,
and a casual observer might have supposed that she had not
heard him at all. But she was a poor actress, and could not
prevent her throat working uncomfortably, or her tongue
darting out to moisten her lips.

'Do you mean, perhaps, he had differences with his parents?' said Walter, gently, but with absolute determination.
When she still did not reply he continued:

'You can imagine, I am sure, Mrs. Bennett, how difficult it
has been to find anyone with reliable information about his
early life. So anything you can tell me . . .'

'I really know very little,' she said, reddening, her eyes
cast down. 'But . . . but – by all accounts – his mother had an
uncontrollable temper.'

Walter's gaze suddenly lost its focus, and drifted past her.

'Like a gale,' he murmured.

'I beg your pardon?' said Mrs. Bennett. I knew Walter well enough to see that her words had recalled to his mind something he had heard or thought before, but she seemed uncertain whether or not he was joking, and half-smiled at him tentatively.

'Like a gale,' he said more loudly, returning her smile.

She nodded (though I think she was still puzzled, for her expression continued to hover between seriousness and jest) and said:

'She was, I believe, a great trial to him and his father, and died mad.'

'Really?' said Walter. 'She was committed, you mean?'

'Yes.' Her voice was barely audible. 'To Bethlem Hospital, I think. Though I – I'm not certain.' She hesitated a moment; and when she went on again it was with a kind of breathless urgency that made her sound, for the first (and last) time, harassed and defensive. 'He never spoke to me about it. We all knew that he confided in my father, but it was too sacred a subject to be openly discussed.' She wrung her hands, as if she despaired of making us see. 'What you must understand, Miss Halcombe – Mr. Hartright – is that he was more like one of our family than a friend. And no family can long survive if its members do not respect each others' sensitivities and secrets.'

Walter stared at her for a moment; and then nodded and laid down his notebook and pencil.

'Shall I pour out some wine?' he said.

'If you please,' said Mrs. Bennett, with a grateful look.

At the mention of the word 'wine', I noticed, her husband held out his hand in readiness, and kept it there patiently until Walter tapped his wrist to alert him, whereupon it closed on the proffered tumbler like a sprung trap. He did not drink, however, until we were all similarly provided, and Mrs. Bennett cried:

160

'We should do as we always did! Raise your glasses, everybody! Here's health and happiness to us all!'

To listen to the Right Reverend Bishop of This, and Her Majesty's Secretary of State for That, telling us that *innocence* must at all cost be preserved and protected, you would think that no virtue excited greater public admiration; yet can we imagine a man of the world, or a woman of fashion – or a costermonger, or a lady's maid, come to that – freely admitting to being *innocent*, or thanking the man who so describes them? No, for to be *innocent* is not merely to be blameless – it is also, is it not, if we are entirely honest, to be childish, and foolish, and ignorant (horror of horrors!) of *how things really go on*? Yet sitting there, a tumbler of brown sherry in my hand, and seeing Mrs. Bennett's unfeigned joy at the sunshine playing on the murky water, and the caress of the cold air on her cheek; her delight at the company of friends yet living, and the memory of others now dead, I could not but reflect that *we* are the fools – for have we not, in our thoughtless desire to seem *practical* and *sensible*, taken strength for weakness, and weakness for strength? Here was an elderly woman, who had known her share of the tragedies and reverses that befall us all; and yet somehow, miraculously, they had not embittered her, or – whatever marks they had left upon her outer form – corroded the girlish loveliness of her soul. She still (you could hear it in the exuberance of that strangely young voice) took simple pleasure in the mere fact of being alive, in loving and being loved, in wondering at the beauty of God's handiwork – and surely that made her stronger, and more fitted for existence, than the most worldly-wise cynic on earth, who thinks he has seen the essential hollowness of life, and seeks only to while it away as agreeably as possible before it is taken from him?

'Health and happiness to us all!' we called back, as lustily and unselfconsciously as children, and quite impervious to the quizzical looks of the captain and his mate in a passing tug.

'Now, Miss Halcombe,' said Mrs. Bennett, taking up a plate, and searching in the basket for cutlery. 'Let me help you to something. Some beef and salad?'

'Thank you.' I had half-forgotten the purpose of our expedition already, and would have been quite content if no-one had mentioned it again all afternoon; but Walter was not to be so easily deflected, and pursued his quarry with a doggedness which – though I had seen it before, when he had been fighting for Laura's happiness and honour – still took me by surprise. Setting down his glass, and reaching once more for his notebook, he said:

'You saw him often at your house, then?'

'What, Turner?' cried Mrs. Bennett. 'Oh, yes, constantly! It seems, indeed, when I look back, that all my earliest recollections are in some way bound up with him. Truly, Mr. Hartright, you never met a merrier creature!'

The food was quite forgotten again, and she settled happily back in her seat. This, you could see, was the Turner she loved to talk about: not the madwoman's son, but the light-hearted playfellow.

'He would romp endlessly with us children,' she went on, 'making houses for us with wooden bricks, and then knocking them down, or letting us wind and unwind the long cravat about his neck as if he were a maypole.'

Walter laughed. 'And did you continue to know him in later life?'

'Oh, certainly. For a few years, indeed, we saw more of him than ever, for he built a little lodge for himself and his father at Twickenham – I can't remember when exactly, it must've been 'thirteen or 'fourteen, I suppose, there's a Miss Fletcher there now; and so we became neighbours, after a fashion, and we were forever meeting at either our house, or his, or getting up picnic parties together on the river.' She impulsively stretched a hand towards her husband, and smiled at him, though he could not see her, with her head on one side, and her eyes bright with tender recollection. 'Charles there, and his brother Tom, who became a surgeon, and me and my sisters, and our father, and Miss Phelps the singer, and Ben Fisher, who went to India, and Sam Fisher, who joined the army, and Mr. Maxwell –'

'Humph!' said her husband, loudly, startling us all; for (save when he had raised his hand to drink) he had been as impassive as a statue, and this was almost the first sound he had uttered.

'My husband did not approve of Mr. Maxwell,' said Mrs. Bennett, with a teasing laugh – which seemed, nonetheless, to contain some undercurrent of sadness, or regret.

'Why not?' I began; but she silenced me with a sharp nod towards Mr. Bennett, which plainly said: *Wait, and he will tell you himself.*

And, sure enough, after a few seconds, he said, in a ponderous, wheezing voice:

'Not so much I didn't *approve* of him, my dear. He depressed my spirits, that's all, with all his talk of rocks and bones.'

'What, he was a geologist?' said Walter.

The old man nodded. 'Every generation has its own trial. For mine it was geology.'

'Not *all* your generation, my dear,' said his wife, with a weary smile that suggested this was an old dispute, rehearsed between them many times before. Then, evidently determined to wrest the conversation back from him, she hurried on, before he had time to reply: 'It certainly wasn't a trial for Turner, Mr. Hartright. Mr. Maxwell told me he might have been a geologist himself, so great was his understanding –'

'Turner was not obliged, as I was, to sit by a dying woman,' said Mr. Bennett, suddenly, the passion of his words curiously at odds with their slothful delivery, 'and try to persuade her that she could still trust in God's love for her, and for the dead infant at her breast, despite the discovery of so much evidence that seemed to contradict His word. If He has lied to us about the age of His world, why should we believe His promise of redemption?'

There was something plaintive, even desperate, in his tone, as if the perplexity was his, and he was hoping we might ease it; but what comfort can a layman – and a stranger, at that – bring to a clergyman whose mind has become a muddy battlefield, so trampled by the ceaseless advance and retreat of faith and doubt that every argument and counter-argument must already seem wearyingly familiar? No-one spoke for a few moments; and then Walter said cautiously:

'Was Turner not, then, much occupied with religion?'

Mr. Bennett shook his head. 'He was a pagan!'

'He came to church with us, when he was staying,' remonstrated his wife, gently; but the old man only shook his head the more, and gave a disgusted 'Hah!'.

'I never discussed theology with him,' said Mrs. Bennett, pursuing her theme with some warmth now, 'but no-one could have felt the sufferings of his fellow-creatures more keenly, or tried harder to obey our Lord's injunction to love his neighbour as himself.'

This seemed to reduce her husband to speechless incredulity; for he could not make a sound, but merely continued shaking his head so vigorously that I feared he must become dizzy, and faint.

'There are, I think, some who would be surprised to hear you say that,' said Walter, mildly. 'Many people think he was cold, and mean, and –'

Mrs. Bennett reddened – she was incensed – her friend was under attack, and she must fling herself into the task of defending him, even if it meant forgetting her manners, and not allowing Walter to finish.

'They would not think so if they had known him as I did,'

164

she said. 'He could appear rough and suspicious sometimes, I know – that was a deficiency of his early upbringing and education. But look within – and there you'd find the truest, most affectionate heart that ever beat.' She paused, searching her memory for some telling incident or characteristic to prove her point. At length she found it; and burst out:

'Another man, for instance, might have neglected us, in favour of more fashionable acquaintances, as soon as he had become wealthy, and much sought-after, might he not? History, I am sure, is full of men who have done so. But not Turner – his feelings for us were as a son for his father, and a brother for his sisters, and were not to be changed. The day my father died, Mr. Hartright' – her voice rose, and became more animated, as if this was the *coup de grâce*, and proved her case beyond all reasonable doubt – 'Turner wept like a child, and threw himself into my arms, sobbing, "Oh, Amy, I shall never have such a friend again!"'

It struck me that if Turner had been the paragon she was suggesting, he might have shown more concern for her loss, and less for his own; but Walter merely nodded, and said:

'So you never found him morose, or taciturn?'

'The kindest of us can be morose sometimes, Mr. Hartright,' she replied, glancing at Mr. Bennett. 'I've seen Turner gloomy, particularly in his last years. Once or twice I recollect coming upon him looking melancholy, and asking him the matter, and being told' (here she adopted a gruff voice, with a distinct cockney twang), '"I've just parted with one of my children, Amy" – by which he meant he had sold a painting. But how I remember him best – out here, in a skiff, or cooking dinner on the bank with the rest of us, or' – pointing to the shimmering park that stretched away from us, until it seemed to vanish beyond a flimsy muslin haze at a bend in the river – 'lying up there in the hay, – no! Never! He was always singing, or making jokes – though often no-one else could understand them. If he was quiet it was because he was looking at the effect of light on the water, and trying to draw it, or struggling to write a poem.'

'A poem!' said Walter, surprised.

'Oh, yes, he loved poetry.' She hesitated, and then – with a faint blush – went on: 'Once, after a picnic, I found a scrap of one of his verses on the bottom of the boat, and – I know I should have given it back, but please remember, I was very young! – I kept it.' She reached inside the collar of her dress, pulled out a little gold locket on a chain, and opened it. 'I carry it still, to this day,' she said, removing a tiny pellet of folded paper and handing it to Walter. 'Here.'

As if, in that simple act, she had broken the spell that tied her to the past, and brought herself back into the mundane present, she laid a hand on my arm and said: 'Now, I am being a miserable hostess, Miss Halcombe, and' – raising her voice, and calling indulgently – 'yes, I know, my dear, a miserable wife, too. We must all eat, without delay.' She handed me the plate she had already prepared for me, and quickly filled another. 'Mr. Hartright, would you be so good as to pass that to my husband?'

But Walter was still engrossed in reading, and seemed not to hear; and when she repeated the question he said:

'Would you mind if I transcribed this?'

'No, not at all,' said Mrs. Bennett. 'But I fear my husband will die of hunger.'

'Why don't you let me do it,' I said (for Walter, being seated in the middle of the boat, was the only means of conveying anything back and forth), 'and you can resume your proper function as a waiter?'

So he handed it to me; and I copied into his notebook the following lines:

                                    pure and clear
Past ~~meadows sweet meadows~~ tree-fring'd mead-
ows and
    blessèd golden glebes
Where linger still the shades of Pope and
Thomson;
And Albion's mighty workshop, ~~wreath'd in black-
est smoke~~
    industrious yet,
And wreath'd in blackest smoke; until at length
He flings the fragile barks of ~~HOPE and~~ BEAUTY,
HOPE
    and JOY
Into the raging sea, where th'ensanguined sun
~~bloodies~~
    bloodying the clouds
~~Tells~~ Speaks of the storm to come

When I had done, Walter and Mr. Bennett were eating
voraciously; while Mrs. Bennett, having taken one-and-a-
half mouthfuls, had quite forgotten about food again, and
was in the middle of a story about Turner and Miss Phelps. I
had missed most of it; but it seemed to concern a debate
about the refraction of light from floating objects, which
Turner had tried, finally, to resolve by dropping a lettuce-
leaf into the water. Standing on the bank, however, he had
lost his balance, and fallen into the river himself, flapping
his arms, in the vain attempt to save himself, like the wings
of a bird – at which Miss Phelps (here Mrs. Bennett began to
giggle at her own anecdote, something any etiquette book
will tell you you should avoid doing at all costs) had cried:
'Ah, Joseph *Mallard* William Turner!'
    I could not help reflecting, as I pictured the scene, and saw

the simple pleasure it still brought Mrs. Bennett after so many years, on my own upbringing. Had Papa (dear man that he was) been right to protect me quite so assiduously from the unregulated company of male friends? Would I really have come to so much harm – looking at Amelia Bennett it was hard to think so – if I, too, had been allowed to mix with intellectual young men on terms of easy equality?

The meal over (most of Mrs. Bennett's disappeared over the side of the boat as she was carelessly stacking the plates, as if it had finally despaired of ever arousing her interest, and decided in a fit of pique to give itself to the ducks), she took up her guitar, and announced that she would sing us some of 'the good old songs that Turner loved'. She did not, like some amateur performers, bully and embarrass us by insisting that we join in; and yet we did, of our own volition, whether we knew the words or no – for only a block of stone could have heard such unconstrained delight and remained untouched by it. It seemed, indeed, for a moment, to reach even into the depths of her husband's soul, and to bring a ray of warmth to the lump of ice that had formed there – for after half a minute or so, to my immense surprise, his wavering baritone, too, swelled the chorus.

I had never, to my knowledge, heard any of the songs before, and I can remember nothing about them now (beyond a general impression that they were all remarkably silly), save for the refrain of an absurd ditty about a nun and a gondolier:

> He fiddled like the mad emperor Nero
> And sang: 'O Lady, if you'll be my Hero
> I'll be Leander
> Tho' I stand a
> Simple gondolero!'

Or something to much the same effect.

Lulled by the music, and the wine, and the sunshine and fresh air, I at length lay down, and half-closed my eyes, and allowed fancy to carry me back forty years. The same river, the same songs, the same voice: not hard to imagine (the idea suddenly filled me with a strange, intense feeling, in which joy and longing were inextricably intertwined, that rose from the pit of my stomach, and plugged up my throat, and disturbed the motion of my heart, like a finger laid against the pendulum of a clock) that I, too, was of that same party of young people, lolling in the long sweet grass, and talking of great things, when Amelia Bennett was yet a girl, and the trees of Arcadia covered in their summer green.

It was already twilight when we again reached the boatyard. Walter seemed unnaturally silent as he shipped the oars, and helped the Bennetts ashore, and I wondered whether the afternoon might have fatigued him, or made him disconsolate for some reason; but when I glimpsed his face by a flare of light from the open shed, I saw he was merely preoccupied with his own thoughts, for his skin was taut and highly coloured, and his shining eyes kept wandering off in pursuit of some new idea. I was not surprised, therefore, when he politely declined Mrs. Bennett's invitation of a glass and a light supper, and said we should be on our way – for he intended to walk along the river, and it would be quite dark before we got home. She, for her part, absolutely refused his offer to carry the basket and the rugs back to her house, saying she would not dream of taking more of our time, when we had so little to spare, and would give sixpence to a lad from the yard to go with them. And so we thanked and *not-at-all*ed each other for a minute or two, until Mrs. Bennett suddenly shook Walter's hand, and (to my astonishment) kissed me on both cheeks, and said 'Goodbye', and turned on her heel, and hurried her husband into the night without another word or a glance over her shoulder.

I had imagined that Walter would break his silence as soon as we were alone together, but he barely spoke at all until we had gone a mile or two, and were passing a little waterside tavern, with welcoming yellow lamplight in the windows, and a wooden balcony carried out over the water on knock-kneed piles that looked as if they were about to give up the ghost, and tumble into the river, and drift off towards France. Stopping by the door, he said abruptly:

'Shall we have something to eat?'

It was not the kind of place I should normally have expected Walter to choose (or not, at least, since Laura came into her fortune), but I fancy that this evening he had had it in mind to stop here, or somewhere like it; for as we made our way through a bar parlour smelling of smoke and river-mud, where little knots of boatmen, their faces ravaged by weather and drink, turned curiously to watch our progress; and past a poky kitchen, from which the heat blasted like a furnace; and upstairs, finally, to the coffee-room, he had the satisfied look of a man whose life is unfolding perfectly to plan.

'Let's order chops,' he said, with a conspiratorial smile, as we sat at a table in the window. 'They're hard to spoil, even in a kitchen like that. And we'll have porter, don't you think, in honour of Turner?'

If I touched his skin, I thought – looking at his flushed cheeks, and feeling their warmth even across two feet of tablecloth – it would resonate like a drum, or the rind of a ripe melon: he is so *full*, so buoyed with wild excitement, that it must break out in a mad rush of words, or a flamboyant dance – or else he will strike some unsuspected rock, and explode, and all will go to waste, soaking into the barren soil.

'So what do you think? What do you think?' he said. 'Is

Ruskin right?'

'About what?'

'Turner. Was he a tortured genius?'

'A genius, certainly,' I said, cautiously. 'As to *tortured* ...
Well, what do you think?'

He dismissed the question with a shake of the head.

'Come on,' he said. 'What kind of a man was he?'

'Well,' I began tentatively (for I did not wish to deter him
by offering a view very different from his own, and so
prove, unwittingly, to be the rock myself), 'what do we
know? He was humbly born; a little eccentric, perhaps – but
no more, probably, than anyone else so dedicated to his art;
a man who loved England – its countryside, its coasts, its
people.'

I looked questioningly at Walter, who nodded enthusias-
tically, giving me the courage to continue more confidently:

'He was somewhat rough-and-ready – that we must
attribute to his troubled childhood – and could appear stern,
or even rude, sometimes – but at bottom kind-hearted, I
believe, and a loyal friend.'

Walter nodded again; but then a shadow seemed to cross
his face, and he said:

'And what of his morals?'

'His morals,' I repeated slowly. His gaze was so intense
that I had to look away, and was too confused for a moment
to reply. Then I said:

'I wonder – I wonder, Walter, in all sincerity, whether it is
possible to be a great artist, and yet live a life of monastic
seclusion and purity?'

I could not tell whether he was amazed or appalled at
what I had said, or merely indifferent to it, for his expression
changed not one iota, and he continued to stare at me.
Eventually (for I found it embarrassing to be scrutinized in
that way, and doubly so when the scrutinizer was my own
brother) I looked past him through the window at the

Thames. The fog was silently returning, and casting a white film over the river – so you could barely see it at all, but only trace its course by the chain of reflections from gas-lamps, and oil-lamps, and the red glow of a ship's boiler, smeared on its surface like broken fruit.

At length Walter turned to see what I was looking at, and at once let out a gasp.

'Wouldn't Turner have loved that?' he said. 'The ghostliness. The *imprecision*.'

'Yes,' I said.

'Not just a great artist,' he said, facing me again, and taking my hand. 'The *greatest* artist in the history of the world!'

XX

Letter from John Farrant to Walter Hartright, 1st October, 185–

20 Trotter Street, Farringdon

Dear Sir,

I have heard you intend a life of the late Mr. J. M. W. Turner, and cannot rest easy until I have told you what I know of him; for I fear you shall never have the truth from his 'fellow artists' – I mean, Mr. Jones, Mr. Davenant &c., &c. – or from the polite ladies he kept company with at Isleworth and Brentford. They saw only the face he cared to show to the world; I saw the other.

I was an engraver by trade – and would be to this day, if my sight had not failed me. You will not, I hope, think me proud when I tell you that I had a name for a good eye and a sure hand, for any who knew my work would say the same; and it was on account of that that Mr. Turner heard of me, and asked if I would make some plates for him. This

172

was, I think, in the spring of 180–. He told me that a publisher had engaged with him for a set of coastal scenes, to
be engraved and printed in a book; but they had quar-
relled, and he had decided to publish them himself. I
should, I suppose, have taken warning from this history,
but I was young, and little acquainted with the ways of the
world, and gratified that a coming artist like Turner should
have chosen me to execute his design. He seemed reasonable enough, and quite businesslike, and we soon agreed
terms: he would etch the outlines, and then pass the plates
on to me to add aquatint, mezzotint, and any further
engraving that might be necessary. For this I was to receive
eight guineas a plate.

The life of an engraver is a solitary and an arduous one,
even at the best of times; you spend twelve or fourteen hours
a day in the closework-room, poring over a plate with a
magnifying glass, trying to realize an artist's most brilliant
conceptions by carefully removing small pieces of metal –
and then, quite often, when you at last come to 'prove' it,
you find there is some small deficiency in the plate, which
obliges you to efface the effort of many days, and do it over
again.

Do not think I exaggerate when I tell you that, with Mr.
Turner, this hard existence became a kind of hell.

Item. He did not keep his word about the outlines, but
required me to do them, saying 'he was too occupied with
other matters to attend to them'. He thus loaded me with a
deal more work when I scarce had time enough to do what I
had already undertaken with him; but when I asked for a
deferment he grew angry, and said 'if I could not accommodate myself to his requirements, he believed there were other
engravers in London who would be glad to do so'.

Item. He constantly found fault with my workmanship,
demanding that I should re-do plates in which neither I, nor
my wife, nor any other person could discern any imperfec-

173

tion whatever – so that I might have done five engravings for anyone else in the time it took me to complete one to his satisfaction.

Item. All this might yet have been tolerable had he treated me as an artist like himself, engaged with him in a common endeavour; but his manner towards me was always that of an irascible master towards a wilful, good-for-nothing servant. One day in November, soon after I had sent Mr. Turner the proof of a plate over which I had laboured long hours, and of which I was – I think justly – proud, and expected great things, I came into the parlour to find my wife (who was then carrying our first child) crying. On my inquiring the matter, she showed me a letter that had come that moment from Mr. Turner, in which he thanked me stiffly, and said (I still remember his words, tho' it is more than fifty years since I saw them) that 'he noted that I had extended the aquatint into the sea, an indulgence for which he had not asked; and he was sorry so much time had been lost, for it would not do, and I must rework it'.

My wife said she could bear no more, and begged me to go and see him, there and then, to see if I might adjust matters between us; and fearing for her health, and for that of the child (which we lost, indeed, less than a month later), I did as she asked. And so we come to the meat of my story.

Mr. Turner was living then at Harley Street, where I found him at home; but when I tried to explain to him the difficulties I was under, and told him I thought I should have ten guineas a plate, instead of eight, for all the extra work he had put me to, he grew livid, and flew into a rage, and seemed unable to speak, but only trembled, and ground his teeth, and slammed the door in my face.

I was, as you may imagine, too agitated to go straight home to my wife, and went instead to a public at the end of the street, where I had something to steady myself; but far from calming me, it only made me feel the more aggrieved, and emboldened me to think I should return to Mr. Turner's house, and confront him once more with my demands – matching his anger, if necessary, with my own.

Whether I should really have had the courage to carry this plan through I cannot now say; for as I approached his door – my legs feeling heavier, I must confess, with every step – it suddenly opened, and Mr. Turner himself emerged, dressed in his tall hat, and a long coat, and looked about him surreptitiously, as if satisfying himself that he was not observed. I was no more than fifty yards from him, and he would surely have recognized me – but for the fact that it was dusk, and a fog was starting to form, and I had the presence of mind to turn quickly into another doorway, from which I was able to watch him without his seeing me.

Mr. Turner glanced this way and that two or three times more, and then set off down the street at a quick pace. After scarcely a moment's hesitation, I began to follow him. Even at the time, I remember, I was puzzled by my own actions, and justified them to myself by reasoning that some opportunity might present itself to speak to him again, when he should not find it so easy to escape me. I now realize that this was a young man's self-delusion, and that my real motive was the hope that I might learn something which would give me greater power over him, and so assist me to redress the imbalance between us which I felt so bitterly.

Without a backward glance, Mr. Turner turned east into Weymouth Street, and, crossing Portland Road, made a dog-leg into Carburton Street, and then turned again into Norton Street. Here he took me by surprise; for, about halfway along, he stopped suddenly before a certain house, and again looked about him suspiciously. I only avoided discovery by dodging quickly behind a passing brewer's cart, and crossing the street; from where I saw him disappearing into the hall, and the front door closing behind him. My first thought was that this must be a bawdy house or an accommodation house, for why else would he wish to conceal his business there? Yet only the lower windows were lit, and I saw no-one else either entering or leaving; and after only a few minutes Mr. Turner himself came out again – too soon, I imagined, for anything in that way to have happened. He still seemed to fear detection, however; for he had taken pains to disguise himself, by putting on a heavy cloak in place of his coat, and winding a muffler about his face; and before he finally stepped into the street he once more glanced furtively about him.

He did not return to Harley Street, but instead turned back on to Carburton Street and continued east, walking with the same quick, darting gait. Wary of being taken unawares a second time, I decided to follow at a greater distance, so that if he stopped suddenly again I should be able to conceal myself; but I did not make sufficient allowance for the fog, which grew so thick, as the night came on, that I lost him altogether in Fitzroy Square. I ran to catch him up, and after half a minute or so made out a murky figure ahead of me on Grafton Street, but it seemed a little too tall for Mr. Turner, whom I concluded (or rather guessed), therefore, must have turned on to Upper John Street; and so I went that way myself. And I was right, as luck would have it, for I had not gone fifty paces – still running, and choking on the cold unwholesome air – when I came upon him suddenly.

I shall never, as long as I live, forget the picture he made standing there, the mist swirling about him, before a shabby door with the number '46' painted on it (I see it still, the '4' not quite straight, and the '6' blotched and disfigured, as if it was being consumed by mould). His hand was already on the handle; but even now he hesitated, and peered over his shoulder to make sure that no-one saw him, his little bird-like eyes turned yellow by the sulphurous haze, and burning with the most malevolent expression I have ever seen. For a moment I thought he had recognized me, for he started, as I appeared, like a frightened animal; but I immediately lowered my gaze, and hurried on, and when I glanced back he was entering the house.

There was a small public on the other side of the street, which commanded a good view of number 46, and I found myself a place by the fire, and settled there to watch. But an hour passed, and then another, and still Mr. Turner did not come out, and no-one else went in; and at length, thinking I could delay going home to my wife no longer, I told the landlord I thought I had seen a friend enter a house opposite, and asked him, as casually as I could, if he knew who lived there. He could not meet my eye, but blushed (for he must have thought my 'friend' was Mr. Turner), and looked down at the mug he was wiping, and mumbled:

'There's a young widow there, sir, a Mrs. Danby. She's kept by an artist, they say, who treats her, if you'll pardon me speaking plain, as his whore – and none too kindly, by all accounts.'

This is all I know for a certainty, and I shall not lie to you, or pretend to more understanding than I have. I have heard from others, however, that in later years Mr. Turner's habits of secrecy and dishonesty became ever more vicious, until at length he deceived even his closest friends – living, unknown to them, under a false name, in a poor little cottage in Chelsea. Do not, I beg, allow yourself to be deterred by certain persons from doing your duty, and discovering what this extraordinary conduct was intended to conceal.

For my part, I can say only that J. M. W. Turner was the most tight-fisted, black-hearted devil of a man I ever met. I see him still in my dreams, and wake thanking God that he now has no other power to hurt me and my family.

Yours very truly,

John Farrant

XXI

Letter from Miss Mary Ann Fletcher to Marian Halcombe, 1st October, 185–

Sandycombe Lodge, Twickenham

Dear Miss Halcombe,

I shall be delighted to receive you and your brother here, any morning you please. I should warn you, however – lest, like the generality of visitors, you imagine it to be some great villa, that can profitably occupy you for a day – that Sandycombe Lodge is only a house in miniature, and you will be done in no more than half an hour.

I do believe, though (but you may perhaps consider me partial!) that you will find it well worth the journey: it is a charming little curiosity; and affords an interesting glimpse into Turner's mind, and into his unusual mode of life.

Yours very truly,

Mary Ann Fletcher

XXII

Letter from Walter Hartright to Laura Hartright, 2nd October,185–

Brompton Grove,
Saturday

My dearest Laura,

Your strange letter arrived by this morning's post. You silly girl! How can you think – let alone write – such things? Do you really imagine that *I* can bear this separation any more easily than you (who at least have little Walter and Florrie to comfort you)? – or that I would willingly protract it an hour longer than was necessary?

It grieves me – as it would any man – to hear that our children ask, 'Has Papa forgotten us? Does he not love us any more?'; but what wounds me a thousand times more is that you say you are at a loss how to reply. Great God! How can you be at a loss? Does not your heart answer for you: 'Of course not, my darlings; he thinks of you, and misses you, every minute of every day; but he is engaged on some great undertaking that shall one day make you proud of him.'? Or do you think so poorly of me that you no longer believe it yourself, but really suppose that I care nothing for family and home, and that I linger in London, like some shallow, worthless man of the world, merely to indulge the whims of idleness and pleasure?

You say that my letters no longer sound like your 'old dear Walter' – that while they are addressed to you, you feel I am really directing them to someone else entirely. My dearest – have I not explained?! I have not time enough to keep a journal *and* to write to you (if I did so, I should be always at my desk, and have to delay my return still further!), and must consequently depend on my letters to preserve a record of my thoughts and impressions. So, yes, others (God willing!) shall one day read some of my words – but would you sooner I confided them all to a diary, and so excluded you, my life's companion, from the very marrow of my experience?

This book – let me state it plainly, when I should have hoped I had no need to – is very dear to my heart. Through it, I believe, I shall be able to say something of true value about the life of a great artist, and about the nature of art itself. If I do as you ask, however, and return to Limmeridge now, all my efforts (and the hardship we have both endured) will have been in vain; for there are more doors I must open, more corners I must peer into, more questions I must ask, before I can confidently reach a judgement on this elusive man and his work. I shall not, therefore, deceive you (as I unwittingly did before) by saying: I shall be home in so many weeks. I shall be home when I have done what I must do; and that – trust me – will be as soon as I can possibly contrive it.

My love as always, and kisses to the children.

Walter

XXIII

From the notebook of Marian Halcombe, 5th October, 185–

Sandycombe Lodge, Twickenham

Neat, plain, geometrical

Whitewashed walls, low slate roof

So small, at first think it's a *real* lodge – expect to see gate, and long drive, with great man's house at end of it

Only inside see it for what it is – Lilliputian classical villa, conceived on different scale from modern houses surrounding it (presumably not there in Turner's time?)

Even on a dull day – first impression (like Turner's paintings): Light

Tiny hall – barrel-vault ceiling – simple decoration – entrance to an elegant dolls'-house

To left: curving staircase, lit by oval skylight, up to two bedrooms

Beyond hall, transverse corridor: dining room at one end; library at the other; in the middle, Turner's studio, with a great window overlooking garden. Light! light! light!

Miss Fletcher – answered door herself. About 40 – long, pale, anxious face, eyes rather close together. Frail, trembled, as if with cold. Sat with her while Walter went outside to sketch house and garden.

Semi-invalid – amuses herself finding out 'all I can about Turner, and his odd mode of life here'. Thinks he was 'a funny little man'. [There – 'funny' again]

Turner moved here 1813.

Why Twickenham? Air. Light. View of Sir J. Reynolds' house – also poet James Thomson's.

Solus – Solis

Blackbirdy

'Billy'

Pony & trap – sketching

'Daddy' or 'Old Daddy' – looked after house

Also gallery [strange!]

Market gardener – cart – gin

Left 1826

House sold to Mr. Ford – sold to Miss Fletcher's fath

From the diary of Marian Halcombe, 5th October, 185–

I have sat here a full hour, and written no more than '5th October' – and shall soon be obliged to change even that, for looking at the clock I see it now wants but ten minutes to be *6th* October. Walter depends on me for an account of the day's events, and all I shall finally be able to give him is my notes.

And yet as soon as I start to write for myself rather than for him – see! – the words begin to come. Why? Do I all of a sudden no longer feel at ease with him? No longer trust him?

Certainly I was puzzled, and not a little embarrassed, by his manner today. He was so withdrawn, so wound about with his own thoughts, that for whole minutes together he said nothing at all, but acted as if he were quite alone, opening a cupboard door, or unfolding the shutters on the window, without question or comment. Miss Fletcher seemed not so much offended by this off-handedness as astonished by it; perhaps assuming that such behaviour would be considered quite normal in London society, she watched him open-mouthed, like a child bemused at the strangeness of the adult world but determined to learn its secrets. Only once did she try to engage him in conversation, as he stood sketching the fireplace in the dining room, and she burst out admiringly: 'Oh! I wish I could draw like that! How fortunate – to have the Muse of Art as well as of Literature!'

To which Walter did not reply at all (surely a modest 'You overstate my talents, I'm afraid', or a polite 'I'm sure you have remarkable gifts, Miss Fletcher', would have cost him little enough?); but merely looked away, with a half-smile that seemed to say: *Yes – you are right – I am infinitely your superior; and you are of so little consequence that I needn't waste breath denying it.* The poor woman was left staring and gulping like a stranded fish; until at length, unable to bear the humiliation any longer, she was forced to resort to the pitiable fiction that she had been talking to me the whole time, and muttered:

'Hm, Miss Halcombe?'

'Yes, indeed,' I said. I was debating whether to add, 'But sad that the Muse of Good Manners seems to have deserted him completely,' when Walter forestalled me.

'I think I shall go outside now, if I may,' he said suddenly. I should have liked to go with him, but decided to stay and talk to Miss Fletcher instead – partly to show my anger with him, and partly my sympathy for her.

'You must forgive my brother if he seems a little distracted,' I said as he left. 'He is very preoccupied with his book.'

'Oh! – no – I quite understand!'

'Turner is proving a difficult subject.'

'Yes, yes,' she said sorrowfully, as if living in Turner's house somehow made her responsible for his vagaries. 'But I suppose that's the privilege of genius, isn't it? To be a little odd?'

'Do you think you would have liked him?'

'What, Turner?' she said, surprised (as, indeed, I had intended she should be; for jolting her into another train of thought was the only way I could conceive of avoiding a none-too-original lecture on the artistic temperament). 'I really don't know.' She thought carefully for a moment. 'It all depends, I think. Sol*us* or Sol*is*.'

'I beg your pardon?'

'I don't know why he later changed the name to "Sandycombe Lodge", but when he first moved here he called the house "Solus" . . .'

'"Alone",' I said.

She nodded. 'But my brother thinks he meant "Solis", S-O-L-I-S. "Of the sun." Or perhaps just "Sunny". Turner'd barely been to school, you see, and didn't have Latin, so it would have been an easy enough mistake for him to make.'

My mind's eye was suddenly dazzled with the array of suns we had seen at Marlborough House. 'That seems likelier, doesn't it?'

'Perhaps,' she said. 'But you'd certainly suppose he wanted solitude, for he put bars on all the windows, and made the garden a thicket of willows.'

I looked outside. A few yards away I recognized the top of Walter's head. Beyond it, sure enough, was a thick wall of trees.

'And the boys called him "Blackbirdy",' said Miss Fletcher, 'because he wouldn't let them bird's-nest.'

That might, I thought, have simply been because he liked blackbirds; but before I could say anything she went on:

183

'And there were only the two of them in the house.'

Two? Was there a wife, then? A young Mrs. Booth? I could not, for a moment, think of a delicate way to phrase the question; but she must have see it in my face, for she said:

'Turner and his father.'

'His father!'

She nodded. '"Billy" and "Daddy".'

'And not even a servant?'

'Daddy *was* the servant, Miss Halcombe. I know – an eccentric arrangement, but there it is – while Billy was out in his pony and trap, sketching, Daddy was here, taking care of the house and garden. And as if being his son's cook and valet weren't enough, he was also expected to stretch his canvases, and varnish them when they were done, and go up to London to open the gallery.'

'What gallery?' I asked.

'Oh – did you not know? – Turner kept on his house in Queen Anne Street, even while he was living here; and there was a gallery there, where buyers could view his work. And Daddy, of course, was a tight-fisted old man – it was something of a family trait, as I'm sure you've discovered – so to avoid paying the coach-fare he'd give a market gardener a glass of gin to take him into town on his cart.'

She started to laugh, but then stopped abruptly as Walter entered the room. All through my conversation with Miss Fletcher, one part of my mind had been silently composing a thinly veiled rebuke to him, with which I hoped, on his return, to jar him back to some semblance of politeness; but I at once saw that it would not now be necessary. His languor and aloofness seemed to have evaporated like mist before the sun, and he was once again – as he'd been on his return from Petworth, and during our visit to the Bennetts – all enthusiasm and attention. I couldn't imagine the cause of this transformation, but I quickly realized it was not simply a bad conscience: there was an unmistakable sense of direction in his manner as he sat next to Miss Fletcher on the sofa, and complimented her on her garden, and amused her with a silly anecdote about a black kitten which had leapt on him from behind a currant bush, and half-killed his boot. After a minute she started visibly to relax, and shot me a glance so brimming with gratitude – *See! He likes me, after all!* – that I shuddered with pity.

'What I was wondering', said Walter – after a tiny pause that told me that this was his true purpose – 'was where are the kitchen and the other offices?'

'Ah, yes!' said Miss Fletcher eagerly. 'A good question, Mr. Hartright. Let me show you.'

She rose, and led us back into the miniature hall.

'There,' she said, pointing to a plain, inconspicuous door beneath the stairs. 'Turner's triumph. You'd never guess it was there, would you, if you didn't know?'

'No,' said Walter.

And I must own that I hadn't noticed it before, either, and that if I had I should have assumed it was nothing more than a modest cupboard.

'Why his *triumph*?' I asked.

'Why, he designed the house,' she said, with the complacent air of a woman giving a well-tried performance, and seeing from my startled expression that it was having its usual gratifying effect. 'Oh, yes, he quite fancied himself the architect. So this' – reaching for the handle, and turning it – 'must have been in his mind.'

I confess I couldn't (and still can't) imagine what 'this' might have been – unless it was that Turner, the master of *chiaroscuro*, having contrived to make the upper floors wonderfully light, decided, by way of contrast, to leave the basement as dark as possible; for beyond the hidden door you could see nothing but the top of a mean spiral staircase, which disappeared after two or three steps into the gloomy grey haze of a dungeon. Any urge I might have had to

185

explore further (and I felt little enough, faced by this uninviting prospect) was immediately quelled by a sickly waft of cold air, laced with the smells of stale cooking, which rose from the darkness like the breath of a dying animal; so I contented myself with turning back to Miss Fletcher and saying:

'Yes, very ingenious.'

But Walter was not to be so easily deterred; pressing past me and Miss Fletcher (who seemed on the point of closing the door again), he descended the first few steps. After a few seconds he stopped, and cried, 'This is remarkable!' and then continued on his way.

'You are wise to stay here, Miss Halcombe,' said Miss Fletcher, backing away from the doorway. 'It's rather cold down there, I'm afraid, and you might easily catch a chill.'

I have wondered, since, whether there was anything in her manner – some hint of foreboding or secret knowledge – that might have alerted me to what was about to happen; but all I can recall is a frail, hunched woman, her hands crossed and rubbing her arms, and a smile of humorous apology on her thin lips.

It cannot have been more than two minutes before we once again heard Walter's footsteps on the stairs. I shall never, I think, forget his appearance as he re-emerged a few moments later: the vigour of his movements, the vitality of his form (which seemed suddenly to have expanded, so that it risked bursting out of his sober town clothes); above all, his face, which bore an expression I have never seen before, and don't know whether I should wish to see again – an expression compounded all at once of excitement, of satisfaction, and (as it seemed to me) of a kind of wild, desolate terror.

Perhaps this is the true root of my uneasiness: in that instant, I recognized Walter's features well enough – but not the mood, the beliefs, the thoughts they expressed. Only last week, I thought he had truly become himself again, for the first time in years (and congratulated myself, poor vain wretch that I am, on having engineered this transformation, by introducing him to Elizabeth Eastlake); now I wonder whether what then *seemed* his true self was no more than a temporary phase – not a terminus, as it were, but merely a small station, through which he has already passed on his way to somewhere else. And that somewhere else is a place I do not know, and will make him a stranger to me. Or –

Later

Heavens! Why did I stop again? A strange storm in my head – my thoughts all lashed together, so I could not unravel them.

It is now past two in the morning, and still Walter has not returned.

He told me he was going to Mayall's photographic studio in Regent Street. He cannot still be there now. Where is he?

Perhaps my anxiety has deprived me of the power to think and write about him.

This will not do.

Concentrate.

One question, naturally, preoccupied me as we got into our cab, and left Sandycombe Lodge.

What had Walter seen in the basement?

Yet I felt I could not ask him directly, for fear that in doing so I might drive him further from me. The truth was, I suddenly realized, I could no longer predict how he would behave. If I revealed that I had seen how deeply he had been affected, he might, indeed, confide in me; but I could as soon imagine his airily denying it (*You are too fanciful, Marian; I never thought I should find you guilty of that*); or else becoming embarrassed and confused.

For a few minutes I said nothing at all, hoping that he might be moved to fill the silence himself, and so spare me the necessity of declaring my curiosity; but he only sat quietly staring out of the window. At length, unable to bear it any longer, I said:

'A pretty little house, I thought. Or at least the parts of it I saw.'

An irresistible invitation, you would suppose, to describe the parts I *hadn't* seen; but he merely nodded absently. I must either hold my tongue, or be more direct.

'What was the basement like?' I asked.

You would think he had been struck deaf.

'What *is* it, Walter?' I said. 'Why won't you tell me?'

But again he said nothing; and after a minute or two opened his notebook, and began studying the drawings he had made.

It was intolerable – I *must* discover what he had seen – and yet I was at a loss to know how to prise it from him. It was clear, however, that the more desperately I pursued him now, the more stubborn he would become; so I resolved to ponder the matter in silence.

What might one find in a basement, to excite such a response?

Something that Turner had left there – an undiscovered picture, or pictures. But in that case, surely, Miss Fletcher would have shown them to us, or at least mentioned their existence?

Evidence of a crime – a bloodstain (heaven help us!). Hard to believe – but it was undeniably odd, was it not, that Miss Fletcher seemed to be the only person in the house? Suppose she'd fallen out with the housekeeper, and taken an axe to her in the scullery? Or perhaps she'd had a lover, and he had spurned her?

No, no – inconceivable – if there had been anything of the kind there, she would not have allowed Walter to find it, and he could not have remained silent about it.

Why was my mind running on such terrible things? Was it just that the place made me think so powerfully of a dungeon?

A dungeon. A dungeon. A lightless room. A barred door. Dripping walls, covered in moss. A set of rusting manacles –

The cry of a hawker in the street brought me out of my reverie, and I looked out of the window and saw that we were entering Putney. The road was crowded with carriages and carts; the pavements thronged with dull, decent people thinking of nothing save whether it would rain, or where the cabbages might be best and cheapest. If they could see *my* thoughts, they would indubitably suppose I was mad.

I was somewhat chastened by this reflection (for if I have had nothing else to boast of, have I not always prided myself on my good sense?); but then it struck me that I could turn my new-found weakness to my advantage, by making light of it.

So was there a prisoner in chains there, Walter? Did you find Old Dad, still locked up after fifty years, and raving piteously about varnish?

I turned cautiously towards him, rehearsing the words in my head. He was still engrossed in his notebook, adding a line here, or a scribbled word there, whenever the motion of the cab allowed. Something in his posture, the obstinate set of his neck and shoulder, told me, beyond doubt, that he would not be amused, and I should fail again.

I was suddenly overcome with tiredness – sleep seemed to ambush me, whether I would or not, pressing me to my seat, and turning my eyelids to lead. No dreams of horrors – no dreams of anything, so far as I can recall; and I was woken again after only a few minutes – for we had gone but a mile or so, and were still a little way from home – by a sharp slapping sound. The cause, I soon discovered, was Walter's notebook, which had slipped from his lap on to the floor. I

189

was surprised, for an instant, that he did not bend forward to retrieve it; then I saw that he, too, had fallen asleep, and I picked it up myself.

We are brought up to believe that letters and diaries are sacrosanct, and that it is the blackest dishonour to violate their secrets – but what of a notebook? Surely (I told myself) that is something else entirely – a mere collection of facts, as neutral as a column of figures, which cannot be held to belong to any person in particular. It was only as I lifted the first page that I suddenly imagined what *I* should feel if the situation were reversed, and I found Walter making free with *my* notebook without my permission.

I stopped myself, but not before I had glimpsed one of his sketches. It was not the gloomy interior I had expected, but an outside view of the garden front. There were the two little single-storey wings, with their stucco walls and trim slate roofs; there in the centre Turner's studio, where Miss Fletcher and I must have been talking even while Walter had drawn this (indeed, I could just make out two ghostly little crescents in the window, which might have been our heads).

But below it was another window, which I had not seen before: a lunette, protected by an iron grille, half hidden by a tangle of bushes. Beyond it must lie the basement.

It reminded me of something – something unexpected, though for a moment I could not say what it was. The curved top; the glass (at least in Walter's drawing) so shadowed that it looked like an empty socket – why did they seem familiar?

And then, with the force of a physical shock, it struck me: the half-buried arches in *The Bay of Baiae*.

Later still
He is back. I cannot imagine where he has been – I do not wish to imagine – but he is back. Thank God.

The sound of the door woke me. I had somehow persuaded myself that I had finished, and fallen asleep at my desk.

I have just re-read what I wrote. I had *not* finished. I had not described our homecoming.

As we descended at last from the cab, I missed my footing. Walter caught me, but not before I had twisted my ankle. The pain must have shown on my face, because, as I hobbled towards the door on Walter's arm, the driver said:

'Your missus all right, sir?'

So kindly meant. And yet those words laid bare my heart so mercilessly that even my poor self-deluded eyes could not fail to see it.

Oh God, I am so miserable.

XXIV

From the journal of Walter Hartright, 6th October, 185–

Am I mistaken? Could I be mistaken?

There is something about a photographic studio that makes you doubt the evidence of your own senses. There is the painted backdrop, telling you that you're in the library of a country house or a garden strewn with statues; there are the clamps, half hidden by a curtain, that fix the subject in a pose of apparent naturalness for long minutes together.

But surely it is childish superstition to distrust a man simply because he lives by creating illusions?

Considered rationally, is there any reason why Mayall might have lied?

I cannot think of one. He appears a plain, unaffected, business-like sort of man. Being American, he has no connections here. If he is now the most successful photographer in London (that was, I am sure, Sir William Butteridge I saw emerging from his studio), he has become so entirely through his own efforts, and the excellence of his work. It is true that he suddenly seemed more obliging when I mentioned Lady Eastlake's name, but that, I am sure, is because she has taken such an intelligent interest in his profession.

So what exactly did he say?

'Turner came to my *atelier* several times in 'forty-seven, 'forty-eight and 'forty-nine. There was something rather mysterious about our early meetings. In one of them he told me led me to believe he was a Chancery Court Judge, and he did nothing to dispel this impression, later on.'

Led me to believe. Odd, but not inconceivable that it was simply a misunderstanding of some kind. Turner was, after all, an old man (he must have been what? – seventy-two? – when they met?) – perhaps his weak eyesight prevented him seeing the puzzlement on Mayall's face, or he mis-heard a question.

And yet . . .

'He came to see me again and again – so often, indeed, that my people used to think of him as "our Mr. Turner". And every time he had some new notion about light. One day, I remember, he sat with me three hours, talking about its curious effects on films of prepared silver. The whole subject seemed to fascinate him. He asked whether I'd ever repeated Mrs. Somerville's experiment of magnetizing a needle in the rays of the spectrum, and said he would like to see the spectral image copied.'

Not the conversation of a man with failing faculties. Nor, indeed, you would imagine, of a Master in Chancery. Surely Mayall must have been curious enough to question him further? 'If I may say so, sir, you know more about optics than any judge I ever met . . .?'

That would have been the moment for Turner to disabuse him, if it had been an honest mistake. But *he did nothing to dispel this impression, later on.*

It is true, of course, that Turner made no attempt to conceal his name – but then there was little chance it would betray him: there must be thousands of Turners in London.

What, then, of the pictures?

'At first he was very keen on trying the effects of light let in on the figure from a high position, and he sat for the studies himself. Later, I took several daguerreotype portraits of him. In one, he was reading – a favourable position for him, because his eyes were weak and bloodshot. There was a lady who accompanied him [presumably Mrs. Booth] and I recall that he gave one of these pictures to her.'

But none of the portraits was full-face; and when I asked Mayall if he still had any of them (for, apart from the early self-portrait Ruskin showed me, I have still seen no image of Turner, and can form no mental conception of him in his later years) he replied:

'Alas, no. I did set aside one curious portrait of him in profile, which of course I immediately looked up when I found out who my mysterious visitor really was. But unfortunately one of my assistants had effaced it [did Mayall hold my eyes a little too fixedly here, as people do when they lie?] without my permission.'

And how *had* he found out who his 'mysterious visitor really was'?

'Oh, I met him at the *soirée* of the Royal Society, in – I think – the spring of 1849. He greeted me very cordially, and immediately fell into his old topic of the spectrum. Then someone came up and asked if I knew Mr. Turner, and when I told him I did, my informant said, rather significantly: "Yes, but do you know that he is *the* Turner?"

'I was rather surprised, I must confess. I ventured to suggest that I might be able to help him, by carrying out some experiments for him on his ideas about the treatment of light and shade, and we parted on the understanding that he would call on me. But he never did call on me, and I never

193

saw him again.'

Perhaps I *am* mistaken, then. If Turner's intention had really been to deceive Mayall, then surely he would not have acknowledged him at the *soirée*.

And yet and yet and yet . . .

We are still left with this:

- During his visits to the studio Turner pretended to be a judge.
- He allowed himself to be photographed, but avoided poses in which he could easily be recognized.
- Once Mayall knew his identity he never called on him again, despite having undertaken to do so.

Geniuses are not like other men.

But is not this all of a piece with Sandycombe Lodge?

You are an artist – you worship the sun – you know that no man since the beginning of time has caught its moods and effects with such fidelity and power.

You build a house so full of light that any visitor must say: *This is a temple to the sun.*

But what if Farrant is right? What if this is only the face you care to show the world, and there is another, concealed behind an almost invisible door?

As I stood in that basement, and stared out through the cavern-mouth window with its fearful iron bars, was there not but one thought that overwhelmed me: *This house was designed by a man with a secret*?

Farrant may be lying, of course. I must remember that. A letter so at odds with everything else I've learned may simply be the product of a diseased and envious mind. If that's all it is – which, let me not forget, was certainly my assumption when I first read it – then all this speculation is mere fancy, and I have evidence of nothing more sinister than eccentricity.

But if he is telling the truth . . .

There is no help for it. I must go and see him.

A mere five hours has passed since I last closed this book –
but what a five hours! In that time I have changed my coat
for another – changed my *name* for another – gone from the
Reform Club to a low tavern, and from there to the Marston
Rooms in Piccadilly (a place that even a week ago I could not
have conceived of entering), where I sit now, next to a
woman and a late theatre-goer at the neighbouring table
who laugh drunkenly at each other's remarks as – I presume
– they negotiate terms. (Small wonder that London is so full
of vice, when a man seeking rest and refreshment late at
night is forced to resort to an establishment such as this.)

And what to make of it all? I cannot tell – too many
impressions, and speculations, and novel experiences. I
must try simply to set it all down, and trust that some pattern will emerge.

The notion that Farrant was the key to resolving all my
doubts had struck me with such force, and filled me with
such nervous agitation, that my only thought as I set out
was: *Find him!* It was only after I had gone half a mile, and
the raw fog had cooled my excitement, that I realized how
precipitate I was being. Suppose I *did* find him – what then?
My object was to discover why he had written to me, and
whether his charges against Turner were true; but a man
who had lied to me on paper could as easily do so in person.
Try as I might, moreover, I could think of no way to phrase
the question (my best effort was: 'A story so extraordinary is
hard to credit, Mr. Farrant') that would not imply I did not
believe him, and so risk antagonizing him – which I was particularly anxious to avoid, since he might well be of further
service to me.

But some impulse that would not be denied drove me on.
I knew that if I abandoned the quest now, and returned

home without the truth – or, at least, the satisfaction of knowing I had done everything in my power to get it – I should find no rest there. I had no choice but to keep going, and trust to fate and to my own wits to guide me.

This resolution seemed to clear my mind, and I immediately saw that I must consider my situation with the cool strategy of a general on the eve of battle – survey the landscape, assess the strengths and weaknesses of my forces, and order their disposition accordingly. What was at once apparent was that a direct attack would fail: if Farrant knew – or even suspected – who I was, or my motive for talking to him, I was lost. My only hope, then, was to approach him at a tangent, finding – if I could – some pretext to engage him in conversation and nudging him towards the subject of Turner. If he repeated the same story then, to a man who – so far as he knew – had no interest in the matter save natural curiosity, and no power to influence the views of others, then there must be a strong presumption that it was true. And if he *was* lying, I might detect it in his manner – for a liar often betrays himself with tell-tale gestures of unease, either revealing his dishonesty by weak smiles and fidgets, or trying to conceal it by too great a display of frankness.

My first aim must be to appear as inconspicuous as possible, so that I might enter his street, and, if necessary, station myself for some time before his house, in order to observe his habits, without drawing attention to myself. And here, at once, I encountered a difficulty: for a man dressed for business in the West End and an evening at the Reform Club cannot hope to escape notice in the back-alleys of Farringdon. I had other clothes at home, of course, but they were too formal, or too rural, or too bright – none of them suggested that sad air of straitened respectability that alone, I felt, could make me invisible.

I wrestled with this conundrum for twenty minutes or more, all the while continuing at a fast pace – for if I faltered,

I knew I should be lost. I must be like the Pilgrim, confident that if my faith was great enough – but only then – every obstacle could be overcome.

And so, indeed, it turned out. As I approached Covent Garden, it suddenly struck me that Hand Court was no more than a quarter of a mile away, and that I might go by it with only the smallest deviation from my way. To see Turner's birthplace once again; to view it, this time, with the eyes of knowledge and experience rather than of ignorance – surely this might deepen my understanding of the man, and help me better to evaluate what I learned from Farrant?

Or so I argued to myself at the time; but now I wonder if I was not prompted by something else: a memory so apparently inconsequential that it could not make itself known at once, but must adopt another form entirely, until the moment when I should be able to recognize it. That moment came when I turned into Maiden Lane – and saw, of a sudden, in an illuminated shop front, three red balls on a blue ground. There! – Eureka! – the answer to my problem! The place was kept, of course, by the mother of my young guide on my last visit, and there was always the chance that she might remember me – but what if she did? She would hardly refuse to do business with me on that account; and if she questioned me directly I would simply deny I had ever been there before. Tonight I must become another man altogether; and it would be a useful test of my powers as an actor to see if I might carry off the transformation now.

As is often the case in such establishments, there were two entrances: one facing the street, and the other through a little court to the side, where those who yet retain some pride may slink in (so they hope) unobserved, and surrender their remaining treasures in the seclusion of a private booth. This second door was locked, presumably because it was thought that only the most desperate would need to avail themselves of a pawnbroker so late in the evening.

Even though no-one who knew me as Walter Hartright could possibly have seen me, I confess that I hesitated a moment, and went through the pitiful charade of looking in the window, and pretending that I was contemplating buying the stuffed pheasant in a glass case, or one of the cheap rings and brooches neatly laid out like geological specimens on a card, before I finally summoned the courage to go inside.

The only gas-jet was at the front of the shop, where it could cast its light into the street, and act as a beacon to the poor souls seeking its bitter succour. The rest of the interior was lit by two oil-lamps, whose soft glow gave an unfamiliar romance to the pyramids of depressingly mundane objects – a clockwork spit, watches and snuff-boxes, cups and dishes and vases – clothing them in tantalizing shadows, and creating the illusion that somewhere among them you might stumble upon something rare and wonderful. Behind the counter were shelves lined with ticketed bundles, and another door, its presence marked only by an irregular rim of light, which must lead – I deduced from the murmur of voices beyond it – into domestic quarters.

An automatic bell announced my presence, and all at once the voices stopped, and the door at the back opened, and a figure appeared. Not the woman, but – I knew it instantly, from the slender form of the silhouette, and its rapid childish movements – the girl herself. She stopped and stared when she saw me, but whether because she recognized me (the brightness of the gas-lamp was behind me, and must have made my face indistinct) or merely because she was surprised to see such a well-dressed man in the shop at such an hour, I could not say.

'Good evening,' she said after a moment, with a tentative smile.

I removed my coat. 'I should like to leave this,' I said (and was surprised to hear that, without conscious thought, I had dropped once again into the voice I had last used at Petworth). 'And take another in its place.'

She seemed puzzled, and glanced uncertainly behind her.

'Come on, girl,' I said. 'It's worth a pound, at least. You can allow me five bob for it; and must have something I could take, doesn't matter how old, older the better, for a shilling or two?'

Perhaps she wondered if I had stolen it (a thought that must occur to a pawnbroker ten times a day); for she ran her gaze over my tie and waistcoat and boots, as if to see whether they were all of a piece with the coat. At length, evidently satisfied, she said:

'What is it, then? Trouble with the 'orses?'

'That's it,' I said, simultaneously grateful that she had supplied me with a story, and angry with myself for not having had the foresight to invent my own. 'But my luck'll change tomorrow. Meantime, a man needs money to drink.'

'Yes,' she said; and then, turning her large brown eyes directly upon mine, and with a knowingness that seemed to penetrate me like a blade of ice: 'And for somethin' else, I shouldn't wonder.'

Did she, in that moment, know who I was? Had her mother convinced her, after all, that my purpose in befriending her on that earlier visit had been to debauch her? Or was this what life had taught her to assume of any man who came into the shop at night in need of money?

I looked away, affecting not to have heard her. 'So, girl, what do you say? Five bob?'

I thought she might say she needed to ask her mother; but she instantly replied, with the confidence of a seasoned haggler:

'Four.'

In truth, I should have been happy enough to take a penny, provided I could have a satisfactory replacement to go with it; but I could not tell her so, so I gruffly answered:

'Let's see what you got, then.'

She was back in a moment, with two coats. One was long and black, well cut from a fine worsted cloth, and speckled with neat darns and patches; and I was tempted to take it, for I knew it would keep me almost as warm as my own. It was so old-fashioned, however, that it could not fail to look odd on a man of my age, and in the end I chose the other – a cheap confection of brown serge and cream piping, with bound pockets and turned-back cuffs, such as a clerk with aspirations to fashion (if such a thing exists) might wear.

'That one's dearer,' said the girl. 'Three-and-six.'

I think she expected me to try to beat her down, but this was not the moment to argue, so I merely nodded and said:

'Very well.'

She handed me the ticket for my own coat, and a sixpenny piece. 'You won't get much for that,' she said, with the same knowing look, and a smile that was almost a leer. 'Couple of pots of beer, and off 'ome to your missus.'

For all I remember now of the route I took to Farringdon, or of what I saw and heard upon the way, I might as well have been sleep-walking. My every thought – beyond that required to place one foot in front of the other, and to avoid obstacles – was devoted to but one object: to try to concoct a plausible story. My want of one in the pawnbroker's shop had caused nothing worse than embarrassment – indeed, thanks to the girl, I had been spared even that – but with Farrant it would certainly prove fatal. But how to devise something that would meet every eventuality? *I am looking for a friend, who told me he lodged here.* What if he had no lodger – or, worse, *did* have one, who said he'd never seen me before in his life? *Cousin Farrant! Do you not know me? True – I was only a child when we sailed for Australia, but surely – ?* No – the stuff of melodrama; and, besides, I knew nothing of his family circumstances. In the end, I decided I must simply gather as much intelligence as possible; and then rely on fate to give me a pretext for talking to him, and my own resources to furnish me with a character appropriate to it.

Trotter Street, it turned out, barely deserves the name of 'street' at all; it is no more than a row of tall, pinched, grey houses overlooking a long straggle of workshops and builders' yards and odd pockets of waste ground. There is but a single line of gas-lamps, which seem scarcely equal to the task of lighting it – at least on a night like tonight, with no moon, and with a heavy fog rolling up from the river; and even when your eyes have adjusted to the darkness, there is little enough to lift your spirits. The road is rough and treacherous, the cobbles broken here and there by black puddles; and at one end of it – just at the point where you think you should be able to turn a corner, and escape to somewhere less desolate – you find your path barred by the locked gates of a blacking works. Farrant's story might yet, of course, prove to be true; but it was easy enough to imagine how a man living here might *fancy* he had suffered a thousand wrongs, when his real grievance was against life itself, for condemning him to such a cheerless place.

Number 20 was almost indistinguishable from its neighbours, save that the painted figures on the door had faded, and you could identify it only by observing that it stood between number 19 and number 21. There was a dim glow behind the fanlight, and a brighter one in the first-floor window, but otherwise the building was dark. I looked about – as had Farrant himself, if he was to be believed, when *he* was pursuing Turner – for an inn or public, where I might make enquiries about him, and take shelter while I was watching the house; but there was none to be seen. I leaned against a buckled fence on the opposite side of the street, hoping I might see someone going in or out; but after ten minutes all that had happened was that my hands and feet had grown numb with the cold. Time, I decided, to take some other action.

There was no light in number 19; and when I approached number 21 I heard, from inside, the sound of a glass breaking, and two voices – a man's and a woman's – trying to outdo one another in drunken argument. I edged away, therefore, all the while keeping my eye on Farrant's house, and knocked at number 18. After a moment, a woman of thirty or so opened the door a foot or so and peered out.

'Yes?'

'Mrs. Farrant?' I said.

Her forehead creased, and she drew in her lower lip and shook her head.

'Mr. Farrant does live here?'

'You got the wrong house,' she said.

'Oh, pardon me. Then . . .?' I pointed down the street, and raised my eyebrows.

'What you want with him?' she said. 'You a dun?'

'No,' I said; but before I could go on a child's voice behind her said:

'What is it, Ma?'

'Ssh!' she said; but the boy squeezed past her skirts, forcing the door wider open, and stood in front of her, looking up at me. He was about eight, with fair curls and curious blue eyes.

'I think he may be my uncle,' I said.

'*May* be!'

'My ma always said she had a brother who was an engraver in London,' I said. 'Only they had a difference, when they were young; and last thing she said, when she was dying, was: "Find your uncle, and make it right with him."'

If I had expected this affecting tale to melt her, I was mistaken; for she continued to skewer me with a suspicious gaze in which there was no hint of a tear. The boy, however, at that moment came to my aid.

'Who's he talking about?' he said, tugging at his mother's

apron. He completed the question by forming the thumb and forefinger of each hand into a circle, and then holding them before his eyes.

'You didn't ought to make fun of him,' said the woman. 'What with all his kindness to you.'

I remember feeling a great tiredness pass through me, weighting my legs and sapping me of the will to go on. It was late – it was cold – I had come all this way, and learned nothing for my pains save that Farrant had once been kind to a child, and there seemed no prospect that I might learn anything more.

But then, the next instant – it all happened so quickly that it is still confused in my mind – the boy darted out on to the pavement, before his mother could grab him; shouted, 'Come on, I'll show you!'; ran two or three steps; and then abruptly stopped.

'There!' he said, pointing to a figure moving slowly away from us. 'There he is!' Something in the way he braced himself and tilted his head told me that he was intending to call out; but I stopped him just in time.

'Hush,' I said. 'I want it to be a surprise'; and then, before he could question me, or protest, I handed him the sixpence the girl at the pawnbroker's had given me, and left him and his mother staring after me as I set off in pursuit.

More than half a century ago, Farrant had followed Turner through the fog; now, here was I, following *him*. This symmetry, for some reason, exhilarated me, as the resolution of a piece of music may please the ear, or the perfect balance of a composition (think of Turner's own *Ulysses Deriding Polyphemus*) satisfy the eye. I was so distracted by it, indeed, that I became careless, and almost gave myself away; for – somehow foolishly conceiving him still to be the strapping young fellow he had been then, and imagining that it would be all I could do to keep up with him – I started at a tremendous pace, and came upon him far too quickly.

Hearing my footsteps, he stopped and turned, and looked about him like an old bear sniffing the air; and would, I am certain, have seen me, save that – as I saw at once from his heavy spectacles, and half-closed eyes – his sight was now too weak. I stood quite still, holding my breath, until at length, hunching his shoulders, he lumbered on again, feeling his way with a stick. I had learned my lesson – as he, I recalled with a smile, had learned *his* in Norton Street; and waited half a minute or so before setting off once more, this time being careful to keep a prudent distance.

I did not have to continue in this manner for long. At the end of the street he turned into the main thoroughfare, and then, after fifty yards or so, into a small public house – which I must have passed on my way there, though I had no recollection of it – called the White Post. Fearing that, if I went in after him immediately, he might associate me with the footsteps he had heard, and correctly guess that I had been following him, I decided to linger outside for a few minutes. To the left of the door was a low, uncurtained window through which I could see a crowded parlour hazy with tobacco smoke, and hear the cheerful chime of glasses and the ebb and flow of laughter and conversation. Although I could not stand directly before it without being noticed, I found that if I pressed myself against the adjacent wall and craned my neck, I still had a clear view of one half of the room – some rustic prints; the end of a long table (the people sitting at it were largely invisible, but I could just see an assortment of elbows, and two tankards, and a hat); and a small modern fireplace, bright with coals. In the chimney corner were two comfortable chairs – one empty, the other occupied by an old man with a grimy red neck-tie and a round, beef-red face. Something in the way he tapped his fingers, and then looked up questioningly, made me suppose he was waiting for Farrant; and so indeed it proved, for a few seconds later my quarry shuffled into view, and shook the old man's hand.

I say 'the old man's'; but as he removed his cloak, and gently eased himself into the vacant chair, I saw that Farrant was in fact the older of the two. Time had made sad work with him, but he must once have been an impressive figure: even now, bent and frail though he was, his large girth and broad shoulders made him seem almost too big for the little room, and his big-nosed, wide-mouthed, craggy-browed face gave him the imposing presence of a Roman emperor – an impression accentuated by his skin, which the cold had turned as white and luminous as marble.

Within a few moments the two men were talking intently – Farrant leaning forward, and rotating his hand to emphasize his words; the other nodding in agreement (though there was a certain wariness in his eyes, it seemed to me), and drumming his fingers ceaselessly against his wrist. When the barmaid brought their mugs of beer, Red-tie looked up and smiled at her; but Farrant appeared not to notice her, and continued speaking without pause. I waited for two or three minutes more, and then, when Farrant at length sat back and cast about for his drink, concluded that I might safely go in.

Two or three of the men sitting at the table glanced briefly at me as I came through the door, but otherwise my appearance seemed to provoke no response at all, and I knew that about the coat, at least, I had made the right decision. The smoky warmth pressed against my face, as tangible and stifling as a blanket, and made me suddenly aware how chilled I had become. It required no great feat of acting, therefore, as I picked my way between chairs and stools, to shiver and rub my hands and mutter 'brrr' under my breath – or not, at least, until I started to come within earshot of Farrant's conversation, and heard (so I thought), amongst a torrent of words I could not make out, one that stopped me dead: 'Turner'.

My first impulse, naturally, was to stand still and listen;

205

but to do so would be to risk alerting them to my interest; and with a great effort of will I forced myself to continue my dumbshow. They fell silent as I approached; but Red-tie looked on with a kind of distant amusement, like a man who happens by chance upon a street-entertainer, while I stationed myself before the hearth, and began stamping my feet, and blowing on my hands, and shaking the steam from my mist-sodden clothes.

'Evening,' I said, at length, seeing that if I was to get into conversation with them I must initiate it myself. They nodded, but did not reply; and after a moment – as if he thought this small show of ceremony had concluded their business with me – Farrant leant towards his companion and said, in a strangely light, womanish voice:

'Undoubtedly it would have greater weight from you.'

Whether because he felt uneasy at continuing their discussion in my presence, or merely because he was curious about me, I cannot say; but Red-tie ignored him, and continued to watch me. After a few moments he said:

'You been out all night?' He looked towards Farrant. 'You see him, Jack? He's wet as a dog.'

Farrant screwed up his eyes to look at me. The effort made him frown; but any appearance of sternness immediately vanished when he drew in his breath with a soft whistle of pity, and said:

'Oh, you poor chap. What happened to you?'

'Missus threw him out of the house,' said Red-tie, with a laugh, and I started to join in; but Farrant silenced us by lifting his big hand, and shaking his head.

'No,' he said gravely. He continued to look at me, not unkindly, as if giving me the chance to explain myself.

'I came to see my sister,' I said. 'Only she wasn't in.'

Farrant nodded. 'Where's she live?'

'Trotter Street.' That, I knew as I said it, was a mistake; but I couldn't immediately bring to mind the name of any other street in the vicinity. Cursing my own carelessness, I waited for him to ask me what my sister was called, and which her house was; but he merely nodded again, and went on:

'And where do *you* live?'

'Other side of town. Putney,' I said.

'That's a fair way,' said Farrant. He looked about him, and prodded the air with his foot until he struck a stool, and then hooked his boot under the stretcher and drew it towards me. 'Here. You don't want to stand after a walk like that.'

'Thank you,' I said, sitting down.

'Something urgent, was it?' said Farrant. 'I could give her a message, if you like. I'm just at number 20.'

For a moment, I had absolutely no idea how to reply; and then, as if someone had suddenly set off a flare, illuminating a landscape that until now had been lost in darkness, I saw with perfect clarity what I must say:

'That's very kind of you; but the fact is I'm just back from Petworth.'

Did I imagine it, or did Farrant and his companion exchange furtive glances? I went on:

'Her boy's in service at the house; and I came to tell her how he goes on there.' I paused, but neither of them spoke – though they seemed to be watching me so keenly that I felt I must comment on it, or again risk rousing their suspicion. 'Do you know Petworth, then?' I said, looking from one to the other. 'In Sussex?'

'Only by repute,' said Farrant, with a dry smile.

'Lord! you should see it! Regular catacomb of a place. Most of it empty, and the servants kept running one end of it to the other from morning to night.' I laughed. 'My nephew, he's a droll young fellow, he says it's no wonder they call them *foot*men, for that's the bit that does most of the work.'

The barmaid, a thin, dark-haired girl of eighteen or so, came to take my order. I wondered whether to offer them something, but decided it would seem too forward.

'Put a drop of something in it, Kate, to warm him up!' Red-tie called, as she was leaving. 'Else he'll take and die of a chill!'

She turned and shouted something over her shoulder, but it was lost in a sudden spasm of laughter which spread through the room, and ended with Red-tie himself.

'I'll be honest,' I said, 'I was hoping to get a position there myself; for Paul's a good boy, and I thought they might be happy enough to take another from the same stable, so to speak. But –'

Farrant raised his hand, and craned towards me. 'A position as what, Mr. . . .?'

'Jenkinson,' I said. 'Oh, you know, an upper servant. I was the under-butler in my last place' – I paused here, for effect, and lowered my voice – 'but the old man died before I could get a character from him.' I laughed – or rather Jenkinson did, for I could barely recognize the sly, cynical, man-to-man sneer that issued from my lips as my own. Red-tie chuckled too; but we were quickly shamed into silence by Farrant, who refused to ingratiate himself by joining in (surely the fellowship of facile heartlessness is the largest gentlemen's club in the world, and resisting its blandishments must have required some courage), and continued to regard me with the same unsmiling expression.

'But turns out Colonel Wyndham – that's the master now – only wants people that have come with them from their old house.' I winked at Red-tie. 'His wife's an Evangelical, you see, and very particular about the servants' morals.'

The girl brought my porter; and I winked at her, too, for good measure.

'Your health, gents.'

Farrant gravely raised his glass, but did not drink.

'I'd have done well enough there in the old days,' I said. 'If what Paul says is to be believed. Place was full of people,

208

painters and poets and what-have-you, and Lord knows how many women – not a corner or a cubby-hole didn't have a Royal Academician in it, or one of his lordship's bastards.' I shook my head, conveying – I hoped – my deep regret at having missed such colourful goings-on.

'You're talking of the Third Earl's time?' said Farrant.

'Yes,' I said – making, I think, a fair show of surprise. 'Why? Were you acquainted with him?'

'I knew his name,' said Farrant. 'Everyone knew his name then, leastways in my line of business.'

'Indeed?' I was on the point of going on: *Are you an artist, then?* when I thought better of it. My 'guesses' must not appear too accurate, and I must not seem too eager to ingratiate myself. I glanced at Red-tie; and then, with a waggish little smile, and in a manner bordering on the insolent, said:

'And what business is that, Mr. . . .?'

Out of the corner of my eye, I saw Red-tie's lips twitch. Farrant still looked at me impassively, but I noticed the broken veins on his pale cheeks starting to colour.

'Farrant,' he said. 'I'm an engraver.'

'Ah,' I said, with an air of indifference. I took a deep draught of my beer, and grinned at Red-tie. 'That fortifies you, Mr. . . .'

'Hargreaves,' said Red-tie, laughing.

'Better than a warming pan.' I barely heeded the critical voice in my own head saying *That sounds foolish – warming pans don't fortify*; I was too busy trying to think of a way to direct the conversation back to Petworth, and then to artists, and then to –

'Did they say anything of Turner?' Farrant asked suddenly.

I could scarcely believe my good luck. 'Turner?' I said.

'The landscape painter,' said Farrant, looking not at me but at Hargreaves, with a meaning expression that seemed to say: *See, I know what I am about.*

'Yes, as it happens,' I said, laughing. 'Though I don't know how much of it to believe.'

Farrant leaned forward. 'Why, what did they tell you?'

'Oh,' I said, 'that he was a strange, secretive little devil, who locked himself in the library, and would admit no-one save the Earl.'

Farrant nodded. 'Is that all?'

'He had a housemaid for a . . . friend – you know the kind of friend I mean, Mr. Hargreaves? – and gave her a little picture to remember him by. That part's true at least, I think, for her daughter showed it to me – the poor girl's soft on Paul, I fancy, and thought no doubt she'd impress his uncle.'

Hargreaves guffawed lewdly.

'And I'll tell you, the funny thing – what do you think it was?'

Hargreaves shrugged, and looked away; while Farrant was so intent on hearing the end of my story that he could not bear any distraction from it, and shook his head impatiently.

'What you or I'd have done is leave her with a sentimental miniature, wouldn't we, Mr. Hargreaves? Or a peaceful country scene? But not Turner – he had to give her a blood-red sunset, and a rising storm. "Here you are, darling. Something to remind you of me."'

Hargreaves began to laugh again, but Farrant cut him short.

'That does not surprise me,' he said. His voice was quiet but tremulous, and he clenched his fists like a man struggling to keep some great passion in check. 'Nothing of what you say surprises me – save that he gave her anything at all.'

'Why?' I said. 'Did you know him, then?'

'Well enough,' he muttered. 'Well enough.'

I said nothing, waiting for him to go on; but after a few moments he shook his head and said:

'Anyway, it is no matter.'

'No,' I said; and then – thinking it was at last safe to do so – 'I should like to hear.'

He shook his head again. 'What good's tittle-tattle? I tell you what I know, and you tell the next man, with a bit added here, and another there, to season it; and he does the same in his turn, and soon there's a hundred different stories, and no-one believes any of them. I want people to have the truth, here, in front of them, black and white. And they will, soon enough.'

His face was so grave, and his voice so urgent, that it was impossible, in that instant, to believe he had lied to me.

'What,' I said, 'are you writing a book?'

'No,' he said darkly. 'But there are others interested in Turner.'

My skin prickled, as it does at the onset of a fever. Was *others* just a rhetorical flourish, or did he mean *more than one*? If he had found out about me, of course (which was clearly the case, although I did not know how), was it not reasonable enough to suppose that he also knew something of Thornbury, and had perhaps communicated with him? But what if there was a third – or even a fourth – biographer, of whom I had never heard at all?

'Really?' I said, as casually as I could. 'Who?'

He took a leisurely sip from his glass and then set it down again, wiping the suds from his mouth. 'You will forgive me, sir,' he said with a sigh, avoiding my gaze, 'but I barely know you; and this is a delicate matter.' And I could not help noticing – dear God! how complex are our emotions, and how contradictory! – that while his shoulders were bowed under the weight of some great burden, yet his eyes shone with the consciousness of the power he enjoyed at that moment.

'The truth is,' said Hargreaves, with a wheedling smile, watching Farrant closely all the time, 'there's a value now, to stories about Turner. There's a gentleman as pays good money for them. What Mr. Farrant's saying is, you want him to tell you, you'll have to put your hand in your pocket –'

'No!' roared Farrant, so loudly that the room suddenly fell quiet, and every face turned towards us. 'I don't care anything about that. I want the facts straight, number one; and number two, no-one knows about them till they're published. That's the first rule of war: don't give your secrets to the enemy.'

'Who are the enemy?' I said.

Farrant didn't reply at once, but instead stared thoughtfully before him. At length he turned abruptly to me and said: 'Turner had powerful friends.'

'Indeed –' I began; but Farrant was already preparing to leave, pulling his coat about him and searching for his stick. 'Oh, please,' I said, touching his arm. 'Don't go. Let me buy you a drink.'

He knocked my hand away and shook his head emphatically. 'I shall wish you good night.'

My palms felt dry and empty – I longed to clasp them round his rough sleeve, and drag him back to his chair – but I knew nothing would be gained by it. If he was not angry with me yet (and it seemed to have been Hargreaves, rather than I, that had provoked him), he soon would be if I persisted in trying to detain him. All I could do, during the unconscionable time it took him to get ready, was to stare at the fire, and exchange sheepish grins with Hargreaves. At last, he fastened the final button on his coat, and without another word, began his stately progress towards the door.

'You can buy *me* a drink,' said Hargreaves, when Farrant was out of earshot. 'And I'll tell you what I know.'

'About the gentleman?'

His face took on the surly, puzzled look of a slow-witted man who suspects he is being mocked. 'What gentleman?'

'The gentleman who pays good money for stories about Turner.'

'Oh!' He clearly hadn't expected this; and he frowned as he wrestled with the troubling question of why I should want to know. Fearing that I had gone too far, and given too much away, I said hastily:

'I was thinking of my nephew. He could spin him a tale or two.'

'Ah, I see!' He smiled and nodded, and for a moment I thought he was going to tell me, for he gave me a crafty side-long glance that seemed to say, *I get your meaning now; you're a man of the world like me*, which I interpreted as a prelude to doing business. But then he suddenly looked away and said: 'I won't deceive you – I know no more than Jack Farrant told me, and that's little enough.'

'His name?'

Hargreaves shook his head.

I cursed inwardly. Could it have been Thornbury? That was the likeliest explanation, but it failed to explain Farrant's letter to me. An author might naturally give a use-ful informant money; but he would scarcely pay him to send his story to a rival. Perhaps there *was* someone else . . .? Or perhaps Farrant had merely heard about me from Davenant or George Jones (for did not his letter mention both their names?) and had written to me on his own account, for his own reasons? I should gladly have given fifty pounds for the answer, though I knew better than to say so. Something of my feelings must have shown, however, for, before I had time to speak, he went on eagerly:

'But I'll tell you something else – a sight tastier – about Turner.'

I forced an indifferent smile on to my face, and said lacon-ically: 'As good as the housemaid?'

'Oh, better!'

'Very well.'

He shook his head, and wagged a finger at me. 'Drink!'

I summoned the barmaid. The question of what he should

213

order at my expense seemed to exercise Hargreaves terribly, and he agonized over it for some seconds before finally saying:

'A pot of porter, if you please, and a tot of brandy' – here he leered comically at me – 'just to keep it company on the way down.' And then, as if he feared I should cavil at this extravagance, and withdraw my offer, he laid his grimy fingers on my cuff, and said: 'It's worth it, Mr. Jenkinson. You'll see.'

And so, indeed, it proved; for this, as near as I can remember it, is what he told me – his face thrust forward, his eyes gazing up into mine with the anxious look of a dog that expects another biscuit if its master likes its trick, and a kick if he does not:

'I'm a waterman by trade; I was a hog-grubber once, but, what with the new bridges, there's no living to be made on that stretch of the river now; so the last fifteen year or more I mostly been plying Wapping. And that's where I saw him – oh, must've been a dozen times, at least.

'He was a rum one – you knew that the minute you laid eyes on him – not much taller'n a child, with a big hat, and a long coat. You couldn't see his face clear, for he'd wrap a scarf around it, to keep the cold out o' doors, as he'd say, and besides, it was dark more often than not; but I remember his big Jew's nose, and his eyes looking at you like a ferret, and his grey hair sticking out under his hat – for he was already an old fellow by this time.

'He liked me, he said, on account I'd been a sailor; and usually he'd ask for me special, to go to Rotherhithe. It was always the same: I'd take him across of a Saturday night, and bring him back again Monday morning. General, he wouldn't say much, just sit staring over the side of the boat, as if he was looking for something in the water; and once . . . once or twice I saw him take out a notebook, and scribble in it.

214

'I didn't know who he was – he never told me a name – but I wouldn't have guessed it was "Turner", for one time, as we was putting in at Rotherhithe, an old seaman who'd had a bit to drink came up to him and says: "Back again, Mr. J.? Lord, give the girls a chance!" Might have been "Jay", I suppose, but it didn't sound like that – too quick, if you know what I mean. So perhaps he went by "Jones", or "Johnson".

'But then one time, he's going ashore at Wapping, and another gentleman steps down to take the boat, and sees him, and says: "Why, Turner!"; but he just shakes his head and marches off without a word. When the other gent's settled himself, he says: "You know who that was? Turner, *the* Turner! J. M. W.? R.A.? I'd heard stories about his adventures, of course, but I never believed them before now."

'So I says, "What stories, sir?" And he says: "Why, that he'll finish painting on a Saturday night, and put a five-pound note in his pocket, and go and wallow in some low sailor's house by the river till Monday morning!"

'And the rummy thing is, after that, I never saw the old man again.'

My mouth was dry; I could hear my own heartbeat throbbing in my ears; I was filled with that strange tumbling excitement you feel when your wildest intimation suddenly becomes a certainty. Hargreaves must have seen the effect he had had, for he concluded by exhaling dramatically, and sitting back with a triumphant glint in his eye, as much as to say: *There! What did I tell you?*

'Well,' I said, still striving to sound nonchalant, even if my glowing cheeks betrayed me. 'That was tasty enough, I suppose.' I got up, squinting at the clock above the bar counter.

'Worth another pot?' he said quickly.

I hesitated, and then laughed and said:

'Oh, why not? But you'll drink it alone; for I must off home.'

It was while we were waiting for the barmaid that Hargreaves suddenly leaned over and tugged my sleeve.

'I'll tell you what,' he said, looking round to see that we were not overheard. 'The funniest thing. Fair turned my stomach. One time, we was nearly at the south bank, and Turner looking in the water as usual, when he suddenly points to something and says: "Over there! Row over there!" "What is it?" I says; for I couldn't see nothing; but he just says: "Row! Row!" And he takes out his little book, and starts to sketch something, frantic like, as if all of a sudden it's just going to vanish away.'

Hargreaves looked about him again; and when he turned back to me there was such disquiet in his eyes that I realized he was telling me this not for gain, but to unburden himself.

'I didn't see what it was until my oar struck it, Mr. Jenkinson. So help me, it was a body – a poor girl, couldn't have been more than sixteen, as'd drowned herself. And there was Turner, lost to the world, drawing her face.'

XXV

From the private notebook of Walter Hartright, 7th October, 185–

Others may read a journal.

No-one must read this.

What is a man who slips like mercury between the fingers, who is never where you think to find him, who goes abroad under an assumed name and a borrowed identity?

A man who never marries; and maintains no household; and even in those places where he hides from the world has secret chambers in which to conceal himself still more completely?

A man who consorts with whores in stinking taverns? A man who responds to seeing a corpse not with some pious exclamation of pity, but by taking out his notebook and drawing it?

He is a genius.

Last night, for the first time in my life, I was like mercury.

I have never been so free.

Leaving the White Post I might have –

What?

Gone anywhere. Done anything. Walked to the docks, and taken passage for Java. Returned to Maiden Lane and found a girl, and enjoyed her in the alley where she stood. No-one could have said: That was Walter Hartright. No-one could have blamed me. No-one could have blamed *me*.

Gravity held me by a thread. At any moment I might have snapped it, and drifted away altogether.

But I let it draw me homeward, as a child draws a kite.

Until I reached Piccadilly. And the Marston Rooms.

I did not seek her.

But I did not send her away.

I had set down my journal. I was so tired I had lost all sense of time. I was watching a drunk man lurching towards the door.

She said: 'A penny for your thoughts.'

I turned. She was perhaps twenty-five, wearing a close-fitting blue dress and crinoline. She had thick fair hair pinned loosely over the nape of her neck. She smelt of musk.

'What are you about?' she said.

I smiled, and weighed the open journal in my hand.

'What, are you an author, then?'

I said nothing.

'Must be lonely work, being an author. I expect you feel

like a bit of company, don't you, sometimes?'

I nodded.

'That's good,' she said, sitting beside me. 'I'm fond of company, too.' She leaned close. She was warm. I smelt the hot biscuit tang of powder on her cheeks.

'You going to buy me a drink, then?'

I jerked my head at the waiter.

'I like champagne,' she said. 'It makes me gay.'

The drunk man had finally stumbled into the street. Through the window, I saw a woman in a wide-brimmed hat accosting him.

'I'm Louise,' said my companion. She pouted teasingly, and gave a little nod that invited me to tell her *my* name.

I said nothing, but merely looked at her and smiled.

'Gentlemen are often shy about that,' she said. She put her head on one side and appraised me, running her tongue over her blood-red lips. 'What about *Leo*?' she said at last, in barely more than a whisper.

'Leo,' I heard myself say.

She spread her hand on the open page of my journal and caressed it, as if she might coax the meaning from it. 'So, Leo, what are you writing?' When I did not reply, she suddenly seized the book and began to read at random:

'What's this – "wallow in some low sailor's house by the river"?' She broke off, laughing. I snatched the book back.

'You bad boy,' she said. 'Is that what you get up to?'

The waiter came. His smile said: *I know what you're doing.* I wanted to hide my face in shame. I wanted to acknowledge his gaze, and bask in the warmth of his admiration.

'Champagne,' I heard myself say.

'Very good, sir.'

'And something for yourself. Make the night go a bit sweeter.'

'He's a gent, ain't he?' giggled the woman, catching the waiter's eye.

218

His smiled deepened. 'Thank you, sir.'

When he had gone, she took my wrist in her hot fingers and leaned closer. Her breath smelled of licorice and wine.

'I like to wallow,' she whispered.

'I bet you do.'

How can I explain it? I cannot say it was not my voice. But it was the voice of a me whose existence I had never suspected. He must have been there always, sealed away in some blackness so profound that I had never thought to try to penetrate it. But now the shutters had been thrown open, and we could see and hear each other.

'I know a nice place,' she said. Her lips brushed my cheek, and she whispered in my ear: 'What would you like to do with me?'

We were poised, Leo and Walter; balanced on a pinpoint.

It's natural enough, ain't it? A man and a woman were made to give pleasure to each other.

Think of . . .

~~*You can't pretend you don't feel*~~

You can't pretend you only want to fuck your wife.

I could see the pulse in her throat, as if some tiny creature were trapped beneath the skin.

See? Her heart's pounding, too.

If I go with her, I shall cease to be me.

Isn't that the point?

'Mm?' she murmured again. 'What would you like?' She drew my ear-lobe into her mouth, nipped it, rolled it on her tongue.

I can imagine. That is enough. I can see, and imagine.

I must freeze this moment; I must stop time; I must hold my breath; and be as adroit as an acrobat with a pole.

I laid two sovereigns on the table, and left without another word.

XXVI

Letter from Laura Hartright to Marian Halcombe, 7th October, 185–

Darling Marian,

Walter has written me such a cold, angry letter. Why is he so cross with me? Do you know? I can think of nothing I have done, save to tell him that we miss him, and long for his return. That would never have made the old Walter angry. It would have brought him back to us. I know it would.

I am so unhappy. This morning Florrie said, 'Why are you not pretty any more, Mama?' I could not tell her the answer: that I had lain awake half the night, crying about her father.

Am I – I can barely write this – am I losing him? Has he changed? I pray to God not. But I am so far away – I cannot touch him, or see his dear face, or hear his voice.

You are so much cleverer and wiser than I am. Please – is there anything you can do to make things well between us again?

Your affectionate sister,

Laura

XXVII

From the journal of Marian Halcombe, 9th October, 185–

This cannot go on.

God, is there to be nothing in life but gritting our teeth, and doing our duty?

XXVIII

Memorandum of a letter from Walter Hartright to Mr. Hawkesworth Fawkes, 10th October, 185–

1. Am engaged on *Life of Turner*.
2. Mr. Ruskin tells me you knew him well – would be able to give me invaluable information.
3. Will be passing close to Farnley on Thursday, and wondered if might call upon you?
4. Please forgive me for not giving you more warning. Will of course understand if unable to see me at such short notice.

XXIX

From the journal of Walter Hartright, 12th October, 185–

~~It is as well~~
It is as well I did not write ahead to tell her I was coming, for I shall not now be home tomorrow after all. What delayed me was a strange accident, into which I cannot but read some significance.

Just before we reached Leeds, there was a tremendous bang from the front of the train, and we jerked and rocked and squealed to a halt. My neighbour, a florid, grey-haired man of about fifty, wearing a brown suit and no overcoat, as if his own internal furnace were enough to keep him warm, lowered the window and looked out.

'Can you see what's the matter?' I said.

'Burst boiler,' he replied, turning back. 'I'm afraid, ladies and gentlemen, we're going to be here for a while. They'll need to send another engine.' And with that he leant out again, unfastened the door, and gingerly lowered himself to the ground.

I was sure this must be against company regulations, but I heard no-one remonstrating with him, and after a minute or so I took out my sketch-pad and pencil and jumped down after him – partly out of curiosity, and partly to avoid the purgatory of having to exchange grumbling platitudes with my fellow-passengers for an hour or more.

At first all I could see was a dense swirl of vapour and gritty smoke, which seemed to engulf the locomotive and half of the front carriage; but as I drew closer I could make out blurred figures hurrying about, or standing talking in little groups. Among them I saw my brown-suited companion, apparently deep in conversation with a bearded man in a round cap and white canvas trousers whom I took to be the driver. No-one seemed to have been hurt; and yet there was something undeniably awful about the scene: the flailing rods and pistons; the dreadful spouts of steam shrieking from the split boiler (it is only when they are wounded that you see the terrible power of these brutes); the ferocity of the still-raging coals, glowing red through the fog like the mouth of hell.

Awful, but strangely beautiful, too. I took out my pencil, and started to draw.

I was so engrossed in my labours that I did not notice the approach of the man in the brown suit, until he was standing at my shoulder.

'You're an artist?' he said, after a moment.

I nodded.

'You put me in mind of Turner. He loved mists, and fires, and machines. You're familiar with his work?'

'Yes,' I said. 'I admire it very much.'

'I knew him, you know,' he said. His voice sounded matter-of-fact enough, but he pushed his thumbs into his waistcoat pockets and rocked back and forth on his feet, as if his sense of self-importance, having been denied the outlet of words, must express itself in some other form. 'I'm Elijah Nisbet.'

He clearly expected me to be impressed, and I think my 'Oh!' contrived to suggest that I was, though in truth I had never heard his name before in my life.

'I have some of his later paintings,' Nisbet went on. He glanced at my drawing again, and then nodded approvingly. 'It would be a pleasure to show them to you, if you're ever near Birmingham. A professional like yourself might appreciate them better than my neighbours do.'

'Thank you. I should like that very much.'

'Let me give you my address.' He took the pad, and scribbled on the back. 'There,' he said, returning it to me. 'Now I must go and write a complaint.' He cast a speculative look towards the crippled locomotive. 'The driver's to blame. He reported it "correct" last night, but there must have been some evidence of a flaw.'

He did not explain how he came to speak with such authority, or why it was his business to complain; and I did not ask him, for fear it would reveal that I didn't really know who he was.

It was only after he had gone that I realized I hadn't told him *my* business, either. Why had I been so secretive? Was it merely that he had connected me with Turner not as a biographer, but as a fellow-artist, and I had not wished to disabuse him?

*

The relief engine did not finally arrive for nearly two hours, with the result that I missed the train to Arthington, and arrived in Otley too late to see Mr. Fawkes. I therefore sent a note by the carrier to say that I should call on him in the morning, and have put up for the night at the Black Bull, where I write these words.

It's easy to see why Turner loved this place. If Lord Egremont's Petworth – a Renaissance palace presided over by a Renaissance prince – appealed to the classical side of his nature, then Mr. Fawkes's Farnley must have fed his hunger for the sublime. In the streets of Petworth you are aware, above everything, of the inescapable presence of the great house; in the streets of Otley – which must be approximately the same size – you are aware only of the presence of nature. The town is bounded on one side by the River Wharfe, with majestic moors rising gradually beyond it; and on the other by an enormous hill – called 'the Chevin', according to the driver from Arthington – that seems to blot out half the western sky. The sun was setting behind it as I arrived, and I took out my notebook and did a series of quick sketches, screwing up my eyes and craning my neck to see the clutter of craggy rocks on the summit, until at length it was too dark for me to work, and I approached the inn.

The Black Bull is a solid, welcoming, unpretentious kind of place – constructed, like every other building I have seen in Otley, of rough-hewn local stone smudged with grime from the nearby mills – which stands at the corner of the main square. As I entered, the last few stalls from the day's market were being dismantled by lantern-light, and a pack of small boys was scuffling among the trampled cabbage-leaves and broken turnips on the ground. For a moment I was put in mind of my first visit to Maiden Lane – though here the children's faces glowed with health and merriment, and the cold air was misty with their breath, and rang with the sound of their laughter – and found myself wondering whether Turner had ever seen such a scene in Otley, and been moved by it to the same thought? This notion gave me a sudden start: what images, what private memories and associations – which I could never now know – might then have flitted through his consciousness; and what old pains and needs and hungers might they have stirred? And should I find any traces of this secret, inner Turner here – as I had, for an instant, in Twickenham and Farringdon; or was I fated merely to discover clues to his artistic life, and hear Mr. Fawkes reiterate what I have come to see as the official line: *a strange, eccentric little fellow, but no man could have been more tender-hearted, or a truer friend.*

I was greeted in the flagged hall by a thickset, round-faced man, wearing a heavy apron, and collarless white shirt, with the sleeves rolled back to reveal a pair of massive forearms, and a sprig of grey hair showing at the unfastened throat. Through the half-open door to the right I glimpsed a trestle table lined with plainly dressed men and women, and heard the powerful thrum of twenty or thirty voices. Farmers and their wives, I thought, relaxing after market-day.

'G'd evening, sir,' said the innkeeper. 'Would you be looking for a room?'

'Yes,' I said. 'If you have one.'

'That's just about all we *do* have,' he said – not insolently, but with a kind of good-humoured relish. His eyes searched the row of hooks behind him, and at last lighted on a key.

'You want to see it first, sir?' he said.

'No, I'll take it,' I said hastily, suddenly realizing how tired I was, and how unprepared to trudge round the town looking for an alternative. 'As long as there's a bed, and a table I can sit at, and write.'

'That I think I can promise you,' he said with a smile.

Following him upstairs, I tried to guess his age. He was still hale and strong, but from the deep lines in his powerful neck, and the wisps of silvery hair about his ears, I supposed he must be about sixty. Walter Fawkes, I recalled from my researches, had died in 1825; and Turner had never again returned to Farnley, so his last visit here must have been around forty years ago. Unlikely, therefore – but not impossible. As we reached the landing, I said:

'Do you by any chance remember Turner?'

225

'Turner?' he said, surprised. 'What, th'ironmonger?'

'The painter.'

'Painter! Nay. What, here in Otley, was he?'

'Sometimes.'

He shook his head. 'I never knew him. But see, I only come from Ilkley fifteen year ago, like.' He opened the door to my room, and carried my bags inside. 'Here you are, sir. I'll just set the fire going for you.'

While he worked, I stood by the little casement and gazed out. The room overlooked a side-alley, but beyond it I could see the town stretching away – an irregular horizon of roofs and chimneys, oil-lamps winking in uncurtained windows, and strings of street-lights so feeble that they quickly petered out as they approached the foot of the Chevin, as if they knew they could not challenge its black looming bulk, and might as well give up altogether. Somewhere in that bewitching pattern of light and shade, I thought, there must be somebody who recalls Turner – somebody who knows something about him that will deepen my understanding of the man, and give me an advantage against Thornbury, who appears so far ahead of me in London. I had an empty evening before me; and there and then resolved to spend it trying to find this person, and learning what he – or she – could tell me.

My first thought was to join the farmers, and take my dinner with them; for among them there might well be one from the Farnley Estate, who, if he had not known Turner himself, could at least perhaps refer me to someone who had. When at last I descended again, however, and was about to enter the dining room, I found my way barred by the innkeeper.

'If you care to step into the back parlour, sir, there's a table set for you there.'

'Oh, please don't trouble yourself with that,' I said, thinking they must suppose it would be beneath my dignity to eat at the common board. 'I'm happy to sit with everyone else.'

'It's no trouble, sir,' he said – and I fancy my words had taken him aback, for he flushed, and his voice had a phlegmy edge as he went on: 'Quite the other way about; for they're nearly done in there, and my wife wants it all sided and neat like afore the lasses go home.'

And so I found myself sitting all alone at a white-clothed table before a snug coal fire, in a comfortable little room at the rear of the house. I did not, however, forget my purpose, even when it turned out – to my disappointment – that I was to be waited on by a spotty girl of fourteen or so, who would not only clearly not remember Turner herself, but whose mother had probably not even been born at the time of his last visit here.

'Tell me,' I said, when she had taken my order (standing stock-still, and frowning and biting her lower lip with concentration). 'Who is the oldest person you know in Otley?'

For some reason, this reduced her to uncontrollable giggles; and, quite unable to speak, she shook her head, and retreated to the kitchen. A couple of minutes later, however, as she reappeared with my soup and set it before me, she said:

'Mrs. says to try Druggist Thompson.'

'Why?' I said – unsure whether this was a belated answer to my question, or a reference to some other topic altogether. She froze like a frightened rabbit; so I coaxed her by saying:

'Is he very old?'

She shook her head again, and left without another word; and it was only when she brought my steak pie (a full twenty minutes later) that she said:

'Nay, but all the old folk go to him for their potions an' that. You won't have far to look. He's only out in th'market place.'

And so he was – or, rather, so his shop was; for by the time I had finished my meal, and retrieved my coat from my room, and ventured out again, 'Thompson: Druggist' was firmly closed.

There seemed nothing to be gained by returning at once to the Black Bull, so I decided to take a walk. If nothing else, I should enjoy the childish pleasure I still find in exploring new places – observing the names of shops and taverns, and looking into the houses as I pass, and imagining what it must be like to live in them; and if I was lucky, some chance encounter might yet allow me to discover something of Turner. A raw wind was starting to blow in from the north-west, carrying – above the stench of a nearby tannery – a wild moorland smell that seemed to call out the spirit of adventure; and with a sudden spasm of exhilaration I turned up my collar, and set off down the narrow path at the side of the hotel.

I found myself – as soon as my eyes had adjusted to the darkness – in a maze of mean passages, that turned and twisted and doubled back so unrelentingly that after a few minutes I should, I think, have had difficulty retracing my steps. I was not concerned about getting lost, however; for I knew I must come out somewhere, and that that somewhere could not be very far from the Black Bull, which I would be able to approach by way of the main streets. At every lighted window I peered inside, hoping to see some elderly person sitting alone before the fire – for surely Turner, if he knew of this knot of secret alleys, must have come here again and again, drawn by the opportunities it offered for being unseen and unknown? – and someone might remember him yet, if I could but describe him well enough. Beyond one white-bearded old patriarch regaling a group of younger men in an ale-house, however, I saw nothing but rooms full of children and their mothers (including, once – through gnarled little panes of glass grey with steam – a tin bathtub before the fire, and a baby splashing in it. Why, I cannot say – but this scene stabbed me so fiercely with the recollection of my own family, and the realization of how far they have been from my thoughts lately, that I had to bite my lip to stop myself weeping.).

At length, turning a corner, I felt the wind and a spatter of rain full on my face; and a few moments later emerged in an open yard at the edge of a street I did not recognize. The Chevin rose up directly before me, no more than a mile or so away; and for a moment I had the strange impression that it had grown since I'd last seen it, for its dark mass seemed to reach as far as the eye could see. Then I saw that what appeared to be the 'top' was moving, and was in reality no more than a great black storm cloud rolling towards us at a fearful pace. I wished now that I had paid more attention to the way I had come; for it was clear that if I did not return to the hotel at once, I risked being soaked to the skin, and having to put on wet clothes in the morning.

From somewhere to my left, I heard the strains of music, and thinking there might be a hall or an assembly room nearby, where I might turn my predicament to advantage by sheltering pleasantly until the storm was past, and perhaps falling into conversation with an elderly doorkeeper, I set out briskly in that direction. After no more than two hundred yards or so, I came to a brightly lit, plain stone building which looked as if it had once been a chapel, but which now boldly announced itself to the world – by means of a large painted board above the door – as 'Otley Mechanics' Institute'. The music came from a room on the first floor; and as I drew nearer I was conscious that there was something strange about it, though for a moment I could not have said what it was. The melody was familiar – a piece by Mendelssohn, I think; the playing more than competent, for such an out-of-the-way place; and yet . . .

And then it struck me: I could identify the first two instruments easily enough – a violin and a piano – but what in heaven's name was the third? A piccolo? Too deep. A flute? Too rich and deep.

I was still wrestling with this conundrum – heedless of the rain that was now hammering the top of my head – when the door opened, and a tall, slender man peered out, and grimaced up at the sky. He held an umbrella, which he started to unfurl; but as soon as he felt the wind catch it he closed it again, and set off with no other precaution than a violent shrug to lift his coat higher about his neck and shoulders. He had gone no more than five paces when he saw me. The puzzlement must have shown on my face, for his expression promptly changed from hawkish severity to a broad smile, and he said:

'You know what that is?'

I shook my head.

'Come and see.'

There was a kind of boyish eagerness in his manner that suggested he welcomed the excuse to delay his departure – either because he feared a wetting, or because he was less than enthusiastic about his next engagement; and, before I had a chance to reply, he turned abruptly and led the way back into the Institute. The ground floor was chill and gloomy, with dark-painted doors marked 'Library', 'Reading room' and 'Classroom'; but a cheerful brightness fell on the stairs, as if they rose from this world to the next. And indeed, as we ascended towards the gas-lit landing, we heard – more loudly with every step – the breath-catching tones of a tender *adagio* – which, if not quite an angelic choir, yet seemed heavenly enough in contrast to the sullen drumming of rain on roof and windows.

Directly before us, as we reached the top, was a pair of heavy panelled doors. My guide opened one, and wedged it ajar with his body so that I might see past him. A few people just inside, hearing our arrival – or else feeling the sudden blast of cold air against their necks – turned towards us, greeting me with a stare that was neither hostile nor friendly, but merely curious; and then nodding and smiling as soon as they saw my companion, who smiled and nodded back.

I found myself looking into a long room running the

entire length of the building, and set out as a lecture hall, with tightly packed rows of chairs – every one, so far as I could tell, occupied – and, at the far end, four or five men sitting behind a baize-covered table on a raised dais. The musicians were clustered round the piano at one side of the stage; and one glance was enough to tell me why my guide had brought me here, and why his eyes were even now searching my face, in anticipation of some evidence of astonishment. The piano-player and the violinist were just such a young woman and a young man as you might expect to see appearing in the public hall of any small provincial town; but the third performer was something else entirely. He was no more than eighteen or nineteen, with close-set eyes, dark ringlets and a hook nose. He stood before a music stand, following a score like the others – but his only instrument was his own lips, which he was using to *whistle* his part, with a range, and a depth of feeling, that I should not – had I not seen him – believed possible.

My guide laid a finger on my arm and whispered in my ear: 'There. That's Whistling Albert.'

'*Whistling Albert*?'

'Printer Walker's boy.'

'Ah,' I said, trying to give the impression that I knew who Printer Walker was, and realized that he was an adequate explanation of the miraculous whistler. I was evidently unsuccessful, however; for my companion said:

'You haven't heard of the Printer?'

I shook my head.

'I thought maybe you'd come to see him,' he said. He backed out on to the landing, leaving just his foot in the door, and continued in a louder voice: 'We don't get many visitors in Otley, and most of them are for him. Or Dawson and Payne.'

No point in further pretence. I smiled, and shrugged helplessly.

231

'Why, they make "Our Own Kind",' he said; and then, seeing I was still baffled: 'The *printing* machines. That's what we're principally known for, nowadays, Mr. . . . .'

'Hartright.'

'Hartright. Yes, the Printer says in a few years Otley machines'll be known all over the world. Or rather, "celebrated in every clime and corner of the globe"; for he'll never use a simple English phrase when an ornate Latinized one will do.' He gave a pleasant laugh, with no hint of malice in it. 'He would find it hard, I think, to rise to the challenge I once set myself, of composing a sermon entirely in words of one syllable.'

A clergyman; but of what denomination? A Methodist, like as not, in a place like this. For an uncomfortable moment I imagined his sharp eyes uncovering the secrets of my soul, and making a damning catalogue of all the levity and wantonness he found there. I was relieved when at length he said:

'I'm Joshua Hart, the vicar here.' He held out his hand. 'And what *does* bring you to Otley, Mr. Hartright, if not the printing trade?'

'I'm writing a book.'

'Ah, the printing trade after all – at least, after a fashion. We should have had you here tonight.' He made a gracious little bow in the direction of the hall. 'They always like to hear literary men. Doubtless the thought of all that paper from the mill, and all that occupation for their machines.' He laughed, again without any appearance of ill-feeling. 'And what, may I ask, is your subject?'

'The life of Turner.'

His eyes brightened. 'J. M. W., R.A.?' he said; and then, before I had time to reply: 'Ah, I understand. Farnley Hall.'

'I go there tomorrow,' I said.

He nodded. Encouraged by the warmth of interest in his face – and by the sudden reflection that a vicar should be at least as well placed to advise me as a druggist – I went on: 'I was hoping tonight that I might find someone in Otley who had some reminiscence of him.'

'There, I'm afraid, I cannot help you,' he said, smiling. 'I only came here in 'thirty-sev–'

At that moment, the music ended; and a sudden explosion of clapping made all conversation impossible for the next half minute, during which time we could do nothing but stand smiling impotently at each other. As the applause finally died away, however, his eyes seemed to stray past me; and then he nodded to himself, as if acknowledging some sudden insight. Leaning over and touching my arm again, he said:

'No, I *may* be able to help you.' He held up his hand, signalling me to wait, and looked towards the hall, where one of the men at the table had begun to speak in a deep, treacly voice:

'Thank you, Miss Binney; thank you, gentlemen – a charming musical interlude. We now come to the moment that certain small boys have been waiting for' – laughter from the audience – 'the lecture on electricity by Dr. Kerr and Mr. 'Druggist' Thompson. Ladies of a sensitive disposition should be warned that at some point during the demonstration an electric spark will be used to fire a concealed cannon.' (More laughter, and squeals.) 'If you want to leave now, no-one will think worse of you for that.'

'Come,' said Mr. Hart. 'Let's go before we're trampled to death by fleeing women.' As he guided me towards the staircase, he said:

'When we met just now I was on my way to see three of my parishioners. One of them, Mrs. Swinton, is a widow. No more than sixty, I should guess, or thereabouts. But she grew up at Farnley.'

'Ah.'

'She is in a sad way now, poor woman; very lonely since

233

her husband died, and crippled by arthritis; but some company would do her good, if I can persuade her to it. Where are you putting up?'

'The Black Bull.'

There were footsteps on the stairs behind us. He glanced quickly over his shoulder, and urged me hurriedly to the door.

'If you care to wait for me there,' he said, 'I'll see what I can do, and call in on you on my way home to tell you how I've fared.'

I thanked him, and asked him

Later

Am I just seeing monsters in the dark?

God knows the soberest man might fancy he glimpsed something in the shadows after such an evening as this.

But surely

No. I must keep myself in check.

Once again – record what happened – judgement later.

*

He came for me about ten, when I had almost given him up. His face was tired and weatherbeaten, and his clothes so wet that they had abandoned all pretence of protecting him, and merely hung like dripping rags; but he seemed cheerful enough.

'I'm sorry I'm so late; my first call was a mother who's lost her boy, and these things won't be hurried. But the upshot is, Mrs. Swinton'll see you, if you're still willing. She's a strange old body, and I don't know what you'll get from her; but nothing ventured, eh?'

I followed him like a blind man, guided more by sound than by sight; for the rain was coming down so hard when we got outside that it stung my eyes; and even when I

234

shielded my face with my hands I could see little more than an unbroken sheet of water, which all but hid the buildings on either side of us, and made it impossible to make out where we were going. Beyond the clack of his boots and the gush and gurgle of the choked gutters was another, more distant noise: an ominous rumbling, so vast and portentous that – like the Chevin – it seemed to speak of some power unimaginably greater than ourselves, which might at any moment sweep us and all our puny works from the face of the earth, leaving not a trace behind.

'What's that?' I shouted, pointing towards it.

'The weir!'

'Is it always so angry?'

He shook his head. 'There'll be floods tonight, if this don't let up.'

How long our journey took, I cannot say – for when you are as wet as it is possible to be (a state I attained in less than two minutes); and your clothes stick to you like drowning men clinging to a log; and you can discern no change in your surroundings from one moment to the next, time quickly loses all meaning. At length, however, we came to a row of small stone cottages, with roofs of tattered, dripping thatch, and odd little mismatched windows that looked as if they had been set into the walls anyhow, with no concern for symmetry or proportion. Mr. Hart paused at the second door, and knocked; and then, without waiting for an answer, lifted the latch and went inside.

A smell of smoke and fat and bacon – the feeble glimmer of two or three tallow candles – a brilliant orange fire in the grate, with the dark shape of a cooking pot cut from its heart, and a pair of old bellows hanging to one side: those were my immediate impressions. It was only after I had cast about for a few moments that I noticed *her*. She was sitting in the darkness on the far side of the hearth, wearing a black dress and a grubby old crinkled cap, with her arms protectively hugging a large bowl in her lap, as if she feared we might be robbers, and meant to take it from her. Next to her was a chair laid on its front, with planks placed across the back to form a kind of table. Her bright unsmiling eyes never left me as Mr. Hart said:

'Dolly, this is Mr. Hartright.'

'Good evening,' I said, removing my hat. She did not move or speak, but only nodded. As she did so, the light from the fire caught the contours of her face, showing a broad brow and high cheekbones and a mouth held so tightly shut that it was no more than a black crater between nose and jaw.

'Poor Mrs. Swinton – she finds it difficult to get up now,' said Mr. Hart, as if by way of explanation.

'Oh, please don't stir on my account,' I said – somewhat redundantly, for it was plain she had absolutely no intention of doing so.

'Well,' said Mr. Hart, quietly, holding his hand out to me. 'I'll leave you now.'

'Thank you,' I said.

'I hope some good may come of it.' He smiled. 'If it does, you may recompense me with a copy of your book.' He turned towards Mrs. Swinton, and raised his voice.

'Good night, Dolly.'

'G'd neet, Mr. 'Art,' she muttered – and the sound of her voice startled me, for it was almost as deep as a man's. She watched him leave, as alert as a wild animal; and then said:

''E en't put the sneck 'ome.'

'I beg your pardon?' I said.

'The sneck,' she said. She extended her hand and pivoted it at the wrist, from which I deduced she meant the latch. 'Neet like toneet, wind'll 'ave t'door off 'is 'angers if 'e's not fixed reet.'

As if to prove the point, the door flew open as I reached it, and would have knocked me off my feet if I had not jumped

236

out of the way in time. My struggle to close it again, and to secure it firmly (no easy matter, for the wood was badly warped) must have made an entertaining spectacle; for when I turned back suddenly towards Mrs. Swinton, she was shaking with silent laughter. As soon as she saw she was observed, however, she resumed her previous dour expression; and said:

'Tha's nivver 'Artright.'

'What?' I said, too taken aback to make any other response.

'Tha reet name's not 'Artright,' she said, looking squarely into my eyes.

'What is it, then?' I said, with a sheepish smile, and an uncomfortable tightness in my throat. I held my breath, convinced, for one wild giddy instant, that she was going to say 'Jenkinson'. After studying me for a few seconds more, however, she merely shrugged and said:

''Ahsumiver, tha's sodden wi' weet. Come by t'fire, and get dry.'

I accepted gratefully, even though the stench of burnt lard and dirty clothes and unwashed flesh grew riper and more oppressive with every step. As I drew near – mastering my revulsion by breathing through my mouth, and so contriving to smell nothing at all – I saw that the makeshift table next to her was lined with rows of little freshly cooked cakes; and that suspended from the beamed ceiling was an ingenious kind of rack – much like the 'creels' I have seen in cottages in Limmeridge, save that it was attached to a pulley and a length of rope that allowed her to lower and raise it without leaving her seat – to which she had transferred a dozen or so dry. She must have seen me looking at them, for she said:

''Ayver-bread. Will tha teeaste 'un?'

In truth, the thought of it turned my stomach; but I felt I could not politely refuse, so I reached up to take one.

'Nay,' she said, 'tha oughta 'ave it 'ot, to warm tha guts;

I'll make tha one fresh'; and pulling a piece of dough from the bowl in her lap, she quickly pinched and patted it into a little disc. As she laid it on the bakestone in the fireplace I tried to persuade myself that the dark smears on the surface were a trick of the dim light, rather than grime from her filthy fingers; but it was with some difficulty that I forced myself to take it from her, and bite half of it off, and say:

'Thank you, it's very good.'

'Tha don't want to stand,' she said, gesturing to an old chair – crudely held together with thick wooden slats nailed to the legs and the back, that put me oddly in mind of a child sitting on the floor holding his knees – which was half hidden in the shadows on the other side of the hearth.

'Tha's been to th'Institute, parson says,' she said, as I pulled it out, and sat down. 'What's tha reckon to tha'?'

'I was very impressed,' I said. 'I don't know when I've heard better, even in London.'

'Oh, ay?' she said, with an odd little smile, which I could not decipher, and found slightly unsettling.

'Yes. It's a fine hall. And Whistling Albert is a phenomenon.'

She let out an almost soundless gust of derision – though whether it was directed at me, or at Whistling Albert, or at the Institute, I could not tell.

'Why,' I said. 'What do you think?'

She laughed. 'They reckon as I'm addled. And I reckon as they're a cletch o' gawbies.'

'Gawbies?'

'Don't use their yeds,' she said. 'Tha's what I mean. Think on account they don't see nowt, there b'ain't owt to see.'

Cold as I was, I suddenly felt colder. 'See what?' I said.

Perhaps she had not heard me; for she made no reply, but gazed at the fire, shaking her head sadly, and muttering 'Ay, ay' under her breath. After a few moments she picked up an ember-rake, and absently riddled the grate with it; and then, without looking at me, said:

'Hast tha bin up on t'Chevin?'

'Not yet.'

She nodded, but said no more, merely studying the flames in silence. At length I said:

'Why, what's up there?'

She laughed. 'Nowt, if tha'll credit t'Printer, and Druggist Thompson, and t'doctor man, wi' all their bangs an' flashes.'

'But *you* –' I began.

'Tha ivver 'eeard tell of t'Barguest?' she said, suddenly looking me full in the face.

'The *Barguest*?'

She nodded, and rattled the ember-rake against the cooking pot.

I was bemused for a second or two, but then all at once – miraculously, I think now – seemed to grasp her meaning.

'What?' I said. 'Is he in chains?'

She nodded. She was watching me intently now; and I knew that if my expression betrayed the slightest sign of mockery or disbelief she would clamp shut, and I should get no more from her.

'What kind of a creature is he?' I said. 'A ghost? Some poor fellow that was hanged there years ago?'

She shook her head. 'A beast,' she said, in little more than a whisper. 'I 'eeard 'im once, years sin, when the bairns was small, and we was up there bleggin'. It were a'most dark, and rawky, so's tha couldn't hardly see; and Adam, our boy, 'e were freetenin' th' lasses – tha know, "Best run, or t'Barguest'll get tha," an' sich-like – and I were tryin' to 'ush 'im, when there were this gert noise be'ind us – like a snufflin', tha'd call it, and a tiftin', and –'

'Tifting?' I said.

She pushed her tongue out, and took two or three rapid breaths, before going on: 'And 'e were roarin', and pawin'' –

here she made her hands into claws, and scraped some imaginary surface – 'and jumpin' at 'is chain, so's tha could 'eear it twangin'.'

'How near?' I asked.

'Reet there,' she said, pointing towards the door. 'No more'n ten paces.'

'And did you see him?'

She shook her head. 'We was too flayed to look. We just ran, tumblin' an' bangin' all t'way down; but there were no bones brak, thank the Lord, tho' we was tha' clarty an' moithered comin' 'ome the mester a'most died o'freet to see us.'

I nodded. A dog, presumably – perhaps an escaped mastiff; but if I said so I should indubitably offend her. She seemed to guess my thoughts, however, for she went on:

'Course, all tha doctors and druggists and ranters says t'were nowt – we fancied it, or t'were nobbut a dog, or a doddy, or a sheep, or some sich – but there were summat there, reet enough, an' I nivver 'eeard mortal beast make sich a noise, not afore or sin.'

'It must have been very frightening for you,' I murmured, thinking that a show of sympathy might be enough to reassure her that I took her story seriously, and so deter her from asking whether I actually believed it.

She appeared not to have heard me, however; for she was quiet for a moment, and suddenly laughed and said:

'One of them Methodies says, "Oh, Mrs. Swinton, I'm sure it was just a pow-cat." "A pow-cat!" I says to 'er; "no-one's ivver seed a pow-cat as could 'oller like tha', but there's plenty of fowks seed the Barguest – so which does tha' think is likelier *I* 'eeard?" 'Er says, all reasonable-like, "There b'ain't no sich thing as a Barguest, Mrs. Swinton." "What," I says, "and no boggards, neither, I suppose?" "Nay," she says – jus' like she's preachin' a sermon – "Truth is, there's too mich darkness in the world, Mrs. Swinton; and too mich

240

in our een; and tha's why we 'ave street-lights and schools, so's fowks can see wha's there, and wha' b'ain't. Has tha' 'eeard tell as anyan seed a boggard sin the gas were put in?" So –'

'A boggard', I said, 'is what? A spirit of some kind?'

She nodded. 'I says to her, "Course they won't come when there's mickle light, or mickle gabble."' She sat back in her chair and scrutinized me through shrewdly narrowed eyes, trying to decide – I supposed – whether she could trust me with some still greater confidence. I held her gaze, and consciously relaxed the muscles of my face. At length, she leant towards me again.

'Oft-times, at neet,' she said, so softly I could barely hear her, 'I see the mester, a-sittin' in tha chair as tha's in now. An' I nivver leets a cannle, then, for I knows I'd only freeten him off, an' I like the company.'

I shivered – I could not help myself – my damp clothes felt suddenly as close and clammy as a shroud, and I longed to shake them off. It was all I could do not to turn, and see if the mester was standing at my shoulder, waiting to claim his place. I forced myself to breathe normally; and resolved to change the subject.

'Mr. Hart says you grew up at Farnley,' I said, my dry tongue sticking and clicking against the roof of my mouth.

She nodded.

'Do you by any chance remember Mr. Turner, the painter?'

'Ay, I remember 'im,' she said gruffly, not meeting my eyes. She took up the poker and busied herself with the fire. I waited for her to go on.

''E knew,' she muttered at last.

'Knew what?'

'Awlus about, a' sorts o'weather, he were,' she said, as if this answered my question. 'Muckier t'better. Up t'Chevin. Out on t'moors in t'rain.' She jabbed a finger towards the shuttered window. ''E were 'ere now, tha's where tha'd find 'im.'

'I imagine he was drawing, or painting–' I began.

'Ay, tha's wha' 'e said.'

'He loved stormy effects –'

She stopped me with a vigorous shake of the head.

'Why,' I said, 'what do you think he was doing?'

''E could make it come to 'im, an' do 'is biddin',' she said.

'What?' I said. I could not conceive what she was talking about. The Barguest? The *weather*?

She was silent for a few seconds; and then she said:

'Tek 'em bellowses, and give t'cowls a bit o' puff.'

I knelt before the fire. As the first shower of sparks erupted, she gave a murmur of satisfaction, as involuntary as the purr of a cat. Then she cleared her throat; and speaking in a slow, gentle voice said:

'I knew a lass once, Mary Gallimore. More like a sister to me, she were, 'an a friend; for we lived anent each other as bairns, an' was awlus lakin' together. She were nivver quite reet – a bit gaumless, tha know, cuddy-wifted, an' couldn't climm a set o' keckers wi'out she'd get ankled up at t'top, and fall down 'em again. But t'kindest body tha's ivver met. Wouldn't 'urt neeabody or nowt, would Mary.'

She paused. I turned to look at her. She was shaking her head, and exhaling in a kind of sad noiseless whistle that was oddly affecting. She caught my eye, and continued:

'Once, I seed 'er tek th'ole mornin' tryin' to get a tom-tellalegs from out the ass-nook, for fear it'd be burned when her mother mek t'fire. Th'other bairns laughed at 'er, but she wouldn't let it bide. Tha's the way she awlus were.'

I replaced the bellows, and sat down again. Perhaps there was some impatience in my manner; for she said:

'Ay, I've no' forgot tha' Mr. Turner.'

'No, no,' I said. 'Please. What happened to her?'

'Well, owd Mr. Fawkes, 'e were a gradely man, after 'is

fashion – 'e tek a interest in 'er. 'E knows she won't nivver be like rest o' us young roisters; so he says to 'er mother: "Tha send 'er to the 'all when she's thirteen, and we'll find a place for 'er there." So tha's wha' she does; an' Mary fetches up as under-'ousemaid, tekkin' out slops an' sich-like a' t'big 'ouse.'

There was an odd stirring of dread and excitement in my stomach.

'Ay,' she said. 'Yon's where she met 'im. Back-end o' th'year, it were –'

'Which year?' I said, taking out my notebook – and silently congratulating myself for having had the foresight to wrap it in oil-cloth.

'Oh, 'eleven, I should say, or 'twelve, mayhap. November, any road; for t'last time I seed 'er we was out chumpin' for Bunfire Neet, my brother an' me, down by t'river.

The last *time! Dear God! Where is this leading?*

'I'll nivver forget – we come on 'er all sudden-like, reet anent t'bank, atween a pair o' willows. We mun've freeted 'er; for she jumped an' bloddered when she 'eeard us, and a'most fell i' t'water; and when she turn' round, she were a' spew-faced – save her een, which was red fro' cryin'. "Lor', Mary," I says, "wha'ever is t'ma'er wi' tha?"; but she can' say nowt reet off, but just shaks 'er yed. So I puts my arms round 'er; an' after a minute or two she tells me.'

She paused, and fiddled with the fire again, even though it was burning brightly now, and had no need of her attentions. For a moment I felt a flush of anger: she was deliberately tormenting me by making me wait, for no good reason other than that it pleased her to do so. And then I reflected how rare this experience must be for her – to have another person hanging on her every word, and to read in his face the dramatic effect of a story that no-one else, perhaps, had ever accounted of any interest – and realized that her enjoyment was innocent and understandable enough, and that it would be churlish to begrudge it.

'There now,' she said, sitting back. 'Well, first thing she says is, "Am I a bad lass, Doll?" "No, doy," I says, "course tha b'ain't – whyivver should tha be askin' tha'?" "I's yon Mr. Turner," she says, "as is stoppin' a' th'ouse. I goes in 'is room this mornin', an' 'e were tha" – she couldn't barely speak – "'e were tha' maungy to me." "Why?" I says, "whativver'd 'e do?" She just sniffles an' shaks 'er yed; but I coaxes her, like, and ends up she says: "'E called me names – said I were a beltikite, and a buffle-yedded greck, an' sich."'

Whatever the truth of the rest of it, I could not believe this – for if Turner had been moved to speak at all (and he was, of course, famously taciturn with strangers), he would surely not have resorted to local terms such as 'beltikite' and 'buffle-head', which must have been as unfamiliar to him as they were to me. Again, Mrs. Swinton seemed to guess what I was thinking; for she said:

'I don' reckon tha's reet – I reckon as tha were summat else, but she were tha' ashamed she couldn' bring 'ersel' to say it.'

'You mean you think he behaved improperly towards her?'

She shrugged. 'What does tha think? 'Im an' a thirteen-year-old lass, in a sleepin'-room?'

It was possible – I had only to remember the girl at Petworth to realize that. But surely it was at least equally likely that she had merely disturbed him while he was working; and that her description of the response this had provoked – an outburst of (to her) quite unaccountable anger – was accurate enough, even if she had translated the actual words Turner had used into her own dialect?

'Ahsumivver,' Mrs. Swinton went on, 'I couldn' get nowt more from 'er; so I kisses 'er, an' I says: "If tha's fashed about owt, doan' keep it to thasel', else it'll go bad on tha – what tha's to do is tell Mr. Fawkes, for 'e's a fair mester, an' a good man. Will tha promise?" An' she does; an' at-after she's a bit bruffer, an' ivven shows us a lahtle smile when we bahn.'

Her voice wavered suddenly, and her breathing became jerky, as if the need for air and the urge to sob were struggling for mastery of her. She steadied herself by bunching a corner of her apron in her hand, and continued:

'Nex' morn, I sees tha Mr. Turner, walkin' till t'Chevin in 'is long black coat, no' lookin' to left nor reet of 'im, an' goin' tha' quick tha'd think Jack Lob were after 'im. Soon after, it comes on to rain; an' then it's teemin', jus' like toneet, so thick tha can't see tha nose afooar tha; an' a' the talk's o' floods, an' t'farmers start movin' t'beeas fro' the cloises by t'river.' Her lips trembled, and she drew them between her teeth for a moment, and clenched her fist again.

'Tha' neet, we 'eeard as 'ow Mary were missin'; an' t'men ou' in t'storm wi' lanterns, lookin' for 'er. They foun' 'er in the mornin', no' far fro' wheear we seed 'er. All ankled up in t'weeds an' willows, she were, drownded.'

'Dear God!' I said. 'What a terrible thing.'

'They carried 'er to a byre, and set 'er i' t'fodderem. And tha Mr. Turner, so I 'eeard, went there after, and drawed 'er liggin' there.'

Yet again, I thought. *Why?*

'I'm very sorry,' I said.

She said nothing, but watched me unflinchingly, as if waiting for me to draw some obvious conclusion from the evidence she had laid before me. A fearful idea suddenly struck me.

'Surely', I said, 'you don't think he was somehow *responsible* for her death? It was clearly a tragic accident – you said yourself she was clumsy, and it's all too easy to see how such a girl . . .' My voice trailed off in face of her implacable stare.

'When I were a lass,' she said slowly, 'there were an ol' woman a' Pool as could put th'evil eye on a pig, and make t'rain come.'

'Are you . . .? You're not suggesting – that Turner could – that he would . . .?'

She smiled, and I hesitated, wondering if she were laughing at me. But it was not, I decided, that kind of smile – rather the martyred, resigned grimace of a woman who sees what others are blind to, and is accustomed to being mocked for it.

'I'm sorry,' I said – knowing that in that instant I was joining the ranks of doctors and druggists and Methodists, and feeling a spasm of guilt for it – 'but I cannot believe that.'

And I couldn't. Yet as I went on to make polite small-talk for ten minutes (conscious, all the time, of her sullen coldness, and knowing that I had caused it, and that nothing I could say now would mend matters); and then at length rose and thanked her and left, and blundered back through the rain to the Black Bull, I could not get what she had told me from my thoughts.

Was it just the fact of the drowned girl, with its echoes of Hargreaves' story, and of Mrs. Booth's account of Turner's last days? Or was it the idea of Turner as a wizard, which strangely recalled Davenant's description of his behaviour on Varnishing Days:

If a savage had seen it, he'd have sworn it was magic.

I remember a young Scotch fellow watching it once, and muttering something about sorcery.

I don't know.

I must go to bed.

XXX
From the journal of Walter Hartright, 13th October, 185–

God! What a night!

I dreamed I was by a lake. It was black, and unnaturally

still, but fringed by half-submerged trees, from which I knew it had but lately flooded. As I watched, the moon came up, and I saw that there was something white stirring beneath the surface. At first I thought it was a great shoal of fish; but then I noticed that it did not move, but merely seemed to ripple in some invisible current. And then, all at once, I knew: these were bodies – hundreds, thousands of them – broken from their graves by the deluge.

In the same moment, I became aware that a man was standing next to me. He was short, and wore a long black coat and a black hat. It seems obvious, now, that he was Turner; but in my dream, although he appeared faintly familiar, I thought he was an undertaker. I sensed he was burdened with some great sadness, some terrible apprehension. At length, he let out a dreadful sigh, as if he could no longer put off the fatal moment, and began to whistle.

As though in response, a girl – so white, so dazzlingly white I could not look at her – rose from the lake; and I knew (though how, I cannot say, for no voice spoke) that she had been summoned to accuse her murderer.

I waited. I felt sick. I could not move.

She pointed at me.

As she did so, the Last Trump sounded.

I woke – I half-woke – in my room at the Black Bull. I could still hear the horn: it was coming, quite distinctly, from outside. I went to the window and peered out, but it was quite dark, and I could see nothing. I lit the lamp, and looked at my watch. It was just past five. I had slept for little more than ninety minutes.

I returned to bed and lay down; but still the horn sounded, and in my fuddled condition I could not rid myself of the idea – even as, in some part of my brain, I recognized it as ridiculous – that it was calling me. Knowing I should not sleep again, I got up after a few minutes, and dressed, and went down into the street.

I cannot account for my behaviour during the next hour, save by saying that it was as if I were simultaneously awake and asleep. My waking self knew that I was in Otley; that the storm had blown itself out overnight, leaving the cobbles wet and shiny, and tearing great rents in the clouds, through which appeared a scattering of stars; that this was the cause of the shimmering black expanse I saw before me; and that the noise I heard was made by a mortal agent, who almost certainly did not even know I existed, and was blowing his horn for some rational reason (though I could not guess what it was) that had nothing to do with me at all. And yet, at the same time, I was still in my dream; and the black expanse was the dark lake; and the horn was speaking to me alone, and drawing me, for good or ill, towards my destiny.

I could not see the pied piper; but I could hear him clearly enough, making his way through a tangle of small streets to the east. As I set off in pursuit, lights appeared in bedroom windows to either side of me, as if to confirm that I had chosen the right direction, and to show me the path ahead. After a few minutes, however, I realized that the sound of the horn was growing fainter; and when, at length, I came out in a broad thoroughfare, it had become so distant that I could no longer say with any certainty where it was coming from, or whether I must go left or right to follow it. My waking voice said: *You have lost him; go back to bed*; but to my dreaming self it seemed evident that the horn had brought me here for a purpose (for there are no accidents in the world of dreams), and I at once looked about to see if I could discover what it might be.

Before me, in the middle of the road, was a tall column like a maypole; beyond that, the louring, inescapable blackness of the Chevin. And as I looked at it – saw the knife-sharp line of its ridge; and the jumble of rocks at the top, as grim and ugly as a clot of blood – I was suddenly seized by the overwhelming conviction that I must climb it. If I could but conquer that darkness, my confusion would evaporate, and I should at last be able to see clearly.

The first mile or so – past a gasworks, and a tannery, and through an orderly little orchard, where the trees stood as still and uniform as soldiers – was easy enough; but with every pace the Chevin bulked larger and more fearful; and when at length I reached the bottom, and saw nothing but an apparently unrelieved wall of rock and scrub, I wondered if the task I had undertaken was, after all, impossible. My waking self (conscious that in a few hours I must present myself at Farnley Hall, and that I should not cut a very respectable figure if my eyes were bleary from lack of sleep, and my clothes torn and mud-stained) was all for giving up; but the hero of my dream – for whom the greatness of the obstacles to be overcome merely demonstrated the importance of the quest – would not hear of it. After a minute or two I found a narrow gap between two overgrown bushes, and saw a jagged black scar scored into the hillside above it; and concluded that this must be a path.

And so, indeed, it was, for perhaps two hundred slippery yards; but then, as the slope grew rapidly steeper, it became little more than a muddy waterfall, with last night's rain still trickling down its miry face. I hauled myself up, clutching at tufts of gorse and bramble, and feeling for rocks with my feet, until the incline eased again, and I was able to walk (arms outstretched for balance, and gingerly testing the ground with every step, in case it suddenly slid away from under me) for a hundred yards more, to the next waterfall, where I had to begin my struggle with rocks and tufts afresh.

I cannot say how long I continued in this manner, climbing and slithering, climbing and slithering; but at length the going underfoot seemed to become easier, and a cold wind started to finger my sweating face. I dimly saw, not a quarter of a mile away, the tops of three or four stunted misshapen trees jutting above the ridge; and I knew that they must be on the other side, and that I was approaching the summit. And then, without further warning, I was there, and upon the rocks.

They were larger than I had imagined, and blacker – for the dawn had just begun to lighten the sky, and they towered above me in chaotic silhouette. My first response, on seeing them this near, and realizing their size, was to wonder at the tremendous force that had placed them there; for they seemed to have been strewn along the crest as carelessly and easily as pebbles thrown by a child. But it was not this that made me pause and tremble – rather a curious, disturbed jolt of recognition. It took me but a moment to identify the cause:

What I had taken for rocks was, in fact, an enormous dragon.

I blinked, and looked again. It was unmistakable: there was its blunt head (which only a moment before I had seen as a huge crag), the mouth pulled open by the weight of the jaw, surveying the town below; behind it lay the spikes and folds and billows of the curled body.

I knew it was not a dragon; and yet I knew, in the same instant, that it was, and that I must defeat it.

I clambered to the very top, over its rough pitted skin, the bony spines of its wings, and stood there shivering. After a minute or two, the rim of the sun appeared to my right, streaking the sky with violent orange. As its first feeble rays spread along the valley, they caught the façade of a house on the other side of the river – no more than a speck of white at this distance – which I knew from its position must be Farnley Hall. A few minutes later it was gone again, lost behind a haze of vapour rising from the sodden ground. Soon the whole scene was covered in a brilliant diaphanous mist, through which blotches of brown and yellow and green appeared – pure colour, detached from any object; and I knew with absolute certainty that Turner must have stood here on such a morning as this, and taken from nature those very effects which his critics thought most unnatural.

I looked down at my feet. No scales. No wings. No talons. I was standing on rock.

I laughed with relief.

The landlord of the Black Bull made a passable job of cleaning and drying my clothes. His wife mended a tear in my sleeve.

At breakfast I asked the girl about the horn-blower.

'Oh, that's John, sir,' she said, giggling. 'Does that every mornin', when 'e knocks off t'night shift. Tell them's 'as work to go to it's time to get up.'

I was at Farnley by 11.00; but when I explained my business to the old man at the lodge he sucked his gums and shook his head. 'Tha can try, sir. But I've 'eeard as t'mester's bahn abroad today.'

It was a blow; but there was nothing to be gained by turning back now, when I had already come so far. There was always the chance that the old man was mistaken, or that, at the least, Mr. Fawkes would be able to spare me half an hour before he left; and I set off down the drive at a brisk pace.

But I had not been going five minutes before I saw, coming towards me, a black carriage and pair. *Perhaps it is only a visitor*, I told myself; but even as I did so I had to admit that the evidence of my own eyes gainsaid me, for there was something in the easy movement of the horses and the relaxed attitude of the driver that made it clear they were on home ground. The carriage slowed as it drew near; and then – when I had stepped out of the way to let it pass – halted beside me. A square-jawed man of about sixty, with wavy white hair, lowered the window and looked out.

'And you're Mr. Hartright, I'll be bound,' he said.

'Mr. Fawkes?'

He nodded. 'I had your note, sir,' he said, extending his hand. 'And should have replied, had I known where you were putting up. The damnable fact is I have to go to London today.'

'I ought to have stayed a few days longer, then, and seen you there,' I said.

He laughed, and opened the door. 'If you'd care to come with me to Arthington, we can talk on the way, and afterwards Hayes can take you back to Otley, or where you will. That, I'm afraid, is the best I can offer you.'

'That's very good of you,' I said, setting my foot on the step, and preparing to seat myself opposite him. As I entered, however, I saw the place was already taken by a thin, bilious-looking manservant, who shrank away from me as nervously as if I were a leper. He looked anxiously at Mr. Fawkes.

'Shall I sit with Hayes, sir?'

'If you'd be so good, Vicary.'

The man bolted through the door on the other side, and stood buttoning his coat and drawing on his gloves against the weather. Mr. Fawkes knocked on the glass, and held up his watch.

'If you please, Vicary.'

The man scuttled up on to the driver's seat.

'I fear I'm an uneasy traveller,' said Mr. Fawkes, as the carriage set off again with a lurch. 'I never much relish going from home, and always fancy a wheel will break, or one of the horses will cast a shoe, or we'll be set upon by brigands.' His face broke into a frank smile, making him appear the very image of the bluff good-hearted Englishman – until you saw that it did not reach his eyes, which remained guarded and full of shadow, as if life had indeed taught him to expect the worst. 'So I always leave early, and generally end by having to wait half an hour at the station, which vexes the servants dreadfully.' He laughed, and wagged a finger at me. 'But you, at least, should be satisfied, for it means we shall have longer together.'

And he was right; for, in the end, despite everything, I did not fare so badly. The circumstances of our meeting deprived me of the chance to see the pictures at Farnley, of course; but – by way of compensation – they seemed to have a strangely galvanic effect on Mr. Fawkes. Confined within the swaying carriage, and keenly sensible of the pressure of time, he told me more in fifty minutes than he would have done in as many hours surrounded by the distractions of a busy household. My only difficulty was that the constant motion, and the necessity of letting him speak without interruption (for the smallest pause might cost me a vital piece of information) made it hard for me to keep adequate notes.

So here, as well as I can remember them, are the most important parts of our conversation:

HF: I wish to God now I'd paid him more heed, Mr. Hartright; but you know what boys are. I cared precious little for art, I fear, and far too much for foolishness and pleasure – with the result that my early memories of him are mostly of the fun and frolic and shooting we enjoyed together. [A sweeping gesture of the hand, indicating the moors]

WH: Was he a keen sportsman, then?

HF: Keen, if not entirely accurate. [*Laughs*] He once contrived – Lord knows how – to bring down a cuckoo. We taunted him mercilessly for weeks afterwards, but he took it in good part. Indeed, he was often the first to allude to it, and tell the story against himself.

I don't know what others have said to you of his temper and disposition, but in our hours of relaxation together I always found him as kindly-minded a man, and as capable of every kind of fun and enjoyment, as any that I ever knew.

[*There – I was right – the official line.*]

WH: Was he well liked by the servants?

[*HF shrugs. Plainly considers it a strange question. At length:*]

HF: They may have thought him a little eccentric.

WH: Do you remember a girl called Mary Gallimore?

HF: No. Why? Did she complain of him?

WH: She said he insulted her once in his room.

HF: *Insulted?* You mean . . .?

WH: Called her a fool.

[*HF laughs.*]

HF: He hated to be walked in on when he was working.

WH: Why?

HF: There's nothing very mysterious about it. He liked to work alone, that's all. Perhaps he feared people would think him odd, for his mode of painting was, undeniably, strange.

WH: Can you describe it?

HF: I can, as it happens; for I was once lucky enough to see it. [*Wonderful! – at last!*] One morning, at breakfast, my father challenged Turner to make him a drawing that would give some idea of the size of a man-of-war. Turner chuckled, and turned to me, and said: 'Come along Hawkey, and we will see what we can do for Papa.'

And for the next three hours I sat and watched him. At first you would have supposed he was mad; for he began

254

by pouring wet paint on to the paper till it was saturated, and then he tore and scratched and scrabbled at it in a kind of frenzy – ripping the surface with his thumbnail, which he kept long for the purpose – and the whole thing was utter chaos. But then, as if by magic, the ship gradually took shape; and by luncheon time it was complete, every rope and spar and gunport perfect, and we carried it downstairs in triumph, and Turner said: 'Here we are! *A First-Rate Taking on Stores!*'

WH: He had no model to work from?

HF: None.

WH: Then how . . .?

HF: I've often asked myself that question; and the conclusion I've come to is that it was an unusual faculty of the brain. Just as some musicians can repeat a piece from memory after hearing it once, so he could retain an image. And then, of course, he refined his gift still further by constantly drawing and taking notes on everything he saw – so that when he stood before that piece of paper, all he had to do was move the colours about until they resembled the picture already printed on his mind.

WH: Not magic, then?

HF: [*Laughing*] It *seemed* magic, that's all I meant, to a young man. On another occasion – I must have been twelve or thirteen – I remember him calling me to the window to see a thunderstorm. It was rolling and sweeping and shafting its lightning out over the Chevin; and he was saying, 'Isn't it grand, Hawkey? Isn't it wonderful? Isn't it sublime?' and all the time making notes of its form and colour on the back of a letter. I suggested some better drawing-block, but he said:

'No, this does very well.' Presently, when it was finished, he said: 'There, Hawkey! In two years you will see this again, and call it *Hannibal Crossing the Alps.*'

And so I did. He had remembered it so exactly that he could reproduce every last detail.

[*Perhaps why we see the same motives again and again in his work? Once they were rooted in his mind he could not expunge them?*]

HF: My father, I believe it's fair to say, was Turner's closest friend while he lived; and after he died Turner couldn't mention his name without the tears coming into his eyes. It's for that reason, I think, that he never came back here in later years, even though he was often enough invited. As a result, I only saw him on my infrequent visits to London; but up to the very last time, about a year before his death, he was always the same to me – addressing me by my boy name, and showing me the greatest kindness, as if in doing so he could continue to express his attachment to my father, and his glowing recollections of his 'auld lang syne' here.

[*The official line again.*]

Yes, but that does not mean it is untrue.

Who is more likely to describe Turner accurately? A man who knew and loved him for fifty years; or one who glimpsed him once or twice in moments of weakness?

I have seen dragons where there are only rocks.

One more night at the Black Bull, to purify myself of my folly.

And then, tomorrow, home.

XXXI

Letter from Walter Hartright to Marian Halcombe,
22nd October, 185–

Limmeridge,
Sunday

My dear Marian,

You were right – I confess it (and when were you ever not?) – this was for the best. The quest for Turner *had* temporarily disordered my mind somewhat, and to be here with my darlings is the best cure possible. I feared they would not know me – that I should not know my*self* in the gentle light and domestic calm of Limmeridge, but would mope about the house like a spectre at the feast, carrying my darkness with me. But the darkness is gone, and the spectre with it. I am truly myself again – even Florence is happy now, and as sweet and natural with me as if I had never been away!

As for Turner: I am painfully conscious of how much time I have wasted chasing shadows – and of all that, in consequence, remains undone. (I torment myself at night sometimes, imagining what Lady Eastlake would say. *Is this all you have discovered, Mr. Hartright, in almost five months? That Turner was a strange man?*) It chastens me that I must therefore accept your offer – but accept it I do, with a grateful heart, and the certain knowledge that man never had a truer or a more generous sister. You promise to write to me regularly with your discoveries; I, for my part, swear to treat them as judiciously and dispassionately as a palaeontologist treats the bones of a dinosaur. Like his extinct titan, mine shall be resurrected on the basis of facts alone. No more unruly imagination!

Your devoted brother,
Walter

Book Two

XXXII

From the journal of Marian Halcombe,
October/November 185–

Monday
Nothing.

Tuesday
Letter from Walter. Sat down to answer it, but could not find the tone. At length overcome by such lassitude I could not keep my eyes open.

Tomorrow.

Wednesday
Another blank day. Tomorrow I *must* begin my work.

Thursday
This afternoon, at last, I found the courage to call. Or perhaps it was not courage, but merely foolishness; for I had finally persuaded myself, after a good deal of self-interrogation before the looking-glass, that I could carry off an interview without betraying either myself or Walter. Some part of me, I think, must have known all along that I was deceiving myself – it was Elizabeth Eastlake, after all, who drew from young Mrs. Ruskin the secrets of her unhappy marriage; and it was ludicrous to suppose that so penetrating a mind would have much difficulty in uncovering *my* misery; but without this pitiful little sop to my *amour propre* I should probably not have been able to force myself to go at all.

It was not long before I got my come-uppance.

'Marian!' she said, taking both my hands in hers. 'What a

great pleasure! Tell me you are here on serious business.'

'I am, as it happens.'

She gave a gratified nod. 'Stokes, I am not at home.' She touched my arm and began leading me towards the boudoir. 'I was bracing myself for Mrs. Madison, or any one of a hundred other doughty matrons.' She waved, in passing, towards the drawing-room table. 'What do you think of my *aide-conversation*?'

I turned and saw a small unframed picture of a Madonna and child lying on a folded cloth. It was badly cracked and faded, but you could still see the graceful line of the Virgin's neck and the sweet simplicity of her expression.

'Filippino Lippi,' said Lady Eastlake. 'It came back from Italy with us. I shall be sorry when it goes to the Gallery, for it's been a social godsend. The dullest woman will coo at it for minutes on end, and then embark on an animated monologue about babies.'

I felt I was expected to make an amusing riposte; but my poor tired brain stubbornly refused to produce one. Lady Eastlake affected not to notice, and busied herself with clearing a pile of papers from a chair; but as soon as we were sitting down she looked at me steadily and said:

'Are you quite well, my dear?'

'Yes, thank you,' I said – aware, as I did so, that my words had a kind of leaden sluggishness that belied their meaning. 'And you?'

'Oh, yes! – I've been very blessed. Two months of mountains and buildings and pictures, and not a single dinner or at-home to irk us. But one tires eventually of all the dirt and the corruption. So it's a second blessing to come back again, and find oneself once more in a place where things are tolerably well ordered.' She smiled; but her eyes, never straying from my face, seemed to pin me to my seat, denying me the freedom to speak.

'And what of your brother?' she went on after a moment.

'He . . . he . . .' My voice was calm enough – I had rehearsed this speech again and again, to give it just the right air of nonchalance – but I could feel my traitor cheeks starting to burn, which flustered me, and caused me to lose my way. I quickly recovered myself; but it was clear from her unwavering gaze that Lady Eastlake had not missed my confusion.

'He has had to return to Cumberland for a few weeks,' I said.

She nodded, as if she knew it already, and understood the reason without my having to say it.

'I confess I did feel some anxiety about him – about both of you – while I was away. I couldn't help wondering if, after all, it was perhaps not a kindness to have asked him to undertake this book.'

'Oh no! You mustn't think that!' I said. 'He . . . he . . . he's very happy!' It was so obviously a lie (for I could not look her in the eye, and my tongue rebelled, and made me stutter) that I thought she must challenge me; but she only said:

'Well, I am glad to hear it. But I fear it may have demanded more than either of you suspected. No man should be separated from his family for months at a time, if it can be helped – even the best of them finds it unsettling. And there is undoubtedly – I should probably have warned your brother of this more clearly, but I did not want to prejudice him – there is undoubtedly something disturbing about Turner. There are few people who could come close to the details of his life, and not be affected by them.'

She paused. I wanted to deny it, but it would have been as unavailing as trying to halt an advancing army by throwing sticks.

'Has that been your brother's experience?' she said.

'Perhaps. A little.'

She nodded again. 'Whom has he spoken to so far?'

I told her. She was silent for a while; and then, as it became clear that I had finished, a faint look of puzzlement crossed her face.

'No-one else?'

'Not so far as I know.'

Should I say more? Should I tell her the truth: that I could not be certain, because I had still not dared to ask Walter what he had done, or whom he had seen, on the evening of our visit to Sandycombe Lodge? I had hoped (or half-hoped and half-dreaded) that he might volunteer it; but since he had not done so, I would not force him into a position where he must either lie to me, or else tell me something he would sooner I did not know.

'And what of you, Marian?' she said. Her voice was so soft and solicitous, so removed from its usual bantering tone, that I knew at once she must somehow have looked into my very soul, and seen the desolation there. And suddenly it seemed to me that further pretence was futile – I had resisted as best I could, but the citadel had fallen, and all that remained was to surrender, and confess the secrets she had already guessed. Surely, indeed, it would be a blessed relief to do so – to share the burden of my wretchedness with another human being, and not merely with an insensible book?

I formed the words – I opened my lips – I closed them again. I could not speak without condemning Walter, as well as myself; and that I had no right to do. Or so, at least, I told myself then; but now, as I write, it seems to me that my dominant feeling at the time was *fear* – fear, I suppose, that I should become an object of pity. Dear God! how tenacious is pride, and what forms it takes to deceive us!

'It is easier for me,' I said. 'I am only his amanuensis. I merely have to gather facts for him, without reflecting on their significance. He –'

'Oh, what nonsense!' she said, laughing. 'I don't believe it for a moment!'

'No – indeed – that is why I am here,' I said (and was surprised to hear the animation suddenly returning to my own voice). 'Inevitably, most of Walter's informants remember Turner from his middle and later years. He now has the difficult task of reviewing everything they told him, and forming it into a coherent picture. I, meanwhile, am to stay in London, and learn what I can of Turner's early life and career.'

Her eyes narrowed disconcertingly. 'Personally, I should have thought *that* would have been *harder*.'

'Only in a practical sense,' I said. 'Everyone who knew Turner then is presumably dead. All I am looking for is any scraps of evidence – memoirs, letters, private papers – that may have survived, and could yield a useful insight or detail. The only art will be in knowing where to search, and getting permission to examine them. The actual business of reading them, and noting down anything of interest – that's something any competent clerk could do.'

She was not convinced. She stared at me steadily, her lips set in a kind of sceptical half-smile that seemed to say: *Very good. Now tell me the truth.* I held her gaze, however, and at length she relented.

'I am not the person to help you, then,' she said, ringing the bell. 'You should talk to my husband. He knew Turner and his circle, socially *and* professionally, for more than forty years.'

I could not help wondering why, in that case, she had not introduced us to him before; but the next moment she gave me the answer.

'I hate to trouble him, when he is so heavy-laden.' She shook her head. 'So many responsibilities – and they seem to grow more every day. He was at the palace this morning – dines with Lansdowne tonight – and tomorrow, I believe, goes to the House of Lords.' She suddenly seemed to lose her accustomed self-confidence, and turned to me with an almost pleading expression. 'He is not a young man, Marian, and I confess I fear dreadfully for his health. But what can I do?'

I was spared the necessity of replying; for at that instant the footman arrived, and Lady Eastlake, immediately recovering the habit of command, said:

'Ah, Stokes. Would you ask Sir Charles if he can spare the time to join us for a few minutes?' She was silent and thoughtful for a moment after he left; then – hoping, I fancy, that by convincing me she would convince herself – she said:

'But perhaps it will do him good, don't you think? To lay down the burdens of office for a moment?'

And certainly, from the alacrity with which Sir Charles appeared, and the affability of his manner as he greeted us, and shook my hand, you would suppose that she was right – or, at least, that *he* thought so, for he managed to convey the impression that he had but been waiting for our invitation to release him from the drudgery of duty, as a prisoner may wait for the precious few minutes in the day when he is allowed outside and can feel the sun on his face. At first I assumed that Elizabeth Eastlake – with that superior understanding that sometimes seems to exist between husband and wife – had simply judged the right moment to interrupt him; but I soon came to see that the explanation lay not in her character, but in his. He is, I think, one of the most charming men (in a quiet, melancholy, English way) that I have ever met. Not, certainly, the most handsome – his eyes are too deep-set, and his mouth too wide, for that; and yet his whole face seems to glow with such intelligence and sympathy and gentle humour as to make mere physical perfection seem shallow and commonplace next to it. It is easy to see why he has risen to such eminence, and is so much in demand; for when you are in his presence he contrives to make you feel – be you the Prince Consort, or a Royal Academician, or merely his wife's spinster *protégée* – that at that moment he would sooner be with *you* than with

266

anyone else on earth.

'We are depending on you, my dear,' said his wife, as he seated himself opposite me, 'to help us save Turner.'

'Indeed?' he said softly, looking at me with an amused smile.

'At the moment, as you know, he is languishing in the clutches of the wretched Thornbury.'

'Poor Thornbury,' said Sir Charles, in an undertone.

His wife did not appear to hear him. 'Miss Halcombe's brother', she went on, 'has valiantly undertaken to rescue him, by writing a biography of his own.'

'Ah.' He still smiled; but – seasoned diplomat though he is – could not conceal a twitch of surprise.

Heavens! I thought. *Has she not told him even that?*

To my astonishment, Lady Eastlake suddenly blushed and started to laugh softly, like a naughty child guiltily acknowledging her misdemeanour. Sir Charles caught her eye, and gave a rueful little laugh in reply – though what the cause might have been, I could not possibly imagine.

'It must, I am sure, be difficult for him,' he murmured, turning back to me. 'I feel for any man who takes on Turner's *Life*. Even Thornbury.'

'Sir Charles is too tender-hearted,' said Lady Eastlake. 'He'd plead for the life of a rat. Thornbury is a scoundrel – and a scarcely competent one, at that. He deserves to be publicly flogged and transported.'

Sir Charles smiled and shook his head.

'A criminal colony would be just the place for an author of his sort,' said Lady Eastlake. 'With so much sensational material to hand, he'd barely have to trouble his powers of invention at all.'

'Turner is not an easy subject,' Sir Charles remonstrated good-humouredly. 'I know nothing of your brother, I'm sorry to say, Miss Halcombe, save what Elizabeth tells me' – oh, dear! poor Walter would be mortified! – 'but I'm sure he is admirably qualified. Does not he, nonetheless, occasionally find himself confounded by all the mysteries and contradictions?'

I recalled Walter's strange journey over the past few months – the moments of elation and despair, of boyish enthusiasm and silent incomprehension; and, anxious though I was that they should think well of him, and retain confidence in his abilities, I could only reply:

'Yes.'

'I sometimes think,' said Sir Charles, 'that Turner left a deliberate legacy of confusion.'

'That is, you must admit, a partial view,' said Lady Eastlake. There was a hard edge to her voice that surprised me – and perhaps it surprised her too, for she leant impulsively towards him and said more gently: 'Though, of course, entirely understandable in the circumstances.'

What circumstances? I hoped Sir Charles, realizing that I could not very well ask, might take pity on me, and explain; but he merely smiled wearily and shook his head.

'He always loved riddles and enigmas, my dear,' he said. 'Think of his pictures. They're full of puns and arcane references.'

'*What You Will*,' said Lady Eastlake, dryly.

Sir Charles nodded and laughed. (It is only now, as I write this, that I see why. How slow and blind I have been!) 'Are you familiar with the painting, Miss Halcombe?'

'I don't think so.'

'It's a scene from *Twelfth Night*. Sir Toby Belch – Sir Andrew Aguecheek – Olivia and her attendants – trickery and concealment in the garden. The play had recently been illustrated by Stothard –'

'She won't know Stothard, my dear,' said Lady Eastlake.

'No, indeed. An older member of the Academy. Known for his stone deafness. And for being an enthusiastic follower of Watteau.'

He paused, and smiled at me expectantly. Clearly there must be some significance in what he had said, but try as I might I could not find it. At length Lady Eastlake came to my aid by prompting me:

'What is the alternative title of *Twelfth Night*?'

'*What You Will.*'

She nodded at me encouragingly.

'*Watteau?*' I said, utterly bemused. '*Watteau You Will?*'

They both laughed.

'The whole picture,' said Sir Charles, 'is a humorous allusion to Stothard. And, at the same time, Turner's own oblique act of homage to Stothard's master.'

I felt – as one sometimes does in dreams – as if, without warning, I had been led into a world governed by a different system of logic: a world of odd, tantalizing blind alleys and half-echoes, where a piece of string may have three ends, and none of them can ever be securely tied together. It was, undeniably, startling and disconcerting; yet exhilarating, too, for all at once it seemed to offer a possible key to understanding (if only in the most topsy-turvy way) some of the pictures and *motives* that had so baffled me since I had seen them at Marlborough House. Perhaps, indeed – it struck me – Sir Charles might even be able to explain *The Bay of Baiae*, and why it was so troubling. A month ago I should have asked him directly, without a second thought; but now I found I had not the courage to do so. Was he not, after all (I argued to myself) both Director of the National Gallery and President of the Royal Academy; and would I not be putting myself at an even greater disadvantage with him, and risking the good opinion of his wife – who had done me the honour of treating me as a friend, and as an intellectual equal – if they saw the depth of my ignorance and perplexity? There is nothing like losing your own self-respect to make you fear forfeiting the regard of others!

'Many artists do much the same, if not quite so convolutedly,' said Lady Eastlake. 'Rembrandt. Titian.'

'But it wasn't just his art,' said Sir Charles. 'You could see the same tendencies at work in his life. When he dined with us, during his last years, did he not go to extraordinary lengths to keep from us where he was living?'

'That is scarcely surprising,' said Lady Eastlake, 'when his circumstances there were so unrelievedly squalid.'

Sir Charles shook his head. 'He was always the same. Ask him at the outset of a tour where he intended to go, and like as not you'd get an evasive answer, or a downright lie.' He suddenly smiled, and laid a hand on his wife's arm. 'You won't remember this – you were still astonishing the burghers of Norwich – but in 'twenty-five or 'six he went to the continent, and while he was away there was a terrible powder explosion near Ostend. His poor father was convinced Turner must have been killed, for he'd said that was where he was going. There was even a report to that effect – in, as I recall, the *Hull Advertiser*, for some impenetrable reason. But when Turner came back, it turned out he'd gone another way altogether.'

Lady Eastlake laughed. 'You may ascribe that', she said, 'to mere perversity of character.'

A wild, barely conceivable notion, composed as much of images – the fish-jaw rocks of *Ulysses Deriding Polyphemus*, the rock-dragon of *The Goddess of Discord* – started to form in my head. I thought it would drift away before I could grasp it; but at that moment Stokes entered with the tea tray, giving me a moment to reflect. As he withdrew, and Lady Eastlake began to pour, I was startled to hear myself say:

'No – I think I see – his *life* was a kind of pun. Isn't that what you mean, Sir Charles?'

He nodded, but it was no more than a gesture of courtesy – he clearly had no idea what I was talking about. And, indeed, I had little enough myself as I went on:

'The essence of a pun, surely, is that one word, one sound,

has two meanings – or more than two?'

'In that case, Turner's life was the very reverse of it,' said Lady Eastlake, laughing. 'One meaning and two words: Turner and Booth.'

'No, but . . . no, but . . .' I began, feeling my cheeks burning again, and inwardly cursing myself for having spoken.

'No, I think that's a very interesting point, Miss Halcombe,' said Sir Charles gently. 'All those contradictions contained with the same being. It *is* like a kind of pun. Would you care for some tea?'

'Thank you.'

I silently God-blessed him for his gallantry in rescuing me; but I couldn't help feeling disappointed (and not a little humiliated) that I had been so obviously in *need* of rescue. Had my observation really been so nonsensical? For all that I was embarrassed, I did not think so – and I still do not think so now, looking back.

'*Perverse*', said Sir Charles, turning to his wife, 'seems altogether too small a term for Turner. There have been times, recently, when I've found myself remembering that his mother was mad.'

Perhaps she was moved by the weariness in his face, and the sad sincerity of his voice; for instead of laughing, and saying he exaggerated (as I expected), she only looked at him in silence, her eyes wide and solemn – and lustrous, it seemed to me, with tears.

'Is it not mad, Miss Halcombe, to leave your entire fortune to charity, and your pictures to the nation – and yet to begrudge paying a few pounds to a competent lawyer to draw up your will, so that it ends up in Chancery?'

'No,' said Lady Eastlake, before I could speak. 'It is merely a poor kind of joke. Not hugely amusing, I grant you – and even less so, I know, when you're caught in the unenviable position of trying to interpret his wishes to a literal-minded judge. But a joke, nonetheless.'

Her husband made to speak, but – clearly determined to take charge of the conversation – she went on:

'I am very conscious, my dear, that we are keeping you from your work. Miss Halcombe needs to know where she may find information about Turner's early career.'

Was I imagining it, or had the talk of madness – indeed, our whole discussion about Turner's character – made her uneasy? It was, surely, exactly the kind of subject that would normally have engaged her interest, and spurred her to heights of brilliant speculation; and yet she had shied away from it as fearfully as one of those dull, unintellectual women she loves to mock.

'Well, *I* first met him', said Sir Charles, 'when I was still little more than a boy, but for many years afterwards I lived in Rome, and saw him only infrequently. We did spend a few months together in 'twenty-eight and 'nine, when he was visiting Italy – he shared my studio, and subsequently put on an exhibition of his works at the Quattro Fontane.' He laughed. 'The foreign artists, and the critics, had never seen anything like them – not just the yellowness of the pictures themselves, but how they were shown; for to save the cost of framing he nailed a length of rope round each one, and painted it ochre.'

'Turner was already past fifty by then,' said Lady Eastlake. 'Scarcely *early*.'

I thought perhaps Sir Charles had taken offence; for he did not reply at once, but stared at his long pale hands, as if he were trying to imagine how to paint them. At length, however, he looked up at his wife and said:

'What became of Haste's family?'

'Haste?'

'He kept a journal, I believe.'

'Not one, I'm sure, that gives a very flattering portrait of the art world.'

Sir Charles shrugged. 'Well, as to that, my dear, I think we

272

must trust Miss Halcombe and her brother to form their own judgement. At all events, nothing else occurs to me at the moment. They're all dead – Farington, Girtin, West – all of them.' His voice trailed off, and he shook his head, as if the completeness of death's victory had ground him into despairing silence.

'And how might I find Mr. Haste's relatives?' I said quickly – for Lady Eastlake's face was set into a petulant frown, from which I could only assume she still disapproved, and might yet try to deter me.

'Well . . . well . . . Wasn't his poor son –?' muttered Sir Charles, half to himself.

'Poor!' snorted his wife.

As if to forestall an argument, Sir Charles suddenly got up. 'I shall make enquiries, and let you know.' He bowed to me, extended a languid hand to his wife, who reached out and touched the ends of his fingers; and then, murmuring how delightful it had been to meet me at last, left to return to his work.

And that is how we left matters.

After I came home I had another thought of my own. It was prompted, trivially enough, by no more than a flickering gas-jet in the hall, which sent grotesque shadows over the print of *London from Greenwich Park*, so putting me in mind of the original in Marlborough House, and then – by a natural progression – of my conversation there with Lady Meesden. She, surely, I thought, would be able to tell me more of Turner's early years; and I sat down there and then and wrote to her daughter, explaining my situation, and asking if I might call.

There. Two strings to my bow. Perhaps I shall not fare badly as a detective after all.

Friday
No post this morning.

After luncheon sat down and tried again to write to Walter. Still could not do it. I feel like a river which suddenly finds itself barred by a dam, and, no matter how hard it batters and rages, cannot break through. Perhaps I will do better when I have something definite to report.

At least, though, I have begun to feel calmer. It is a small, quiet blessing – but a blessing nonetheless – to know that I may walk easily about the house, without the dread of coming upon him unexpectedly, and feeling that awful jolt against my breast, and trying to force my thick dry tongue into making some light remark. Indeed, if I am honest, it is a relief to know that I shall come upon no-one else at all. Perhaps. (Strange that I should catch myself writing that! Are the Davidsons 'no-one'? No – they are good kind people, and as sincerely fond of me, I believe, as I am of them; yet the invisible barrier that separates their world from mine is too strong to be breached. Whatever their private thoughts, they would never say or do anything that put me at risk of revealing my true emotions, or demand anything more from me than my instructions for dinner.) Perhaps the solitary life – if that is to be my fate – may have something to commend it after all.

Tonight a letter from Sir Charles, who, as good as his word, has found where Haste's son lives (not far from Turner's birthplace in Covent Garden, it seems) and written to him to say he may expect to hear from me. Before I go to bed I shall write to him myself.

Saturday
There are many doors closed to a woman that a man may pass through freely. That, as I recall, was how Lady Eastlake explained her reluctance to undertake this work herself; and

274

if I have discovered nothing else today, I have learnt that on that score, at least, she was right. Walter could have accomplished what I did in half the time and with a quarter of the effort. I only hope that in the event the prize turns out to be worth the trouble of getting it.

Cawley Street is a narrow little street to the east of St. Martin's Place, which – from the rigid regularity of the houses – looks as if it was intended to run in a straight line, but then had to be bent in order to fit the available space. The tall windows and delicate fanlights give the impression that it might once have been a fashionable address; but now the poverty is palpable. You can see it in the battered paintwork and rusting railings and dull windows – many of which, I noticed (either to keep the warmth in, or the prying gaze of passers-by out), were shuttered even in the early afternoon.

There was no bell at number 8, and the knocker was so arthritic I could barely lift it, with the result that, for all the noise I was able to make, I might as well have stood there clearing my throat. A young man in the street – from his peaked cap and neat brass-buttoned coat I took him for a railway guard – saw my predicament and stopped.

'May I be of assistance, miss?'

'Thank you.'

It was a struggle, even for him; but at last he managed to deliver two resounding knocks which shook the frail door. The echo from inside was so loud and vibrant that I assumed for a moment Sir Charles must have been mistaken, and the house was unoccupied; but then we heard distant footsteps descending an uncarpeted staircase.

My saviour took this as his signal to withdraw. I was on the point of offering him money, but the suave efficiency of his manner somehow conveyed the idea that he regarded helping me as no more than an extension of his official duty; and – remembering the prohibition on giving gratuities to railway staff – I thought I might offend him. Searching his

275

face, I convinced myself that I was right, for what I saw there was not hope or disappointment but merely professional satisfaction at a job well done; but at that moment the door opened behind me, and his expression promptly changed to one of outright incredulity.

I turned, and saw a man of about fifty standing in the doorway. There was, unquestionably, something unusual and unsettling in his appearance. He was not above average height, but his body had a kind of thickset fleshiness that in other men might have suggested lethargy but which gave him an air of animal strength and menace – an impression accentuated by his moth-eaten black coat, which was far too tight and looked as if it was about to give up the long battle to contain him by bursting apart at the seams. His head was almost entirely bald, save for a close-cropped patch of silver bristles above each ear, and the veins on his throat and brow stood out so fiercely that you could see them throb. *Blood*, indeed, was the first thought that struck you when you looked at him – he seemed as full of it as a sated leech, and you could not help supposing that the smallest nick in his stretched skin might bring forth an unstoppable red torrent.

'Mr. Haste?' I said.

He did not reply, but merely scowled at me.

'I am Marian Halcombe. Did you receive my letter?'

His look went past me. 'Who's that?' His voice was loud and querulous and unexpectedly high.

I turned back. The young man was still waiting in the street – not, I am sure, for money, but only to see if I needed further help. And, indeed, I was far from confident that I didn't; but I could not very well enter the house with a railway guard in attendance, so I nodded and said:

'Thank you again.'

The young man hesitated a moment; then, raising his fingers to his cap, he said, 'Very good, miss,' and went on his way.

Haste still said nothing. He gazed at me with narrow, appraising eyes, tugging distractedly at a handkerchief clutched tightly across the knuckles of his left hand. Then, without a word, he abruptly stood aside and held the door for me.

I walked past him into a narrow hall in which there appeared to be no furniture at all. He closed the door behind me and started upstairs, the sole of one of his shoes – which had split from the upper – flapping noisily on the wooden steps.

'This house isn't fit for a lady,' he said, as we reached the landing, looking over his shoulder at me. 'It isn't fit for a gentleman, either. It isn't fit for a dog.'

He gestured roughly towards a room overlooking the street. For an instant I thought he meant me to enter; but then I realized that he had shown me merely to prove his point, for it was completely bare, and he was already on his way to the next floor.

I followed him with growing trepidation, for every step brought more evidence – the ghostly outline of a chest against the faded walls, a solitary hook abandoned on a picture rail – that the house was empty, and we were alone in it; and my unease turned into outright fear as we reached the very top and I saw before me a plain narrow door fastened with a staple and padlock. All at once – I could not stop it – I found myself thinking of the story of Bluebeard; and, while I did not imagine I should find the bodies of his previous wives inside, yet I could not help wondering why he had brought me here, or reflecting that if he meant to harm me I should be powerless to protect myself or to summon help. But I reasoned that it would be pointless to try to leave now: for if he intended anything untoward, he would certainly catch me before I made my escape; and if he did not I should miss my only certain chance of finding out more about Turner. And I took some courage, too, from *his* behaviour;

277

for surely if there had been any grounds for my anxiety, he would have been aware of it, and at pains to reassure me – and yet as he absently took a key from his pocket, and unlocked the door, and threw it open, he barely seemed conscious of my presence, let alone of my feelings.

We entered a long dingy room, as mean and functional as most attics, and yet not entirely devoid of comfort; for a frugal fire in the unadorned little grate took the edge off the cold, and a handsome old chair before it seemed to promise some respite from the prevailing atmosphere of drudgery and want. There were books, too, most with cracked spines and flaking gilt lettering – I quickly noted the plays of Shakespeare, and the *Aeneid*, and Wordsworth's *The Waggoner* among a hundred more whose titles had rubbed clean away – all squeezed into a miniature bookcase ingeniously constructed to fit against the low sloping ceiling.

'A man says you want to read my father's diary,' said Mr. Haste, staring at the dormer window.

'A man! You mean Sir Charles Eastlake?'

He did not reply, but took what appeared to be a broken chair-leg from a box by the hearth, laid it on the fire and knelt down to blow the embers into life. He had not invited me to sit down, so – uncertain what I should say or do – I waited by the door and looked about me. For all its sparseness and poverty, the room had a surprising air of neatness and purpose which saved it from seeming squalid. The mattress that served as a bed was covered with a clean white counterpane, and the stacks of papers on the floor and on the small table had clearly been arranged according to some method – although what it was I could not have said. The only discordant note came from a huge unframed painting set at an awkward angle across the end of the room (it was too big to fit the wall flat), which seemed to belong to a different order of reality, and was as intrusive and out of place in this pinched world as a giant entering a hovel. It showed

King Lear on the heath, hands raised, beard matted with rain, railing at the storm as a savage fork of lightning cracked the sky.

I felt Mr. Haste's gaze upon me. 'Is that your father's?' I said.

He nodded. 'All the bailiffs left me. I secured it here and stood at the top of the stairs with the poker and told them if they tried to enter they should be sorry for it. That deterred them – they were pitiful little fellows – but I dare say they'll be back.'

So that accounts for the padlock, I thought: he must always fasten it as a precaution before answering the front door. I felt a rush of relief, and an odd sense of gratitude to the picture for providing me with such a straightforward explanation, which made me suddenly absurdly determined to like it; but when I looked at it again I could not help feeling disappointed. Perhaps it was just the oddity of seeing it here, but something about it seemed not entirely right.

'It's very striking,' I said.

If he had heard the equivocation in my voice he showed no sign of it. 'My father was a genius,' he said. 'But to be a genius in England, of course, is not enough.'

'Indeed?'

He shook his head. 'If you want to get on you must learn to grovel, and fawn, and hold your tongue. Like that man.'

'What man?' I said – realizing, in the same instant, that he must mean Sir Charles. 'Why will you not say his name?'

'Come here,' he said, moving to the window. 'Do you know what that is?'

I craned my neck to see what he was pointing at; but it was at such a sharp angle I could not manage it without standing where he did. He saw my predicament, and promptly made way for me.

'Large building. Stone,' he said.

I could just make out a square grey rim above the

rooftops. 'The National Gallery?' I said.

He nodded. 'And the Royal Academy. Do you know what is behind it?'

I shook my head.

'St. Martin's workhouse. They could not say it plainer, if they carved it in stone above the door. *That is what a man of genius may expect, if he fails to ingratiate himself.* What does he want you to do?'

'I beg your pardon?'

He rounded on me suddenly. 'That man! Why did he send you here?'

I felt my temper rising. I wanted to tell him that his misgivings were misplaced – that Sir Charles had no other motive than kindness to me – but I feared I should only make him angrier. And I knew that if it came to a contest between his anger and mine I should assuredly lose, so I edged back into the middle of the room and said mildly:

'Did he not say in his letter?'

'A biography?'

I nodded. 'Of Turner.'

And I told him, as simply as I could, calculating that any hint of flattery or dishonesty would only inflame his suspicions more. And I think I was right; for, if he did not seem entirely convinced when I had finished, yet he did not immediately expostulate with me either, but lapsed into a pensive silence, pulling abstractedly at the handkerchief about his hand.

This, plainly, was not the moment to press him further; so I left him to his thoughts and looked about me again, discreetly searching for some clue that might help to explain his fury, and the sorry state in which he had been reduced to living. As I did so, my eye caught the papers on the table. They were of different sizes, and in different hands; and from the way they had been written and laid out it was evident that they formed the text of some magazine or journal, which in due course would be delivered to a printer. Several paragraphs bore headings – 'An Honest Man'; 'His Highness' Magpie' – in the manner of articles; and on the top sheet was written 'The Eyeglass', which I took to be the title of the publication, although I had never heard of it.

'Two shillings a day,' he said suddenly.

I could not imagine what he was talking about – unless perhaps it was the cost of the magazine, or the pittance he received for working on it. I turned towards him, with what I knew to be a foolish grin. He was clearly in the throes of some great inner turmoil, for his jaw worked, and he pulled so hard at the handkerchief that the skin about it turned white.

'Rent,' he said.

'Rent!'

'For the diary.'

The blood rose to my cheeks. Walter, I was certain, had never been expected to pay for information, and it had never occurred to me that I might be. Did Haste feel free to make such an insulting suggestion merely because I was a woman?

'I did not suppose this to be a commercial arrangement,' I said stiffly.

He started to tremble, though whether with fear or rage I could not tell. 'If a man inherits his father's house, no-one thinks ill of him for letting it.'

It was true – I could not deny it – and yet surely (I told myself indignantly) this was not quite the same? When I tried to identify the difference, however, I could not immediately do so, and ended by saying lamely:

'A diary is not a house.'

'It is all my father's estate,' said Mr. Haste. 'That and' – he gestured to the picture and the books – 'what you see here. The duns have taken the rest. Am I not to get some profit from it?'

He drew himself up, and thrust out his chest; but I was more sorry for him than afraid, for his eyes were dull and despairing, and he could not stop his hands from shaking. He looked, indeed, more than anything like a large frightened dog that hopes to win the day by a show of aggression, but is all prepared to run if its opponent stands firm. He must have seen the pity in my face, for his voice suddenly became more urgent and appealing.

'I have lost everything, Miss Halcombe. Even my family.'

'Your family!'

He nodded. 'My wife was not brought up to this, as I was. She tried, but she had no stomach for it; and at length was driven out, and took our girls to live with her sister in Surrey.'

'Oh, how dreadful!' I said, remembering the change that only a few weeks' separation from Walter had wrought on Laura and her children – and that without any of the distress of poverty, or any doubt that he would one day be returning to them.

'And there they must stay,' said Mr. Haste. 'Unless our fortunes mend.'

'And is there any prospect of that?' I asked, conscious, as I did so, that I was weakening my own bargaining position, but unable to harden my heart and affect complete indifference, as perhaps a man might have done.

'Not if . . . certain men have their way,' he said, with a grimace that was almost a smile, though a bleak and cheerless one. He waved towards the pile of papers on the table. 'But they shall not take my hope, as they took my father's.'

'What *is* that?' I said.

'A new venture.'

'A magazine?'

He nodded. 'They will try to silence me, as they have before. But even if they succeed, it will not be for long. I shall merely start another. And then another, if necessary. And another.'

Was this madness, or the heroic fortitude of a wronged man? I could not tell; and was so curious that – fearful though I was that it might only provoke a torrent of imagined grievances and fantastical allegations – felt I must try to discover more.

'What is the subject?' I said cautiously.

'Oh, my subject! My subject is always the same, Miss Halcombe. Folly and dishonesty and corruption.' He gave a sharp barking laugh, more like a cry of pain than of merriment. 'It is my destiny, it seems, to fight against them until I die.'

Mad he might be – and if, as seemed to be the case, he numbered Sir Charles Eastlake amongst his 'foolish' and 'corrupt' enemies, then mad he most undoubtedly was – and yet I could not but feel a certain admiration for his courage and determination in the face of adversity, as well as a natural sympathy for his unfortunate circumstances.

'Very well,' I said, smiling as graciously as I could. 'I agree to your terms.'

His face immediately relaxed, and took on a quite different demeanour, in which relief and triumph seemed equally mixed.

'Where is the diary?' I asked.

He pointed to six uneven volumes on the top shelf of the bookcase. I calculated that it would take me about a day to read rapidly through each, and to place a mark where I found anything of interest; and then perhaps another two or three to transcribe the passages I had selected for Walter. To be charitable (and also, I confess, to avoid the embarrassment of asking for change) I took a sovereign from my reticule and held it out to him.

'Here,' I said. 'I will take them for ten days.'

'*Take!*?' he said, suddenly reverting to his bullying. 'You cannot *take* them, Miss Halcombe. You must read them here.'

It was outrageous – unreasonable – out of the question;

and yet I knew I had brought it on myself by being kind to him, and so encouraging him to think he could take further advantage of me. It was time, however apprehensive and reluctant I might feel, for me to stand firm.

'No,' I said. 'Where would I work?'

'I will find you a table and chair, and put them downstairs.'

'You have scarce enough furniture for yourself,' I said. 'And what' – I started to laugh, with a confidence I did not feel – 'what if the bailiffs come?'

He shook his head, and made to protest; but before he could speak I went on:

'Besides, how shall I keep warm?'

'I'll buy coals – you must give me extra for coals,' he said; but the bluster in his voice was already being undermined by an edge of dreadful eagerness, which threatened at any moment to degenerate into outright pleading.

'Mr. Haste,' I said. 'I am not going to work in this house. I came here today in good faith, and have made what I believe is a generous offer. I'm afraid you must take it or leave it.'

'They are all I have!' he said pitifully, snatching the handkerchief from his knuckles and winding and unwinding it frenetically around his index fingers in consternation. The back of his hand, I noticed, was covered in little scabs, as if he had scraped it with a brick.

'What is it that concerns you?' I said. 'You think this is some ploy by Sir Charles to get hold of your father's diary so that he may destroy it?'

He let out an involuntary gasp, as if he had been struck, from which I deduced that I had guessed rightly.

'If that *were* Sir Charles's intention,' I went on, 'and he were prepared to act so dishonourably – which I can assure you he would not – do you really suppose he would have no better recourse than to send me?'

He could not answer, but merely stood staring at me.

'If you will trust me with them, I promise I will take good care of them; but if that is not good enough for you, then I am sorry, but I must leave empty-handed.'

He looked so desperate that I feared for a moment he would snatch the money anyway, or strike at me in a rage; but he neither moved nor spoke. Seeing the dumb misery in his eyes, I almost relented; but then I steeled myself, and – with no more than a cool 'goodbye' – turned and left the room.

Disappointment and relief – those, in about equal measure – were my dominant emotions as I began to descend the staircase, and both seemed to deepen with every step I took. But then, when I reached the last flight, I suddenly became frightened again; for above me I heard the sound of the padlock closing, and then the clatter of his footsteps following mine. What if he had decided to try to stop me? I quickened my pace, clutching my skirt in one hand and the banister in the other. I had reached the door, and was fiddling frantically with the chains and bolts, when he reached the first-floor landing and shouted:

'Wait!'

But I did not wait. I let myself into the street, slamming the door after me, and then hurried to the corner and stopped in front of a house with brightly lit windows and a cheerful sound of laughter and voices within to catch my breath.

And it was there he caught me. I had thought I was safe, and did not hear him approach. I felt his hand on my arm, and almost shrieked in terror.

But when I turned I saw I had no reason to be frightened. His shoulders were sunk in defeat, and the heat and passion had left his face, making it suddenly deathly pale. He held the diaries towards me like a supplicant.

'Here,' he said.

I gave him his sovereign, and hailed a cab.

I have not opened them yet. What if, after such an adventure, they prove worthless?

Sufficient unto the day. I shall look at them tomorrow.

Sunday

Bad news. A letter from Mrs. Kingsett: her mother is very ill. I may call when she is better, but that is not likely to be for some weeks – if, that is (I cannot help thinking, in view of her age), she gets better at all. I curse myself for being such a prig at Marlborough House, and so failing to learn more then.

Prayed for Lady Meesden's recovery in church. Of course there is an element of selfishness in my prayers. I hope I may be forgiven.

Still could not bring myself to open the diaries. They are my only hope at the moment, and if they are disappointing I shall fret and be unable to sleep for worry, which will help no-one.

Tomorrow morning. I swear it.

Monday

Missing days – missing weeks – an entire missing decade – and little enough (so far, at least) about Turner. But I am not entirely despondent. Sir Charles is right: if nothing else, I am learning something of the art world fifty and sixty and seventy years ago, which can only be helpful.

And what a world it is! So different from our own! Here is the first mention of Turner's name, on 18th April, 1793:

Dined at the Old Slaughter Chop House with Perrin, then drew at the Academy from 7 till 8. Afterwards, Perrin, Hynd and Larkin came to tea, and we ended by talking half the night. Perrin was much excited by a 'young genius', William Turner, whose work he had seen yesterday. The boy is not yet eighteen – has won the Great Silver Palette for landscape drawing – is 'the bright hope of the British school', etc. etc. I said that in that case he must prepare himself for disappointment; for in a few years, when the novelty has gone off, he will find himself neglected, and another 'young genius' sought to fill his place.

'No matter!' cries Larkin (who I think was drunk, for he and Hynd had been drinking together; though it made him maudlin and reckless, not merry) – 'in a few years we shall not want hope for a British school, or for a British anything; for history has set its seal upon us, and soon we shall have come to nothing, like Venice before us.'

'Oh, what damned nonsense!' roars Hynd, like a red-faced bull.

'The world's turned upside down, and you're blind if you don't see it!' rejoins Larkin, growing heated. 'Twenty years ago, who'd have supposed that in so short a space we should have lost America, and the French king his head!'

'As to that,' says Hynd with a grim laugh. 'There's heads nearer to home might get the same treatment, and we should be none the worse for it.'

And if Perrin had not at that moment proposed a glee, and at once begun to sing, it might have come to blows.

For my own part (God forgive me!) – only grant me success, and the world may turn, or tumble, or fall about my very ears, for all I care!

This makes me think that perhaps I was right about Turner's *The Decline of Carthage* being intended as a warning to England. He painted it much later, of course; but the impressions made on a youthful mind stamp it for life; and perhaps he never lost the fear which comes from being born into a time of desperate wars and revolutions, when the very survival of your country seems in doubt.

Nothing more of note, then (save for the trials and disa-pointments of Haste's career), till we come to 1799:

1st December. An idle day. Did not work as I should.

Met Perrin tonight at Lord Meesden's. He tells me young William Turner is elected an Associate of the Royal Academy, and has removed from Covent Garden to Harley Street, having been assured by his fellow-Academicians that it is a more respectable situation.

It is painful, as I close, to reflect on our respective ages, and on our different prospects; for Perrin says that Turner, though he is but four-and-twenty, claims he has more commissions in hand than he knows how to execute, while I, nine years his senior, and with a wife and children to support, have no com-missions at all, and must make up the rent for this very *unre-*spectable lodging by painting my landlord's cat.

God grant me strength to strive harder, that I may succeed in my great task. And keep me from the sin of Envy. Amen.

Poor Haste. As I read these words, I cannot help seeing the image of his son, and that mean little attic, and the strange overblown painting of Lear, and concluding that his petition went unanswered.

But at least he mentions Lord Meesden! That is heartening – though only, of course, if Lady Meesden lives.

Should I pray for her again? Or do we corrupt our prayers, when we want what we are asking for too much?

I must ask Mr. Palmer next Sunday.

Tomorrow I accompany Haste into the nineteenth century.

Tuesday

All morning with Haste. Sometimes I can scarcely bear to read him, so relentless is the torrent of failures and accidents and misunderstandings. And, to make it worse, as often as not they are not merely dreadful, but dreadfully *comic*, so that I find myself laughing even as I cry, and end by reproaching myself for lack of feeling.

For some reason, there is nothing at all for 1801, save a short entry for 31st December:

31st December. And what is left but once again to repent my vices, weaknesses and failings of the year past, and to pray for greater strength in the year to come?

Tonight I re-read Reynolds on Poetry and Painting. Poetry, he says, 'exerts its influence over almost all the passions', including 'one of our most prevalent dispositions, anxiety for the future'. It 'operates by raising our curiosity, engaging the mind by degrees to take an interest in the event, keeping that event suspended, and surprising at last with an unexpected catastrophe'. Painting, by contrast, 'is more confined, and has nothing that corresponds with, or perhaps is equivalent to, this power and advantage of leading the mind on till attention is totally engaged. What is done by painting must be done at one blow; curiosity has received at once all the satisfaction it can ever have . . .'

My pictures should rise to this sublime challenge – they should amaze – they should dumbfound – they should at a single unanswerable stroke attain all that a poem achieves in ten or twenty or a hundred pages.

But do they? Alas! I fear they do not. God make me worthier of the sacred cause to which you have called me.

Was not Turner, too, an admirer of Reynolds, and a lover of poetry? Might not those same thoughts have been in *his* mind?

In 1802, Turner himself reappears:

27th May. This afternoon, just when I had given up all thought of seeing him again, Sir George Beaumont called. To my shment, he acted as if there had been no uneasiness or

astonishment, he acted as if there had been no uneasiness or estrangement between us, and our relations were as cordial as ever. On entering my painting-room he stood a long while before Lear; and my heart beat so wildly as I awaited his judgement that, had he asked me a question, I doubt if I could have answered it. At length, however, he made no comment at all, but merely asked whether I had seen the present exhibition at the Royal Academy.

Scarce able to speak – for I was starting to wonder if he might have gone mad – I said I had not; and then, pointedly, asked if he would care to give me his opinion of *that*. He plainly did not understand me; for, in the politest manner possible, he said: 'Indeed, Haste. There are some fine things there; but I don't like what I see of young Turner and his imitators. They lack *finish*.' (Was I to be denied a certain grim satisfaction at hearing this?)

And then, without a word about my work, he left, leaving me too dumbfounded to call after him.

And two years later, in 1804:

19th April. Sir George called with Perrin, who is full of Turner and all his works, having but yesterday been to the opening of Turner's private gallery. He was as excited as a child who has just seen the king. 'It is seventy feet long, Haste – and twenty wide – and stands behind his house in Harley Street, and its neighbour in Queen Anne Street' – and more in the same vein, as if a catalogue of architectural facts were the most interesting topic in the world. At length, to my relief, Sir George stopped him by saying: 'That's all very well, Perrin; but he should not shew so many pictures together. And his skies are too strong, and do not correspond with the other parts.'

'What, then,' says Perrin, aghast. 'Do you not think he has merit?'

'He has merit,' said Sir George, 'but it is of the wrong sort. There is a perversity about him – he is too rough and unnatural, and neglects the example of the immortal masters, merely for effect. The danger of it is that he may lead others into the same errors, for there's no denying his seducing skill; and that's why all men of taste and sense should oppose him.'

There were red spots on Perrin's cheeks, and I could see he wanted to take issue with him; but he held his tongue – fearful, no doubt, of losing his own commission. But I was emboldened by Sir George's words to screw my courage to the sticking-place and ask him, at last, straight out about my Lear – for here was a work built solidly on those very everlasting principles he had just so warmly praised, and – though he had not yet offered an opinion – yet surely he would not have spoken so if he had not meant to approve it?

He seemed surprised, at first, that I should even mention the matter; but then he stood and gazed at it for a minute or more. At length he said: 'It is too big, Haste.'

Too big! – I could scarce believe my ears! I should have been as politic as Perrin, and said nothing; but my indignation was roused, and the words fairly forced themselves from my lips: 'If you will recall, Sir George, it was *you* who considered my original plan too small, and asked me to paint it the size of life!' To which he made no direct response at all, but merely said: 'I should not have the space for it,' and left.

A moment later Perrin put his head back in at the door and said laughing: 'You must build a gallery to accommodate it.' And then he was gone again before I could reply.

Was ever an artist more abused? My rage and despair were so terrible I wanted to dash my own brains out, or take a knife to the picture and cut it to ribbons, but my poor Alice heard the commotion, and restrained me.

She is an angel in my distress. God bless her, and reward my exertions in spite of all!

Twenty-three months, and still he had not finished his Lear! However many years must it have taken him? Seldom can a man have laboured so long to so little effect. Or rather, not *little* – for if it is the picture I saw in the attic, no-one could complain it was too small – but rather *unsatisfying*. The style is too bombastic – the figures disproportioned – the whole somehow less than the sum of its parts. I do not agree with Sir George Beaumont about Turner, but I can fully understand his reluctance to applaud *Lear*.

But *why* do I not agree with him about Turner? Is it merely our natural inclination to venerate the past? For Beaumont, the ideal was the style of the Old Masters (who doubtless, in their turn, were reviled for flouting the accepted conventions of *their* time), and anything that diverged from it was seen as 'error'; while for me, Turner himself is already hallowed by age, and his works seem to glow with a natural beauty entirely lacking in the sickly confections of the present.

It cannot be wholly that (for otherwise, of course, I should equally admire the *Lear*); and yet it is undeniably true that I find an enchantment in Haste's world – a world of Regency bustle and elegance, in which Islington was still a village, and beaux still paraded at Vauxhall – which has not been entirely banished by the knowledge that it was vicious and depraved, and the evidence in Haste's own journal that it was as full of suffering as our own. Why are we so perverse?

Wednesday

Almost ten barren years – barren both for me and for Haste, for there is no reference to Turner, and nothing (save the birth of his son) but debt and failure for him – but at last, in 1813, I find this:

15th February. Turning into Queen Anne Street met Calcott, who had evidently just emerged from the first house. A plate by the door read: 'Benjamin Young, dentist', so I rallied him, saying: '

What! Have you broken your tooth then on Sir George's leg?'

He gave a smile that barely deserved the name and said: '
That is nearer the mark than you know. No, I am just come
from Turner's.' And he pointed to a door next to the first, which
I had supposed led to the dentist's mews. 'That is the entrance
to his gallery.'

'I thought it was by the house in Harley Street.'

'He has moved round the corner here, and taken the next
house along; and had this door made through the dentist's, so
that people may reach the gallery more easily. Which is a matter
of material concern for him at present; for if he is to find pur-
chasers for his work, it is here he must find them.'

I asked him why; and he replied: 'Why, because of Sir
George Beaumont. He's so implacably furious with us – with
Turner, for leading us all astray, and with me, for being led –
that he's trying to stop people buying our work. Result: neither
of us has sold anything at the Academy exhibition for some time
now. Last year, he cut me dead at the private view, and deterred
Lord Brownlow from taking one of my landscapes. And even
Turner, for all his reputation, had difficulty securing a good
position for his *Hannibal Crossing the Alps*.'

'That', I said, 'is nothing to do with Sir George. It's to do with
the Hanging Committee's being a spiteful little cabal, riven with
petty jealousies and intrigues.'

Calcott did not respond – they never do, but merely sulk, for
the thought that anything might be the fault of the Academy
itself, and not of the patrons and connoisseurs, wounds their
pride. He shrugged, and said stiffly: 'At all events, I am resolved
to send nothing in this year, and Turner is minded to do the
same.' And off he went, in a pet.

Perhaps I should not have spoken so; but I cannot, even now,
see a great injustice and not cry out. For what is the proper
object of an institution such as the Royal Academy, if not to seek
out talent, wherever it is to be found, and to encourage it for the

glory of art, and the renown of the country? And what does it do
instead? It acts as a closed club, whose sole purpose is to pro

mote its own members (when they are not too occupied with fighting each other) – by, for example, appointing one of their number to the position of Professor of Perspective, and then not requiring him to carry out his duties. So are men of genius excluded, and compelled to starve, while their inferiors occupy the places that should by right be theirs.

Reading that last paragraph, I was struck by how different in tone it seemed from what had gone before, as if Haste had suddenly decided to stop writing his journal and embark on a tract instead. It was little surprise to find, therefore, when I reached the entry for 11th November that year: 'Today began my satire on the Academy'; and, three months later, 'Today my satire is published. God help it to find its mark.'

He wrote under an assumed name, a rare piece of discretion for Haste, announcing his aim as 'the wholesale reform of this corrupt body'. I hope he did not suffer by it; but I know him well enough now to fear that he did.

Thursday

A letter from Mrs. Kingsett. Her mother died three days ago. A great blow for her, and – I confess it – a dreadful disappointment for me. My head is full of names that I found in Haste – Calcott, Beaumont, Perrin – and as I read I tantalized myself with the prospect of talking to someone who could speak of them from first-hand experience. And that is quite apart, of course, from what she might have told me of Turner himself.

But I must not waste pity on myself, when there are others so much more deserving of it. Mrs. Kingsett herself sets me a fine example, for even in her grief (I am touched to find) she thinks of me, and my far smaller loss, saying that I may call next week, and look at Lady Meesden's letters and papers before they are dispersed or destroyed. I shall go, and be grateful.

All afternoon and evening with Haste. I have now reached 1827. Nothing more of Turner – nothing at all, in fact, save almost unremitting misery, made only worse by the occasional snippet of praise or promise of a commission, which raises him up just enough to ensure that the inevitable disappointment, when it comes, plunges him into yet deeper despair. He is, of course, discovered as the author of the attack on the Academy, and finds that he has contrived to alienate himself, at a stroke, from almost everybody who could help to further his career. More and more, as the years go by, and one grandiose scheme after another comes to nothing, he sees 'the great Cabal', and his own fearless honesty in denouncing it, as the cause of all his troubles.

But two small points of interest, which perhaps go some way to explaining his son's strange behaviour. On 15th May, 1814, he records:

A young artist named Eastlake called. He is still little more than a boy, but has more sense and judgement than many twice his age. He is but lately back from Paris, and as he stood before my *Caesar*, I could see what thought was passing through his mind: 'At last! – an *English* history painting worthy to hang next to those of Italy and France!'

And on 1st June, 1828:

Dear God! how corruptible are even the seemingly noblest spirits! Eastlake called to 'pay his respects' – so he said – before returning to Italy. His true purpose became apparent when I asked him to commit himself to my cause; for while conceding that the Academy 'is far from perfect', he urged me to desist from publicly attacking it, on the grounds that 'there is nothing to be gained from needlessly offending people'. 'What!' I cried. 'Is the sacred name of Art then nothing! – and the war that must be fought to protect her "needless"!?'

When he saw he would not persuade me, he soon left, with
out even remarking on my *Pilate*. It would not do to concede the
power of *my* work, when you are a newly elected Associate of
the Royal Academy, and hope to become a member.

Oh, dear.

Friday

It is just past eight at night, and I have this minute closed
Haste's last volume. I knew I should find no more of Turner,
for during his last years Haste had time and energy for nothing but the ever-growing inventory of his own sufferings –
his imprisonment for debt; his desperate pleas for help; his
rejections and increasingly public humiliations. I feel as if I
have been sitting by a sick-bed, these last few days, helplessly watching the decline of some dear but troublesome
friend, and that death has taken him at last.

He has gone, but the two last entries, in 1837, haunt me
yet:

11th January. Called Arthur to me, and made him promise that,
whatever may become of me, he will continue to fight for what
is right, and to secure for my name that justice which, after forty
years' ceaseless struggle, is its due. He was like a boy again,
weeping, and begging me to remember him and his mother, and
for their sakes to do nothing rash. At eleven he left, swearing to
return in the morning, bringing, if he could, some hope or
promise of relief.

God bless me through the troubles of this night.

12th January. I am resolved at last. My hand has been stayed by
thoughts of my poor family – but now I am persuaded that
when the initial pang is gone they will live easier without this
great burden that has so oppressed them.

God forgive me. Amen.

I do not like to think of what happened next, but cannot put it from my mind.

Saturday

I feared I should have nightmares about poor Haste, but – as so often happens – my sleeping mind took me by surprise; for in the event the only incident from his diary that found its way into my dreams was something I had considered entirely trivial, and already almost forgotten.

I was in a street, and saw two doors before me. One was the entrance to a dentist's; the other, though it was unmarked, I knew led to Turner's gallery. As I hesitated, wondering whether I should enter, the door opened of its own volition, and I went inside. I was not frightened – only mildly irritated that Turner had somehow contrived to admit me while remaining invisible.

The hall was dark, and completely bare. When I reached the end, I expected to find a door into the gallery before me; but instead there were only stairs down into an unlit basement. Again, I felt no fear as I descended; but I was vexed by the growing conviction that Turner was there, but would not let me see him.

At the bottom was a crude stone arch, and beyond it a kind of cave or grotto cut into the bare rock. It was suffused from above with a dim white light, which made the specks of mica in the granite glitter like a constellation in the night sky, and gave it an eerie, seductive beauty. It seemed no bigger than a cellar, but I soon realized that was deceptive; for when I reached what I took to be the end wall I found there was a small opening to the left, through which the cave continued. As I stooped to enter it, the figure of a man started from the shadows, as flittery and imprecise as a bat, and as quickly disappeared again, like a startled animal scuttling for shelter. I had barely seen him, but I somehow knew who it was: not Turner, but Walter. And my annoyance turned to outright anger: he had come here before me, and kept it a secret from me.

At length – after how many twists and turns I cannot say, and with the passage growing narrower and darker with every step – I saw a hazy yellow light before me, and a moment later found myself in an octagonal chamber. On each of the eight sides there hung a picture, but although they blazed with the familiar Turnerish golds and oranges and reds, I recognized none of them. Until, that is, I came to the seventh; for it was *The Bay of Baiae*.

At last! I thought. *I shall understand!* I stood close and studied it carefully. It was just as I remembered it. There were the sea and the sweet-smelling hills and the great tree; there the serpent and the rabbit and the skull-like ruins. And there the figures of –

I stopped suddenly; for while the figure of Apollo *was* undoubtedly there, the Sibyl was nowhere to be seen.

I awoke, angrier than ever, unable to shake off the disagreeable sensation that Turner and Walter were both making a fool of me, and that I was abetting them by failing to see something that was before my very eyes. It was there, like a word you know perfectly well, whose shape hovers half formed on the air, whose rhythm you can almost hear, that yet somehow eludes you. Although it was not long after four, I determined to get up, and try to discover what it was.

It was too cold to sit at the table, so I gathered my diary and notebooks and returned with them to bed. I started by thinking about the picture, looking again at my original description of it at Marlborough House, and searching for some significance to the missing figure; but, try as I might, I could not find it. I set the question on one side, therefore, and turned my attention to Queen Anne Street.

Why had I dreamt of that? Was it just chance – or was it, as I still felt strongly, even now that I was fully awake, a clue to some riddle? In real life, of course, the gallery would have been quite different – on the ground or the first floor, and lit by windows. Was there a reason for my imagining it in the basement? Or had my mind merely somehow confused it – as is the way with dreams – with Sandycombe Lodge, and Walter's experience there? Certainly, that might explain my sense of anger and frustration: for my unease with Walter dates from that moment, when – for the first time – he appeared like a stranger, and refused to confide in me. (And, if I am quite honest, I must acknowledge that it was the day, too, when *I* first discovered feelings in myself that I could not confide to *him*.)

I found the notes I had taken during my interview with Miss Fletcher, and laid them side by side with Haste's account of his meeting with Calcott. On a first reading, I could see only one connection: the fact that – according to Miss Fletcher – Turner's father had travelled from Twickenham to Queen Anne Street every day to take care of the gallery.

Why should that matter? I could not imagine. I read through it again, and was on the point of giving up, when I noticed the dates.

Miss Fletcher says Turner moved to Sandycombe Lodge in 1813.

Haste says that in 1813 Turner had only recently moved to Queen Anne Street.

So: he moved to two houses at almost the same time.

And then it struck me – with a sudden rush, like stones dislodged from a river-bank – that this was not an isolated incident, but part of a broader pattern. For when Turner died, had he not been living in Chelsea, but maintaining Queen Anne Street as well, and trying to persuade the world that he lived *there*? And as a young man – if the disgruntled engraver Farrant was to be believed – did he not keep a house in Harley Street, and another in Norton Street, to which he repaired in secret?

Of course, there are families that have a house in town, where they come for the season, and another in the country; but Turner had no family (save for his father), and did not live in that way. For most of his life, moreover, *both* the houses he kept were in town – for Sandycombe Lodge was the only one that might truly be considered rural.

What, then, of women? Is it not customary for a man to install his mistress in her own establishment? Might that not be the explanation?

For Norton Street, perhaps. And possibly for Chelsea, although it is difficult to see Mrs. Booth, for all that she and Turner were not married, in the character of a 'mistress'. But not, certainly, for Twickenham; for there – Miss Fletcher was categorical on this point – there was no-one in the house but Turner and Old Dad. It is hard to avoid the impression that this tendency to live in two places at once was not merely a response to the particular circumstances of the moment, but sprang from some deeper impulse.

And what might that be? A desire to remain enigmatic – to prevent people from knowing precisely where you are?

Too fanciful? Think of Sir Charles's story about Turner's visit to Belgium. Would not his behaviour on that occasion fit perfectly with such an explanation?

I have no idea whether it is important, or even what it means, but I cannot deny a feeling of satisfaction that I have at last discovered *something*.

Sunday
At church this morning prayed for Haste, for his poor son, and for Lady Meesden. Nothing to sully the purity of my motives now.

Tuesday

Last night I was too tired even to think about writing my diary, so this entry must serve for yesterday. A day, I have to say, that I have no desire to relive, for it evokes in me nothing but feelings of weariness and frustration and unease – but relive it I must, else I shall forget the details.

The Kingsetts live in one of those large, thick-porticoed new stucco houses north of Hyde Park that look as if they have been made out of icing, and will melt entirely away at the first sign of rain. Outside, everything square-edged and dazzling white; inside, by contrast, all drapery and gloom, and glum-faced servants tip-toeing about so quietly you would think they feared a sudden noise might bring Lady Meesden back from the dead, and provoke some unpardonable breach of etiquette. When at length Mrs. Kingsett appeared, and spoke to me in a normal voice, it sounded indecently loud.

'I am glad to see you again, Miss Halcombe,' she said simply, as we shook hands. The skin about her eyes was grey and swollen, and her black dress made her appear deathly pale, but she managed a small smile, in which there was a glimmer of real warmth – and even, I thought (though I could not then imagine why) something akin to relief.

'This is very kind of you,' I said.

She shook her head quickly, as if even so slight an acknowledgement of her distress might threaten her composure, and touched my arm.

'I wasn't sure where to put you,' she said, starting to lead me back into the hall. 'But in the end I decided you'd be most comfortable in the library.'

But she was wrong. I knew it the instant we crossed the threshold: this was a foreign country. The atmosphere was both chilly (for although the fireplace was the size of a small Grecian temple, the pitiful little heap of coals in it would not have heated a bedroom) and stifling, with a dense pall of stale cigar smoke that hung in a marble haze before the half-curtained window, and made it almost impossible to breathe. In the centre of the room was a square table covered in a baize cloth, and strewn with newspapers and cigar-boxes and an open copy of *Punch*. There were, indeed, books lining the walls, but they looked so stiff and formal and unused that it was difficult to avoid the impression that they were as much strangers to the real life of this gentlemen's club world as I was, and that they had been kept merely for decoration, or to justify retaining the name 'library' for what was, in effect, now a smoking room.

Perhaps Mrs. Kingsett sensed my hesitation, for she said, almost apologetically:

'It's not ideal, I'm afraid – but you'll understand, I know, that in the present state of affairs it's difficult to arrange everything as –?'

'Of course,' I said. 'But shall I not be in your husband's way?'

'It is at his insistence,' she said, so softly that the words came out as a startling snake-like hiss. I glanced towards her: the muscles in her jaw were tight and bulging, and she clutched at her own wrist, as if trying to steady herself. And then, in an instant, she relaxed again, and said more loudly:

'I'm sure, though, that you'll do well enough here.'

She guided me towards the far end of the room, where a small table and chair had been placed next to the window. Behind them stood a lit standard lamp, and on the floor beside them were two long drawers, filled almost to over-flowing with papers, which had simply been removed wholesale from a large chest. As I approached, I felt Mrs. Kingsett falling behind; and when I turned I saw that she had stopped and was staring at the floor, as if she feared even the sight of her mother's correspondence would be too painful.

'I've made no attempt to organize them, I'm afraid,' she said.

'Would you like *me* to try?' I said. 'I could at least arrange them chronologically.'

'That would be kind,' she said dully. 'Though it might be rather a waste of your time. Mauritius thinks we should just burn them.'

'Oh, no!' I cried, before I could stop myself. I should not, of course, have offered an opinion at all, for this was, in the eyes of the world, a matter for her family alone; but I was truly appalled at the idea of such wanton destruction, and no less so that such a spirited woman should feel – as the hopeless resignation in her voice suggested she did – that she must accept it merely because it was the wish of her husband. It was, after all, only three months since we had met at Marlborough House – and then it had been *she* who had seemed in control, and *he* who had been obliged to accommodate himself – however grudgingly – to *her* wishes. Had the death of her mother not only left Mrs. Kingsett grief-stricken, but also (in some obscure way I could not begin to understand) shifted the balance of power between them in her husband's favour?

'At all events, I hope you will find them of some use,' she said, in the same flat tone, edging towards the door, as if I had again raised an unwelcome subject, and she was anxious to make her escape. 'Do ring if you need anything.' And then, with a perfunctory wave at the bell-pull by the fire-place, she was gone.

I sat down, feeling suddenly alone and dreadfully exposed, like the girl in a fairy story who finds herself in the giant's castle, and fears he may return at any moment. Irrational though I knew it to be – for had he not, according to his wife, proposed this arrangement himself? – I could not rid myself of the idea that he would be angry if he found me here, and angrier still if he caught me reading his mother-in-law's correspondence. It must have been a full minute before I finally mastered myself, and reached into the near-

303

est drawer (still, I must confess, with the uneasy sense that I was trespassing), and took out a thick sheaf of papers.

The next moment, my anxiety vanished – or rather, it was temporarily dulled, as diversion may dull a toothache, by more urgent emotions – for there, in my hand, was a note from Leigh Hunt; and another from Lord Alvanley; and three or four from people I had never heard of, but supposed to be equally eminent; and an order of service for the coronation of King William. Scattered among them, to be sure, was a good deal of duller matter, such as you would find in anyone's effects – lawyers' letters, and bills of sale, and a folded page from *The Times*, on which I could see nothing of interest at all – but it served only to show off the gems to better advantage, and make them seem all the more brilliant.

My fingertips tingling, like those of a child trying a lucky-bag at a fair, I put my hand in again, and felt, beneath the scattering of loose sheets strewn across the surface, three or four tightly bound bundles. These, presumably, were what Lady Meesden herself must have considered her greatest treasures. Trembling, I took one up at random, and set it on the table before me.

It was bound in faded red ribbon of the kind used on legal documents, and consisted of about forty letters, all in the same hand. The most recent, at the top, was dated 1823; the earliest, at the bottom, 1802. Those in between were not evenly spaced, but grouped in little clusters: 1804, 1806, 1809, 1811. It surprises me, now, that I did not pay more attention to this irregular distribution, and wonder what it might mean; but I was too occupied with trying to guess the writer's identity. Most of the letters were signed merely 'Caro'; but as I reached the last few I found two or three that bore the name 'Caroline Bibby' – and one, written in 1803, that ended: 'I cannot tell you how eagerly I look forward to next week; when I may at last sign myself, not merely your *true friend*, but your *loving sister*.' There was nothing to indicate *what*, exactly, had occurred the following week; but from that expression, and the solicitous tone of the rest of the letter, I could only assume that it must have been Lady Meesden's wedding, and that Caroline Bibby had been Lord Meesden's sister.

I took out my notebook, laid my pencil beside it, and picked up the first letter. It was my firm intention merely to cast my eye over each page in turn, and to pause only when I saw a direct reference to Turner, but after two minutes I had been waylaid into reading and relishing every word. Here, at last, was the breezy world I had hoped to find in Haste – of rides in the park and boat-trips to Greenwich; of breakfast parties and assembly-room balls; of *soirées* crowded with French *émigrés*, and ageing macaronis, and noble bankrupts, and pinks of the *ton* so tightly squeezed into their breeches that they could barely sit down, and could only hobble away discomfited when their dress was criticized, or they were worsted in repartee – and all described with the most engaging simplicity and charm. Within the space of a single day, Caro (from the beginning, I could not think of her by any other name, and soon imagined that she was *my* friend, and all this written for *my* amusement!) plays whist with a countess who loves nothing but dogs and gambling, and will not go to bed, but sleeps wherever she happens to be when she dozes off, so the servants have no idea where they will find her in the morning; calls on an old man with a rouged face and diamonds in his wig, who collects snuff-boxes, and tries to persuade her to return that night for an assignation in his *garçonnière*; and then, on her way to the theatre, is stopped by a stone-throwing mob in Westminster, who think her carriage is Lord Castlereagh's, and when they discover their mistake chalk 'Liberty' on the doors. And yet nothing seems to spoil her, or shock her, or ruffle her good humour.

I had just started to read her account of an evening at

Almack's, and was so utterly engrossed in it that I had forgotten where I really was, or my purpose in being there,
when I suddenly became conscious that I was no longer
alone. I looked up: Mr. Kingsett was standing in the doorway. I could not clearly see his face, for my eyes had grown
accustomed to the lamplight, and could not immediately
adjust to the gloom beyond, but his stance – stock-still, one
hand on the handle – was that of a man who had supposed
he was entering an empty room, and was flabbergasted to
find that it was already occupied. I told myself again that –
unless his wife had been lying – he must have expected me
to be there; and said, as easily I could:

'Good afternoon.'

He did not reply, but after staring at me for a few seconds
more suddenly closed the door behind him, took a newspa-
per from the table, and settled himself in a chair by the fireplace. His posture suggested that he was reading, but it was
plainly too dark for him to do so.

'You will strain your eyes, Mr. Kingsett,' I said – sound-
ing, I hoped, good-humoured, but not over-familiar. 'Why
don't you ring for someone to light the lamps?'

Again, he said nothing; so I went on:

'Would you like me to do it for you?'

Surely, I thought, he *must* answer me now – but he merely went on with his charade of reading, and showed no sign
of even having heard me.

I was determined not to be intimidated, and forced myself
back to work; but I felt so unnerved by Mr. Kingsett's presence, and so slighted by his behaviour towards me, that I
found it almost impossible to concentrate. All at once, *this*
had become the real world again, and Caro's – which before
had seemed merely a romantic version of my own, like a
particularly enchanting stage-set – now appeared as alien
and perplexing as China or Japan. Several times, as I reached
the end of a sentence, I realized I had taken in barely a word

of it, and had to start again.

I had struggled through three or four letters in this way, and was beginning to wonder whether there was any point in continuing, when, as I turned a page, my eye fell upon the words 'Turner's Gallery'. I looked again, to make sure I had not made a mistake, and then – my excitement suddenly returning – copied the reference into my notebook:

All in all, my dear, I think you may count yourself fortunate to be *there* and not *here*. The only *évènement* of note that I'm sorry you missed – for I think you would have enjoyed it – was the opening of Turner's Gallery, which was splendid indeed. Never have I seen so many magnificent works by one man, in one place. The effect on walking in was rather like seeing all the members of a particularly handsome family – of whom you have previously only met two aunts and a younger son – gathered together in a single room. And there was the *grand génie* himself, the father of them all, darting about like a song-less bird, presenting his favourites to the guests.

Sur ce sujet-là – I was startled to learn from Mr. Perrin, whom we met on our way out, that Turner's own mother died, not a week ago, in Bethlem Hospital. Turner is always taciturn (save, so you tell me, when he is in his cups!), and in hindsight it did strike me that perhaps he had been even quieter on that occasion than usual, but you would certainly never have supposed from his manner or his appearance that he had recently suffered such a grievous blow.

When I had finished, I turned back to note the date – 21st April, 1804 – and then set my pencil down to continue reading. As I did so I caught a movement out of the corner of my eye, and, turning slightly, saw Mr. Kingsett getting up from his chair. I fervently hoped that he was going to leave again; but instead he took a cigar from a box on the table, lit it, and then started deliberately towards me. I affected not to notice, and pretended to be getting on with my work; but when he came to a halt at my shoulder I could no longer ignore him, and glanced up.

He was standing with his back half towards me, one hand in his pocket, the other languidly holding his cigar, as if he had simply decided to stroll over and look out of the window, and was completely unaware that his vantage point was no more than six inches away from another human being. I could not think what to do: it seemed preposterous to continue acting as if he weren't there, and yet if I spoke to him, and he again refused to acknowledge me, I should feel even more embarrassed than I did now. It was only when I felt my eyes starting to smart from his cigar smoke that I decided I must say something: to have remained silent would have been tacitly to accept his violation of the normal social rules, and so put myself beyond their protection.

'Would you like me to move?' I said. 'I fear I am in your way here.'

He turned and looked at me with a kind of incredulous scowl, as if I had said something unimaginably offensive. Then, without a word, he leant his head close to mine – so close, indeed, that I was forced to crane my neck to avoid our cheeks touching – and studiedly started to read what I had written in my notebook.

I felt for a moment I must be dreaming: such astonishing conduct, in the library of a house to which I had been invited as a guest, was quite outside my experience, and seemed totally inexplicable. I wondered for a moment if he was simply exceedingly drunk, but – although he stank of tobacco – I could not detect the faintest smell of wine on his breath; and his rudeness had none of the casual bluster of a drunkard about it, but seemed rather glacially precise and calculated. And that made it all the more frightening: for drunkenness, at least, is the devil you know, and there is a certain predictability to its effects, and to the kind of chaos it may bring; but if a sober man were prepared to act so outrageously, there was no telling what else he might do.

This is worse, I suddenly thought, than being at Haste's: for here I have no chance of escape, and no assets with which to bargain, and no possibility of redress if I am insulted further. And that realization made me bold: for I knew, with utter certainty, that I must assert myself now, or lose all hope of restraining him.

I took up my notebook and closed it.

He breathed in sharply, but said nothing, and did not look at me. The hand holding the cigar trembled slightly, shaking a cylinder of ash on to the pile of letters. He returned the cigar to his mouth, and then reached down unhurriedly to pick up the notebook.

I reached it before he did, and laid my hand on top of it.

Now, for the first time, he looked me in the face. I met his gaze steadily. I should, I know, have been afraid, but the instant I saw his pig-nose and weak mouth and the expression in his eyes – quite rational, but puzzled and uncertain – I knew that my will was stronger than his. After a moment, he turned away, and walked slowly from the room – trying to salvage his dignity by affecting a weary nonchalance that said: *I don't care: your notebook isn't worth the trouble of getting it.*

But I knew my victory was only temporary. I still had no idea what his motive might be, but it was inconceivable that, having created such a battle-line between us, he could now simply retreat from it. He would think twice, I imagined, before choosing to challenge me again directly, but would look for any opportunity to spite me when I could not defend myself. This meant, in all probability, that he would wait until I had left, and then remove or destroy the papers, or merely instruct the servants not to admit me again. I wondered briefly whether I might persuade Mrs. Kingsett to let me do as Haste had, and take the letters with me; but her husband would certainly forbid it, since part of his mysterious purpose had clearly been to keep them, and me, in this room, even though our presence here plainly infuriated him. And if I encouraged her to defy him, I should only end by making matters worse between them, and so adding to her misery.

For a moment, I lost sight of Turner and Walter altogether, and could think only of my struggle with Mr. Kingsett, and of how utterly intolerable (I was astonished by the savagery of my feelings on this point) defeat would be. And all at once, I knew what I must do: I must remain here for as long as necessary, and not go until I had finished.

I took out my watch: it was just past three. I looked at the two drawers, trying to estimate how long it would take me to work through them. With only the most cursory reading of the contents, I decided, perhaps two hours each. Allow a further two hours – more or less, depending on exactly what I found – to copy down any relevant references. That would take me till after nine. The Kingsetts dined, I imagined, at about seven, and would certainly expect me to leave by then; but if Mr. Kingsett could disregard convention, then so could I – and I solemnly promised myself that I would not move unless Mrs. Kingsett personally asked me to do so, or else I were physically ejected.

There was no time to reflect on this plan – I must just act on it, without delay. I skimmed the rest of Caro's letters – painfully conscious of the delights I was forced to pass over in my single-minded quest – and, finding no further mention of Turner, tied them up again, set them to one side, and picked out another bundle. This time, though, not only could I not discover the identity of the writer, but – so crabbed and cryptic was the hand – I could barely even make out one word in three. I started trying to tease out the meaning by using the characters in words I recognized as a model for deciphering the rest, but I soon realized this was a luxury I could not afford, and quickly gathered the sheets together again to re-tie them.

As I did so, something struck me: most of the dates on them were within a few days of those on Caro's letters. And almost in the same moment, I understood why: people had only written to her at length, of course, when she – or they – had been away from home. The contents of these drawers – like the negative of a photographic image, or the fossilized marks made by some vanished ancient creature – were the impressions left by *absence*.

This realization made me almost weep with frustration; for if these were only the leavings of Lady Meesden's life, how much more would I have been able to learn had I had the foresight to come here two months ago, and actually talked to her? Even as it was, thanks to Mr. Kingsett, I could not get the best from them, but must rush through at break-neck speed, picking out only the most obvious points.

For an instant, I felt close to despair; but then I rallied myself, and went on.

The next few hours are more or less undifferentiated in my recollection – an unbroken pattern of ink and paper and dust, and sore fingers, and sorer eyes – in which almost any moment might stand for them all.

With, that is, one solitary exception. I had completed my search of the first drawer, and had just taken another bundle (the last, as it turned out) from the second, when I heard Mr. and Mrs. Kingsett talking together in the hall. I could not make out what they said, but there was a kind of suppressed urgency in their voices that might, you imagined, suddenly break free of all restraint, and erupt into angry shouting. I could not but suppose that I was the subject of their conversation, and that at any second one or both of them might enter and oblige me to stop, but I willed myself to keep going.

It was not, as it happened, as hard as it might have been;

for something about the new package immediately excited my interest. It was tied in a brittle black mourning ribbon – only the few notes from her husband enjoyed the same distinction – and beneath the knot someone (presumably Lady Meesden herself) had slipped a card with the name 'O'Donnell' on it. At the top was the torn and stained manuscript of a short play called *The Man of Taste* – among whose *dramatis personae*, I was intrigued to see, was a 'Mr. Over-turner'. Beneath that were perhaps fifteen long letters, written in the same strong, clear hand. The first, I saw – with a small thrill that not even my present circumstances could entirely dampen – was dated 1799, which made it the oldest document I had so far discovered. It began: 'Sweet dearest Kit', and was signed 'Your doting Richard'.

I hesitated – but only, I must confess, for an instant: for surely, if Lady Meesden had not wanted the letters to be found, she would not have kept them; and neither she nor her lover would come to much harm by my looking at them now. Before I had read more than a sentence, however, the door opened, and Mrs. Kingsett came in. As she moved into the lamplight, I saw that her eyes were red-rimmed and wet, and she was dabbing at her nose with a handkerchief.

'We are about to dine,' she said. She sounded hoarse, and could no longer even attempt a smile. 'Will you join us?'

'I'm afraid', I said, 'that I've already inconvenienced you and your husband enough.'

She did not try to gainsay me. 'But it's late. You must be tired.'

'A little. But I shall soon be done.'

'Would you not be better to come back tomorrow?'

Her voice wavered ominously. She seemed on the brink of breaking down altogether. Hoping to deflect her, I laughed, and said as lightly as I could:

'Two hours. And then, I promise, you will be rid of me for ever.'

She stared at me, as if she had exhausted all her resources, and was at a loss to know what to do next. And then her expression changed from stupefaction to fear, and – as if drawn by some unseen force – she looked towards the door. And in that gesture I suddenly thought I saw the ugly explanation of her husband's behaviour.

He was punishing her. Punishing her for creating a life in which he had no part, and protecting herself from him too effectively. Her complete indifference had reduced him (as he saw it) to no more than a cipher in his own household, robbing him even of the power to wound her. Now, at last, fate had taken his part, delivering the blow he had been incapable of inflicting himself, and leaving her, at the same time, hurt, vulnerable, and deprived of her most formidable ally. This was his chance of revenge, and he had seized it with relish. Hence his insistence that I should be in the library, and his manner towards me. By humiliating *me*, he was humiliating *her*; by demonstrating *my* powerlessness, he was exposing *hers*.

Seeing the blotches and tear-stains on her pale cheeks, the frantic working of her hands, the uncontrollable tightening of her mouth, I almost relented. Had she turned back to me again, and made one last attempt to persuade me, I should have packed up at once. But she was defeated, and left without another word.

It is as well for me she did.

So hastily did I write everything down, and in such a topsy-turvy order, that I have only the haziest idea of what I have got. Today I was too exhausted to read through it all again – or, rather, too fragile, for I dread finding that after all my discoveries are worthless, and the whole ordeal of getting them consequently a waste of time. And that, when I think of what I endured – and, even more, of what I compelled poor Mrs. Kingsett to endure – would be hard to bear.

Tomorrow I shall be stronger.

XXXIII

Extract of a letter from Lord Meesden to Kitty Driver, 2nd October, 1802

Beaucoup de monde à Paris – or you might simply dispense with the 'coup' and the 'de', for the whole *beau monde* is here, or has been – Fox, Lansdowne, Morpeth, a clutch of duchesses, Ladies Conygham and Holland, and a thousand more. And all, to me, the most tremendous bore; for none possesses the only quality that can arouse my interest – being *you*.

In search of diversion from my *you*less state (no horse, I swear, ever felt the want of a driver more) I went yesterday to the Louvre. It was as tedious as being in society, and for much the same reason – whatever their merits, Titian and Rembrandt and Raphaël never painted the one face in all the world I long to see.

While there, I found your friend Turner skulking by a Poussin, and feverishly scribbling hieroglyphs into a notebook. He started when he saw me, and would, I think, have tried to make his escape if I had not gone up and asked him when he intended to return to England. I had thought perhaps to entrust him with this letter (or with the unborn twin I should then have written, beginning 'I send this by the hand of Mr. Turner'), but he seemed so displeased at being recognized that I repented of the idea. As we parted, I said:

'You know, Mr. Turner, you are the only man in Paris I envy.'

'Why?' he growled, in a suspicious sort of way.

'Because you will see Mrs. Driver before I do.'

XXXIV

Extract of a letter from Lord Meesden to Kitty Driver, 15th May, 1803

Copley tells me his tiresome compatriots are again making trouble for the King – but now, having won the colonies, they are no longer content with fighting there, but have carried the war home, to the Royal Academy. The Philadelphian President, West (I begin to fear men named after cardinal points – *North* loses us America; *West* brings the insurrection here; what mischief may we expect from Messrs. *South* and *East*, when they appear?), has taken up arms, demanding that the Academy Council should be answerable to its own General Assembly, rather than to the Crown. I confess I can see very little purpose to its being the *Royal* Academy, if the King is to have no power within it, and his only function is to be a convenient scapegoat, on which indifferent painters may vent their fury at their own want of success; but Copley fears the democrats will carry the day.

Among the most incendiary of them, it appears, is your friend Turner, who plots against the royalists like a veritable Robespierre, and cannot contain his rage and loathing whenever he meets them. Are you certain we should invite him to the wedding? He may end by fomenting the tenants against us, and forming a committee, and turning the church into a People's Court, and declaring our bodies independent of our heads.

XXXV

Extract of a letter from Lord Meesden to Lady Meesden, 2nd February, 1809

Turner, it seems, has again excused himself from carrying out his duties as Professor of Perspective. No woman that I know would let a man off so lightly, who still showed such reluctance to enter the conjugal bed, more than a year after the ceremony; but the Academy has not even hinted at lawyers and doctors and divorce, but merely smiled demurely, and said it will be well enough for him to start *next* year.

XXXVI

Extract of a letter from Lord Meesden to Lady Meesden, 22nd January, 1810

Still the trembling bride awaits. Turner protests he has a headache, and cannot begin his lectures for a further year.

XXXVII

Extract of a letter from Lord Meesden to Lady Meesden, 1st February, 1811

Must end, & get Perkins to preen me for tonight – but before I do, a piece of droll intelligence: The marriage is consummated at last! – Turner has made his first public appearance in the character of Professor of Perspective! – & Larkin (whom I met at the B.'s) tells me it is quite the most amusing thing in London – quantities of comic business

with papers, illustrative drawings &c. – sentences starting
confidently in one direction, & then taking another, & so by
degrees finding themselves in a dead end, by which time
both the audience & Turner have long since lost any idea
what they may mean, save that it plainly has nothing to do
with perspective. There isn't a farce or a comedy comes
close, says Larkin – the Academy could sell tickets at a
guinea apiece, & would be turning people away.

XXXVIII

Extract of a letter from the Hon. Miss Lydia Bolt to Lady Meesden, 1st September, 1827

Speaking of which, dearest Mama, Mr. Turner is here, and
not at all as I had supposed him to be – not brusque or
withdrawn, but charming in a shy, birdish, kind of a way,
and with an interesting observation to make on almost any
subject, from *Childe Harold* to the reflection of light from
wet feathers. He found me in the garden, trying to sketch
the sea and Portsmouth beyond. I was, I own, embarrassed
that *he* of all people should see it, but he was very kind, and
took great pains to help me, without a single word of dis-
couragement or criticism.

He, by the by, painted one of our *conversazziones*. Imagine
a scene by Watteau, blurred by the rain before it is dry, and
you have it.

XXXIX

Extract of a letter from Cynthia [Lady?] Abbott to Lady Meesden, 13th April, 1813

I wish you had been with us last night – we dined at the
Nuthampsteads' – the dinner indifferent enough, but great
hilarity – young Mr. Smiley, *qui veut devenir artiste*, as he
says, entertained us hugely with his imitation of Turner
giving a lecture at the Academy. His napkin became
Turner's notes, which he proceeded to 'lose', and discover
at last under my chair – one of the footmen was transformed into Turner's assistant (to whom, apparently, he
invariably delivers his oration, rather than to the audience)
– and his words, when they were audible, had Turner's
jumbled sense and execrable pronunciation to perfection. I
cannot remember everything he said, but an orange, I
recall, was a 'spearide form' – the (semi-circular) arch on
the window a 'semi-ellipsis' – and the 'young gen'lmen' of
the Academy were 'hex'orted to raise the hart of landscape
to the poetical 'eights of 'istory painting, for the glory of
Britain hand 'er Hempire'. There was a deal more in the
same vein, but I missed much of it, alas, *de trop rire*.

XL

Extract from Act II, scene ii of *The Man of Taste*, a privately performed farce by Richard O'Donnell [1810?]

[Tom Wilde sees Lucy Luckwell at the theatre, and falls
in love with her. He follows her to the country house of
her guardian, the connoisseur LORD DABBLE, where he
gains admission by presenting himself as an artist, and

offering to paint Lucy's portrait. Instead of being left alone with her as he had hoped, however, he is constantly interrupted by a stream of painters and connoisseurs offering advice.]

Enter SPEED.

SPEED: No, no, no, no, no.

TOM: Why, what's amiss now?

SPEED: It's too small.

LUCY: Oh, no, Mr. Speed, surely not!

SPEED: And can you not dress her as Boadicea, or Britannia? Portraits aren't worth a fig, unless you *dignify* 'em, as Sir Ocular said. *History*, now, that's the thing. Wait. I'll fetch a crown, and a ladder.

Goes off.

TOM: Dear Miss Luckwell!

LUCY: Dear Mr. Wilde!

TOM: Dear Lucy!

Takes her hand.

LUCY: Oh! oh! oh!

TOM: I have, I fear, a confession to make.

LUCY: Oh, pray, don't be fearful! I shall be happy, dear, dear Mr. Wilde, to receive *any* confidence you may care to repose in me.

TOM: Why, then, I am not really –

Enter OVER-TURNER *and* COLD-CUT. *They stand stock-still, staring at the picture.*

TOM: Well?

COLD-CUT: *(looking at Over-Turner)* Um um um um um.

OVER-TURNER: It wants yeller.

COLD-CUT: Indeed, yellow would improve it mightily.

OVER-TURNER: An' a burnin' sun.

COLD-CUT: A sun! Of course!

OVER-TURNER: An' a sea-monster.

COLD-CUT: The very thing I was about to propose.

OVER-TURNER: Where's your colours?

Tom hands him his palette.

OVER-TURNER: Cold-cut, you make out the bill. Now then.

He starts mixing paints furiously with his brush. Enter SIR
GILES BOOMER *and* MR. MEASURE.

SIR GILES: No! No! No! No! No!

TOM: What's the matter now?

SIR GILES: Ho! Stop! Seduction!

TOM: (*aside*) What, am I discovered?

SIR GILES: Mr. Wilde, you must not allow yourself to be
led into unnatural error!

TOM: Error it may be, Sir Giles, but nothing connected
with Miss Luckwell could be considered unnatural.

SIR GILES: Let me see. Where's my Claude-glass,
Measure?

*Measure hands him a Claude-glass. Sir Giles examines the
picture through it, slowly walking backwards.*

OVER-TURNER: Claude? 'E does misappre'end, as Sir
Ocular 'ad it, taste may usurp genius, all is bespoke,
nothing allowed, when that which 'eretofore is 'eld
up as perfection.

SIR GILES: Your picture is fine, Mr. Wilde, very fine – I
would only say it could be browner, especially in
the skin and teeth, for Nature, you know, is *exceedingly* brown, as the Old Masters taught us, though a
common eye may miss it. But all in all I should say –
only avoid the excesses of Over-Turnerism, and you
will be the great hope of the British School!

TOM: But as I was just trying to explain to Miss Luckwell –

SPEED: (*off*) I thought *I* was the great hope of the British
School!

Enter SPEED, *carrying a ladder, with which he inadvertent-*
ly hits Sir Giles, knocking him to the ground.

SIR GILES: That was last year.

XLI

Extract of a letter from Richard O'Donnell to Kitty Driver, 4th September, 1799

William Turner is also here. Do you know him? He certainly knows *you* – has seen you in everything, and is evidently
a great admirer of yours, but won't come out and say so
directly. I hope I have no cause for jealousy – it would be
displeasing indeed for a man to know he had been usurped
by a dwarf. The last I knew of him, he was painting scenes
at the Pantheon in '92, but now it seems he is quite the coming artist, and has been engaged by Mr. Beckford to make
watercolour drawings of the estate.

And why, you are doubtless wondering, am *I* at Fonthill?
Because Mr. Beckford stands in pressing need of monks; and
finding himself unable to procure the real thing (to which his
avowed atheism, and his enthusiasm for catamites, have
proved an obstacle), has turned to a popish Irish theatre
manager to coin some counterfeits. Every morning, I assem-
ble the 'lads', as Mr. Beckford calls them, in a vast unfinished
hall, and drill them in chanting and singing and processing
until I can no longer keep my temper with them – which
happens often enough, for they are the least apt pupils you
ever saw, having been selected more with an eye to their
fawn-like looks than to their thespian ability.

And what does he want with monks? you say (nay, you
whisper it, you trollop; I hear you as I write) – why, he wants
them to fill his house, which when it is finished is to be the
greatest gothick palace in the world – 350 feet long, and with

a tower taller than the spire of Salisbury Cathedral. He plans *une grande ouverture* next year – though what he will do for guests I cannot conceive, for he is so notorious for keeping butterflies that no respectable member of society will set foot here – and work continues day and night to get it ready. Last evening, after dinner, I looked from my window, and thought I had never seen a more ridiculous scene: the labourers scuttling back and forth by flickering torchlight; Beckford, dressed as an abbot, prowling among them, with poor Wyatt, the architect, hovering in attendance like a nervous novice; and Turner behind, shrinking into the shadows as if they were his natural home, then darting out again like a little elf, drawing so quickly that his hand was but a blur. I should have laughed out loud, had I not recalled that this monument to folly is being erected on the poor scarred backs of those wretched Negroes in the Indies, from whom all Beckford's fortune comes.

XLII

Extract of a letter from Richard O'Donnell to Lady Meesden, 4th September, 1829

Jollet is a good man – cannot do much for me, but makes me as comfortable as he can, tho' he knows he won't be paid for it in this world.

You know your time is near when patterns start to complete themselves before your eyes. Today I had a fancy to see the sea again, and Mme. Sylvestre's son pushed me in my chair to the harbour. Some English passengers arriving – one seemed familiar – a little red-faced fellow in a long coat and scarf, pressing forward with some other purpose in his gait than mere pleasure. I thought for a wild moment he must be a dun, sent here to persecute me before it was too late. And then I knew him.

'Turner,' I said.

He did not recognize me, or pretended not to, but hurried on his way.

It must be thirty years to the day since I last wrote to you of Turner.

It is a hard thing to die. When you hear I am gone, wait a little while, and I shall come to you again.

XLIII

From the journal of Marian Halcombe, November 185–

Wednesday

Have just finished reviewing my discoveries, and find myself less disheartened than I'd feared. A distinct feeling that I've made progress. But *what*, exactly?

To begin with – confirmation of what I already knew:

- Turner's mother *did* die mad, as both Amelia Bennett and Sir Charles told me. And I have a date for it: April 1804.
- Turner *was* vilified by Sir George Beaumont and other connoisseurs – Haste's diaries and O'Donnell's play (Turner/Over-turner, Boomer/Beaumont) bear each other out on this point.
- He was – or at least was perceived as being – tight-fisted. ('Cold-cut, you make out the bill.' And Sir Charles's account of his 'begrudging a few pounds' to have his will properly drawn.)
- He did move about a great deal, and disliked people

recognizing him, or knowing where he was, when he
did so – a peculiarity attested to not only by Sir
Charles, but also now by Meesden and O'Donnell.

Such corroborations are encouraging – they point to a
modest foundation of fact on which I can build.

And what else?

I feel (to my own great surprise) that in a small, haphazard
way I am starting to *know* him. Where before all was
obscure, I now see unexpected glimmers of light.

Take, for instance, his elusiveness. Since it is mentioned
in the earliest letters we have, the roots of it must presumably lie in his very early life – about which I still know
almost nothing (beyond the fact that he was a scene-
painter), and have little prospect of learning more. And yet
might not part of the reason also be the knowledge that (as
the letters to Lady Meesden make clear) he was regarded as
a laughing-stock, and knew that whenever he appeared in
public *as himself* he might be derided for his dress, or his
tradesman's manner, or his inability to express his
thoughts?

As time went on, moreover, he must have become increasingly aware that these eccentricities were adversely affecting
not merely his social relations, but also his professional
prospects. Why, for example, was Charles Eastlake (who,
though a dear man, is not a quarter the artist) knighted, and
elected President of the Royal Academy, while Turner
received no formal recognition at all? It can only be because
gentlemanliness, rather than talent, is the key to preferment.

All of which, surely, would be enough to breed habits of
secrecy and concealment in *any* man – particularly one so
painfully sensitive and shy?

His supposed meanness, too, seems more understandable
when you know something of the world in which he
worked. To be an artist in the first years of the century – as

evidenced by the example of poor Haste, which Turner must have had constantly in his mind – was a perilous undertaking, in which your name and your fortune might at any moment be destroyed at the whim of a powerful connoisseur. Only by making yourself independent could you hope to defy a man such as Sir George Beaumont, and so continue following the dictates of your own genius – and the cost of that independence must be to practise the utmost economy, and allow no indulgence either to yourself or others.

It is undeniably satisfying to be able to ascribe comprehensible motives to behaviour that had previously seemed unaccountable, or even mad. But I must not be too pleased with myself – there is still much I do not even begin to understand.

And what of the *pictures*?

Thursday
An exhilarating day – but its fruits so tantalizing and insubstantial I scarce dare write them down, for fear they turn out chimeras, and evaporate before my eyes.

I had intended copying out what I have gathered so far and sending it to Walter (for after my recent adventures I can no longer content myself with being merely a scribe, but have begun to seek Turner on my account; and to part with my notebooks now would be the equivalent of a detective throwing away his evidence); but I was diverted from my plans by two letters. The first was from Haste's son, reminding me that I have now had his father's diaries for more than ten days, and demanding to know – with a kind of frozen rage that cut me like an icicle – when he might have the honour to expect them back again. In truth, I had not exactly forgotten our agreement; but had somehow persuaded myself, in the excitement over Lady Meesden's papers, that I need not adhere to its exact terms, and that a delay of a day or two would not be fatal. It pained me to realize what I should have known all along – that by this thoughtlessness I had only justified his suspicions, and left him feeling more embittered and besieged than ever; and I resolved that after luncheon I should call on him in person, and try to make amends.

The second letter was from Mrs. Kingsett:

My dear Miss Halcombe,
    I found this today on my mother's writing table, and thought it might be of interest to you.
    Yours very truly,
    Lydia Kingsett

My first response was not so much curiosity as relief – for although there was no mention of what happened on Monday, yet the mere fact that she had written at all suggested that her husband had not yet entirely succeeded in breaking her spirit, and that she was not (as I had feared) aggrieved at me for being so stubborn, and so unwittingly adding to her difficulties. Her note, indeed, seemed a kind of salve to Mr. Haste's anger, from which I was still smarting; and I re-read it two or three times before finally unfolding the sheet she had enclosed, to see what it was:

> *1 Oliver Buildings, Hammersmith,*
> *15th September, 185–*

Dearest Kitty,
    Pie and pheasant both arrived in excellent health – and we did not neglect to pledge *yours*, you may be sure, as we despatched them! How good you are to me! I do not believe you have once forgotten my birthday in more than sixty years. It seems little short of a miracle that you still remember your Romeo after so long.
    I often think fondly of our days together in Drury Lane

and Dublin. I won't say they were the happiest of my life, for –
thank God – most of my days have been happy; but I'll swear I
never knew a handsomer woman than you were then, or a
truer friend.

May God bless you always,
James Padmore

I was, for a moment, frankly puzzled as to why Mrs.
Kingsett had sent this to me (I must have been particularly
slow-witted this morning, though I like to think I have made
up for it since!); and it was only when I reached the words
'Drury Lane' on the second reading that it struck me. A great
wave seemed suddenly to break over me, tumbling me this
way and that, leaving me feeling excited and giddy and sick
all at once. Here, at last, was what I had given up all hope of
finding: someone who had known the world of Turner's
youth. But in the two short months since his letter had been
written, sickness and death had already cheated me of its
recipient. Might not the writer now also be dead, or at least
too ill to speak to me?

Without delay, I scribbled a short note to Mr. Padmore,
saying I intend to call on him tomorrow; and an even short-
er one to Mrs. Kingsett, to thank her for her help. Then I
asked Davidson to take them to the post, and myself set out
for Cawley Street with Haste's diaries.

It is strange now to look back, and reflect on my thoughts in
the cab. They revolved entirely around Mr. Haste: whether
or not he would be at home; whether – if he was – I could
expect a civil interview, or must prepare myself for abuse
and recrimination; and whether, in the latter case, I should
respond by abjectly apologizing (which might mollify him,
but might equally only enrage him further; for the sorrier I
seemed, the more reason I should be giving him for supposing he had been deeply wronged), or alternatively by adopt-

ing an air of mild surprise that he should make so great a fuss about so small a matter.

In the event – how pitiful our belief that we can foresee the future, and our attempts to prepare for it! – Mr. Haste's behaviour proved of almost no consequence to me whatever, and the most important outcome of my visit had nothing to do with him at all.

He was, indeed, at home, and (perhaps in anticipation of my return) had even made the small concession of greasing the knocker, so that I was able to rouse him without having to press-gang a passer-by into helping me. I heard him clattering down the stairs, and then charging through the hall so furiously that I feared he must be in a very paroxysm of rage, and unable to defer even for a moment the opportunity of venting it. If he was, however, it was plain that I was not its object; for he started, as if he were surprised to see me, and then immediately glanced up and down the street, clearly looking for someone else. And not, I fancy, the bailiffs this time – for his expression was not surly and defiant, as it had been before, but rather eager and impatient.

'I am sorry I could not come sooner,' I said. 'It took me longer than I'd expected to finish. There was so much of interest, and your father wrote so well.'

If I had hoped this explanation would please him, I was disappointed; for he merely nodded and grunted, mechanically reaching out his hands for the books even as his eyes continued to search the street. His fingers, I saw, were stained with ink, and there were two or three little blots on his shirt.

'I hope you will accept another ten shillings, by way of compensation,' I said.

He nodded again, and extended his palm, still gazing past me.

It was as I rummaged in my reticule that something at the corner of my vision caught my attention. It was nothing more than a triangle of split and splintered floorboard, dully illuminated by the afternoon light; but it suddenly rekindled a powerful and unexpected memory. This was the bare hallway of my dream; and for a brief vivid moment I again saw it not as the way to Haste's attic but as the entrance to a mica-spangled subterranean grotto where, I knew, I should find the secret of Turner's paintings.

'What is below here?' I asked, handing him a half-sovereign.

'Hm?'

'A basement? A cellar?'

He nodded distractedly.

I gazed down into the cramped area. The windows were grey and opaque with dirt, and one of the panes was broken, and had been roughly reinforced with a board. A tangle of almost leafless ivy spread up the walls, insinuating itself so aggressively into every gap and fissure that the bricks were starting to buckle and crack, and you could already half-see them as the ruin that they were destined to become in fifty or a hundred or two hundred years.

I was conscious of rapid footsteps behind me, and then a breathless voice calling 'I'm sorry. Sorry. Sorry. Sorry.' I turned and saw a plump man, as bald as Haste himself, hurrying towards us, clutching a carpet-bag filled to overflowing with papers. Haste admitted him, and then closed the door without another word to me, or a glance in my direction.

But I did not feel affronted – I was too elated for that. For I suddenly thought I had understood what it was that had been nagging me about *The Bay of Baiae*.

I had instructed the cabman to wait, thinking I might need to make to a quick escape; and now I told him to take me as fast as possible to Marlborough House. It was a nightmare journey – I could not remember what time the exhibition closed, and feared I should arrive too late to see the picture today; yet every time we seemed to break free of the traffic and pick up speed, we shook to a standstill again after only a few moments, and remained there for what felt like an ever-longer eternity. As we approached Trafalgar Square, the tangle of omnibuses and carriages and horses became so knotted and impenetrable that I decided it would be quicker to walk; and, having paid my fare, I got out and set off into the *mêlée*.

I was in luck. Fighting the great tide of humanity one moment, being swept along by a counter-current the next, I found myself in less than ten minutes at the end of Pall Mall. The gallery was still open, the painting where I remembered it. And when – after a good deal of gentle shouldering and 'excuse me'ing – I had breached the wall of people before it and could see it plain, I knew in an instant that I had been right.

It was so obvious, indeed, that I marvelled that I had not grasped it before. *The Bay of Baiae* is not one picture, but two. On my first visit here, I had been struck by how out of place the figures of Apollo and the Sibyl had seemed – as if they had been transposed from another scene altogether; and seeing them again now, I realized that that is exactly what had happened. For Turner portrays *them* at the start of their story, when the Sibyl, still young and beautiful, has been granted her wish, and is sifting the grains of sand in her hand, and counting the years of life she is to have; but the landscape, with its half-hidden serpent, and broken columns, and skull-like arches, shows the inevitable end: the destruction and decay to which she must eventually come.

A letter from Walter when I got home. Why has he not heard from me? I cannot write to him now.

Friday

No matter it is late. I am like a general, who, flushed with success, feels he must press on to final victory before his fortune changes.

First: Mr. Padmore. Thank God! – he is still alive, and well, and in possession of his wits – or, at least, he was until three hours ago. And more than that – has told me more than I could have possibly hoped.

From the name, I had imagined Oliver Buildings to be a dingy, stinking tenement; but in fact it turns out to be a group of single-storey alms-houses, built in red brick in the gothic style, and arranged around three sides of a grassy square, with a wrought-iron gate and a railed fence on the fourth.

My heart was beating so hard as I knocked at number 1 that I could feel it in my throat, and feared I should have difficulty in speaking normally; but there was something so soothing and reassuring about the answering 'Come in!' that I at once began to relax. It was, I know, irrational: there was no guarantee that the speaker was Mr. Padmore, for if he had died, another resident might have been given his place; and yet from those two words I felt certain that it *was* him, and that we were destined to be friends.

I entered, and found myself in a neat room, running the whole depth of the little house, that seemed to serve as parlour, kitchen and library all at once. The fire was a kind of open range, with a small oven to one side of it, and a deep grate so crammed with glowing coals that the atmosphere was as oppressive as a hothouse. To the left of it was a bookcase, and to the right a dresser lined with stout red-and-gilt china that glowed prettily in the light from the back window. A slender-legged table covered in a clean white cloth stood in the centre of the room. It was spread with cups and a sugar-bowl and a pile of papers – among which I recognized my letter. Around it was an odd assortment of oak and

331

walnut chairs. In one of them – a heavy, old-fashioned piece with brawny arms and splayed feet, that looked as if it had been designed to accommodate the greedy squire from a Fielding novel – sat a very old man so thin that he occupied barely half the seat. He had clearly been expecting me, for he immediately said:

'Miss Halcombe?'

He tried to get up, but having pulled himself to a half-sitting position he could go no further. He looked so uncomfortable, with his head poked forward and his hands clutching the scrolled ends of the chair arms, that I immediately begged him to sit down again; and he at once subsided with a grateful smile.

'The spirit is willing,' he said. 'But the joints now – they're the sticking-point.' He held out his hand. 'How'd you do?'

'How do you do?' His fingers were as light and fleshless as a bird's claw, as if nature, resolved to waste nothing on a body so close to the grave, had reduced everything to its barest function.

'I am very glad to see you,' he said. He pulled a clean red handkerchief from his pocket and held it towards me. 'Would you be so good as to place this in the window by the door?'

'Of course,' I said, trying to sound as if this were the most natural thing in the world, and exactly what I should have expected. But he must have seen my perplexity; for as I took it he said:

'It is our *billet* for tea.'

I hung it on the casement latch, where it drooped unimpressively like a limp flag; but the effect seemed to satisfy him, for he nodded and said:

'Thank you. Will you sit down?'

I took a chair next to him, and at once nearly cried out; for now that I saw him steadily I realized that he was not merely old – he was unimaginably, impossibly ancient. I should have noticed it before, save for the trouble which – presumably in my honour – he had taken with his appearance. His well-cut, brass-buttoned blue coat suggested a much younger man, until you saw how his body had shrunk away from it, leaving great empty folds about his chest and shoulders. His sparse hair, as fine and lustrous as spun silver, had been skilfully trained across the top of his head to disguise the freckled scalp beneath. Most striking of all were the discreet dabs of rouge on his cheeks, which I confess I found quite shocking – until I saw the sweetness in his eyes, and realized that what had prompted him to adorn himself in this way was not vanity, but a gracious desire to look as agreeable as possible within his limited means. (A cynic might argue that the two motives are the same; but the object of vanity, surely, is to inspire admiration? – while his, plainly, was merely to give pleasure to a guest.)

I was prepared for a long preamble of pleasantries and idle reminiscences, such as is generally necessary with old people who live alone; but, as if to confirm my good opinion of him, he at once said:

'My memory's well enough, ma'am, at least for the old days; but I tire easy now, I fear – very easy. So don't stand on ceremony – just ask what you will.' He laughed. 'Else by the time we get to the meat, you'll find I'm asleep.'

'Very well, then. I was wondering if you could tell me about Covent Garden? When you were a young man?'

'Covent Garden – oh, well, now! Just imagine – a boy no more than eighteen – seen nothing of the world but Hampshire and Margate – suddenly whisked to London, and taken to the greatest theatre in the land, and given the *entrée* of the house. All the great names of the day. Charles Bannister. Mrs. Gibbs.' He shook his head, still marvelling at his good fortune. 'I was giddy, Miss Halcombe. The smell of it! Even now – mix me a bit of sawdust and a bit of paint, and the fumes of a lamp or two – not gas, mind, it must be the old

oil, warm and smoky – and I can't quell a flutter down here.'
He pointed to his stomach, and chuckled.

I hadn't, of course, meant the theatre, but rather the area in
which it stood; but I felt I could not say so now without seeming rude.

'Did you live nearby?' I asked.

'I was with my brother at first, in Holborn. But then I had
rooms of my own, in Maiden Lane.'

'Indeed?' I said, trying to keep the excitement from my
voice. 'And who did you have for neighbours?'

'Well, now.' His eyes narrowed with the effort of recollection. 'Downstairs we had a German musician, what was his
name? – Herr, Herr . . . I forget – and a man who made flutes,
and Potter the bone-doctor, and – Schussel, that was it, Herr
Schussel, lived with an Irish woman, she wasn't his wife,
Mrs. Malone . . .'

'And what of the rest of the street?' I said.

'Oh, we were a pretty mixed company, taken all in all.
Actors and actresses; a plasterer; a poet; an architect; two or
three tavern-keepers; a coach-maker; shopkeepers; fair . . .
fair' – he hesitated, and the rouge on his cheeks was reinforced by a tinge of natural colour – 'fair Cyprians, if you
take my meaning?'

'Women of . . . ?'

He nodded. 'There was a deal of those.'

'And do you recall any of the shops?'

He took a deep breath, and then let out an unsteady sigh.

'Miss Halcombe,' he said, lightening his words with an
indulgent smile. 'I feel I am being made to play "Twenty
Questions", and cannot guess the thought in your mind. I
pray you, for your own sake – be plain with me.'

And I was. For the first few seconds I hesitated and stumbled; but I soon heard myself talking about Turner and
Walter and my own research with an ease and directness
that startled me – for I had not spoken so freely to *anyone*

334

since the day of our visit to Sandycombe Lodge, and could not conceive why I suddenly felt able to be candid with *him*. And I still cannot account for it now, save that I was drawn on by the interest and sympathy in his face – and perhaps by the knowledge that a crippled old man in a Hammersmith alms-house would be unlikely to betray me.

I had just finished when a short, thickset woman suddenly entered without knocking. She wore a grey dress and a crimped bonnet, and carried a white apron, which she started to tie about her waist even as she leant against the door to close it.

'Betty,' said Mr. Padmore fondly. He looked at me, and pointed to the handkerchief in the window. 'Whenever we hoist the signal, Betty takes pity on us. Betty' – turning back to her – 'this is Miss Halcombe. Miss Halcombe, Mrs. Chambers.'

'How do you do?' she said briskly, extending her hand. She was about seventy, with a heart-shaped face that might once have been very striking, but now looked weatherbeaten and neglected – as if, once her beauty had started to fade, she no longer thought it worth the trouble of tending. There was no trace either of insolence or deference in her manner, from which I deduced that she was not a servant; and yet if she had been a member of Mr. Padmore's family, surely that is how he would have introduced her?

'I live over there,' she said, as if by way of explanation, pointing out of the window.

'Ah.'

She must have seen my puzzlement; for she went on:

'With the women.' She took a kettle from the hearth, and filled it from an enamelled water-jug. 'You learn to care for one another in a company.'

'A company?' I said.

She nodded, and set the kettle to boil on the fire.

'Do you mean, then, that everyone here is an actor or an

335

actress?' I said, half-laughing with surprise, and with an odd kind of delight at the idea.

'*Was*,' she said. 'We are all *decayed*.' She began to laugh, and after a moment Mr. Padmore joined in.

'Or so the Theatrical Benevolent Society tell us,' she said, reaching down a tea caddy from the mantelpiece.

Mr. Padmore seemed so absorbed in watching her preparations that I feared I had lost him; but, just as I was about to try to nudge him back to our conversation, he said:

'No, I have not forgotten.' He closed his eyes, and collected his thoughts in silence for a few moments. Then he looked at me again and said:

'You are in luck; for I remember the barber's shop quite distinctly.'

I gave a little yelp of triumph – I could not help it – which surprised even myself, and startled Mrs. Chambers so much that she almost dropped the teapot; but Mr. Padmore merely smiled and nodded.

'Yes, indeed,' he went on. 'Several of the older men went to Turner, or engaged Turner to come to them; and I thought I could do worse than go there myself. So I took my wigs to him, until I noticed the young whips were no longer wearing them; and then I grew my hair, and took *that* to him instead.' He shook his head. 'I wish I had the power of painting myself, Miss Halcombe, so I could show it to you. There was a long low window on the street, full of grinning dummies in bob and cauliflower wigs; but you couldn't go in that way – you entered by a side-door in the court – the name's gone, I fear . . .'

'Hand Court?'

'Yes, that was it.' He shut his eyes again, and began tracing an invisible plan with his hand. 'A narrow hall – stairs up and down – the shop in a dark little room to the left. Rows of blue bottles against the wall – a table here, with towels, and razors, and a bowl – a spiral machine there, for frizzing, I suppose – and all about powder-puffs, and crimping-irons, and braiding-pins, and leather rolls for making curls, and heaven knows what. And the *smell*. Scorched hair. Soap. Pomade.' His nostrils twitched, trying to recapture some long-lost fragrance. 'And *powder*. Yes.' He opened his eyes suddenly. 'Do you know the smell of wig-powder, Miss Halcombe?'

I shook my head.

'Not unpleasant. Sneezy. And there always seemed to be the most tremendous noise, at least when I was there. As much inside as out. Water boiling. Tongs clacking.' He laughed. '*Tongues* clacking. Oh, yes, a deal of tongues.'

'Was Mr. Turner very garrulous, then?'

He inclined his head, and scratched the lobe of his ear, as if it might stimulate thought or memory. After a moment he said:

'Do you know, I can't recall? But *someone* must have been; for there was always talk. Or so it seems, at any rate, when I think back to it now.' He smiled wonderingly, like a traveller who has paused in his journey to look behind him, and is amazed to see how far he has come. 'We did not want for subjects – the colonists in America, the *sans-culottes* in France. Or for men of consequence to discuss 'em.' He leaned a little towards me, as if confiding a secret. 'I once saw a portly-looking gentleman coming out, with the whitest wig I ever set eyes on; and Mr. Barrington, who was with me, said he was the Prince of Wales' private chaplain.'

'Really?' I said; for it is hard to imagine so exalted a person today going to a dingy establishment in Maiden Lane (or at least one where he does not fear to be recognized) and being obliged to rub shoulders there with impoverished actors and tradesmen.

Mr. Padmore nodded solemnly. 'And Dr. Monro, who was the King's –'

'Mad-doctor!' I cried, remembering Mrs. Bennett.

He nodded and beamed – not, I think, with admiration at my knowledge, but rather with satisfaction at the discovery that his world had not yet entirely vanished, and that a man who had been famous in his time was still remembered in mine.

'Did you know', I said, 'that he was one of Turner's first patrons?'

He shook his head. 'But I'm not surprised to hear it; for he was known as a collector, as I recall, and as something of an artist himself. And he must have seen the boy's drawings at the shop, for old Mr. Turner used to pin them up in the window and around the door, and sell them for two or three shillings apiece. He was also, did you know –?'

But at that moment Mrs. Chambers set the tea before us; and he stopped talking, and watched appreciatively as she poured.

'There, now,' she said, when she was done. 'It was a pleasure to meet you, Miss Halcombe.' She collected the handkerchief from the window and handed it to me. 'Perhaps you'd be good enough to show this again when you leave, and I shall know to come and tidy up.'

'Bless you, Betty,' murmured Mr. Padmore, as she left. 'She is so . . . she is so . . .' And then, quite suddenly, his eyelids fluttered and drooped, and his head dropped forward.

'You were saying . . .' I began loudly; but he did not stir.

The thought that sleep might succeed where death had not, and deprive me at the last of some vital piece of information, reduced me to a kind of panic, and without pausing to consider I leapt up and tapped him on the shoulder. It was enough, thank God. He twitched, and opened his eyes, and looked up at me. For an instant he did not seem to know who I was; but then he said:

'Ah, Miss Halcombe, Miss Halcombe, forgive me. Were we progressing?'

'Indeed,' I said, feeling the tears start in my eyes.

He laughed apologetically. 'I grow foolish, I fear. I entirely forget where . . .'

'Dr. Monro.'

'Oh, yes, yes. He was a great connoisseur –'

'Yes,' I said, impatience getting the better of me. 'But you were about to tell me something else about him.'

'Was I?' He frowned thoughtfully. 'Ah! He tended the King during his –?'

'I know that!' I tried to soften the effect by laughing, but he seemed somewhat taken aback, and sank into perplexed silence.

I vowed I should not interrupt him again. And I was rewarded, for after a few seconds he said:

'The Hospital?'

'What Hospital?'

'I must have mentioned that. Or perhaps I assumed you knew? The *Bethlem* Hospital.'

'What of it?'

'Why, Dr. Monro worked there. He was director, or physician, or some such.'

I knew his words had some great significance – I knew they closed a circle I had thought destined to remain incomplete – but I was too busy writing them down to see their full implications. At length, Mr. Padmore himself saved me the trouble; for after gazing out of the window for half a minute or so, he said falteringly, as if he had only just grasped it himself:

'And do you know, that was a strange coincidence; for Mrs. Turner herself went mad, I believe, and ended up under his care.'

My mouth was dry with excitement, and I forced myself to take a sip of tea before asking:

'Do you remember her at all?'

'Barely. I think perhaps she was kept out of sight; for by all accounts she had an ungovernable temper, and might have troubled the customers. I do recall . . . I do recall . . .' He paused and grimaced, visibly struggling to retrieve the fragments of something that had happened almost seventy years ago. At length he nodded, as if he were finally satisfied that he had got them in order, and said:

'The family, I think, lived mostly in the cellar or basement. And I do recall one day hearing the most blood-curdling screams and howls coming from downstairs. Mr. Turner was setting my curls, or something like – he was a spry, cheerful little fellow, always bouncing about on his toes, like a sparrow; and at first he just laughed and tried to make light of it. But then the boy came rushing up, white as death, and ran into the street; and Turner made some excuse, and went down to soothe her.'

'When was this?'

He shrugged, as much with his eyebrows as with his shoulders. "Eighty-nine. 'Ninety. 'Ninety-one. I don't think I ever saw or heard anything of her again. But a year or two later Turner did tell me his son had taken a painting-room at the other end of the court, and I remember thinking it must have been to get away from the mother.' He paused, and sighed. 'Oh! but Bethlem Hospital, Miss Halcombe. That wasn't kind. It is more humane now, I believe, but then it was a hell – as I can testify, for I went there once, to see a poor friend of mine, who after hanged himself. In the winter he was shut up like a stalled beast, with a straw mattress to lie on; in the summer he was purged and bled and doused in cold water.' He shook his head, as if that were the only protest he could make. Tears filled his eyes, and his voice broke as he went on: 'Our Saviour cast out demons, but not by bleeding or half-drowning the wretches they tormented.'

'I'm sorry,' I said. 'I did not mean to distress you.'

He shook his head again, and started to weep silently.

'Let us talk of something else,' I said. 'The theatre. Lady Meesden.'

He nodded; but then, as suddenly as before, his eyes closed, and his chin sank to his chest; and all at once the agitation left his face, and he became so still that – save for his breathing – you might have supposed that he had finally crossed the almost imperceptible boundary separating him from death.

I did not try to rouse him again. I set the handkerchief in the window, and left.

*

I wrestled with myself all the way back to Kensington. Should I, or shouldn't I? It was late – I was tired – I had done enough for one day. And yet my curiosity would not be quieted. In the end, just before we turned into Brompton Grove, I stopped the cab, and told the driver to take me to Maiden Lane.

I repented of my decision the moment we entered the street. It had started to rain, and the wheels bumped over mounds of rotting leaves which had washed down from the market, filling the air – I could smell it even through the closed windows – with the stench of putrefaction. Crowds of blank-faced children stared in as we passed. Two middle-aged drunkards, their eyes as dull and slithery as oysters, leered and pointed from the steps of the Cider Cellar tavern. Realizing how vulnerable I should be if I got out, I hastily reduced the scale of my ambitions, and told myself that perhaps it would be enough if I saw the shop from the cab.

But since I knew from Walter that it was no longer a barber's, my only hope of picking it out was to discover which of the dark little alleys leading off the street was Hand Court – and this, try as I might, I could not do: for some were unmarked, and the names of the others so worn and covered in soot that I could not read them from so far away. When we reached the end, therefore, I told the driver to turn round, and to stop outside a pawnbroker's shop I had noticed as we passed, which I thought I might safely enter (for while my apparent motives might be discreditable, they would at least be easily understood, and not open me to unwanted attentions), and where I could expect a civil answer.

No sooner had I closed the door behind me than a girl of thirteen or fourteen appeared from the back of the shop. She had large brown eyes, and a pale pretty face that was already hardening into calculation and suspicion. She looked at me unsmilingly, saying nothing.

'I wonder', I said, 'if you could tell me where Hand Court is?'

She jerked her thumb towards a narrow arch on the other side of the street.

'Thank you,' I said.

'You want to see old Jenny?' she said, as I reached the door again. 'I'll take you for a tanner.'

'No, thank you,' I said (for the thought of leaving this twilight world and plunging into the evil-smelling darkness of the court filled me with horror). 'But here's sixpence for your trouble.'

She took the money without a word, and scowled at me as I left, as if she feared I had somehow got the better of her, and duped her into parting with something at less than its true value.

I asked the driver to wait a minute or two more, and crossed the street, pulling my cloak about me to protect myself as best I could from the fine penetrating rain. The entrance to the court was a plain classical arch with a heavy keystone; and through the iron gate barring it I could see huddles of people talking in the dull lamplight glow from doors and windows. I had no trouble identifying which had been the barber's shop – for had not Mr. Padmore said it was to the left of the hall, which meant it must have been the building on the left-hand side of the gateway? – but the 'long low' window of his description had long since disappeared, and been replaced by a tall modern double sash extending the full width of the house.

But what caught my attention was what lay below it. For there, at right-angles to a grating set into the pavement, was an elliptical basement window, covered with a prison-like iron grille.

The echoes were unmistakable.

Sandycombe Lodge.

The Bay of Baiae.

Thursday

Six days – almost a week – since I last opened this journal. Six days in a darkened room, with Mrs. Davidson almost always at my bedside. Six days of chattering teeth, and a thirst that would not be satisfied, and delirious dreams – of which I can remember almost nothing, save that for some reason I felt horrified by the thinness of my own sheet, which I experienced not only as a chill against the skin, but also as a sick numbness in my mouth, and as a kind of warped moral quality, as if it were the work of the devil.

I should not have gone to Maiden Lane. That is what Dr. Hampson says. To get wet in such an insanitary place, when I was already tired from days of reading and writing and staying up half the night, was little short of madness. The fever could well have proved fatal. I must think myself lucky, and treat it as a salutary warning.

I try to do as he says, and thank God with a grateful heart. Too often, though, I think of it as a week lost, and of how easily I might have avoided losing it, rather than as a life gained.

But at least today I was finally able to send a note to Walter. I excused myself from recounting all my adventures, on the grounds that I am still too weak to write at length. Which is, indeed, true enough; but I cannot deny that I am also aware of a certain reluctance in myself to tell him everything, though I am at a loss to explain it. Am I just being petty-minded and mean-spirited, or will I be more forthcoming once I am confident about my own conclusions?

Tuesday
On Sunday I worked for two hours – yesterday four – today six. Dr. Hampson would not approve, but I must note down my thoughts while they are still in my mind.

There will always be mysteries about Turner. And yet I feel I have come closer to the truth than I could have possibly hoped only a month ago.

What follows is no more than conjecture; but does it not make sense of what we know?

His first memories of the world were of a dark basement, and of a wild, uncontrollable woman who terrified him. She could not give him the love and comfort that any child must crave from his mother – and yet he was powerless before her, and could not escape.

Any wonder, then, that he seems to have had a lifelong horror of intimacy? Or that in later life he painted women not as living individuals, with all the wondrous beauty and variety that he found in landscape, but rather as pale, inert objects – corpses, or dolls, or the dummies he remembered seeing in his father's window, which had no power to hurt him?

Any wonder, too, that basements and cellars and caverns were always especially sinister for him (think how all those stories of dragons and monsters in caves must have struck his childish mind!), and associated in his work with menace and ruin? Perhaps that is why, when he came to design his own house, he effectively hid the basement out of sight, so

344

excluding its troubling presence from the light-filled rooms where he lived and worked. (Is this what Walter saw when we went to Sandycombe Lodge? Did it make him suppose that Turner was trying to conceal some shameful secret, rather than the painful memory of his own childhood?)

To the same cause, I think, we may ascribe the beginnings of Turner's taste for mystery and elusiveness. To be at home, as a boy – or in any place where his whereabouts were definitely known by his mother – was to risk, at any moment, having his fragile world invaded and destroyed by a hurricane. Hence his early decision to move to the other end of Hand Court, and then – when he could – to Harley Street. Hence his insistence on privacy, and his anger at being disturbed. Hence his travels, perhaps, and his reputation for reclusiveness, and his flitting back and forth between two or three places, often without letting even those closest to him know exactly where he was.

What now of the pictures? Does what I have learned help me to say anything more about them?

I think it does. For might not the genesis of all those storms and shipwrecks and avalanches lie in his mother's madness? (Is it even possible to see, perhaps, in those bleeding suns and dripping sea-monsters, a tortured reflection of her eventual fate?)

The tempests he could not subdue at home he sought to portray – and so to master – in his paintings. This may seem fanciful; and yet is it not a very natural human impulse?

At the same time, paint gave him mastery of another world: a glorious, sun-filled Eden where, for a while, he could take refuge. But 'in the midst of life, we are in death'. Is that not the meaning of *The Bay of Baiae*, and all those other ruin-infested landscapes? Flee and work and hide as you may, sooner or later the outbursts of a disordered mind and a violent nature, or merely the ineluctable progress of Time and decay, will find you out and destroy you.

We know he had friends – men and women who were able
to take him as they found him, and offer him some of the
domestic comfort and security he could not find in his own
home. These people aroused in him what were perhaps his
strongest human emotions – feelings of gratitude and affection so intense that in many cases (Amelia Bennett's father;
Walter Fawkes; Lord Egremont) they seem to have been
undiminished even by death itself.

But what of his family?

His *art* provided his family – a substitute for the human
family which (aside from his father) he never had as a child,
and never acquired as an adult. Did not Amelia Bennett say
he spoke of his pictures as his 'children', and mourned them
when they were gone? Did not Caro Bibby use the same
image, in her description of his gallery? Might it not have
been the intensity of his parental feelings that drove him to
treat the unfortunate engraver, Farrant, with such uncharac-
teristic harshness? – for any mother may become a tyrant
when she feels her young are threatened. Even gentle Laura,
I am certain, would kill, if she had to, to protect Florrie and
little Walter.

The idea holds, I think, when we turn to the Royal
Academy. Surely his concern for its affairs and traditions,
and the deep (if eccentric) seriousness with which he took
his obligations as a teacher there, suggest that he felt bound
to it by ties far stronger than mere self-interest – as if it were
his fellow-practitioners, rather than his parents and uncles
and cousins, who constituted the body which most pro-
foundly defined him, and which commanded his most abid-
ing loyalty?

We know that – whether or not he liked them, and
whether or not he admired their work – he refused to criti-
cize other artists, and so inflict on them the pain he had suffered himself. Such heroic restraint – which must have been

immensely hard to maintain in the gossipy, back-biting, hot-house atmosphere of the Academy – is surely consistent with the idea that he viewed them more as relations (the tiresome aunt we loathe, but must nonetheless tolerate for the sake of family unity) than as professional rivals?

To whom do we leave our possessions? To our families.

Did not Sir Charles say that Turner's will left his 'children' to the nation, and his fortune to provide for his 'brother' artists in distress?

Such despair. Such loneliness. Such bitterness. Such devotion. Such meanness. Such generosity.

Such hope that he might at length be understood.

To take such a man, at the end of his days, and by patience and kindness and devotion to overcome his suspicion, and penetrate the dark thickets that have grown up about his heart, and free the love imprisoned there – that is no mean achievement.

Poor Turner.

His poor mother.

Good Mrs. Booth.

Wednesday

An idle morning. Tired from yesterday.

This afternoon Elizabeth Eastlake called, to ask after my health. My mind was still full of Turner; and so eager was I to put my conclusions to the test that I thoughtlessly started to tell her about them over tea. By the time I realized how foolish I was being, it was too late to stop; and I blundered on, desperately hoping I could still somehow avoid the trap that I had created for myself.

But no sooner had I finished than she drew me into it. Giving no indication of whether or not she agreed with what I had said, she asked:

'These are your views, or your brother's?'

'Both of ours,' I said, having already decided that this was the lesser of two evils. 'But predominantly his, naturally.'

In reality, of course, Walter has not even heard them yet; and – as I am only too uncomfortably aware – may well disown them when he has. But the only alternative would have been to claim them entirely as my own, and so risk suggesting that the book's central conception – if he *does* accept them – is more mine than his, which would be a devastating blow to his pride.

I am not sure, even so, that she believed me; for she searched my face intently, and there was a caustic edge in her voice as she said:

'Well, he *has* certainly made great progress since we last spoke. Remarkable to think that it came merely from sitting in Cumberland, and reflecting. Something in the air, perhaps.' She smiled. 'At all events, please give him my congratulations, and tell him this is exactly what I had hoped for. Perhaps you and he would care to come to dinner with us next week, and discuss his ideas further?'

It cannot be helped – we must go, and he must make a good impression; or Lady Eastlake will lose confidence in him, and the whole undertaking will be jeopardized at precisely the moment we begin to make headway.

As soon as she had gone, I settled down and wrote to him, saying he must come back.

A small but disquieting epilogue. Davidson had taken the letter to the post, and I was heeding Dr. Hampson's advice by taking a rest after my exertions, when I heard the doorbell ring. It seemed late for someone to be calling, but I got up and readied myself to receive a visitor. After a minute or two Mrs. Davidson came in, and began making up the fire.

'Who was that at the door just now?' I said.

'A woman, miss.'

I waited for her to go on, but she merely busied herself making a good deal of unnecessary racket with the poker. At length I said:

'What kind of woman?'

She hesitated, and swallowed noisily. 'Not what you'd call respectable, miss. And nervous.'

'What did she want?'

'She wanted to see Mr. Hartright,' she said, so quietly I could scarcely hear her.

'Why?'

'She would not say, miss.' She turned, and her eyes briefly met mine, as if she hoped I would see the disapproval in them, and so spare her the necessity of putting it into words. 'Except to Mr. Hartright.'

'Is she still there?' I said, moving towards the door. 'Let me see her.'

'I sent her away, miss. I did not think you should be disturbed.'

But I am disturbed. I cannot help it. Six months ago I should have assumed she *was* simply some poor wretch Walter had helped, and thought no more about it. But now . . .

But it is no use dwelling on it. We must get this book finished, and out of the way – and pray that we can do so without causing lasting damage to our own lives.

Book Three

XLIV

Memorandum of a letter from Walter Hartright to Mr. Elijah Nisbet, 1st December, 185–

1. May remember we met when locomotive broke down near Leeds.
2. Very kindly suggested might call to see your Turners.
3. Shall be passing through Birmingham *en route* to London next week. May I accept invitation then?

XLV

Letter from Walter Hartright to Marian Halcombe, 1st December, 185–

Limmeridge,
Friday

My dear Marian,

You are a marvel! To have made such astonishing progress, in less than two months!

Unfortunately, I shall not be able to return in time for the proposed dinner on Monday. I realize this may place you in a difficult situation, and I am sorry for it; but since I had not heard from you for so long (please do not take this as a criticism – I can quite see that it would have been impossible to write, when you have been so occupied), I naturally had no idea of what, if anything, you had discovered, and no inkling that you might have made plans involving me. I have, in consequence, been pursuing my own independent research, which I fear obliges me to stop in Birmingham on my way back to town. Would it be possible, do you think, to postpone our engagement with the Eastlakes for a few days?

With love from your devoted brother,

Walter

XLVI

Letter from Walter Hartright to Laura Hartright,
4th December, 185–

Heaven knows where,
Monday

My dearest love,

    See! I am being as good as my word! – though with some difficulty, I must confess – the train lurches from side to side like a ship at sea – can only put pen to paper in half-second when it is equidistant between the two. But now or never – for when we arrive at Willenhall (shortly) must go directly to the inn, and thence to Mr. Nisbet's. So please forgive brief note. More tomorrow, I promise.

    Meanwhile – don't be anxious about me. I am well. I have forgotten nothing. I love you.

Walter

XLVII

From the journal of Walter Hartright, 4th
December, 185–

The rest can wait for my letter, but this, I know, would upset her.

    When he came in from seeing the poor fellow, Nisbet was clearly shocked – his face pale beneath the smudges of soot, his left hand grasping his right wrist, as if for support. He looked out of the window at the vision of hell beyond; and then steadied himself, and shrugged, and turned back towards me.

'The price of Progress,' he said. 'Everything has its price.' He nodded, as if this catechism had restored his faith. 'Turner knew that. Now, will you take a glass of wine, Mr. Hartright?'

XLVIII

Letter from Walter Hartright to Laura Hartright, 5th December, 185–

A little past Rugby,
Tuesday

My dearest love,

The North-Western Railway, thank God, is kinder to correspondents than the Birmingham and Derby. My writing-box stays on my knee (most of the time) of its own volition; the pen makes only occasional unauthorized forays across the paper; and my elbow even has the luxury of unimpeded movement, thanks to the seat next to mine being empty. All in all, in fact, aside from the cold, I'm almost as comfortable as I should be in my study at home. So here, at last, is a proper letter.

I had always supposed that the name 'Black Country' was a kind of poetical exaggeration, but it turns out to be as bald and literal a description as 'Canal Street' or 'Station Road'. The ground is black with coal and cinders – the air with smoke – the very trees and blades of grass are black with soot, with just a flash of green here and there to remind you of their former state, like an old bright handkerchief glimpsed unexpectedly amidst the drabness of a workhouse. Mr. Nisbet, it transpires, is an iron-master; and while his house – a nightmare confection of gothic spires and Tudor windows, standing not half a mile from his works – is barely ten years old, it is already so caked with dust that you can only tell by the close-mesh pattern of the mortar that it is built of brick rather than stone.

The door was opened by a middle-aged woman, who led me into a large octagonal hall. The walls were bare, save only for a few sombre portraits, and a picture of Nisbet and his family on the monumental chimney-breast. In the centre of the room was a huge table that might have been intended for King Arthur and his knights, but otherwise it was sparingly furnished, with a few seats set against the sides, and three wing-chairs arranged in a semi-circle in front of the fire blazing in the great stone hearth. A smoky light filtered down from a ring of small windows in the tower above, giving the place a kind of airy solemnity, like the interior of a church.

'I'll tell the master you're here,' said the woman.

But she had not gone three paces before Nisbet himself entered, talking animatedly to another man who – from his heavy boots, and coal-stained brown suit – I took to be his agent. Nisbet was red-faced, and repeatedly shook a sheaf of papers in his hand for emphasis; while his companion listened gravely, head bowed, occasionally nodding, and all the time casting his eyes about the room, like an animal searching for some means of escape. In due course, they fell on me, and settled there; whereupon Nisbet paused, and glanced towards me to see what he was looking at.

'Ah, Mr. Hartright,' he said. 'I shall be with you directly.' He turned back to the man in the brown suit. 'Tell him to think of his wife, Harkness,' he said. 'Tell him to ask her opinion. He must understand – they must all understand – I will not have it.'

Harkness flushed, and stared at his feet. I thought for a moment he was going to protest; but at length he nodded abruptly, and started towards the front door at such a pace that the woman had to scuttle behind him to keep up.

'Now then,' said Nisbet, giving my hand a perfunctory shake. 'How are you?' He did not meet my gaze, but merely looked about the hall, as if making an inventory of its contents. After a few seconds he sat down before the fire, indicating with a casual wave that I should do the same. 'We'll do well enough in here for the time being, I think,' he said. 'My father-in-law's dozing in the library, and I don't want to disturb him.'

His tone was pleasant enough, but there was no hint of apology, and he did not even pretend to consult my wishes, but simply assumed I should fall in with his. I was conscious, too, that he was looking at me in an odd way, staring at my legs and hands and at the back of my chair, with as little embarrassment as a farmer examining a horse he has been offered for sale. At length he sat back, with a faint air of puzzlement, and said:

'So, did you work it up?'

'I beg your pardon?'

'The locomotive?'

'The loco–?' I began. And then I recalled the circumstances of our last meeting, and realized that he must be talking about my drawing of the broken railway engine.

'No,' I said, without pausing to think. 'I've been engaged in other things.'

'Yes?' he said impatiently. His eyes started to search the area round my chair again.

And all at once I knew: he was looking for a portfolio. He had assumed I was a professional artist, and I had not corrected him; and now he supposed that I had come here to try to sell him something. Hence his off-hand manner towards me – a manner which I had last experienced, it suddenly struck me, as a young man, when applying for the post of a drawing-master, and which implied that while

I was something more than a tradesman, I was certainly less than a guest.

How to explain the truth, without embarrassment to us both? Matter-of-factly, making nothing of it? Humorously, with an easy laugh at such a foolish misunderstanding? I was still trying to decide when he went on:

'Anything in the same vein? Engines? Machines?'

'No,' I said. 'Not at the moment.'

'Have you then nothing to show me?'

I shook my head. 'I simply came to see your Turners, since you were kind enough to invite me.'

I had not meant to sound reproachful, but perhaps I did; for he at once said:

'Oh, of course! of course!' He nodded and smiled. 'Forgive me if I mistook your purpose, but men in your line of business seldom lose an opportunity to advertise their wares, I find.'

Perhaps, even now, I should have told him what my *real* purpose was, but having just disavowed one ulterior motive I felt I could not very easily admit to another; so I merely laughed, and said:

'Even Turner?'

'I knew him only as an old man,' he replied. 'When he had no need to play the salesman. But even then he liked his money.' He frowned, and thrust out his lower lip, as if making some nice judgement, or recollecting some disagreeable memory. 'If truth be told, he was something of a miser.'

'Indeed?' I said – as innocently, I like to think, as if the idea were entirely new to me.

He nodded. 'He'd never part with a penny unless he had to, or spend sixpence to save a shilling. The –' He stopped himself, reluctantly, I thought. 'But there. You don't want to hear about the man. You want to see the pictures.'

'No, please,' I said. 'He is something of a hero of mine.'

He went on immediately, like a machine that needs only the smallest nudge to set it in motion again.

'Well, the gallery in Queen Anne Street was a sight to behold. I have workmen keep their houses in better repair.' He shook his head incredulously. 'I was passing once when it came on to rain, and I thought I'd take shelter inside; but when I got upstairs it was so wet I had to keep my umbrella up. Water coming through the broken skylights – water in puddles on the floor – water streaming down the pictures. The wall-covering – some kind of red fabric – was coming off in handfuls. There was a painting of some great classical scene – Carthage, I think it was – and when I got close I saw the sky was all cracked like breaking ice, and in some places it was peeling away altogether. Another canvas was being used as a kind of door, covering a hole in the window, through which the cats would come and go.'

'Cats!'

'Oh, yes, they were everywhere. The place stank of them. They belonged to the housekeeper – a hag of a woman, to give you nightmares.'

'What, Mrs. Booth, you mean?'

'No, Danby, her name was. Hannah Danby.' He mimed wrapping a bandage about his head. 'Her face was so disfigured she had to keep it covered.'

It was all I could do not to laugh at such a relentless catalogue of gothic detail; but he seemed deadly serious as he went on:

'The cats, I suppose, were the only creatures who could tolerate her company. And she rewarded them by letting them walk and sleep where they pleased, and sharpen their claws on the picture-frames, and harry visitors. While I was standing there one of them jumped without warning on my neck, making me drop my umbrella in surprise – and suddenly four or five more appeared, attracted by the noise, and began pressing themselves about my legs.'

He must at last have noticed my efforts to keep a straight face, for he smiled in response, and said: 'And if it wasn't the cats it'd be Turner himself, creeping out of his studio and taking you unawares.'

He chuckled, which I took as a licence finally to laugh myself; and we both guffawed, egging each other on, until we had half-forgotten the original cause of our merriment. After thirty seconds or so, however, he stopped abruptly and said:

'But I shouldn't make fun of him. I wouldn't have lived as he did – but then I couldn't have painted as he did, either. And for all his oddities, he was a pleasure to do business with. Always absolutely straight – you'd agree a price, or a date, and he'd stick to it without fail.' He paused, and pondered a moment, and then acknowledged some new thought by raising his finger. 'I'll tell you something else. He was the only painter I ever met who could talk intelligently about *my* world. The uses of different kinds of coal for smelting. The design of a new pump-engine. He was always fascinated by those kinds of subjects. He had an unshakeable belief in the industrial progress of our nation. As you'll see in –'

He suddenly stopped, and cocked his head. For a moment I could not imagine what had disturbed him. And then I heard it myself: a hubbub of cries and shouts and clanking metal, some way off but impossible to ignore, like the clamour of an approaching army.

Nisbet drew in his breath sharply, and jumped to his feet. 'Excuse me,' he said, barely audibly; and started to leave at a run. But after a few steps he made a visible effort to master himself, and slowed to a walk.

'Come on,' he said, turning to me with a grim smile. 'Dad must be awake now anyway.'

He led me out of the hall and into a square room at the back of the house. It was plainly meant as a library; but it felt more like a small museum or gallery, for half the shelves were taken up not with books but with architectural and mechanical models, and there were pictures covering every scrap of wall. An elderly man in high boots and a plum-coloured riding coat sat before the fire, with the wide-eyed look of someone who has been startled awake.

'What is it?' he asked Nisbet.

Nisbet shook his head brusquely, and strode to the window. The curtains had already been drawn, but he threw them open again, and looked out.

Do you recall the picture of Pandemonium in my father's copy of *Paradise Lost*? If not, find it in my study; for it will give you some idea of the scene that now confronted us. My immediate thought was that the earth itself must be on fire; for, beyond a line of bare trees at the end of the garden, I could at first see nothing but flames, and plumes of black smoke, and some heavier, yellowish vapour that curled this way and that across the ground, as if it were too lethargic to rise into the air. As my eyes grew more accustomed to the dusk, however, I could make out huge black mounds, as big as hills; and the silhouettes of tall chimneys, and engines with great wheels for winding up the coal, and clusters of sheds and cottages and stables – all strewn about as if they had been placed there with as little thought for order or beauty as pins stuck in a pin-cushion.

At the centre were three or four raging furnaces, surrounded by a tangle of tramways lined with laden trucks – which were probably carrying nothing more fearful than blocks of limestone, but might, from their appearance, have been conveying the souls of the damned to hell (an impression accentuated by the rhythmic thump of the engines, which sounded as solemn and ominous as a death march). As we watched, men seemed to be running towards them from every direction – yelling, dropping tools and buckets and gesticulating as they went – and gathering in an ever-bigger knot about something, or someone, on the ground.

I heard Nisbet mutter, under his breath, 'Damn!'

'Is it another accident?' said the old man. He was still in his chair, twisting his head towards us, as if he was too frightened to see the truth for himself.

'Looks like it,' said Nisbet, flatly.

'Oh, Eli!' said the old man, shaking his head. He looked very pale. A strand of thin white hair fell into his eyes, but he did not try to remove it.

Nisbet looked down at his hands, flexing the fingers abstractedly; and then turned to me with a brittle smile and said, with a creditable attempt at normality:

'You'll see, Mr. Hartright, that I've not done a great deal for authors and booksellers.' He waved towards the half-empty shelves, and then to the paintings crowded between them. 'But your fraternity has no reason to complain of me.'

Looking around, I saw that there were perhaps thirty pictures altogether – oils and watercolours, prints and drawings, in almost every conceivable size and shape and manner. The only principle linking them seemed to be their subject matter: every one of them showed a machine, or an industrial process.

'You see my taste,' said Nisbet, trying to sound humorous. 'It's the taste of a man with an interest in two railways and a shipping company.'

'Eli,' said the old man, before I had time to reply. 'Should you not go out there?'

'I'm not going to faffle about like a woman,' said Nisbet quietly. He narrowed his eyes, and looked out of the window again. 'There's a bridge-stocker there. There's a manager. There's Harkness. They know where to find me if I'm wanted.' He returned to me, and, touching my elbow, moved me towards a picture over the fireplace. 'There you are. There's a Turner for you.'

It was a large marine scene: a turbulent grey sea, churned

up by the wind, with an embattled steamer struggling against the storm. Everything was extraordinarily imprecise, even by Turner's standards – the waves no more than a few thick, ridged swirls laid on a brilliant white ground – the ship a fuzzy black blur, of which the most clearly defined feature was the torrent of smoke streaming from its funnel. And yet the effect was somehow so vivid that you could feel the lurch of the deck under your feet, and the sting of the spray on your face, and smell the hot sour reek of coal-smoke, and hear the wheels thrashing and the engine throbbing in your ears.

'What do you think?' asked Nisbet.

'It's very fine.'

'Is that an honest opinion?'

'Yes,' I said, somewhat taken aback by his bluntness.

'Then you must fight the whole neighbourhood. Including my father-in-law.' He turned to the old man. 'This is Mr. Hartright, Dad. Mr. Hartright, Sam Bligh.'

'How d'ye do?' said the old man. His hand trembled as it took mine.

'Mr. Hartright's an artist, Dad,' said Nisbet. He pointed towards the Turner. 'Tell him what you think of that.'

Mr. Bligh attempted a smile. 'It's all froth and splutter,' he said, like a child encouraged to repeat some amusing remark before visitors.

'And you'd as soon . . .?' prompted Nisbet.

'I'd as soon sit in the laundry, and watch the bubbles on the copper.'

'There,' said Nisbet, laughing. 'That is what I must contend with. And his daughter's no better. She thinks –'

But I never discovered what Mrs. Nisbet thought; for at that moment the man in the brown suit entered without knocking. He was out of breath; his hair was wet and tousled, his red face blotched with dirt; and there were scorch-marks on his sleeves.

'What is it?' snapped Nisbet.

Harkness glanced covertly at me. 'I think you should come, sir,' he said softly.

'What *is* it?' roared Nisbet. He was white and shaking, and spat out the words so furiously that he had to wipe the spittle from his mouth with the back of his hand.

I struggled to hold my tongue; for poor Harkness had clearly been through some terrible ordeal, and Nisbet's behaviour seemed akin to the Roman tyrant's monstrous practice of killing the bearer of bad news. But Harkness himself appeared quite unmoved by it – as if, having bolted the doors and put up the shutters to protect himself against some great catastrophe, he was not now going to be intimidated by a mere show of temper.

'Well, sir,' he said, drawing himself up and looking his employer calmly in the eye, 'I told him what you said. And *he* said, he was a free man, and if you wouldn't have him there's others as would. And he stormed off.'

'Is that all?' said Nisbet, his eyes lightening, like a condemned man who had suddenly glimpsed the possibility of reprieve.

Harkness shook his head. 'There was a barrow by the filling-hole, barring his way. He couldn't see it clearly, what with the dark, and him drunk. I suppose he must have thought it was full, for he seized it with all his might, to throw it clear. But it was empty, and gave way too easily, and the force of his own movement sent him into the furnace.'

'Oh!' whimpered the old man, turning away, and pressing his fingers anguishedly against his brow. Nisbet's gaze did not waver; but his face paled and seemed to tighten, as if some unwelcome presence had insinuated itself beneath the skin.

'Two of the other men pulled him out again, almost at once,' said Harkness. 'But he's bad. Very bad.'

'Has the doctor been called?' asked Nisbet.

'Of course,' said Harkness. 'But . . .' He dropped his eyes, finally admitting defeat.

'And what of his wife?'

Harkness shook his head.

'Give her five pounds, and tell her I shall see her tomorrow,' said Nisbet, shooing him towards the door. He started to follow, then stopped and turned to his father-in-law. 'Dad, look after Mr. Hartright, will you?'

But, try as he might, poor Mr. Bligh had not the heart to play the host; and after enquiring where I had come from, and where I was going, and making two or three feeble observations about the pictures, he gave up altogether, and gravitated towards the window, where he stood with his hands clasped behind him, like an elderly Bonaparte surveying the field of Waterloo. Secretly relieved (for I did not feel much like making conversation myself), I lingered at the other end of the room, and tried to divert myself by looking at the remaining Turners. They were, undeniably, magnificent – the interior of a foundry, a dazzling contrast of dark and light; and a fiery railway train appearing through a curtain of smoke and rain – but even their drama seemed somehow flat and lifeless compared with the tragedy unfolding outside, and after a few minutes I found myself standing next to Mr. Bligh and looking out.

The commotion by the furnace seemed to have died down – the swarming throng had stabilized, and ordered itself into a long line, as dark and immobile as a wall. As we watched, it slowly parted, and four minuscule doll-figures emerged carrying what looked like an untidy heap of blankets on a gate. They moved at a regular, deliberate plod, without urgency, towards a horse and cart standing at the edge of the crowd. Clearly, the victim was either out of danger – or, as I feared, beyond help.

I looked away, but a pitying moan from my companion

made me turn back immediately. It took me a moment to make out what he had seen: a woman, running and stumbling across the rough ground, who hurled herself down before the makeshift litter, forcing the men to stop. She hugged herself – then threw her arms in the air – then rose again, and did a strange distraught dance, stamping her feet, and flinging her head from side to side. We, of course, saw this only as a kind of dumbshow, for she was too far away for us to hear the accompanying wails and sobs – which (contrary to what you might suppose) actually made matters worse; for it heightened our feelings of powerlessness and detachment, while underscoring the awful solitariness of human suffering.

But enough – I do not want to distress you, or myself. Suffice it to say that I felt I must avert my eyes, and yet knew that I must not. For a moment I was paralysed by this *impasse*; and then I suddenly saw that by *drawing* the dreadful scene before me I might somehow make it tolerable. I could not be of material aid to my fellow creatures; but it seemed to me that by bearing witness to their agony I might – in some tiny, mysterious way – share it with them, and give it meaning.

My notebook was too small to be serviceable; so I turned to Mr. Bligh and said:

'Do you think I might have some paper?'

I think he, too, was glad to be doing something; for he at once went to the writing table in the corner, and brought me five or six sheets – and then, seeing the speed at which I worked, went back for more, and stood attentively at my side, like the assistant who turns the pages for a musician, in case I should run out again.

I do not know how long I stood there, or how many drawings I made, but I was still labouring when Nisbet at length returned. He seemed shaken, but after a minute or two recovered somewhat, and, recalling his duties as a host, offered me a glass of wine – which I was only too happy to accept. As he handed it to me, his eye fell on my drawings, and he picked them up, and silently scrutinized them for a minute or more. At length he returned them to me, saying:

'Send me a sketch of the finished painting when you've done it. The locomotive, too. I might be interested in buying.'

Heavens! We are almost there! My love to you always, and to the children.

Walter

XLIX

Letter from Laura Hartright to Walter Hartright, 7th December, 185–

Limmeridge,
Thursday

My darling boy,

Your letter quite frightened me. Such a horrible accident! That unfortunate man, and his poor wife! I scarce dare think about it.

Please, my darling, be careful.

Your loving wife,

Laura

L

From the journal of Walter Hartright, 10th December, 185–

Prepared the canvas today. Reviewed my drawings. Worked up two or three preliminary watercolour sketches.

But I cannot settle to it.

There is something disturbing about being back in London. Sometimes – most of the time – I still feel myself. But occasionally I seem to glimpse the world through the eyes of someone else entirely – someone I supposed I had cast off for ever, but who appears to have been waiting for me here, and to have gained strength from my return.

Perhaps I am just suffering from wounded pride. For I feel I have been ordered here like a performing animal, to go through my tricks before Lady Eastlake, and parrot Marian's views as my own.

I must force myself back to the picture. If I can but make *that* work, I shall truly know more of Turner than they ever could.

LI

From the journal of Marian Halcombe, 13th December, 185–

Thank God. My prayers have been answered.

How easily do we lose our sense of proportion. Twelve hours ago, had I been able to foresee the circumstances in which I write this, I should have been utterly distraught. But my heart, instead, is full of gratitude – for what I have lost, I can see, is as nothing compared with what I *thought* I had lost, and has been miraculously restored to me.

Now. I must be as good as my word, and set to work.

From this side of the abyss, it is hard to recognize the woman arriving in Fitzroy Square last night as myself. I observe her coldly (as a stranger would) being helped by Walter from the cab, and glancing expectantly towards the front door, and then devoting a full minute or more to smoothing her dress, settling her bonnet, and hoisting her skirts above the mire, as if a wrinkle or a stray hair or a muddy hem were the worst disaster that could befall her. There is something contemptible about such a petty display; and yet it moves me to pity, too – for I know what she in her blithe ignorance cannot even suspect: that her vanity is about to get its come-uppance.

I had supposed, from Elizabeth Eastlake's invitation, that we should be dining with them alone; and I was therefore surprised to find, on entering the drawing room, that there were two other people already there. At first glance you might have supposed them to be an elderly couple; for both were grey-haired, and they shared a kind of plain, no-non-sense demeanour that marked them out as members of the high-minded, rather than the fashionable, portion of the Eastlakes' acquaintance. Something in the way they stood, however – she talking animatedly, he stooping formally towards her, with the intent expression of someone who has difficulty hearing, but does not want to admit it – suggested that they were people who did not know each other well; and as they separated and turned towards us, preparing to be introduced, I saw that in fact she was a full twenty years older than he was. Her lively spirits, plainly, had enabled her to preserve the manner and appearance of a much younger woman; while he (by some strange law of comple-mentarity), though still only in his fifties, seemed to be hur-rying into old age as fast as his stiff limbs could carry him.

'Mrs. Somerville,' said Sir Charles. 'I don't believe you know Miss Halcombe?'

But of course I knew her name (it is impossible to spend

ten minutes in the company of a blue-stocking like Elizabeth Eastlake without hearing it mentioned at least once), and was keenly conscious, as we shook hands, that it was a great honour to meet her. And yet I could not but feel a spasm of disappointment, too, that the Eastlakes had not considered us worthy of an evening by ourselves, but had merely seen us as one more social duty that must somehow be accommodated with all the others.

'Mrs. Somerville, Mr. Hartright,' murmured Sir Charles. 'Miss Halcombe, Mr. Cussons.'

The next moment, disappointment gave way to outright dismay; for, turning towards Mr. Cussons, I glimpsed out of the corner of my eye another couple arriving. I could not, for an instant, believe my first impression of them; but a second glance confirmed it:

Mr. and Mrs. Kingsett.

I don't know if Mr. Cussons noticed my shocked expression, for it was impossible to deduce anything from *his* face whatsoever. He was a tall, distinguished-looking man, with a high domed forehead fringed with feathery hair, and the alert unsmiling eyes of a bird of prey.

'How do you do?' I said.

'How do you do?'

I was painfully aware of the approaching Kingsetts, and frantically wondering how I should conduct myself towards them; but realizing I could not break free from Mr. Cussons just yet without seeming rude, I lingered beside him, waiting for him to go on. He, however, seemed to feel under no compulsion to say anything more, and merely continued to stare – intently enough, but entirely without interest, so that you felt he wasn't really looking at you at all, but merely keeping watch in case a mouse or a rabbit suddenly broke cover, and scuttled across the carpet. After fifteen seconds I felt I had earned my release – for surely a man must exercise his claim to a woman's attention by speaking within a reasonable time, or else forfeit it altogether? – and, muttering an excuse, bowed to the inevitable, and turned to Lydia Kingsett.

I knew at once that matters had not improved since our last meeting. She looked more worn than ever, and her hands were deathly cold as she clasped mine – although she was, I think, genuinely glad to see me, and even managed a little smile as she said, with pathetic eagerness:

'Miss Halcombe, Miss Halcombe, I'm so . . .'

But then she caught her husband's eye, and stopped abruptly.

'You're what?' I said, laughing, and trying to encourage her with a tone of easy familiarity. 'Come on, tell me.'

She mumbled, shook her head, stared at the floor. I touched her wrist, and bent close to her, as you would to a troubled child.

'Hmm?'

But still she said nothing. In the awkward lull that followed, I felt her husband's gaze upon me, as palpable as heat from a fire, challenging me to turn and discover what had silenced her. I tried to resist, but after a few seconds curiosity got the better of me.

It was disagreeable enough just to see him again, like suddenly smelling some foul half-forgotten odour; but what made it worse was the leering way he was looking at me, which was so frankly insulting that I thought one of the other gentlemen must see it, and come to my defence. Mr. Cussons, however, was still surveying the world from his perch, and Walter and Sir Charles were engaged in conversations of their own; so I had no alternative but to try to deter Kingsett myself, by scowling imperiously at him.

For answer – to my amazement – he protruded his tongue an inch or two from his lips, and ran a finger unhurriedly along it, in a gesture of unmistakable depravity – all the while eyeing me with a shameless smirk. If anyone else observed it (and I pray they did not), they could not but have seen it as evidence of some past intimacy between us; and, although I knew myself to be guiltless, I could not help blushing furiously.

I was, for a moment, transfixed; and then, as I saw him starting to advance towards me, preparing to extend the hand he had just licked, I turned tail and fled. Elizabeth Eastlake was, mercifully, talking to Walter, and I felt no compunction in intruding on them and drawing her to one side.

'Please,' I said. 'Do not ask Mr. Kingsett to take me down to dinner.'

'Why?' she said, surprised, with a surreptitious glance in his direction.

'I'll tell you later,' I whispered urgently – for already he had changed course, and was bearing down on us again.

She nodded, and – woman of the world that she is – promptly turned to intercept Kingsett, allowing me to make my escape. I don't know what she said to him, but when, a few minutes later, she whispered something to Sir Charles, and then slipped quietly from the room (presumably to change the place-names on the dinner table) he made no attempt to approach me again.

I stood in a corner, silently congratulating myself. This was not what I had imagined it would be – it might turn out to be a dull and worthless evening – but at least I had averted the worst harm it could do me.

Or so I thought.

I was spared Mr. Kingsett; but in all other respects the dinner turned out every bit as gruesome as I had feared. The price I paid for my deliverance was to be seated next to Mr. Cussons, who for most of the meal showed as little inclination to talk as he had done before it. I did try to breach the silence with a trivial comment or two, but they were as futile as pebbles flung against a castle wall; for he seemed to regard human communication as an unnecessary distraction, and merely grunted and glowered at me when I spoke, as though I had interrupted an important business meeting between him and his soup.

Sir Charles sat to my right, and was pleasant enough; but *he* was largely taken up with rescuing Mrs. Somerville from Mr. Kingsett, who – under the revised arrangement – was now between her and Lady Eastlake. Kingsett was almost as silent as Mr. Cussons – though not, in his case, out of aloofness, but rather from a kind of sulky petulance. The conversation, when it caught fire at all, was about photography, and prisms, and optical effects; and knowing himself unqualified to contribute to it (it was, quite literally above his head; for Elizabeth Eastlake is at least three inches taller than he is), he did his best to extinguish it altogether. Whenever either of his neighbours said anything, he would sigh, and shift in his chair, and clatter his knife and fork; or gaze absently into space; or appear to listen, with a foolish, put-upon little smile that said: *It's all nonsense, and I won't be taken in by it.* But his principal occupation, which he resumed whenever there was a lull, was terrorizing his wife – staring at her with such undisguised loathing and contempt that the poor woman was almost paralysed with misery and fear, and could only respond to Walter's repeated attempts to draw her out with a few stammered words. I cannot deny being relieved that it was she, and not I, who was the object of this relentless persecution; and yet it left me feeling desperately angry and frustrated, too – as if I were being forced to witness some dreadful unequal battle, while being quite powerless to help the victims.

I was also, I own, haunted by another, less worthy thought: how was I going to explain this disaster to Walter? From his easy, cheerful manner you would never have guessed that he felt there was anything wrong, or that he was less than delighted with the company in which he found himself; but once or twice I caught him looking at me curiously down the length of the table, as if to say: *Why did you summon me back to London for* this? To which I could not think of a reply – save to confess candidly that I had over-estimated both Lady Eastlake's enthusiasm for my ideas, and her regard for me personally. Six months ago I might have made such an admission easily enough – indeed, I should have hastened to do so, knowing that he would reassure me, and soothe my bruised *amour propre* – but now the chasm between us seemed to make it impossible.

On only one occasion did the conversation veer in the direction I had hoped. Mrs. Somerville was reminiscing about Italy with Sir Charles when – suddenly observing that no-one had said a word to me for five minutes – she decided to take pity on me.

'Do you know Italy, Miss Halcombe?'

'Not well, I'm afraid.'

'You should, you should. I am obliged to live there, for my husband's health. But I cannot say it is a great sacrifice.'

She laughed, and Sir Charles smiled and nodded in agreement.

'The buildings,' she went on. 'The landscape.' She shook her head, as if such sublime beauty were altogether beyond her powers of description. 'And the quality of the light. Truly remarkable.'

'That, doubtless,' I said, seizing my chance, 'is why Turner was so drawn to it?'

'Oh, indeed, indeed. I discussed it with him often.'

She paused, busying herself with something on her plate; and, before she could go on, Sir Charles said mildly:

'And you, I think, are fond of Italy too, Mr. Cussons?'

Mr. Cussons glared – his eyebrows shot up – his head jerked to one side.

'I beg your pardon?'

'You are fond of Italy?'

Mr. Cussons sat back – looked about him – settled himself on his perch. He had seen his rabbit. He pounced.

'Not fond!' he boomed, in the over-loud voice of the deaf. 'Filthy dirty. Corrupt. Squalid's not the word for it.'

And then he embarked on a seemingly interminable anecdote about how he had been obliged to go to Naples on business (nothing less would have induced him to set foot in the place); how he had acquired there a Botticelli *Virgin and Child*, of whose true value the shifty peasant who sold it to him had not had the faintest conception; and how he intended to leave it to the National Gallery, together with the rest of his collection – the whole to be known as 'The Cussons Bequest'.

This, at least, answered one question that had been perplexing me all evening: why the Eastlakes had invited such a morose and unsociable individual to dinner? But by the time he had finished, Turner had entirely disappeared from view.

Most hostesses, at the end of such a meal, would have either apologized *sotto voce* to the other ladies while they were withdrawing, or else tried brightly to pretend that nothing was amiss. Elizabeth Eastlake did neither; which surprised me (for I felt the ordeal we had passed through demanded some acknowledgement), until I saw that it arose not from thoughtlessness but from delicacy – for both courses, in this instance, would have only further compounded Mrs. Kingsett's anguish: the first by criticizing her husband in front of other people, and the second by requiring her to affect normality and make polite small talk when she was clearly too upset to do so. Instead, Lady Eastlake calmly helped her friend upstairs (even then, Mrs. Kingsett was so close to collapse that she had to clutch the banister rail like an old woman), and settled her in a quiet corner in the boudoir before returning to Mrs. Somerville and myself in the drawing room.

'My poor Marian,' she said. 'This is not at all what you imagined, I'm afraid.'

'Oh, no,' I said, wondering at my own mendacity. 'It's been very pleasant.'

'Don't lie,' she mouthed, tapping me in mock reproach (at which I heard Mrs. Somerville laughing softly at my side). 'Did you bring your notes?'

'Well . . .'

Her eye fell on my reticule; and she must have seen the bulge of my notebook, for she nodded.

'Only because you asked me to . . .' I began.

She pulled a rueful face. 'I know I did.'

'But it doesn't matter. It can . . .'

'I'm so sorry, my dear.' She touched my elbow impulsively, then turned to Mrs. Somerville. 'I'm afraid I shall have to leave you to your own devices.' She glanced discreetly towards Mrs. Kingsett. 'You do understand . . .'

'Of course.'

She nodded gratefully, then started back towards the boudoir, with the quiet purposefulness of a doctor approaching his patient.

'I dare say we shall manage, Miss Halcombe, don't you?' said Mrs. Somerville. She sat on the sofa, and patted the place beside her. 'Come. Please. I fear nowadays I don't hear very well.'

I sat next to her. She smiled conspiratorially.

'Just think what the gentlemen are having to endure,' she said – with a stress on *gentlemen* that clearly implied: *At least we don't have to suffer that.*

I laughed, and sat next to her. Here at last, I thought, was an opportunity to retrieve something from the evening. I was about to raise the subject of Turner again when she spared me the trouble:

376

'And what, may I ask, do your notes concern?'

I briefly explained.

'The Eastlakes are always so busy,' she said, in the gentle tone of someone trying to excuse a friend's behaviour. 'They try heroically to attend to everything, they really do, but . . .' she shook her head . . . 'but I should be delighted to hear your ideas, if you'd care to tell me.'

And with some trepidation, I took out my notebook.

I began with my (or rather, since I felt I must maintain the fiction that these views were Walter's as well as my own, with 'our') earliest findings; and at first her response was very gratifying. When I spoke of Turner's relations with the Regency art world, and why they might have made him careful about money, she nodded approvingly, and murmured, 'Yes, yes, how true.' My delineation of his character – his sensitivity to criticism; his shyness about his odd appearance and uncouth speech – seemed to please her even more; and she clapped her hands with delight when I concluded:

'Small wonder, then, that he shrank from the eyes of the world; and was willing that people should think him a miser and a fool, if only they would leave him alone.'

'Excellent, Miss Halcombe!' she cried out. 'May I ask – was that your phrase, or your brother's?'

'I beg your pardon?'

'"Shrank from the eyes of the world"?'

'Mine, I think,' I said. 'Though I fear it's an unremarkable enough image.'

'Not at all,' she said. 'Very apt. The watchful eye. The cold eye. The censorious eye.'

Perhaps I looked perplexed; for she smiled, and touched the corner of her own eye, as if to clarify the point. 'That's what he feared. But it's also what fascinated him.'

I only half-saw her meaning; but the ghostly outline of one of Turner's doll-figures suddenly entered my mind, like a

377

bookmark placed in a page that may repay further attention.

'And he was very knowledgeable about it. I have seldom known anyone – besides other scientists – with such a keen interest in optics, and in the theory of light and colour. Or with such a sound grasp of the principles. You'd see him at Rogers', deep –'

'Roger?' I said; and then, before she had time to reply, realized I had misheard her. 'Oh, you mean *Rogers*'?'

She nodded.

'The banker,' I said, recalling that I had heard Lady Eastlake talk of him more than once.

'I think he would have preferred to be remembered as a poet,' she said, with a wistful smile. 'At all events, we all regularly met at his house. My husband and myself; Herschel, Faraday, Babbage, Tom Moore, Campbell. And Turner could speak to any one of us on our own subjects, and with great authority.'

'Indeed?' I said, astonished; for this seemed entirely at odds with the impression I had gained from Lady Meesden's papers.

She nodded. 'Most of the great men I have known – and Turner was, indisputably, a great man – have possessed the same quality. Which leads me to wonder whether genius is not so much a highly developed aptitude for one thing, but rather a kind of general intellectual capacity, that may be more or less equally applied to any field. Certainly Turner might have been a successful scientist or engineer, had he chosen. Anyway –'

'But what, then, of the people who said he was inarticulate?'

She shrugged. 'He could be hard to understand when he spoke publicly. But not when he was relaxed, and among friends.' She paused, struck by a sudden recollection. 'The only complaints you ever heard then were from dullards, who could not soar to the same heights. I remember once we were at a *conversazzione*, and I had been snared by a gentle-man who talked of nothing but the funds, and the price of corn. And Turner came up to me, and plucked from his pocket a yellow handkerchief. "Now, Mrs. Somerville," he said' – and here, to my surprise, she dropped into a gruff cockney voice that I took to be a fair imitation of Turner's – '"what d'you say this is?"

'"Why, a handkerchief, of course."

'He put it back in his pocket. "And where is it?"

'"In your coat."

'"And what colour is it?"

'"Yellow."

'"You're sure?"

'Naturally, I was laughing by this point – I had some idea what was in his mind – but I said: "Of course."

'He wagged a finger at me and shook his head. "A consciousness of the fallacy of our judgement is one of the most important consequences of the study of nature, which teaches us that no object is seen by us in its true place. And that colours are solely the effects of the action of matter upon light, and that light itself is not a real being."

'Well, needless to say, Miss Halcombe, my dull companion had been shifting from one foot to the other during this performance, and rolling his eyes; and now he could contain himself no longer.

'"If you don't mind my saying so," he said, "that's absolute gibberish."

'"Really?" said Turner. "Then perhaps you should read Mrs. Somerville's book."'

She laughed, with a complicit glint in her eye, as if I were in on the joke with her and Turner – rather than (as I had shamefully to admit to myself) in the same predicament as the gentleman who talked of funds and the price of corn.

'I'm sorry . . .' I stumbled. 'I –'

'It was a quotation, almost word for word, from *On the*

Connexion of the Physical Sciences.'

'I'm afraid I didn't quite understand . . .' I said. 'Could you perhaps explain . . .?'

'I was talking about the constraints of the scientific method,' she replied. 'Which Turner, I think, found disturbing. Despite making light of it.'

'Because . . .? Because . . .?' I said, hoping to tempt her into saying something more before *I* had to.

'Because *thought* – the exercise of reason – will only take us so far,' she said at length. 'And then we reach the limit of its competence. For my part, I am content to leave it to faith – the grace and cohesion of what we *do* know, through mathematics, are enough to convince me of . . . of . . .' she hesitated, carefully formulating the right words . . . 'of the unity and omniscience of the Deity. But Turner, I suspect, didn't have that consolation.'

'He was not a believer?'

'We did not discuss it,' she said shortly. 'But I think he saw the chaos and destruction in Nature before he saw the beauty – or rather I think he saw them together, as expressions of the same awful power. And our incapacity to grasp it, to understand it, was humiliating confirmation of our fundamental impotence.'

'That's very interesting,' I said. And I immediately started to explain my conjectures about Turner's childhood – his mother's madness; his terror of storms, both natural and human – which seemed to accord precisely with what she had just told me. To my surprise and disappointment, however, she regarded me with an expression of growing distaste; and, when I had finished, said:

'Forgive me if I am being old-fashioned, Miss Halcombe, but I think a biographer should confine himself to ascertainable facts, and to the recollections of those who knew his subject.' Her tone was measured, but two little angry spots on her cheeks betrayed her. 'This, it appears to me, is neither; but merely unfounded speculation.'

I was about to try to defend myself; but before I could do so the gentlemen entered.

I am unclear exactly what happened next, and in what order; for this (or so it seems, looking back) is the moment when the waking world suddenly gave way to nightmare, and from now on everything has the jumbled logic of a dream. I recall Mr. Kingsett, very drunk, stumbling on a rug by the fire; I remember Lady Eastlake reappearing from the boudoir, and saying, 'I hope, gentlemen, you're going to entertain us; for we've been a bit sombre'; I remember Mrs. Kingsett standing like a spectre in the doorway behind her.

And then we are all sitting, and one of the gentlemen is saying something about a new American medium called Mrs. Mast, who has been doing a brisk trade among fashionable ladies in London – 'for she doesn't use rapping or table-turning like the others, but talks in the voices of the dead themselves'. Lady Eastlake laughs – 'People are so *gullible*' – but Sir Charles mentions a Mrs. Somebody-or-other who swears she heard her dead son speaking to her. 'What's the harm', he says, 'if it gives her comfort?'

Lady Eastlake snorts.

Mr. Kingsett looks at his wife, and says:

'We could employ Mrs. Mast permanently, my dear, could we not? To communicate with your mother. Might improve your spirits, to hear her complaining about me.'

Then confusion: sharp intakes of breath; Mrs. Kingsett crying; Mr. Kingsett saying she is unwell, and must go home; Walter and me both, simultaneously, offering to go with them (for the thought of their being incarcerated alone in a cab together is unbearable); Mr. Kingsett saying it is quite unnecessary; Lady Eastlake thanking us, and insisting on our behalf.

The street outside: helping Mrs. Kingsett into the

Eastlakes' carriage. And then her husband – as if he had not insulted me enough already – suddenly putting his arm about my waist, and saying (why?), '*Please*, Miss Halcombe, we shall do perfectly well by ourselves.'

And then, as I have recovered myself, and put one foot on the step, it happens: a figure appears from nowhere – I am conscious only of a warm, dark bulk too close to me, and the stench of gin and dirty clothes – and there is a tremendous tug on my wrist, and my reticule is gone.

Running footsteps. Two sets of running footsteps. Walter crying 'Stop, thief!', and disappearing after him round the corner of the square.

I wept. I shook. I could not help myself. Elizabeth Eastlake was very kind, and sat up with me, and said I might stay the night; but when Walter had still not returned after an hour, I thanked her and returned to Brompton Grove, thinking I might find him there.

I didn't.

I could not sleep. I sat at my writing table, waiting – as I had on the night of our visit to Sandycombe Lodge – for the sound of his key in the door.

It never came.

I tried not to imagine what might have happened to him, but I could not keep his image from my mind – injured, or murdered, or broken in some dreadful accident; nor the awful reflection that in some way this was my doing.

If only I had been more alert. Taken more care. Never introduced him to Elizabeth Eastlake.

I knew I should distract myself by writing my diary, but I could not do it.

I prayed: *Return him to me, and I will be good. Make normal life possible again, and I will embrace it – joyfully; and never again complain of drudgery, or duty, or the ache of disappointment.*

*

A little before dawn I must have drifted off to sleep. I was woken by a sound from the garden. I looked out and saw a light in the window of his studio.

It did not even occur to me it might be an intruder. I ran downstairs, and outside, and flung open the door.

Walter stood before a huge canvas smeared with black and red. He was unshaven, his cheek bruised, his hair tousled, his eyes bloodshot and unnaturally bright. For a moment he seemed not to know me. Then he said quietly:

'You should be asleep.'

'How could I sleep! I didn't know where you were!'

I cried, and took him in my arms. He set down his palette, and stroked my hair like a child's.

'I have your reticule,' he said. 'There. On the table.'

'Never mind that! What happened to you?'

'I got lost, that's all,' he said gently. 'I'll tell you about it later. Now. Please. Go and rest.'

I could not speak what I felt. I left and returned to my room.

LII
From the private notebook of Walter Hartright, 13th December, 185–

I have crossed the bar. Today. 13th December. A little after 1.00 a.m.

We think we are our own masters, but something drives us or draws us to our destiny.

I thought I was pursuing a common thief. I followed him out of the square, down Carburton Street, across Portland Place. What was in my mind? Nothing – save that I was doing what I must do.

And that luck, or God, was on my side. For every time I seemed to have lost the fellow, I saw him again.

We ran the length of Queen Anne Street, and then my quarry (pilot?) vanished into a small dimly lit court at the end. I went after him, but could not immediately see him, and – since there was no way out but the narrow alley by which we had gone in – assumed he must have entered one of the tenements, where I had no chance of finding him. But then I heard an urgent clacking sound, and, looking towards it, was just able to make out his figure in the shadows. He was desperately rattling at a latch, as if he were intending to escape inside but found the door locked. He glanced over his shoulder as I sprang towards him, and turned to face me.

I should have seen the warning in his eyes. They were not frightened, as they should have been, but satisfied – almost triumphant.

But I had not time to heed it. I pushed him roughly against the wall, seized the reticule, and – fearing he might try to snatch it back – thrust it into my pocket.

Then I heard the door opening, and steps, and hoarse, rapid breathing. I tried to turn, but was jostled off balance. Before I could recover myself, someone was tying my hands behind me. And then someone else slipped a hood over my head, and whispered:

'Come along, sir.'

There was a man on either side of me, and a third behind. They edged me back towards the street, rearranging themselves into single file in order to pass through the alley. When we emerged they stopped for a second or two. I heard the stamp and snuffle of a stationary horse, and murmured voices, and a door opening; and then I felt myself being lifted and bundled into a cab.

Only one man, I felt fairly certain, got in with me; but in my present helpless state I could not hope to tackle even one, so as we moved off I forced myself to stay calm, and await a more favourable opportunity to get away. It was not easy, not only because I was naturally confused and disoriented, but also because my pinioned arms prevented me from sitting back in my seat, so making me prey to every lurch and bump in the road. But I determined not to protest – or indeed to speak at all, unless my captor spoke first; for to do so would have been to throw away the only weapon I had.

I think he must have seen things in the same light; for several times I heard him drawing in his breath, or clicking his tongue, as if he were on the point of saying something – but in the event he always appeared to think better of it, and kept his peace. From which I deduced, first, that he was hoping by remaining silent to break my nerve; and, second, that his own nerve was far from steady – both of which only stiffened my resolve.

I thus had ample time to reflect on who he might be, and why he had gone to such lengths to abduct me. The most obvious motive was robbery – but surely he and his friends might easily enough have accomplished that in the little court? I could think of no-one who might have a reason to murder me – and, in any case, for that, too, the cab was a quite unnecessary contrivance. I could only conclude that he had taken me for someone else, and that in due course – if I had not managed to get away first – his mistake would be discovered.

We had been going, I should guess, about ten minutes, when a particularly savage jolt flung me to the floor, knocking my face (for of course I could not put up my hands to protect it), and wrenching my shoulder. At this, my companion's firmness finally deserted him, and he cried out:

'Oh! Are you 'urt, sir?'

Hurt and dazed as I was, I was conscious of a certain exhilaration at having won the battle of wills between us. I did not reply, which made him still more anxious.

385

''Ere,' he said, helping me back to my seat. His hands were trembling, and his breath was rancid with gin. He laid two fingers against my throat. I felt something hard and sharp protruding between them.

'This 'ere's a spike,' he said. 'You understand?'

I nodded. Perhaps the hood prevented him seeing, for he gave me a small jab and repeated:

'You understand?'

'Yes.'

'Very well, then. Now, I'm going to undo your 'ands, and tie 'em again in front of you, so's you can sit straight. But you tries any dodges, and I swear as you'll get this' – another prick – 'in 'ere. Understand?'

'Yes.'

But for all the bravado of his words, he spoke them with a tremulousness that suggested he was far from confident, and which tempted me, for a moment, to take advantage of my freed hands to try to overpower him. Then I reflected that he could see, and I could not; and that even a drunk and irresolute man might have plucked up the courage to stab me before I had been able to tear off the hood. I therefore decided to bide my time, and meekly let him go about his business – which he conducted with surprising deftness, loosening the rope in a moment, and fixing it again in a moment more, with such assurance that I could only suppose he was, or had been, a sailor. When he had finished, he sat back, and said:

'I'm sorry, sir, but there was no other way to make you see 'er.'

His voice was quite different now: sad, and almost gentle.

'See who?'

'My wife, sir. As 'as something to say to you. She called at your 'ouse, but was turned away.'

'My house!' I exclaimed, suddenly seeing a chance to demonstrate that I was not the man he thought. 'And where is that?'

'Brompton Grove, sir. That's what she told me.'

I was dumbfounded. I had no recollection of sending any-body away. And I could not think of any woman who might have sought me out in this manner. The prostitute I had met at the Marston Rooms? True – I had left her abruptly – but not before paying her, so she had no cause for complaint – unless she had been as consumed with lust as I had been, an idea which I immediately saw was absurd. And how, any-way, could she have known where to find me?

Then I remembered the pawnbroker in Maiden Lane. I might unwittingly have left some evidence of my address in the pocket of my coat. But why might she want to see me? And why had she waited so long?

Finally, at a loss for any plausible explanation, and with a growing feeling of alarm, I said:

'Why does your wife want to see me?'

'She'll tell you that 'erself, sir.'

To have pressed him further would have been to betray my fear, so I held my tongue. I did not speak to him again.

I had long since lost any sense of direction; and without my eyes to help me, had to rely on hearing alone for clues as to where we were going. Once or twice I made out the steady beat and splash of steam-boats, from which I knew we were close to the river; but none of the other sounds I could pick out – the rumble of passing vehicles, a drunken bellow, a barking dog – was specific enough to tell me anything use-ful, save that we were still in the city. I was, however, con-scious of a gradual change in the *quality* of what I heard; for everything – even the thrum of our own wheels, and the clatter of the horse's hooves – seemed by degrees to become softer, as if we were being slowly wrapped in a blanket, and so cut off from everything around us. At the same time, the air grew stiller and colder, numbing my bound hands, and making me long for the gloves and the little flask of brandy in my pocket (though I would not demean myself by asking for them) – from all of which I guessed it must be snowing.

And I was right; for when we at length arrived – after heaven knows how long – I could smell it through the fabric of the hood, and feel it underfoot when my captor helped me down. I heard him mutter something to the driver, and then he took my arm and began to guide me across some rough cobbles, taking care to prevent me slipping. Behind us I heard the cab driving away, at which my heart sank – for with it went any hope that this might only be a short interview, and that they intended I should be taken home immediately afterwards.

We appeared to be approaching a public house, for from just ahead of us came the unmistakable sound of singing and raucous laughter; but we stopped before we reached it, and I heard the secretive patter of fingers knocking on a window, and then, after a few seconds, a door opening. A woman's voice, so quiet that I could barely make out the words, said:

'This the man?'

There was no reply that I could hear, but a moment later I was led into an uncarpeted hall, and thence into what seemed to be a parlour, for I could feel the welcome warmth of a fire. I heard the rustle of the woman's dress as she came towards me, and then felt her fingers quickly squeeze mine – like a strange token of the handshake she would have given me if my wrists had not been bound, and this were merely a normal social occasion.

'I'm the lady of the house,' she said. She spoke softly, with the trace of an Irish accent; and I knew at once that I had never met her before in my life. 'Mary'll do for a name, if you want one. Please sit down.'

The man helped me into a comfortable chair close to the fire. I heard her settle herself opposite me.

'I'm sorry I can't take that off,' she said. 'But I cannot

run the risk.'

I wanted to ask: *Of what?* – but I felt that to enter into conversation would be to suggest that I accepted this situation, and so somehow make it appear legitimate.

'But I'll not be making excuses,' she continued. 'You're wanting something, and I'm going to help you to it.' She paused a moment, for effect: 'The truth about Turner, am I right?'

I still said nothing. She sighed, like a mother cajoling a sulky child – which instantly made me feel a little like one. Finally she repeated:

'Am I *right*?'

'What of it?' I said, as carelessly as I could.

'I knew him,' she said. 'He used to come here.'

'And what is "here"?'

'A lodging-house,' she replied simply. 'Most of the boarders is sailors' women.'

'And he presented himself as "Turner"?' I said, instantly suspicious – for anyone who had really known him would have realized that such recklessness was quite out of character.

'No. I'd no idea who he was, till the fellow who keeps the Ship and Bladebone saw him one day by chance, and said, "You'll never guess who that is."'

'And how did *he* know?'

'Turner was his landlord.'

'What! You mean he *owned* the place?' I cried; although – as I privately had to admit to myself – the very improbability of the idea gave it an odd sort of credibility, for it was the kind of detail no-one would think to invent.

'That's what Mr. Hodgson told me,' she said defensively.

At that moment – as if the mention of a public house had put the notion in his head – the man suddenly mumbled:

'I think I'll just slip next door for a drop of somethin' short.'

He had the shifty, off-hand manner of someone who fears he may be stopped, and thus hopes to escape attention; but the woman was having none of it. As he started to edge away, she said, lethally quiet:

'What, are you still afeared?'

'Don't a man deserve a drink?' wheedled my captor.

'You take another one, you won't be able to stand,' she replied.

'I brought 'im 'ere, didn't I?'

'Afterwards,' she said, relenting slightly.

'Oh, come on!' he said. ''E ain't going to cut it now!'

'In a minute. After he's gone upstairs.'

My skin prickled with contradictory emotions: dread, and outrage, and excitement.

'He had his own ways, Turner,' she said. 'His own tastes.'

'What kind of tastes?' I said.

'You'll be seeing one of his women shortly,' she said. 'She'll show you.'

Show, not *tell*. My mouth was dry. I said: 'May I have some water?'

'Upstairs,' she said. 'In just a moment. But first I wants to tell you something about her. About poor Lucy. She's not got a great head on her, and what she has's been all but fuddled away, for she's a terrible one for the crater. That's why we keep her in, and I lay out her money for her, when her sailor-friend sends it; for she'd drink it all else, and then try to make away with herself after. But you can trust her. She won't lie to you. You understand?'

'Yes.'

'Come along, then.'

She went ahead of me, and the man came behind, pushing me out into the hall and up the stairs. When we reached the landing we paused for a moment, and I heard the woman unlocking a door and opening it.

'Now, Lu,' she said gently. 'You know what is expected of you?'

There was no answer, as far as I could tell; but the woman

must have been satisfied, for I was promptly thrust forward again. All at once, the light outside the hood seemed brighter. I was conscious of the smell of cheap scent and cheap coals – and then, suddenly, of a shrill squeal, half surprised and half amused, which made me fear for my safety – for there was something uncontrolled, even mad, about it.

'We'll come for you in a little while,' whispered the woman, close to my ear. And then I heard the door closing behind me, and the key being turned again from the outside.

The squealing continued for a few moments, but all the time subsiding into giggles, like a pot going off the boil, until at length it had become no more than a kind of breathless, bubbling trill. Then I heard – or rather felt – her approaching; smelt the violet cachou on her breath, and the *eau de Cologne* on her skin, and beneath them both, like a half-buried secret, a rank hint of animal heat. She said nothing; but as she touched my icy fingers she winced, and put them to her lips, and rubbed them to restore the circulation, before finally turning her attention to untying them. As she fiddled clumsily with the knots, I could not but reflect that we had never met – never seen each other's faces – never even heard each other speak; and yet that I was closer to her than I have been to any woman save Laura in my adult life.

She at last managed to free my hands, and then quickly plucked the hood from my head. I blinked; for even the light of the gas-lamp was enough to dazzle me after so long in darkness. She seemed to emerge, in consequence, through a kind of fuzzy mist: first a squat, rather full figure in a low-cut blue dress; then a wide, pale face, puffy from drink or tiredness; deep-set blue eyes and a bright red mouth; the thick brown ringlets untidily pinned up behind her head. She had one hand on the bed – which was not the mean object I should have expected, but a four-poster hung with a dirty chintz curtain. She caught me looking at it, and smiled with a quite uncoquettish frankness, and then shook her head and laughed, as if my presence there still bemused her.

'You got anything to drink?' she said. Her speech was slow and slurred.

I had, of course; but was unsure whether I should own to it. It seemed churlish to deny her; and yet had not the woman downstairs said she was a drunkard, and must be prevented from tippling? She must correctly have interpreted this hesitation as meaning 'yes'; for she immediately said, 'You 'ave, ain't you?' and began rifling through my pockets with the frantic single-mindedness of a dog digging up a bone. When she plucked out Marian's reticule she held it up for an instant like an exhibit in a court case, laughing 'You're a sly one, ain't you?'; and then flung it to one side and resumed her search. Within a matter of seconds she had found the flask, unscrewed the cap and sucked it dry, running her tongue around the little nozzle to catch any stray drops that might have escaped her.

'Nothing more?' she said, before she had had time to catch her breath again.

'That's enough,' I said, conscious even as I did so of a jarring note of priggishness in my voice.

She looked at me curiously, focusing her eyes with some difficulty.

'What's your name?'

'Did they not tell you?'

She seemed surprised that I should ask, and shook her head emphatically – until it seemed to make her dizzy, and she stopped abruptly.

'Jenkinson,' I said.

She drew in her breath sharply; and then her confused expression slowly cleared.

'Ah, I gets it,' she said. 'You likes the same.'

She picked up the hood and the ropes from where she had dropped them on the floor, and dangled them before me. I could not begin to guess her meaning, and merely stared stupidly back at her.

"'Ere you are, then,' she said impatiently. 'Take 'em.'

I did so, and stood holding them helplessly. She turned towards the wall opposite me, where a round looking-glass in a rosewood frame hung above a small chair. Then slowly, without a word, she started to unhook her dress.

I could not move. I thought I should faint. And yet some part of me – the Walter Hartright that the world saw, and that until two months ago I had always supposed myself to be – would still not accept that this was desire, but clung doggedly to the notion that I was there for some perfectly respectable purpose – much as a shipwrecked sailor clings to some pitiful fragment of his smashed boat, in the hope that it will keep him from being swept away. I did not avert my eyes as she let the dress drop to the floor and stepped out of it – I could not; but I tried to persuade myself (God! what madness!) that I was looking simply in order to try to establish her age. From her broad plump hips and thighs, and the slight slackness of the skin on her arms, I guessed between thirty and thirty-five. Though I could barely speak, I said:

'How old were you when Turner came here?'

She did not turn, but her eyes found my reflection in the glass.

"'Oo?'

'The other Mr. Jenkinson.'

'Oh, must've be twelve or thirteen when 'e first 'ad me. 'E come reg'lar after that.'

'For how long?'

She shrugged. 'Five, six years?'

'And how old are you now?'

She giggled; and then unpinned her hair, and shook it free, so that it tumbled down her back. "'Ere, you want to talk, or what?'

I tried to say something.

I could not.

She unlaced her corset and pulled it away, as a sculptor may remove a mould; and then drew her chemise over her head, and laid both on the chair. All she was wearing now was a pair of grubby stockings. She pulled at one of the garters.

'On or off?' When I did not reply she brusquely repeated the gesture. 'Hm?'

'What did . . .? What did *he* . . .?'

'Oh, it were all one to 'im. Weren't my legs as fussed 'im. On or off?'

'Off.'

She bent down and took them off as matter-of-factly as if I had asked her to remove a tea tray.

'There,' she said, flinging them on the chair. As she did so I saw the bounce of her heavy breast, and glimpsed the thicket of darker hair beneath her belly. She appeared entirely unselfconscious, as if she felt no shame in her nakedness, and no pride either.

But to me . . .

To me it was a miracle.

I had never seen a woman undress before.

She threw herself on the bed and lay there, turning her head from side to side, gently rolling her hips so that her legs fell open.

'Come on,' she said.

And then I knew the depth of my own folly. The folly of thinking I might see another life – imagine another life – but not cross the threshold into living it.

The folly of denying my own fate.

For I had not chosen this. I had resisted, indeed, as I have been resisting for months. But fate had overruled me, and delivered me here.

No-one I knew had seen me.

This woman did not know my name.

I was free.

She watched me approach, but then, as I drew near, laid an arm across her face. I sat beside her, uncertain what to do.

'Put it on, then,' she said.

She removed her arm, but kept her eyes closed.

'Put it on,' she repeated.

I slipped the hood over her head. She stretched out her arms in a parody of crucifixion, blindly adjusting them until each wrist was lying against one of the bed-posts.

The meaning was plain enough. I tied one hand with the rope. She did not murmur. For the other I used one of her stockings.

I stared at her. She could not stare back. She had no eyes.

There was so much of her. Such an ocean of skin – as still now as cream, and as smooth, save where it was creased and printed with the stamp of her corset.

Not my wife. Not a woman I knew. Just woman.

I took off my clothes slowly, looking at her the whole time. Why hurry? I did not need to entice her, or persuade her, or ask her permission. She could not escape me. She was entirely within my power.

When I entered her she sighed, and yielded up a cry that seemed extorted from her against her will.

And when I had done she shuddered, and whispered:

'You're more of a man than 'e was. You want to do it again? Or you going to untie me?'

I did not sleep when she did. I have never been more awake. I got up and listened at the door. I heard nothing, except a distant noise of snoring. My captor must have drunk too much at the public, and passed out in a stupor.

I went to the window. The cloud had cleared, and there was a moon. I could see a steep roof, with what appeared to be an outhouse or shed below it, from which – I thought – I could easily enough reach the ground. The snow lay thick everywhere. It would, I thought, break my fall, and muffle the sound of it.

I had no fear. I knew I must trust my fate.

I quietly dressed, put a sovereign on the pillow, and cracked open the casement. It was too small for me to get through fully clothed, so I had to remove my coat and drop it out before me. For a moment it snagged on a broken gutter, but then its own weight freed it and it fell on to the lower roof. And it was as well it did – for when I landed on it, I felt a sharp grazing pain, and found that beneath the snow the whole surface was covered with pieces of broken glass, which had doubtless been put there to stop boys climbing on it. The coat was badly torn, but the reticule and my flask were undamaged, and I sustained no more than a few scratches.

Trust your fate, and no harm will come to you.

I dropped down, and found myself in a little alley behind a row of houses. At the end I could see a line of rickety buildings thrown into silhouette by the moonlight. I made my way towards them, and emerged into a mean street of wharves and taverns and warehouses. I had no idea where I was, or which way I should take; but it seemed slightly lighter and more open towards the left, so I struck out in that direction. And once again fate rewarded me; for after a few minutes I came out in a main road, and almost immediately spied a cab.

The driver hesitated a moment when he saw the state of my clothes, but the sight of my purse soon convinced him.

'What street is that?' I asked him, pointing to the way I had just come.

'New Gravel Lane, sir.'

So I have been in Wapping, where Turner went. I have known the freedom he knew. I have partaken of his power.

LIII

Letter from Laura Hartright to Walter Hartright, 14th December, 185–

Limmeridge,
Thursday

My darling Walter,

You bad boy! Did you not promise you would write every day? Or has dining with Sir Charles Eastlake quite turned your head, and made you forget your poor family altogether!

We are well, save that we miss you so much. Would it were Christmas already – for that will bring us the best present of all.

Your loving wife,

Laura

LIV

From the diary of Marian Halcombe, 14th December, 185–

An odd postscript to yesterday, which I was too tired and upset to note down before I went to bed:

I spent most of the day writing my journal, and resting. About six, having not heard Walter enter the house, I returned to his studio, to ask whether he would be coming in to dinner. I think I took him by surprise; for he was engrossed in writing himself, but stopped as soon as he heard me, and stood before the table, as if he were hiding something from my gaze. He was wilder-eyed and more dishevelled than ever, having plainly neither slept nor changed his clothes since the morning.

'Are you unwell?' I said.

He shook his head. As he did so, the light caught his cheek, and I saw that the bruise there had grown into an ugly swelling.

'Oh, you are! You're injured!' I cried, moving towards him impulsively.

He shook his head again, and put out his hands to keep me from him. Perhaps he was merely being delicate, for he smelt vile, and might have been trying to spare me the stale fishy sweetness that clung to him like a fog, and still lingers in my nose as I write these words; but from the way he flinched, and the coldness in his eyes, it was difficult to avoid the impression that his motive was to protect not me, but himself.

Of course I was hurt. But worse – far worse: I suddenly caught myself calculating the distance between here and the house, and wondering whether Davidson would hear me if I cried out, and come to my aid. I have grown used, these last few months, to feeling I could not completely trust Walter, or guess what was in his mind. But never before have I doubted my own safety with him.

What did I fear he might be capable of doing?

I cannot bring myself to write – to think it, even.

My judgement must have been disordered by anxiety. And lack of sleep. And a night of terrible imaginings.

As I backed away he reached behind him and then moved quickly in front of the painting I had seen that morning. His aim, presumably, was to prevent me from seeing it; but he succeeded only in drawing my attention to it, for it was far too big for him to conceal. It was quite unlike anything I have known Walter attempt before, with none of his customary care and sweetness and faithful attention to detail. The paint seemed to have been flung against the canvas, where it hung in great pools and drips as thick as icicles – as if the artist's job were merely to get it out of the pot, and he had no obligation to do anything with it once it was there. I can only assume he was trying for a Turnerish effect, for there was a jagged red smear in the middle, surrounded by black – but it entirely lacked Turner's lucidity and brilliance. The red wasn't red enough; the black wasn't black enough; they bled into each other around the edges, and suggested no natural object or effect I have ever seen in my life.

But something about it reminded me of another picture. Not the style – not the subject-matter – but the grandiose scale. The *not-quite-rightness* of it.

What was it?

And then I remembered. Poor Haste's huge picture of Lear.

Perhaps Walter saw my reaction; for he snapped: 'It's not finished!' and then, without giving me a chance to reply:

'What do you want?' From the tone of his voice you might have supposed I was a naughty child, who had been told that in no circumstances was Papa to be disturbed.

'I forgot my reticule,' I said hastily – which was true enough, though I had only that moment thought of it.

He nodded towards the table where it still lay. I picked it up, and knew at once that it was too light.

'Where's my notebook?'

He shrugged. '*I* don't know.'

I pulled it open, and looked inside. Nothing else was missing. I took out my purse. Two sovereigns and some change. Just as I remembered.

'Could it have fallen out?'

He shook his head.

'Are you sure?'

'The thief had the string round his wrist.' He rotated his own wrist impatiently for emphasis. I noticed that it was red and chafed, but knew better now than to ask why. 'And after that it was in my pocket.'

'What about when you took it back from him?'

He shook his head again. 'You must have left it at the Eastlakes'.'

'I didn't.'

'You *must* have!' He seemed taken aback by his own vehemence, and made an effort to calm himself before going on, more reasonably:

'It would have been easy enough to forget, wouldn't it? In the circumstances.'

'Perhaps,' I said, moving towards the door; for I could see there was no point in discussing it further. 'I'll write to Elizabeth Eastlake about it.'

And I will. But I still find it difficult to believe that I would have left my notebook there, even in all the confusion – for usually, whether I am thinking consciously of it or not, I am as aware of its whereabouts as I am of my own hand.

Walter did not come in to dinner.

LV

From the private notebook of Walter Hartright,
14th December, 185–

To live as Turner did you need a basement.

I did not think to provide myself with one when I designed the studio. As a result, Marian surprised me today when I was writing, and saw the *Ironworks Accident* before it was ready.

There is not a great deal I can do about the painting, save to deter further visits. But for this notebook there is a simple remedy. I shall go out tomorrow and get a box.

LVI

Letter from Lady Eastlake to Marian Halcombe, 15th December, 185–

7 Fitzroy Square,
Friday

My dear Marian,

Thank you for your note. I am so glad that your brother was able to retrieve your reticule, which has a little restored my faith in Fortune's taste, if not in her morals – for had she deprived you of *that*, after heaping on us all the other disasters of the evening, I should have considered her guilty of vulgar excess, and avoided her society altogether. Did the wretch who tried to steal it escape, or was Mr. Hartright able to deliver him to the police?

No sign, I fear, of your notebook. I have made a fleeting search of the drawing room myself, and made enquiries of the servants, without success; but we shall keep looking, and if the fugitive is found will put it securely under lock and key, and return it to you under armed guard.

We must – we will – meet soon, and make good what we so signally failed to do on Tuesday; though it will not now, I am afraid, be until some time after Christmas.

In haste,
Yours very truly,

Eliz. Eastlake

LVII

From the private notebook of Walter Hartright, 15th December, 185–

I am like an engine. Pulled and pushed by so many conflicting pressures I fear the rivets will break, and I shall fly apart.

But if I can hold myself together this will be a great book. Not just the life of an artist, but – for the first time – his soul.

People will ask me how I know.

I shall say nothing.

They will see the answer in my painting. *Chiaroscuro*.

LVIII

Letter from Laura Hartright to Walter Hartright,
16th December, 185–

Limmeridge,
Saturday

My darling Walter,

Still nothing from you. Is something the matter?

I thought things were well between us again, but now I fear they are not.

Please write soon.

Your loving wife,

Laura

LIX

From the private notebook of Walter Hartright,
17th December, 185–

Sunday

A dreadful night. Dreamed of Laura. She was crying. She said: *If that's what you wanted, you had but to ask.*

Another letter from her this morning. Did not open it. Have not opened the last one.

Tried to reassure myself with Nisbet's words: 'Everything has its price. Turner knew that.'

But what if the price is unbearable?

The worst of it is not being able to talk to anyone. This afternoon, in desperation, I called on Travis. He is a man of the world, I think. But his wife said he had gone to the Athenaeum. I was not dressed for the Athenaeum.

Spent the evening working on the *Accident*. It still would not come; and at length I could not bear to look at it any more, and retreated to my room. But I will not be defeated.

If I have learned anything, it is that victory or defeat is all a question of will. Tomorrow I shall return to it, and *force* it to express what is in my mind.

LX

Letter from Laura Hartright to Walter Hartright, 18th December, 185–

Limmeridge,
Monday

My darling Walter,

Why do you not answer me? I can scarce see the paper for weeping.

Remember my condition.

Please.

Your loving wife,

Laura

LXI

From the private notebook of Walter Hartright,
18th–20th December, 185–

Monday

It is a monster, but I must face it.

Travis appeared about three o'clock. I was doing well enough until then.

'Kate told me you called yesterday,' he said. One raised eyebrow asked: *Why?*

I did not feel I could tell him at once. 'Yes.'

He did not press me, but whistled under his breath, and looked about him at the studio, nodding approvingly. Then his eye fell on the *Accident*. He did not say anything, but gave a knowing smirk that galled me.

'It isn't finished,' I said hotly. I am growing tired of having to explain it.

'No,' he drawled. He did not add: *I can see that*, but he might just as well have done. 'So you are still pursuing Turner?'

'Yes,' I said, wiping my hands, and edging him away from the canvas. 'I am writing his biography.'

'Are you, indeed?' He pursed his lips, and rolled the notion round in his mouth, as a man will savour a wine before pronouncing on its quality. 'What a good idea,' he said at last – in a manner that perfectly conveyed: *Or better, at least, than trying to paint as he did*.

His condescension was insufferable; but I managed to contain my rage, and even to give a fair impression of genial hospitality as I gestured him to a chair, and took one myself.

'And what have you found out?' he said.

'A good deal. Did you, for instance, know that he used to patronize a brothel in Wapping? Where he tied the girls up, and made them hide their faces?'

His response astonished me. I had expected surprise – disbelief – a cry of *Gracious, man! How do you know that?* and then the glorious relief of telling him. Instead, he merely chuckled, and said:

'Oh, yes! – I've heard those stories!'

'You have?'

He nodded and smiled superciliously, like a schoolboy amused at the naïveté of one of his fellows.

'And you do not believe them?'

He shrugged. 'I really don't know. And I don't greatly care.' He took a cigar-case from his pocket and opened it. 'It's not my taste at all. The wilder and freer the better, so far as I'm concerned.' He laughed. 'Smoke?'

'Thank you.'

'It's possible, I suppose. We're all rather strange, aren't we? And Turner was stranger than most.' He lit our cigars, and then meditatively tapped the match until it went out. 'But it's equally possible there are people who want *us* to believe it.'

I almost choked.

'Too strong for you?' he said.

'*Who* would want us to believe it?'

'Oh, I could give you a hundred names. Many of them titled. Most of them powerful.' He shrugged again, as if the point were too obvious to need further elucidation. 'And what else?'

'Wait!' I held up my hand to silence him, while I struggled to order my thoughts. Which was no easy task: for suddenly a whole clamour of doubts and misgivings, which up until now I had successfully kept at bay, breached my defences, and broke in upon my conscious mind.

Had my captors really gone to all that risk and trouble merely in order that I should know the truth? Even the cost of the cab, surely, would have been prohibitive for them?

Was it not far more probable that someone else had paid them to do it?

And then I remembered Farrant. And the man I had met with him, Hargreaves. *There's a value now, to stories about Turner. There's a gentleman as pays good money for them.*

I said:

'Why?'

'Why what?'

'Would they want . . .?'

'Oh, because of the will, of course.'

'Turner's will, you mean?'

'Well, certainly I don't think *mine* would have roused their interest,' he murmured. 'And' – here he looked about him, and smiled languorously – 'forgive me, but I rather doubt whether yours would, either.'

I gritted my teeth. 'And what of it?'

'You don't know?' he said, as if it were the first thing a biographer should have discovered.

'Well, naturally . . .' I began, trying frantically to recall what Marian had told me of her conversation at the Eastlakes. 'Naturally, I realize he made things difficult. By being too mean to pay a competent lawyer to draw it up.'

'And who is your source for that?' simpered Travis. 'Sir Charles Eastlake?'

I could have hit him. 'In part,' I said. 'Why? Is he not to be trusted?'

He shrugged. 'He certainly has an interest in promoting that view.' He hesitated; and then, as if he had finally decided he had played with me enough, stuck his cigar between his teeth, and leant forward purposefully.

'Look,' he said, picking up the cigar case. 'Here is Turner's fortune. Houses, money, and so on. Mm?'

I nodded. He took the matchbox in his other hand.

'And here are his pictures. Some unfinished. Some unsold. But also many of his most famous works, which he's painstakingly bought back over the years, often at excessive prices.' He opened the box, and spilled matches on the table.

'See. There are hundreds of them. Thousands, if you include the drawings. Now' – tapping the cigar case – 'this, apart from a few small legacies, he leaves to charity. To build alms-houses for decayed or unsuccessful artists. While these' – sweeping the matches to one side – 'he leaves to the nation. On condition that, within ten years of his death, a "Turner Gallery" is built to house them. Do you follow me?'

'It's an undeniable challenge, for a man of my limited powers. But I think I can keep up.'

I had landed a small blow. He smiled and nodded – and even, if I am not mistaken, blushed slightly.

'But the family – a gaggle of cousins and what-not, whom Turner hadn't seen for years – contest it. First they claim he was mad. When that fails, they take it to Chancery, saying the wording of the will is too unclear to be understood. After three years there's a compromise. The charitable scheme is overturned on a technicality. So the family get this.' He lifted the cigar case. 'And the nation gets these.' He drummed his fingers on the matches, scattering them across the table. 'Only it doesn't want to go to the trouble of fulfilling his condition.'

'Why ever not?'

'Why do you suppose? Money. Only conceive the unspeakable suffering of one of Her Majesty's ministers obliged to stand up in Parliament and propose spending £25,000 on art! But Eastlake's determined to hold on to them nonetheless.'

'I don't see how he can.'

'By resorting to the most bare-faced sophistry. His argument – he actually had the audacity to say this, can you believe it, to an ex-Lord Chancellor! – is that, since the will was overturned, the National Gallery can keep the collection without having to do anything at all.'

'But surely – it was only because of the will that he got them in the first place!'

'Exactly. As the ex-Lord Chancellor did not hesitate to point out. So Eastlake's in a ticklish situation.'

I nodded. 'But I don't see how blackening Turner's name would help him.'

'Don't you, indeed?' He absently swept the sticks together again. 'Well, now. Just imagine – for a moment – that it's not Turner we're talking about, but the Duke of Wellington. He has made a munificent bequest to the nation, but the government refuses to honour its terms. What would be the result?'

'A public outcry.'

'Yes. Questions in the House. A resignation or two. Articles in *The Times*. *Disgrace*. *Stain on the national honour*. *An Englishman's word* . . .

'Yes,' I said; for it was undeniable. 'Go on.'

'Of course, Turner was only a painter, which any patriotic Englishman knows is a far lesser thing than a soldier. But still – he was, by common consent, our *greatest* painter. So what's poor Eastlake to do? How does he walk the tightrope?'

He gave me a moment to answer; but my mind was in such tumult I could not order my thoughts.

'What view of Turner best serves his purpose?' he prompted.

And then I saw it.

'The flawed genius!'

He nodded. 'If not a genius, then why go to the trouble of keeping his collection? But if not flawed, then how can we justify disregarding his will? Sir Charles, after all, as everybody knows, is a gentleman, and would never do anything dishonourable. So the fault must lie in *Turner*.'

'The problem, you mean,' I burst out, 'is not *our* meanness, but *his*!'

'Precisely. And not just meanness, either. The man was depraved' – here he dropped for a moment into a melodramatic whisper – 'or even mad. So it's quite legitimate for us to flout his wishes. Indeed, seen aright, it is surely our duty to do so, in the interests of public morality?'

He sounded so cruelly like Sir Charles – had captured so perfectly the gentle melancholy, the tone of pious, more-in-sorrow-than-in-anger pain at the folly of the world – that I could not help laughing. But even as I did so I felt myself starting to fall – as if a wall that I had assumed to be quite solid had suddenly given way before my weight.

'*Ergo*,' said Travis, 'Sir Charles, and his trustees, and the government all have a material interest in what you say in your book. If you present Turner –'

'Yes, yes,' I said.

He sat back with a self-satisfied smile, and a little flourish of the hand: *Voilà*.

I could barely speak. It was impossible to think while he was still there. I sat mute while he told me about Sir William Butteridge's rapture at his swooning damsel; and Lady Emery's commission for a fresco; and the favourable reviews of his work, by which, of course, he sets no store at all – could I imagine anything sillier than being called 'the English Botticelli'? Eventually, having exhausted the catalogue of his triumphs, and drawn nothing from me in return but the occasional nod or 'well done, I'm delighted for you', he gave up, and left.

Since when

Since when I have been a battlefield.

At first it seemed irrefutable. I had allowed myself to be comprehensively duped. Even my own picture testified against me. It seemed to glower down on me, reproaching my foolishness and pride. In my self-loathing, I could not take my eyes from it.

But then, as I hesitated on the brink of complete despair, doubts began to set in. They started with Farrant. I had not naïvely accepted his word: I had tested him, quite ingeniously, and found him honest. I was certain I had not been deceived about that.

And then the prostitute's story: it was unsubstantiated – but quite credible, surely, nonetheless? Did it not square with Hargreaves' claim that Turner had *wallowed in sailors' houses*? Had not Gudgeon said that Turner sometimes used the name 'Jenkinson'? And did not the use of the hood seem fitting for a man so anxious not to be seen, and so incapable of painting others?

And what if someone else *had* encouraged, or even paid, the informants? That did not necessarily make what they had told me untrue.

For two hours or more I debated – struggled – fought with myself. First one side, then the other, gained the upper hand; until at length my mind seemed to have been trampled into mud, and I could make out nothing distinctly in it at all.

But I must know.

Tuesday
This is a monster.

So I wrote yesterday.

But then I had only glimpsed the head. I had not penetrated the darkness, and made out the dreadful bulk of the body.

But which monster is it?

This morning I tried to work on the *Accident*, but could not concentrate. No sooner had I composed a figure, or attempted yet another new technique to make the furnace glow, than some word or phrase of Travis's erupted in my head, and I would suddenly find myself again wrestling with the conundrum he had set me. I knew it was hopeless – that I could not resolve it without further information – and yet I could not leave it alone. Finally I saw that I was simply wasting my time, and, bowing to the inevitable, gave up the pretence of painting altogether, and turned my full attention to Turner.

But what could I do? There was no point in returning to the woman in Wapping (assuming, that is, that I could even find her), or to Farrant. They would not say who, if anyone, had paid them. In any case, if it were someone of Sir Charles's stature, they almost wouldn't know themselves, since it was inconceivable that he would have failed to protect himself by using intermediaries.

What I needed, above all, was an accomplice: someone I could confide in – who would tell me if my doubts and suspicions appeared reasonable – who would help me to form and execute a plan of campaign. The obvious choice, of course, was Marian; and for one lunatic moment it did occur to me that I might tell her everything, and throw myself on her mercy. But a half-second's reflection told me that it was impossible, and that – however painful it may be – I must accept that our easy relations are gone for ever, and I must act without her – for the events of the last few days have created a barrier between us that can never be penetrated.

Travis again? No – he would only take it as another occasion to demonstrate his superiority. And besides, I could not trust him to resist the temptation of gossiping to his friends at the Athenaeum about it.

Ruskin? For a minute or so I did seriously think of it. But it would be humiliating to have to confirm his low opinion of me by admitting that I needed his help. And would a man so maddeningly vague and discursive be willing, or able, to give me a straight answer?

In the end I concluded there was but one course of action I could take. After luncheon I must go and see Lady Eastlake.

*

Despite the cold, and the treacherous patches of packed, filthy snow underfoot, I decided to walk. The conventions of polite society, which had always seemed entirely natural to me, now appeared cumbersome and artificial, as if in the space of less than a week I had become a foreigner. I needed time to think myself into them again, and to rehearse what I was going to say. Even in the best of circumstances – and these were very far from the best – it would have been a difficult interview, requiring great tact and perception and mental agility. Somehow I must contrive to hint at the possible existence of a conspiracy, without either revealing my grounds for suspecting it, or naming its probable instigator. I made a little store of phrases: *Delicate matter – you will appreciate – questions of confidence – felt I must apprise you.* Undoubtedly, she would respond no more directly; but from her manner and appearance as she did so (angry or dismissive? blushing or turning pale?) I should be able to gauge whether or not she thought it likely there *was* a plot – and whether, if so, she believed her husband might be involved in it.

In the event, these preparations were in vain. Lady Eastlake was not at home. I was already halfway down the steps again, when a sudden thought struck me:

'Stokes,' I said, turning back. 'Did my sister by any chance leave her notebook here last week? It's small – about so big – red morocco cover?'

He pondered for a second. 'I don't know, sir, but I think I *may* have seen it. If you would just wait a moment?'

He was back in half a minute.

'Is this the one, sir?'

In his hand was Marian's notebook.

'Oh, thank you, Stokes! Miss Halcombe *will* be relieved.

Where was it?'

For a second he forgot his footmanly duty. Smiling, he said:

'Where most things are in Lady Eastlake's boudoir. Beneath a pile of papers.'

Beneath a pile of papers.

All the way back to Brompton Grove I wondered what it meant.

Perhaps there was an innocent enough explanation. Lady Eastlake had found it in the drawing room – taken it to the boudoir for safe-keeping – put something on top, and forgotten it. It was, after all, a small thing, and she was a busy woman.

But then, when Marian had written, surely she would have remembered?

Very well. It was a *servant* who had found it and taken it to the boudoir, on the reasonable assumption that it was Lady Eastlake's. It at once became part of the undifferentiated clutter on the table, and in due course was covered up. Lady Eastlake did not even know it was there.

It was possible.

But at least equally possible, surely, that she *did* know it was there. In which case, why had she not returned it to Marian? Had even, perhaps, gone to the trouble of hiding it – if not very successfully?

I could not immediately think of an answer, so when I got home I wedged the studio door shut with a chair, and then sat down and opened the notebook.

At first I was as baffled as ever. It seemed to contain nothing but Marian's jottings about Turner – what people had told her, or facts she had gleaned from diaries and letters. But then, towards the end, I found a long summary of her conclusions. It was so full of false starts and crossings-out that in places it was barely legible, but I could make out enough to recognize the bare bones of the character sketch of

Turner that she had sent to me in Cumberland. Eight words, in particular, caught my attention:

Poor Turner.
His poor mother.
Good Mrs. Booth.

Poor Turner. *Good* Mrs. Booth. If Travis was right, these were not judgements that would please Sir Charles. Too much sympathy. Too much understanding.

And then, suddenly, a whole torrent of thoughts, each more monstrous than the last, squealed and tumbled into my mind like rats loosed from a cage.

What if Lady Eastlake is not ignorant of the plot, but party to it?

What if *she* is the instigator? What if, knowing how principled her husband is, she resolved to do what his scruples would not permit him to do himself? She is, after all, famously devoted to him, is she not – and jealously protective of his interests?

When she hears Marian's views, then (which she naturally supposes to be mine as well), she is thoroughly alarmed by them. So that when fate presents her with the notebook, she decides to keep it, in order to see the evidence on which they are based, and so be able the more effectively to counter them.

Or perhaps, if she was that determined, she hadn't left it to fate. Until now, I had assumed that Marian's reticule had been snatched merely as a decoy, to lure me to a place where I could be safely captured. But perhaps it had served a double purpose. Marian has always insisted that she would not have left the notebook behind; and certainly there were several occasions when the thief was lost to my view, and he would have had the opportunity to pass it to an accomplice.

At this point, the clamour of the rats abated for a moment;

for I had seen an objection. Neither Lady Eastlake nor any of her intimates could possibly have known my abductor or his wife, or any of *their* intimates; and while it was easy enough to imagine Sir Charles using his power and connections to discover them, and buy their compliance, it was hard to see how she could have done so without running the risk of exposure. Whom could she rely on to act on her behalf, who . . .?

And then another rat appeared:

What if it were Mr. Kingsett?

Perhaps that is why he and his wife were there; and why Lady Eastlake tolerated his appalling behaviour.

Perhaps that is why he touched Marian, and said *Please, Miss Halcombe*, the moment before the thief appeared – so that he should know which reticule to take.

I am giddy. I had hoped for resolution. All I have got is more perplexity.

Davidson has just brought me another letter from Laura. I have put it with all the others. I cannot face it.

These distractions are my enemies. They keep me from my work. I must drive them from my mind, and take up my brush.

Wednesday

Perhaps the monster is what I see when I look in the glass.

Two hours last night I tried to paint, but to no avail.

I went to bed, but could not sleep. I felt myself hemmed in on every side. Disarmed. The will and energy draining from me.

I thought: *You must act, to regain your power.*

So I got dressed again, and went out. I assumed I was entirely alone and unnoticed, but from what came later I wonder now if I was observed.

There was no wind, but the cold took my breath away. It paid no heed to coat and skin and flesh, but straightway touched my bones, as if they were already in the grave, and it were merely claiming its own.

But death at least is certain. Better to walk with death inside you than nothing.

My first thoughts were of the Marston Rooms. I should find my musky whore, and get what I had paid for.

But as I neared the lights and crowds of the Haymarket I began to falter. It wasn't so much the fear of being seen that deterred me – I didn't think anyone would know me in my present state, and no longer cared greatly if they did – but a horror of the dreadful charade of artifice and politeness. She wouldn't say: *Fuck me for five bob* – not in Piccadilly. In Piccadilly there would still have to be preambles: sly glances, giggles, arch comments, drinks and waiters, an exchange of names, a pretence of personal interest. The very thought of it filled me with weariness, and something close to disgust.

Without pausing to consider, I turned south again, and then east into Trafalgar Square. The great blank façade of the National Gallery and the Royal Academy looked as grim as a mausoleum, and as unlikely to yield up its secrets. I raised my hat in passing to Sir Charles, and crossed into Duncannon Street. Ten minutes later I was entering Maiden Lane.

It was impossible to be sure, for the two or three half-hearted gas-lamps did no more than fray the edges of the darkness, but so far as I could tell it was completely deserted. Slowly, slowly, I picked my way over the piles of frozen detritus, looking left and right for any sign of life: a movement, a crack of light in a shuttered window.

Nothing. The gate to Hand Court was shut. The pawnbroker's locked and unlighted.

More slowly, then. More slowly. Give fate time to meet you.

There was a sudden noise behind me. My heart was battering in my ears so loudly I could not tell what it was. I looked back, but there was nothing to be seen. A cat or a rat, probably, I decided, scuttling for safety.

I continued on my way. And then – unmistakably – heard footsteps hurrying after me; and, as I turned, a young, half-whispered voice:

'You lookin' for somethin'?'

I can't be certain it was the same girl, but I think it was. She was dressed as a woman now, and her lips were reddened; but I caught the glitter of her large brown eyes, and her cheeks were still as white and unblemished as a china doll's.

'What you after, darlin'?'

She did not seem to recognize me, but that is no surprise: the light was poor, and the intervening weeks have changed me as much as they have her. I said nothing, but held out five shillings. She had to move and squint to see it; but when she did so, and realized how much it was, she gave a little laugh of pleasure.

'All right.' She took the money and slipped it into a pocket. Then she moved close and put her arms round me – impetuously, inexpertly, like a child thanking her uncle for a present.

'What's your name?'

She must have felt me stiffen and pull away; for she said:

'What's the matter?'

I shook my head. She looked into my eyes, with a little frown of concentration, trying to see what I wanted.

'That's all right,' she said. 'You don't 'ave to say nothin'.' She glanced about her, to see we were not watched, and then lifted her skirt and placed my hand against her quim, wincing despite herself at the cold touch of my fingers. Then, without speaking, she turned and led me back down the street, and through the side-entrance by the pawnbroker's into a little court, and thence into an unlit room on the ground floor.

I could see nothing; and, even if I had, I should not remember it. I remember only the Babel of voices in my head:

How can you do this?

Is she not a whore, like the other?

She is a child, and you sought her out.

There is a price for everything.

Why should she pay it?

She is as eager as I am. Having come so far, I will only distress her more if I withdraw now. And what difference will one man more or less make to her?

What difference to you?

I must be free. Is it not natural – merely one piece of flesh enfolding another? Besides, is it not what Turner did?

Is it?

I feared this ceaseless attrition would sap me, and make me incapable at the last; and so indeed it might have done, had she made any response, or reminded me, by even the faintest gesture, that we were two people, and not merely the impersonal, mechanical conjunction of complementary organs.

But she was quick to learn, and had already understood what she must do. She stood with her back to me, and bent forward, and braced herself against the wall, with barely a movement or a murmur or a sigh. And when I was done, she guided me to the door without a word, and gently pushed me outside, locking the door behind me.

The voices were silent on my way home. I was conscious of nothing, not even the cold. Death itself had forsaken me.

Until I turned into Brompton Grove. For a moment I sensed only an animal apprehension that something was different and unexpected. Then I saw it: standing in front of the house was a black carriage. The windows were curtained, as if for a funeral. A squat coachman in a tall hat sat with his back towards me, so swaddled in blankets that he looked as improvised and immobile as a snowman. The horses themselves were invisible in the gloom, but I could see the haze of their breath on the still air.

I instantly thought of Laura – of the children – of Marian. Somehow, by my faithlessness, I had killed one of them, or made them ill. The horror of the idea stopped me dead, and I had to fight the urge to run away. But then I steadied myself. That was the voice of weakness and superstition. Dr. Hampson would have come by cab. And if someone had died, there would have been a telegram, not a carriage at the door in the middle of the night.

I started walking again, trying to convince myself that for some reason the man had simply decided to rest his horses in Brompton Grove, and that it was nothing to do with me. And had almost succeeded when, as I drew alongside, the carriage door opened abruptly in front of me, barring my path.

'Mr. Hartright?'

It was a high, frail, man's voice that I didn't recognize. I peered into the interior, but could see nothing.

'Mr. Hartright, get in, please. I have something to tell you.'

'Can you not tell me out here?'

There was a small, dry sound that might equally have been a cough or a laugh.

'I should die of the cold.' He paused, as if his supply of breath were exhausted, and must be replenished before he could continue. 'You'll come to no harm, I promise. What could I do, even if I were minded? A brute like you would snuff me out as easily as a candle.'

I hesitated, but only for a moment. If he meant to abduct me, why did he not simply take me by force, as my previous attackers had done? And even if that were his intention, might I not still learn something of value? A few hours' loss of liberty would be a small price to pay, if it helped to end my uncertainty.

'Very well,' I said, pulling myself up.

In the glimmer of light from the street I half-saw a bundle of rugs and wraps and muffs huddled in the corner. I should not have known it was a man, save for the eyes, which appeared for a moment in the narrow gap between fur hat and upturned collar, and immediately flickered away again. They were more shadow than substance, so sunken that they seemed to be trying to retreat inside his skull; and somehow managed to convey, in the brief instant I glimpsed them, an impression of infinite weariness.

'Sit down, please, and close the door.'

I did so. It was now completely dark.

'Thank you.' He had to pause again. I heard the pitiful whistle and splutter of his chest as he struggled for breath. 'I wish to speak to you, Mr. Hartright,' he went on at last, 'on the matter of genius. You are writing, I believe, a life of Turner?'

I did not reply, but waited for him to reveal more of his hand before I showed my own.

'Please, Mr. Hartright,' he wheezed. 'You must assist me. I am a sick man. Every word is a battle. I cannot afford to throw them away.'

'Yes,' I said.

'Very well. I was privileged to see something of him. Something, I think, you will learn from no-one else.'

'Why?' I said. 'Who are you?'

'You may call me Simpson. That will do for now.'

'It is not your real name?'

'Why should a name I choose for myself be less real than the one given me by my parents?'

True, I thought. *Is Jenkinson not as real as Hartright?*

420

'*That* I had to abandon a long time ago,' he continued, 'when an indiscretion obliged me to leave England. Since then I have been living in Venice, and whenever I have returned it has always been under a *nom de voyage*.' He sucked in breath, slowly, so as not to provoke a fit of coughing. When he spoke again, it was in a whisper.

'Can you still hear me, Mr. Hartright?'

'Just.'

'It's better for me to talk like this, if that is agreeable to you. Less taxing. Shan't have to stop so often.'

'Very well.'

'Well, then,' he whispered. 'You will appreciate that a man in my situation must always be careful. Make it his business to learn everything he can of his travelling companions, while giving away nothing about himself. There may be spies. Agents. Hm?'

'Yes.'

'Well, once I was crossing the Alps by Mount Cenis, and there was a small fellow in the carriage with me who at once roused my suspicions. Never said anything, unless someone spoke to him first, and then only brusquely. Never answered questions directly. Spent most of his time looking out of the window, and making sketches, as if he were preparing for a military campaign.'

He had to pause again. I was puzzled. Why was he going to the trouble of telling me this? Did he suppose I had not already heard countless stories of Turner's solitariness and eccentricity?

'Well, it took me a day or two,' he went on, 'but I found him out, little by little. The initials "J. M. W. T." on his valise. A letter interleaved with his sketchbook. A few fragments of conversation, in which he unwittingly let slip that he knew Lord Egremont, and most of the Royal Academy.

'We travelled together several times after that. I never said anything, of course, and he never recognized me – it would have mortified him to know that I had uncovered his secret, when he had failed to penetrate mine.'

'Scarcely a secret,' I said. 'At least in his case.'

His voice was so attenuated that the reply came out as no more than a kind of ghostly sigh:

'Oh, yes! A great secret, Mr. Hartright. The secret of genius.'

My skin prickled, despite the cold.

'I saw him often in Venice. Sometimes when he thought himself completely unobserved. And I can testify that he was a remarkable man. Peep out of your window at dawn, and there he'd be, drawing away. Take a gondola for your evening cigar, and damn me if you wouldn't see him there still, scribbling till the last crack of the sun had gone. And then – then he needs must be away, to make sure that it rose again the next day.'

'Rose again?'

He could not reply at once. I had to clench my fists to prevent myself trying to shake the words from him. Slowly, painstakingly, he drew the air into his lungs.

'You know what sun-worshippers are. Their god must be satisfied with blood, else he will grow angry, and return no more.'

'Blood!'

'I'm talking about girls, Mr. Hartright. It was common knowledge in less conventional circles. I saw them taking one out of the canal myself. There were rope marks on her wrists and ankles, a sack over her face. She'd been held under till she drowned.'

For a moment I could not speak. I could not move. Then I heard myself whispering:

'Why are you telling me this?'

There was no answer. I waited. After perhaps fifteen seconds I felt something brush gropingly against my knee. I put my hand down and found his fingers. They were as cold as

422

stone. The instant I touched them, they started to flutter towards my wrist.

I pulled away, and opened the door, and dropped to the ground.

I did not dream it. There is horse-shit on the ground where the carriage stood.

Can it be true?
  Can it possibly be true?

Who is Simpson?
  Could Kingsett have sent him?

Could it have *been* Kingsett?

LXII

Letter from Laura Hartright to Walter Hartright, 20th December, 185–

Wednesday

I dreamed last night you met a clever woman, who talked to you of all the things I cannot, and took you from me.
  Dreams are often true, are they not?

  Laura

LXIII

From the private notebook of Walter Hartright,
21st–22nd December, 185–

Thursday
Record. I must record.
  Stamp order on the chaos.

Today I went to see a medium.

  As I waited in her drawing room, I could scarce believe I
found myself there. I looked down from the window at the
press of people milling along Brook Street and thought how
easily, even now, I might run outside again and lose myself
among them.

  But then the maid reappeared. 'Mrs. Mast will see you
now, sir.'

  She led me into a small parlour at the rear of the house.
The curtains were already drawn, and the gas-lamps lit. The
fire had burned low, and there was a marked chill in the air.

  Two women sat at a round table in the middle of the
room. One was thin and elderly, long-faced and big-nosed,
so grey and angular she might have been made out of iron.
The other plump and matronly, perhaps thirty years
younger, with pink cheeks and bright eyes.

  'Mr. Hartright, ma'am,' said the maid.

  'How d'ye do, Mr. Hartright?' said the younger woman,
thrusting her hand out as forthrightly as a man. 'I'm
Euphemia Mast.'

  'How do you do?'

  'This is my mother.'

  'How do you do?'

  'She will assist me,' said Mrs. Mast. 'Please sit down.' Her
voice was brisk and businesslike, with a hard nasal
American twang she made no attempt to soften. As I drew

up my chair she asked:

'Have you attended a consultation before, Mr. Hartright?'

'Not of this kind.'

'And why, may I ask, did you come to *me*?'

'I wish' – was I really saying it? – 'to speak – to make contact with a dead man.'

I bit my tongue. I had resolved to disclose nothing about my purpose; for if – as I still more than half-believed – she were no more than a skilful conjuror, who had grown rich by preying on the gullible, she might well be able to construct a convincing 'spirit' simply from what I unwittingly let slip about him. But then I relaxed a little: for, surely, to know only his sex would be a small enough advantage for even the most accomplished fraud?

'We do not call them "dead",' she said, as matter-of-factly as if she were an engineer correcting me for saying 'piston' rather than 'valve', 'but "passed over". Is he someone you have lost?'

'In a manner of speaking.'

'Well, I shall do what I can, Mr. Hartright, but I hope you understand that I can guarantee nothing. I am no more than the channel. Some spirits find it impossible to communicate from the other side. Some do not wish to.' She was suddenly grave and earnest. 'It's most important that you realize that, before we begin.'

I nodded.

'You are a sensitive man, Mr. Hartright' – from the way she said it, you would have thought it was as evident and incontrovertible as the colour of my eyes – 'and sensitive people are sometimes alarmed by what happens when I enter the trance state. So let me explain. My physical body will still be here, but someone else will be controlling it. Most probably it will be one of my guides from the Other Side – Running Deer, or Mops. Just talk to her as you would to a friend. You may find it strange at first, but to her it will seem perfectly normal, I promise you. And as for me: whatever you see or hear, I shall not even be aware of it – so don't imagine that something is amiss, and I need help. Just allow things to take their course, and at the right moment I shall return.'

She waited for me to respond. I hesitated; and then – realizing that there was no point in being here at all if I did not at least pretend to assent to the reality of the spiritual world – nodded again.

'Very well. Have you brought anything with you that belonged to him, or is connected with him in any way? That sometimes helps.'

I knew this to be a usual request; and had anticipated it by slipping the old paintbrush Gudgeon had given me into my pocket before setting out. But now I hesitated. It was a clue – a large clue. Should I risk giving so much away?

She must have noticed my uncertainty; for she said: 'Please give it to me.'

I handed it to her, vowing to reveal nothing more.

'Thank you.'

She held it in both hands, gently running her fingers over the shaft. After a few moments, as if to concentrate better, she shut her eyes. The older woman, I noticed, was watching her closely, occasionally casting a warning glance in my direction that said: *Say nothing*. After a minute or more Mrs. Mast began to slump and nod, like a traveller falling asleep on a train. As if this were a signal, her mother got up, and, moving so quietly I could scarcely hear her, turned off the lamps and sat down again next to her daughter. The only light now came from the dying embers in the grate, and from where I was sitting the two women were no more than a blotchy silhouette.

Almost at once Mrs. Mast started to babble. To begin with it was just a torrent of groans and nonsense words, as if she were talking in her sleep; but then she began to twitch quite

violently, and I heard snippets of two female voices which –
though they indisputably came from her mouth – were
nothing like hers at all.

You –

My –

The Turk –

I help –

Not her –

And then Mrs. Mast's head dropped suddenly against her
mother's shoulder. And one of the voices said, quite clearly:

'There. '*Er's* gone. '*Er* didn't even know what tha wants. *I*
knows.'

It sounded like a girl, eleven or twelve perhaps. Not
American. From the north somewhere, I thought – Yorkshire
or Lancashire, maybe – though some of the words had a
kind of guttural thickness that seemed slightly foreign. The
effect was so strange that I shivered despite myself.

'Go on, then,' whispered the old woman. 'Ask her something.'

Why could I not speak? What was I afraid of?

'Go *on*,' hissed the old woman.

'Who are you?' I said.

'Mops,' replied the voice.

'And why are you talking to me?'

'I goes. For 'er.'

'Who is *she*?'

'Tha knows. Mrs. Wosser. Wossername. Mast. I goes and
finds 'em for 'er. She thinks it's '*er*, or one o' t'others, but it's
awlus me.'

'Find the *spirits*, you mean?'

'Ay, tha's it.' Her tone was surprised, as if she'd supposed
it was too obvious to need pointing out.

Tha. 'Er. Awlus. Where had I heard those words recently?

'Why are you there?'

'Wha', this side?'

'Yes.'

'Ay ay I drownded.'

Drownded.

That was it. The mad old woman in Otley, talking about her childhood friend.

I was drenched and cold with sweat. I said:

'What happened to you? Did someone –?'

'Drownded.' She sounded impatient, as if the subject were distasteful to her. 'I drownded.'

'Is Mops your real name?' I could not remember what the friend was called, but thought I should know it if I heard it.

'Mops. Mobs. Meg.'

Meg. And now it came to me: the friend had been *Mary.* Close – so close it was hard to believe it was mere coincidence – but not the same.

'Meg?' I said, in case I had mistaken her.

'I'm a good lass, I am,' she said, as if she hadn't understood. 'I can 'elp tha. I know what tha wants.'

It was maddening, but there was no point pursuing it. I gritted my teeth. 'What do I want?'

'Tha wants '*e*.'

This sounded like a ploy to draw me out further, so – remembering my resolution – I said nothing, but waited for her to continue.

'I sees . . . canvas,' she said uncertainly, at length. 'I sees paint . . .'

And so would anyone, I thought, *who had first seen a brush.*

'I sees a name . . . the beginnin' of a name . . . I think i's a "T".'

I started; but then told myself it was not such a wonder – 'T' is a common enough letter, and there is a reasonable chance that at least one part of an English name will start with it.

'I' that right?'

'Maybe,' I said.

'Or is i' . . . is i' . . . "J"? Ay, I think tha's i'! "J". An' then "O". No, "E".'

I started again; and this time could not stop myself blurting out: 'Jenkinson!'

'Ay,' she said (though what 'she' was, exactly, I still could not say), '"Jen" summat, all right. Oh, but 'old 'ard.'

'What is it?'

'Sssh!' A pause; then, puzzled: 'I' tha' tha, or 'e?'

'What?'

'That "Jen"? Tha name, or 'is?'

I could not answer. After a moment she said:

'I'm a' felted.'

And then I seemed again to be half-hearing a distant conversation between her and somebody else. But this time the other voice was a man's, gruff and short.

Eerily, I have to confess, as I imagine Turner's.

I forced myself not to reflect on where I was, or what I was doing; but merely to hear and remember what they were saying, like a scientist or a reporter, without judging it. But try as I might, I could still only pick out fragments:

Slippin'

Taste

Why won't –?

Appre'end

'O'?

Windsor

Usurp

Aloud (allowed?)

A moment's hesitation. Then the girl's voice:

'There's no call for tha'.'

I could hear her clearly enough now, but the indignant tone suggested she was still talking to somebody else.

'Ask him,' I said. 'Ask him –'

'Wha'?' she snapped irritably.

'Ask him his occupation.'

A pause. Then:

'P . . . p . . . pain . . .'

Painter. But again, of course, the brush had effectively told *her* that.

'In what medium?'

'Mrs. Mrs. Wosser –'

I shook with frustration. 'What kind of paint?'

'Oi . . . oi . . .'

'Is that all?'

Silence.

'Ask him to name one of his pictures.'

'See . . . see . . .'

'See what?'

'No! *See!*'

'Oh, *sea*! Waves, you mean? Water?'

'Ay . . . ay . . . war. Wa'er. Wa'ercolour.'

I saw I must take another approach, or risk losing my mind altogether. I said:

'Lu.'

She seemed to wait for me to continue. When I didn't, she said:

'Wha tha mean?'

'Did he know a woman called Lu?'

'Mm.' There was a kind of frowning puzzlement in her voice, as if she were struggling to make sense of something – an impression strangely belied by the placid vacancy of Mrs. Mast's face. 'By t'river?'

'Yes.'

There was a murmur I couldn't make out, and then a giggle.

'What is it?' I said.

''E says *Wa'erloo.*'

She laughed again. It took me a second to see why. Then an odd spasm – half fear, half exaltation – passed through me: for surely there was something unmistakably Turnerish about this reply? It could just be coincidence, of course; or it could be that Mrs. Mast was an exceptionally gifted fraud, who had guessed whom I was trying to contact, and had sufficient knowledge of him to make his 'spirit' speak in Napoleonic puns, and refer repeatedly to water – but at that instant, for the first time, I believed I really might be communicating with him.

The thought of it – the hope of it – made me reckless.

'Is it true – is it true,' I said – for a moment forgetting entirely about Mrs. Mast and her mother – 'that he bound her, and placed a hood over her head?'

Silence.

'What does he say?'

"E don' say nowt.'

I wanted to beg. I wanted to plead for my sanity. Only by a great effort of will did I stop myself.

'What of Sandycombe Lodge, then?' I said. 'Why did he design the basement so?'

Silence. I took a deep breath.

'Very well,' I said. 'One question. One question only. What does he know of a man who calls himself Simpson?'

There was no response. I waited, resolving to say nothing more. As I did so, an image drifted into my mind, so suddenly and powerfully that it was as if someone had placed it there directly.

A Turner picture. *Ulysses Deriding Polyphemus*.

But I was not merely watching the scene, I was a part of it. Everything moved before me – the jeering figures on the ship, the horses bearing the sun into the sky, the giant clutching his eyeless face in agony.

I whispered: 'Are you there?'

Still nothing. Just an unbroken silence, that seemed to grow deeper and more final by the second.

Remembering Mrs. Mast's injunction at the beginning, I did not move or interfere. But as the minutes passed I could

431

not help wondering if this were entirely normal. And when at length the old woman – who up until now had remained calm and still – suddenly shifted in her chair, and looked (or so it appeared in the darkness) into her daughter's face, I concluded that something must be wrong.

And then, without warning, it happened. From less than a foot in front of me, the man's voice spoke again. No more than a whisper, this time, and only three words – but they were absolutely clear:

'*Leave me be!*'

I somehow found the strength to sit there quietly as Mrs. Mast returned to consciousness, grunting and muttering as before, and her mother relit the lamps, and the familiar shapes and colours of this world once again formed before my eyes. I contrived to answer politely when she asked if the séance had been helpful, and to offer to pay, and to find two guineas when she told me she did not charge, but would accept a contribution from those she had assisted, in order that she might be able to further her work, and bring consolation to those who mourned.

But once outside I began to weep – to sob and quake and wail uncontrollably, so that people looked strangely at me, and stepped off the pavement to avoid me.

I have no pride left. Tomorrow I shall go to see Ruskin.

Friday
Record.
Just record.

I take a cab to Dennmark Hill. 'Young Mr. Ruskin is not at home. You will find him working at the National Gallery.'

Another cab, to Trafalgar Square. A half-deaf functionary, who at first affects not to understand me. Then he sees murder in my eyes, and conducts me to the basement.

It is dark and humid and close. The walls are lined with boxes, piled two or three high. In the feeble glow of the two gas-lights I can see that behind them the plaster is stained with mould and moisture.

Ruskin sits at a table, working by the light of a single oil-lamp. Before him are stacks of notebooks, hundreds of them – mildewed, tattered, frayed into holes, eaten away by damp and mice. He is painstakingly unbinding one of them, and does not pay us any attention as we enter.

'Mr. Hartright,' grumbles the functionary.

Ruskin raises his head. The blue eyes are as brilliant as ever, but he is pale with tiredness. He stares into my face for a moment – fails to recognize it – looks at the functionary for an explanation.

But the functionary is already leaving. Closing the door.

'The biography of Turner,' I say. 'I came to see you about it, a few months ago.'

'Ah, yes, yes, of course.' He half-rises, leans across the table, touches my hand. 'How are you?'

I say nothing, and he does not press me. He slumps back in his seat, his eyes already returning to his work.

'You said I might talk to you again, when I had gone further.'

He nods without looking at me. He lifts a page from the open notebook, carefully blows the dust from it, and lays it on a sheet of clean writing-paper. I can see nothing of it but a disc of radiant orange dissolving in darkness, but it is enough to jolt me. To shame me.

'Why are you not at home, preparing for Christmas, like the rest of the world?' he says, taking out another page and peering at it.

I have not the energy to ask him the same question. 'I am desperate.'

He sighs. 'I cannot say I am entirely surprised.'

'No. You warned me.'

'Did I?'

There are two other chairs. I clutch the back of one of them, hoping he will invite me to sit down.

'*Sometimes,*' I say, '*we may deceive ourselves into thinking we are capable of some great task which is beyond us.*'

'Is that what I said? Dear me.' He waves a hand at the laden table, and tugs his misshapen mouth into a smile. 'If hypocrisy were a capital offence, my prospects would be poor indeed.'

'It *was* beyond me. I need your help.'

At last he looks at me. 'That is a sad state for any man to find himself in,' he says slowly. 'And if it is the case I am truly sorry for it.'

'What is the truth about him?'

'Ah, the truth!' He shakes his head morosely. 'How do you find the truth about a man who eschewed the literal, and spoke in riddles? It will end by making you mad.'

'I fear it already has.'

He stares deep into my eyes, and then nods. 'The truth about Turner', he says, 'is never direct. Always oblique. There are hints of it in the pictures, of course, but you can never fully comprehend it. It cannot be reduced to its component parts, or to any simple proposition. There will always be something beyond, that defies our attempts to imprison it in words.'

I feel I am about to faint. I drop on to the chair. He appears not to notice.

'Perhaps the same might be said of all of us. I certainly hope it may be said of me. But most of us may be represented by a kind of tapestry, in which the principal elements – honesty, dishonesty, intelligence, stupidity – are clearly visible. In Turner, by contrast, the cloth is twisted and folded and wound in on itself. When you glimpse a thread you never know whether it is a part of the subject, or a chance

434

trick of the weaver's art, or a false trail deliberately woven into the fabric to puzzle or mislead.' He pauses. Examines his own fingers. Fastidiously blows the chalk dust from them. 'You are familiar, of course, with the fallacies of hope?'

An odd expression, but the meaning is plain enough. 'If I wasn't before, the last five months have made me so.'

He cannot resist a smile. 'I was not referring to your own experiences, Mr. Hartright, but to Turner's poetic *magnum opus.*'

'*The Fallacies of Hope*?'

He nods. 'You have not heard of it?'

'No.'

He raises one shaggy eyebrow. I have fallen still further in his estimation, if such a thing is possible. He shuts his eyes, in the effort of remembering, and declaims:

> 'Craft, treachery, and fraud – Salassian force,
> Hung on the fainting rear! – then Plunder seiz'd
> The victor and the captive, – Saguntum's spoils
> Alike, became their prey . . .

'That was the start of it. The caption to *Hannibal Crossing the Alps* in 1812. He'd used verses as captions to his pictures before, of course, but they were always taken from other poets, though often garbled or misquoted. The attribution here was: *MS. Fallacies of Hope*. Thereafter, it appeared on his paintings again and again, each time with a different verse. So what does everyone naturally assume?'

It is too remote from my thoughts for me to grasp it immediately.

He prompts me: 'What is the implication?'

'That . . . that . . . he has – or has written – a poem. An unpublished poem. And is extracting pertinent passages from it, to serve as captions.'

'Exactly. And he must have known that was the impression he was giving. But it wasn't true.'

'It didn't exist?'

'Not in its entirety. He merely composed lines, or adapted them from other writers, when he needed them. It's a false trail, you see?' He lifts his finger, and traces its progress on an imaginary tapestry. 'A flash of colour here – a flash there – you think they belong to the same continuous strand, but they don't. It's an illusion.'

I can barely muster the strength to ask:

'Can we then trust nothing?'

He shrugs, and looks at me curiously, as if he were seeing me for the first time. At length he says:

'What is troubling you, Mr. Hartright?'

And I tell him. I tell him about Farrant and Hargreaves – about our dinner at Fitzroy Square, and my abduction afterwards – about Lucy, and the hood and the ropes. I tell him about Travis, and Marian's notebook, and my growing suspicion of the Eastlakes (at which he cannot suppress a wintry smile). And about my meeting with Simpson, and my uncertainty as to whether or not it was a dream, and the séance with Mrs. Mast. I tell him I don't know what to believe.

But I do not tell him I fucked two whores, thinking it would make me a genius.

He does not even seem surprised. He nods, and then stares at me in silence.

And I am conscious only of the relief of having said so much, and not being vilified or rejected or laughed at for it. And of the intolerable burden of what I have *not* said, which sits in my belly like a small hot coal.

O, God, to be rid of that too! To have said it all – to have revealed those things in myself so dark and terrible that even *I* had not suspected their existence, and to find myself still accepted – that would be a kind of redemption. The only kind I can now conceive.

But it is impossible. Even as I write these words I know

O God

Write. Write. Record.

At length he gets up. He surveys the wall of boxes, finds the one he is looking for, and carefully removes it. Then he brings it to the table and – reaching in his pocket for a key – unlocks it.

'He was, unquestionably, a man of deep, strange errors and failures,' he says. 'And I find myself more and more helpless to explain them. Save that they all arose from his faithlessness, or despair. For this is the century of despair; and it has corroded the greatest minds as perniciously as it has the lowest.'

He opens the box, takes out another notebook, and turns to the last few pages. Sketch after sketch of men and women in bed together. Nothing is complete – a pair of buttocks here, a raised leg there, a hand clutching a bare shoulder – and the faces cannot be seen at all; but it is plain enough to what they refer. Pictures not of people – not even of entire bodies – but merely of an act.

'Yes,' I say. 'It's ugly. But is there any evidence that he – that he could have been capable of . . . of . . .?'

'I am an art critic, Mr. Hartright, not a detective. I can only tell you – as I told you before – that there is a dark clue running through Turner's art, and it is the darkness of death. There is another running through his life, and it is the darkness of England.' He pauses, and shakes his head sorrowfully. 'What he might have done for us had he received help and love, I can hardly trust myself to imagine. But we disdained him. For seventy-six grinding years we tortured his spirit, as we torture the spirits of all our brightest children. And we are torturing it still, now that he is dead.'

'Because of the will, you mean?'

'Ah, yes, the will. We *say* it is the will, because a will concerns money and the law, and those are things we can comprehend. They are *all* we can comprehend. But Turner stirred something deeper in this blind, tormented country – something of which, with our bluff good sense, we are barely aware in ourselves. Turner foresaw our end, which few of us can face. Worse still, he dared to love the light – something without a price on it, which could not be defined and contained in the dreary little counting-house of our minds. And we punished him for it. Whatever he was guilty of, it is we who drove him to it.'

I struggle for breath. I have to whisper it:

'But what do you believe?'

'One thing one moment, another thing the next, like most men. Only *I* accept it, with as much grace as I can. To contradict yourself is no more than to acknowledge the complexity of life.' He gets up again. 'Let me show you something.'

He picks up the lamp, leads me out into the stairwell and into a room on the other side. It is absolutely dark, save for the soft glow of burning oil. Leaning against the wall is a stack of unframed canvases, five or six deep.

'These are his last works,' says Ruskin in a hushed voice, as if we have entered a church. 'The last works of our greatest genius. See how we value them.' He runs a finger down one and then turns it towards me. It is glistening with water. 'See what they tell us about ourselves.'

He hands me the lamp, and slowly pulls the canvases away, one at a time, to let me view them.

~~I have never seen~~

Write

Nothing. Swirls of nothing. Smear

Whirlpools. Pulling you into nothing.

Whirl

Nothing

Whirl

438

LXIV

From the diary of Marian Halcombe,
23rd–26th December, 185–

Saturday

I shall not kill myself.

But I know now why people do.

Nothing rational keeps me from it.

Today we were meant to be travelling to Cumberland, to join Laura and the family for Christmas.

Instead

Some time in the night I was woken by the sound of my door opening. There was a little light left from the fire. The figure of a man crossed before it and then stopped and looked at me. No more than a dim silhouette, but I knew him at once – though to see him there, and at such a time, was as strange as looking in the glass and finding another face where my own should have been.

'Walter?' I said.

He did not answer. I thought perhaps I was dreaming, and reached for the box of matches to light the lamp. Immediately he lunged towards me and put his hand over mine.

'No.'

'Why?' I said. 'Walter, what are you doing?'

He said nothing, but sat on the bed, with his face turned away from me. After a few moments his shoulders hunched and his neck arched and he started to sob.

'What's the matter?'

He dropped forward, his head in his hands, crying almost silently.

'What is it?'

439

He tried to speak, but could not catch his breath. I stroked his back.

'Tell me!'

After perhaps half a minute he said:

'Futile.'

'What is?'

'Life.'

'Your life? My life?'

'Ev–' he began; and then had to gulp for air, and broke off abruptly.

'There! You've given yourself hiccups,' I said, in the smiling voice I have heard Walter himself use, to cajole his children from tears. But instead of soothing him, I succeeded only in provoking a renewed outburst of sobs.

'It's not futile,' I said, hastily changing tack, 'it's not!' – though since I had no idea what 'it' was, I felt as foolish as a doctor trying to treat a wound he could not see.

Walter did not respond at first; but then suddenly turned, and laid his face on my breast.

As a child must on his mother. A man must on his wife.

And like a mother and a wife I comforted him. Without reflecting. I held his head against my cheek. I fondled his hair. I whispered: 'Ssh. There. There.'

He grew quieter. I thought perhaps he had fallen asleep; but then I was conscious that his arms had tightened about me, and he was starting to caress me, as I have never been caressed.

Dear God, what did I think? That he was incapable of harming me? That it was normal for a brother to touch his sister so?

The truth is I did not think anything. I merely obeyed some impulse in me that must have lain slumbering all my life, and now awoke, and told me what to do. I caressed him too, as I have never caressed anyone. There was no beginning to it, and no clear notion in my head of any end. We seemed suspended – as if someone had abstracted us from the world, and set us down in a strange place where we could act without consequences.

Until Walter began pulling at my covers.

'No,' I whispered.

But he did not stop.

'No!' I said more loudly, trying to push him away.

But he was too strong for me. In a moment the blankets were gone, and he was tearing at my nightgown.

'Walt–!' I began; but he drew the nightgown over my eyes and mouth, forcing the word back between my lips, and held it there.

'Do you not love me?' he whispered.

I heard his boots clatter to the floor; and then he was struggling to remove his own clothes. But with only one hand he was slow and clumsy, and at length, in his frenzy, he forgot himself for a moment, and uncovered my face.

All these years I have called him my brother.

He is not my brother. He is –

He was staring at me. Staring at what no man has ever seen. But not like a man. His mouth was wet. He was panting. I thought of a cat about to eat.

I could have cried out again, but what then? The only help at hand was Davidson. How could *he* intervene between Walter and me?

I tried to appeal: 'Walter. Please.'

He dragged my hair across my face, pressing it down so tightly I could barely breathe.

I did not try to speak again. I feared he would hurt me.

I had not known before what the gospels mean by *possession*. I had thought it perhaps no more than a primitive word for *madness*.

But Walter was possessed. A demon had subdued his true nature, and taken control of his faculties and his will. A demon that was not content to destroy innocence and trust and hope, but must enter every cranny, and turn what it found there to evil.

Not only in Walter, but in myself.

For was not this the hellish parody of something that – despite myself – I had thought of? Had I not sometimes dreamed about it, even; and for a moment after I'd woken fancied I felt him beside me?

I had pitied myself for it, and cursed my own folly – but not *hated* myself, for by bearing it alone I was, in my own small way, heeding our Saviour's injunction to take up my cross and follow him. As He had died to save the world, so by my own inward death I might keep those I loved from harm.

But even this consolation was taken from me. For mixed with the horror and the pain – I cannot deny it – there was throb of pleasure too. A mockery – an inversion, like a Black Mass – of the joy I had imagined.

So it was not enough that Walter should betray me, his wife, his children, himself.

I must betray them all, too.

He gave a cry. It was not even his voice, but the desolate yelp of a beast. And then he lay there, so rigid that I thought the demon had fled, leaving him insensible or dead.

I was weeping too much to speak or shout for help, but at length I found the strength to move, and try to push him from me.

At once, without a word, he got up, and left the room.

My sense of time is awry. My sense of everything.

A moment ago Mrs. D. knocked.

'Pardon me, miss, but we were just wondering . . .?'

Wondering what?

I looked at my clock and saw that it was past eleven.

'I'm sorry, I'm not well,' I said.

'Oh, dear. Can I get you anything, miss?'

'No. Thank you.'

'Shall I call Dr. Hampson?'

'I think I'll just rest.'

'Very good.' Footsteps receding, then returning. 'Did Mr. Hartright say he was going out early, miss?'

'Not that I know of.'

'Only he didn't come down to breakfast this morning. And Davidson says he isn't in his bedroom, or in the studio.'

I have washed. And washed and washed. But I cannot look at myself in the glass.

Cannot even pray.

Later

It is after four-thirty. Mrs. D. again. Was I sure she could not bring me anything? Yes. Was there anything else? Yes – could they please telegraph my sister, to tell her we have been delayed? Very good.

A pause. Then: Mr. Hartright has still not returned. Did I think he would be requiring dinner? I could not say.

I hope not.

Let him go hungry. Let him know he can never enter this house again. Let him understand that what he did has put him for ever beyond the protection of society, the comfort of home, the love of family, the respect of friends.

Let him suffer.

Later still

Just midnight. He is still not back.

I feel as if I have just passed two sleepless nights without an intervening day. And now am beginning yet another.

Each has its own mood. The first: horror. The second: rage. The third:

What?

I am standing at the edge of a great ocean, that stretches as far as the eye I can see. If I lived for a thousand years, I should not be able to pass to the other side.

Sadness.

Is he out there somewhere, cold and wretched and at his wits' end? Aghast at what he has done, and utterly at a loss to know what he should do now?

Is he dead, even?

Six hours ago I should have been happy enough to think so. Six hours ago I should have been glad to kill him myself, had I had the means to do so.

To know that he had been punished. That I should never have the anguish of seeing him or talking to him again. That *my* power, in the end, had turned out to be greater than his.

But now I cannot help remembering him, not as he was last night, but as the Walter I knew before. Or rather, the many Walters – for over the past ten years he has been to me teacher, friend, confidant, colleague and brother. And in every one of those characters I would have trusted him – more completely than any man I have ever met – with my honour and my life.

What drove him then to act as he did?

Am I in some part to blame?

Sunday

I can scarce hold the pen.

I have never known such fury or such shame.

He did not return during the night. At nine o'clock this

444

morning I forced myself down to his studio, thinking he might have let himself in by the garden gate and gone there rather than to the house.

But he hadn't. The air was cold and stale. The great murky picture was still on its easel, and looked no more finished than before. When I touched it the paint was not quite dry, but a skin had started to form on the surface.

It was as I turned away from it that my foot struck something heavy beneath the painting table. I could not tell what it was, for it was hidden behind the old sheet Walter uses as a cover. I bent down and lifted the cloth.

There, jammed against the leg, was a small locked deed-box.

I drew it out. It was shiny and unblemished, and so light that at first I thought it was empty. Perhaps Walter had only just bought it, and not had a chance to use it yet. Or removed the contents, and taken them with him.

But as I set it down again, I heard something slither along the bottom, and knock against the end.

Not loose papers. Too solid for that.

A diary?

I scoured the room for a key. I opened drawers, peered into the chipped jug he uses as a brush-holder, looked under rags. Nothing.

I carried the box into the house and ordered Davidson to break it open. At first he was reluctant; but when I said, 'Mr. Hartright's life may depend on it,' he immediately went and fetched a poker, and set to with something like enthusiasm – for he is now desperately anxious about Walter, though he is at pains not to show it, and was clearly relieved to feel he might at last do something to help him. When he was done, I took it to my room, and locked the door behind me.

Inside was nothing but a plain notebook. I opened it at random. The first lines I saw were:

Others may read a journal. No-one must read this.

I felt a small bitter shudder of revenge.

I told myself I should try to be dispassionate, like a doctor examining a patient, with but one end in view: to diagnose the disease that had changed him so dreadfully.

But I could not do it. I would master myself for a few pages, and then come upon something that suddenly swept away my puny defences, and made me weep and tremble. When I reached his account of what happened after my reticule was stolen, I was sick in the wash-bowl.

I still cannot bring myself to set down the details of what I read.

But I think I can now at least partially understand why he acted as he did.

~~And I know I must accept some responsibil~~

When I had finished I went down again to the studio. I found the scalpel he uses to sharpen pencils, and stood before that vile picture, and slashed it until it was no more than a tangle of stained threads.

Then I steeled myself, and wrote to Laura:

Walter is not well.

Must remain in London for the time being.

Return as soon as it is safe to do so.

My poor sister.

Later

After an early luncheon (no more than a plate of soup and some bread; but enough to fortify me, and to persuade Mrs. Davidson that I was strong enough to go out) I returned to my room, and put on a mourning dress. My greatest horror was of people brushing against me, for my skin felt so sensitive that I feared even the slightest contact would make me sick. Wearing black, I thought, would protect me, since people shrink instinctively from grief; and if without warning I suddenly started to weep – as I have done often over the last two days – the veil would both account for, and partially conceal, my tears. I waited on the landing until I heard the Davidsons going into the kitchen (for to explain my appearance to them in the present circumstances would have been quite beyond my power) and then crept downstairs and out into the street.

I had no definite plan: only the certainty that to take action of some kind – however fruitless it might turn out to be – would be preferable to staying passively in my room, with nothing but Walter's notebook and my own tortured reflections to occupy me. I had thought of walking through the park, and hoping some inspiration would strike me; but as soon as I stepped outside I realized that it was too cold, and too slippery underfoot. I went only as far as the end of the road, therefore (where I knew I should not be visible from the house), and looked about me for a cab.

But there was not a cab to be seen. Or, rather, there were hundreds to be *seen*, but none to be *had*; for they were all taken. I watched them pass in an almost unbroken stream: men going about their business; mothers returning from the shops with presents for their children; servants sent out at the last minute to get a bottle of sherry or some more glasses or another side of beef for tomorrow.

All that purpose. All those places to go. What should mine be?

I pondered the question for perhaps a quarter of an hour as I stood there, stamping my feet and rubbing my hands together inside my muff. I had almost given up all hope of finding either a destination or a vehicle to get me there when a hansom drew up on the other side of the street and a woman laden with parcels got out. And all at once I seemed to have the answer.

I struggled across the road and called to the cabman:

'Are you free?'

He nodded. 'Where to, miss?'

'Fitzroy Square. And then to wherever I tell you.'

He looked at me curiously for a moment, and then nodded again.

'Long as you got the money,' he said, with the off-handed assurance of a man who knew he could find another customer more easily than I could find another cab. 'Get in.'

I had, of course, no intention of calling on Elizabeth Eastlake. Wherever else Walter was, he would not be with her. And in my present state she would succeed in prising my secrets from me in ten minutes, whereas I had no prospect of learning *her* secrets at all.

But 7 Fitzroy Square was where this quest began, and I felt a sudden urge to see it again – to see again *all* the places to which the search for Turner had taken us. Partly, I think (though I was barely conscious of it) because of a primitive belief in coincidence, which made me suppose I was more likely to find him again where I had seen him before – as a child will seek his dead mother in the rooms and haunts he associates with her in life. But partly also because, after being trapped for so long in the confusion of my own inner world, I felt that seeing the *outer* world again – the solid, incontrovertible world of stones and bricks, of streets and crowds – would help to clarify my mind, and perhaps offer me a clue to Walter's own thinking, and to his probable whereabouts now. And I think – I hope – I was right.

The last few days have made me a stranger to myself. Before, when setting out to revisit some familiar place, I have generally known what response it was likely to evoke in my breast – elation or gloom, relief or regret. Now, though the register of my emotions is pitifully shrunk, I can no longer predict with any certainty which part of it will be touched. I had supposed that seeing 7 Fitzroy Square again would make me anxious, or depressed, or even weaken my resolve, and tempt me to confide in Elizabeth Eastlake after all; but I had not imagined it would make me angry.

Everything – the imperious windows; the well-swept steps; the wide front door – looked exactly the same, as if it were altogether too grand and self-satisfied even to notice the cataclysm that had struck me in the two weeks since I had seen it last. And I was scandalized by it. I wanted to break the glass – splinter the wood – mar the perfect paint-work.

But I did not get out. After glowering at it for a few moments, with something like hatred in my heart, I told the driver to take me to Queen Anne Street. Turner's house was still there, though (unlike the Eastlakes') it seemed to have borne its share of the world's suffering. It looked careworn and dilapidated, and the windows were covered with a fine dust, which gave them the dull opacity of a blind man's eyes. I wondered whether the gallery still stood behind it – the gallery where Calcott and Beaumont and Caro Bibby had once marvelled and debated. I could not help picturing them there; and thinking how those passionate lives, which but forty years ago had burned so hotly, and felt the causes they espoused so fiercely, were already cold and forgotten – as if a man is of no greater moment than a match, that gives a second's brilliance, and is spent. Somehow, *their* stories, and Turner's story, and our story, worked themselves together into a kind of melancholy thread, and I began to fol-low it, like Theseus – though with no thought or hope of slaying the monster when I reached the end.

I followed it across the sluggish tide of traffic in Oxford Street; and down New Bond Street, where the brightly lit shops were decked with sprigs of holly and ivy, and seemed to taunt me with their promise of innocence and merriment. I followed it into Piccadilly, where I saw the Marston

449

Rooms, and thought for a moment of the woman Walter had met there, and of how even now she must be dressing, and putting on her musk in preparation for her night's work; and then down St. James's and into Pall Mall, and so past Marlborough House, where we had first glimpsed the unimaginable beauty of Turner's work, and its dreadful power.

I followed it into Trafalgar Square, where it wound into the National Gallery and the Royal Academy, and became more complex yet – twisting into itself the machinations of Sir Charles, and the furious martyrdom of Ruskin, and the despair of Haste; and so by a natural progression to Haste's house in Cawley Street, where I stopped the cab. The lower windows were all boarded up, and it struck me with a jolt (the force of my own feelings again took me by surprise; for the thought of it made me cry) that Haste's son must have finally lost his long battle against the bailiffs. But then I glanced up, and saw a defiant glimmer from the attic casement, and felt suddenly quite unreasonably cheered.

I descended from the cab, and gazed up at the tiny flickering light (no gas here; not even a lamp; only a candle) as a storm-lashed sailor must gaze at a distant beacon. Here was a man who had been robbed of almost everything that most people consider essential to human existence, and yet who still had the spirit to fight on. For a moment I wanted to rush inside and join him. Since our last encounter, life had reduced me almost to his level – or beneath it, even, since no-one, at least, had deprived him of his honour; and now, I suddenly thought, we might make common cause. Leading a life of monastic simplicity – labouring together in some great enterprise – might not *that* become my cross, and restore to me my self-regard?

The cabman must have heard my sobs, and observed my efforts to stem my tears.

'Something the matter, miss?' he said.

I shook my head, and turned to climb back into the hansom.

'Take me to Twickenham,' I managed to say.

He stared at me. I took out my purse and shook it like a rattle.

'That weren't what I were thinking, miss,' he said finally; and resumed his place.

And so we followed the thread again: edging our way along the north side of the park – only a stone's throw from the house where Mr. Kingsett had insulted me, and was doubtless still torturing his wife – and into Hammersmith, where Turner had once lived, and where the roads were now clogged with people trudging home to their one holiday of the year, and knots of excited children stood before the brilliantly lit fruiterers, gawping at their displays of oranges and apples and bowls of gold and silver fish, spilling out on to the pavement. And thence through Chiswick to Brentford, and past Amelia Bennett's house (it was quite dark, which startled me, until I remembered that her husband's health required them to spend the winters by the sea); and at length to Twickenham.

I told the driver to stop before Sandycombe Lodge. I looked at the dolls'-house door, and the dolls'-house windows – one of them bright with gaslight; and the plain white dolls'-house walls, and the dark bushes pressing upon them from every side. And I thought of what I could not see: the basement where Walter's madness had begun; its barred window, which had recalled to me *The Bay of Baiae*, and led me (I still believe) to the recesses of Turner's mind; and my stumbling discovery of my own love.

The pain of it took everything from me: speech, tears, movement. And yet as I sat there paralysed, I realized there was worse still to be faced, if I were to follow the trail all the way to the Minotaur. Like a child that can put its finger anywhere but the place that truly hurts, I had gone round the problem without touching its heart.

And in that moment I thought I knew where I should find Walter.

We came back along the river and through Chelsea – past Mrs. Booth's cottage (dear God! had I really supposed that Walter was too delicate to be told of Turner's life there?) and so home. As I paid him, the cabman nodded towards my mourning dress and said:

'I couldn't help noticing, miss. I'm sorry. I lost my own girl a few month back.'

On a sudden impulse, I said:

'Are you working tomorrow?'

He shook his head.

'Got to 'ave dinner, miss, with the missus and the young 'uns. I promised 'em that.'

'Of course,' I said. 'But after that?'

'Well,' he said uncertainly. 'I suppose I could come out for a bit.'

'Would you call for me here? As early as you are able?'

'Very good, miss.' He turned, and then looked back. 'A Merry Christmas to you.'

I managed to slip in without the Davidsons seeing me; but they must have heard me, for a few minutes later there was a knock on my door.

'Do you require anything, miss?'

'No, thank you, Mrs. Davidson.'

A pause. Then:

'Is there any news of Mr. Hartright, miss?'

Her voice was tight, choked with the anxieties she dared not put into words.

'Not yet,' I said. 'But I hope I may have some tomorrow.'

Please God I may.

Monday

I have a photograph of him, taken a year ago. From the openness of the expression, you'd suppose it was a different man. But the features are still recognizable.

I wrapped it in a shawl, to take with me. Then, while I waited, I looked through yesterday's *Times*. Two bodies found in the river. I raced through the descriptions: a pregnant woman, and an old man dressed as a seaman. A relief, of course. And yet I could not help feeling something akin to disappointment, too. Death is at least final. It spares you the need to trouble yourself further.

At last, at four, there was a knock at the door. I went outside. It was already dark, and a heavy fog was hanging in the street. The driver peered at me in the lamplight, and grinned.

"Ow do, miss,' he said, in a mock-pompous voice, touching his cap. 'Compliments of the season.'

I could not laugh. I could not even smile. 'Was it a good dinner?' I said.

He nodded and patted his stomach. 'Very satisfactory, thank you.' He gave a burlesque bow, and gestured towards the cab. 'Where to now, miss?'

I could smell the beer on his breath.

'Maiden Lane.'

The pawnbroker's shop was closed, but a tired-looking woman was just going in by the side-door. I called to her, and showed her the picture.

'Have you seen this man?'

She narrowed her eyes. After a moment she nodded.

'Yesterday. Early. I think it was the same feller. I remembers 'im, on account of 'im bein' so, well, queer.'

'Why, what did he do?'

'I don't mean 'is manner. 'E were a gentleman, there's no denyin' that. But that's what's so funny about it. 'E says: "I

453

wants a new suit o' clothes, cheap as you got." An' 'e takes a worn velveteen tog, and an old shirt, and a pair of kerseymere kicksies.'

'Perhaps he had no money?'

'I don't think that's it. You should 'a' seen the stuff 'e was wearin' when 'e come in. *Very* serious. Must 'a' cost' – she shook her head – 'I don't know what.'

'Did he leave it here?' I said.

She nodded.

'A shilling if you'll show it to me.'

She unlocked the door.

There was no question. Walter's hat. Walter's suit. Walter's shirt, with one of the buttons missing where he had torn it off in his frenzy.

I paid her, and turned back to the cabman.

'New Gravel Lane, Wapping,' I said.

It was a relentless journey, taking us by slow degrees from the power and splendour of the Strand to a world of such abject squalor and despair that even Maiden Lane seemed prosperous and hopeful beside it.

And with every yard I became more convinced that it was the journey Walter had taken.

For what he had done to me was an act of despair.

As we made our way down Fleet Street and Cannon Street and Eastcheap, and past the Tower, and into the teeming rat-cage beyond, I could hear his voice in my head:

That is where I thought I had met my fate.

Nothing will do but to go back there, and meet my fate again, and abandon myself to it.

I should find him there, I knew that now.

But whether living or dead, I could not guess.

After perhaps forty minutes we suddenly stopped. I looked out of the window, but could see nothing but fog and the blur of distant lights.

'Where are we?' I said.

'Ratcliffe 'Ighway. The New Gravel's just over there.' He cleared his hoarse throat. 'What is it you want there, miss?'

'I'm looking for my brother.'

He whistled softly. ''E must've done something bad.'

'Yes,' I said, getting out. 'Find somewhere you can rest the horse, and have some refreshment yourself.' I gave him a sovereign, thinking that if some accident befell me I might not have another chance to pay him. 'And meet me here again in an hour.'

'You can't go there alone, miss!' he protested.

But he took the money anyway. And when he called after me, it was not to urge me to think again, or to offer his assistance, but merely to say:

'Thank you, miss!'

What had I imagined?

Murky, ill-lit streets, half deserted. For today, of all days, surely, anyone who had a family and a home must have returned to them, leaving none but the wretched dregs among whom I thought to discover Walter.

But the desolation I found was of another sort. The people of New Gravel Lane were wretched indeed – but rather than shrinking into the shadows to suffer their misery in isolation, they seemed to have gathered in a great throng to proclaim it in public. I could hear their hubbub even before I could clearly see them: shouts and cries; snatches of song; the squeals of a tormented cat; a bullish roar that erupted suddenly out of the mist and then subsided in uneasy laughter. The beer-houses and taverns were open, and a constant stream of drunken men and women spilled out of them, and staggered bellicosely into the jeering crowd, as loudly and heedlessly as if this were just another raucous Saturday night. Save that some of the shops were closed, in fact, and that the merrymaking had a kind of heightened, feverish, desperate edge to it, there was nothing to suggest that it was Christmas Day at all.

Perhaps this is how they keep Christmas in Hell.

I had feared that I should be conspicuous; but no-one paid me the slightest heed as I entered the press. My first difficulty, indeed, I soon saw, would be to attract anyone's attention for long enough to ask a question; for everyone seemed entirely occupied with bawling and singing and swaggering his own way to ruin. A dizzying procession of faces – sunken and bloated, pale and drink-reddened, scabbed and scarred – propelled themselves towards me out of the fog, and were gone again in an instant. Even had I succeeded in stopping one of them for a moment, the swell of people would have parted us before I had had time to explain my purpose.

At length, I saw a dim forest of masts and spars looming through the mist, and realized I must be nearing the river. The crowd here was slightly less dense, and I saw a knot of capless and bonnetless women talking together at the mouth of the Thames tunnel, like crows waiting for carrion. One of them turned and looked idly towards me as I approached. I raised a hand to detain her.

'I am looking for a man,' I said.

'Ain't we all of us, darlin'?' she said.

The others laughed, and I felt myself blushing behind my veil.

'Here is a picture of him,' I said, unwrapping the photograph.

The woman took it, tilted it to catch the light from the street-lamp, and let out a long whistling sigh.

'I'd be lookin' for 'im, if I 'ad one like that,' she said. She smiled ruefully – and seemed in that moment to age twenty years, for I suddenly saw that she had no teeth.

'Let's cool 'im, Lizzie,' said one of her companions, moving to her side. She stared at the photograph for a moment, and then glanced oddly at me.

'You sure you lost 'im 'ere?'

'Yes.'

'Well, I ain't seed 'im. I'd 'a' remembered if I 'ad.'

The others gathered round, and the picture was slowly passed from hand to hand. Most of the women merely shook their heads; but one – a squat, dark-haired sloven in a torn dress – held on to it for so long, and looked at it so intently, that Lizzie at last burst out:

'What is it, Lu? 'E the one promised to marry yer?'

Lu! Was not that the name . . .?

'*Which* one?' cried one of the others: and they all laughed.

But Lu continued staring at the photograph, and I at her. She *might* have been the woman in the hood, I thought; but the light was so poor, and my mind had suppressed the details of Walter's description so successfully, that I could not be even reasonably sure. I craned forward, trying to make out her features.

'Watch out, Lu, she'll 'ave yer ears off!' Lizzie called out, half jokingly. For a moment I was puzzled; and then – with a shock that made me giddy – I understood: she supposed that I saw Lu as a rival, and was about to fling myself on her in a jealous rage. I tried to dismiss the idea as entirely ludicrous, and found to my horror that I could not do so – for the last few months have broken down the impenetrable wall that I had always supposed separated me from such women. Of course, my relations with Walter were of a different order; and yet had we not both known him in the same bestial, illicit way? And did that not intimately connect us, and give us – at the basest level – a similar claim upon him?

'Give it back, please,' I said coldly, holding out my hand with as much authority as I could muster.

But she glared at me instead, and folded the picture to her breast.

'Come on, Lu,' said Lizzie. 'Give it 'er. She ain't got nothing else.'

Lu still made no response; but at that moment fate intervened, for there was a sudden cry of 'Stop! Thief!' and a second later a boy burst in among us, darting between boots and skirts as he looked frantically over his shoulder. I glimpsed a mat of dirty hair – a pinched face, entirely white save for a great purple sore on one cheek – and then a pair of worn soles as he disappeared into the tunnel.

Lizzie took advantage of the commotion to snatch the picture and thrust it into my hands.

'There you are, darlin',' she muttered hurriedly. 'Off you go, smartish. And good luck to you.'

I did not hesitate, but set off immediately back the way I had come. Behind me, I heard Lu swearing and protesting; but before she could give chase a Jew in a black coat sped past in pursuit of the boy, scattering the women again like startled chickens, and allowing me to make my escape.

I have only vague and disconnected recollections of my adventures during the next half an hour. A black sailor in a fur cap who shook his head sorrowfully as he looked at the picture, and said: 'I have no money' – as if he had supposed I was trying to sell it to him, and would have liked to buy it if he could. Three tars who refused to looked at it at all, and jostled me aside, with oaths and yelps of derision. A little girl, who said she was sure her aunt knew the gentleman; and then led me to a bare room above a shoe-shop, where the air was thick with some sickly sweetness, and a lascar dozed on the floor, and a woman rocked back and forth on her heels, so stupefied that she could not focus her eyes on the photograph, or answer my questions.

At length I was forced to admit that I was wasting my time, and found my way back to Ratcliffe Highway. Whether I had been gone more or less than an hour I could not say; but the cab was waiting. The driver was squinting anxiously into the fog, and seemed relieved when he saw me.

'Well?' he said.

'No.'

'But you ain't 'urt or nothin'?'

I shook my head.

'Where now, then? 'Ome again, 'ome again?'

'No. The nearest police station.'

Of course, I had thought of it before – indeed, it had been almost my *first* thought – but I had been deterred by fear. What if I should walk in, and see a bill proclaiming the discovery of a body that could only be Walter's? What if some gruff sergeant took one look at the photograph and said: 'Oh, yes, miss! We brought *him* in not an hour since. But he don't look like that no more. Twenty-four hours in the river changes a man wonderful.' To learn it there, in the bright lights of a public place, and under the indifferent gaze of a tired official!

But now I saw I had no choice. I *must* know, one way or the other.

I *must* know. As I write those words, I am struck by the irony – for did not Walter use them too, when speaking of *his* predicament? But at the time I was too exhausted and upset even to remark it.

We drove back along the north side of the dock, and then turned south and east again. The streets seemed emptier here, and I could see little beyond the fog until we drew up before the brilliant lamp of the police station. I got out, and opened the wicket gate.

The entrance was lined with the descriptions of people lost and corpses found, but I decided not to torture myself by reading them. Instead, I went straight into the office – a plain, white-walled room that seemed almost impossibly bright and warm after the freezing gloom outside.

Before the desk stood a constable, and two figures I recognized immediately: the boy with the sore on his face, who was cowering and trembling with fear, and his black-coated pursuer. Behind it sat the Night Inspector: a lean, balding man with ginger whiskers, who was writing in a ledger. He looked up as I approached, and said wearily:

'Yes, miss?'

'I am looking for my brother.'

He nodded. From somewhere to my right I heard a soft cough and the creak of a chair. I turned slightly, and out of the corner of my eye saw another man, whom I had not observed before. He was thickset, with a high domed forehead and a fringe of spiky dark hair about each ear. From his neat, sober dress and the open notebook on his knee, you might have supposed him to be a successful lawyer. But he did not seem to be connected with the boy or his accuser; and, indeed, it was difficult to believe that either of them would have been able to command the services of such a man. He watched with a kind of detached curiosity as I set down the picture on the counter – although it was too far away and too high up for him to see it from where he was sitting.

The Night Inspector drew the photograph towards him without a word, and stared at it for so long that I felt certain he must recognize it, and was thinking how best to tell me the dreadful news. But at length he shook his head, and slid it back to me.

I had begun to wrap it again when the young thief suddenly blurted out:

'I knows 'im!' He tried to lunge towards me, but the constable grabbed his shoulder and gave him a cuff that made him squawk with pain.

'What?' I said.

'I knows 'im,' snivelled the boy, between sobs. 'I seed 'im!'

'Where!?'

'I can show yer!'

The constable caught hold of his ear and shook it. The boy squirmed and howled:

'Leave off! Leave off!'

'Please . . .' I laid a hand on the man's arm.

He shook his head, with the worn look of a man tired of having to explain the wicked ways of the world to innocents like me. 'It's just a dodge, miss.'

'It ain't, it ain't!' shrieked the boy. 'I seed 'im! 'E's stalled where I dossed last night! 'E scared me!'

'And where is that?' said a deep, soothing voice. The legal-looking gentleman had got up without my noticing it, and was now standing at my elbow.

'Tench Street crib,' said the boy.

The gentleman nodded, and turned to me. 'My name is Mayhew, madam. And I shall be happy to show you the way.' And with a small bow, first to the Night Inspector, and then to the boy, he ushered me towards the door.

We barely spoke in the cab. My companion – though I sensed he was curious about me, and would have liked to hear my story – was too delicate to question me; and I was too dazed, and too troubled by my own thoughts and feelings, to say anything at all. I dreaded discovering that the boy was wrong; and yet doubted whether I had the strength and energy to do what must be done if he was right – for if Walter *was* there, how should I act towards him? Could I marshal enough civility even to get him away from the place, and take him to where he could be safely delivered into other hands?

After about ten minutes we turned into a dark winding street and stopped at the entrance to a narrow court.

I remember walking through it, and out into an open yard cluttered with barrows and costermongers' carts. I remember entering a huge, smoky kitchen, with soot-blackened beams, and a rude iron gas-jet in the ceiling, and haggard men lolling

461

about on the benches and tables that ran around the walls. I remember one of them crying out: "'Ere's Mr. May'ew, gents!' and a handful of the others breaking into a desultory cheer; and my companion smiling, as if this was no more than his due, and whispering in my ear:

'I provided their Christmas dinner.'

I remember him speaking to the man who had greeted him. I remember the man nodding, and picking up a lamp, and giving it to me; and Mr. Mayhew murmuring, 'Go on!' and urging me on with a wave of his hand, as if he knew this were a quest I must undertake alone.

I remember a barn-like room lined – no, packed – *crammed* – with sleeping-stalls. I remember thinking: *This is what the inside of a slave-ship must have looked like.* I remember peering into the first three or four, and wondering if even a slave-ship could have afforded such images of want.

And then I remember nothing but Walter.

He was lying on his back on a leather cover. In the two days since I had seen him last he seemed to have shrunk, and beneath his unshaven beard his face was as white as parchment. His eyes were open, but he gave no sign of recognizing me. For a moment I feared he was dead; and then I saw him blink.

'Walter?' I said.

He made no response. I moved towards him. As I did so I felt a hand close on my wrist, and heard a voice say:

'Leave it!'

I turned back. A small man with copper-coloured hair and a face marred by giant freckles was leaning out of the neighbouring booth.

'Leave it,' he said again. His nose was running, and he wiped it with the back of his hand. "'E may want it later.'

I looked back at Walter, and noticed a tin plate lying next to him on the bed. All I could see on it were an uneaten potato and a slab of grey that might have been beef.

'Do you mean the food?' I said.

He nodded.

'I won't touch it,' I said. 'I've come to take him home.'

The man nodded again. "E'll die else.'

'How long has he been in this place?' I said.

'Since yesterday,' said the man. 'But 'e won't eat nothing.'

'And how did he come here?'

'I brung 'im. I sees 'im on the bridge, just starin' down at the river. And – I'll be honest with yer – 'e's looking so lost I thinks: *There's an easy one. Why don't you do 'is pocket?* So I'm tryin' to flare' 'is purse, but I can't find it, and while I'm pokin' and pattin' 'e notices me. But stead of shoutin' at me, or tryin' to stop me, 'e just looks at me. There's a namesclop the other side, 'e could 'ave 'ad me just like that, but 'e don't do nothin'.

'So I thinks: *'E must be pretty bad.* And I says to 'im: "You ain't thinkin' o' doin' it, are you? Not – *doin' away* with yourself?"

'But still 'e don't say nothin'. So I says: "You didn't ought to do it, mate. You come with me, and I'll give you twopence for a ticket, and things'll look brighter in the mornin', you see if they don't." And 'e come along as meek as a lamb, as though 'e didn't care whether 'e lived or died.'

He paused, and wiped his nose again; and then, with an almost tender glance at Walter, said:

'And I don't think you do much, do you, mate?'

'Thank you,' I said.

I took Walter's hand, and pulled him up. He was quite unresisting, and did nothing either to assist us or impede us as the pickpocket and I helped him to his feet, and led him towards the kitchen.

I do not recall seeing Mr. Mayhew again on our way out. I do not recall seeing anyone, in fact, until we emerged from the court, and found the driver standing by his cab, stamping his feet and smacking his gloved hands against the cold.

He made no comment when he saw us, but touched his cap, and said 'Good evening, sir', as we helped Walter inside – as if it was the most natural thing in the world for my brother to sleep in a Wapping lodging-house, and he had known all along that this was where we should find him.

On the way home, I at last found the words to say:

'You are ill, Walter. I am going to arrange for you to go somewhere where you will get better. After that, we will return to Limmeridge, and resume our lives. You may talk to me of what happened between us if you will, but neither you nor I will ever mention it to Laura or to any other living soul, and it will never happen again.'

He merely slumped in his seat, and gazed listlessly out of the window. Only when we were almost home did he turn towards me, and – shrinking into his corner, as if to prove he did not mean to touch me – whispered:

'I'm sorry. I'm sorry. You were right. Vacancy.'

'What do you mean? What have I ever said of *vacancy*?'

'My emptiness.'

Fearing he might be delirious, I affected not to hear, and said nothing.

Postscript

From the journal of Marian Halcombe, 15th July,186–

A year to the day since Walter came back to us. The doctors warned us that progress would be slow, and so it has been – agonizingly slow. But week by week he *is* growing stronger – and so, I think, am I. He walks with greater purpose. The children no longer shrink from him in fear. Indeed, he has even begun to play with them again – though with a kind of solemn watchfulness, as if he has forgotten how it is done, and must learn all over again by observing them. And when, a few days since, we entered the nursery, and young Amy suddenly chortled at him, and pointed, and – for the first time – cried 'Papa!', he almost smiled.

As for Laura: she must wonder constantly at the dreadful change in him, and yet I have never heard her complain of it, or ask me its cause. Perhaps she is afraid to do so; or perhaps it is simply her nature to accept things as they are. I fear she is often still hurt and baffled; and yet several times over the last month or so I have also seen her flush with delight, as he forces himself to answer her gaze, or to accept the touch of her hand, or to compliment her with fumbling courtesy on her dress or her hair.

Life here will never be normal again – if 'normality' is how we lived before. There will always be a pain between us. But with every day that passes it feels more like a shared pain, such as soldiers may feel who have endured a battle together. And like the bass notes of a piece of music, it seems to deepen as well as darken our experience. We think and talk less of the past and of the future, and more of the present. Yesterday I found Walter on the terrace, sniffing the smell of rain on earth; and when he saw I smelt it too, and rejoiced in it, we both found – strange the invisible threads that run between us, and the messages they convey! – that our eyes were full of tears.

This morning I heard from Lydia Kingsett. Her husband, it appears, is in prison, awaiting trial (she did not say for what; but how many women would have said even that?) and – for all the shame and embarrassment she must feel – she seems much happier for it. She enclosed with her letter a copy of the *Quarterly Review*, saying there was an article in it by Elizabeth Eastlake – 'which, if you have not seen it already, I think you might find of interest'. I confess I could not bring myself to read it at once, and left it unopened where it lay.

And would, doubtless, have thought no more about it – but that this afternoon, as I was on my way to the garden, I heard a strange sound from the library. *So* strange that I had to stop, and think for a moment what it was.

It was Walter. Laughing.

I opened the door. He was sitting at the table, looking at the *Quarterly*. When he saw me, he got up, and handed it to me.

At first I could not see what had caught his attention. And then I found it: a review of *The Life and Correspondence of J. M. W. Turner*, by Walter Thornbury.

I tried to read it; but it was nothing but a blur of words.

Until Walter pointed me to the last paragraph:

It is even possible that, by requesting some competent friend to draw up a modest memoir of him, and furnishing the necessary information, Turner might have saved himself from the worst of his posthumous misfortunes – that of falling victim to such a biographer as Mr. Thornbury. Perhaps the appearance of this wretched book may be the means of calling forth some writer qualified, by knowledge of the man and of his art, to investigate the truth and to tell it as it ought to be told.

Acknowledgements

I'd like to thank Diana Owen of the National Trust, for showing me parts of Petworth House normally closed to the public, and for her insights into life there in the nineteenth century; Philip and Pat Trower and Gavin and Venetia Young for their hospitality; Pat Hunt and Kate Armitage at Otley Museum for their assiduous research on my behalf; Mark Pomeroy, Archivist at the Royal Academy, for his advice; and Professor Harold Livermore for generously opening his house, Sandycombe Lodge, to visitors. I'm grateful to Dominic Power, Andrew Hilton and Peter Lord, all of whom discussed the book with me in its early stages and made helpful suggestions. And I owe a special debt to Nicholas Alfrey, of the University of Nottingham Department of Art History, who gave me the benefit not only of his immense knowledge of Turner and of his literary acumen, but also of his friendship – listening patiently as I tried to find my way through the complexities of Turner's art and life, reading various versions of the text, and making incisive – and always encouraging – comments.

I am extraordinarily lucky in having both an exceptional editor, Jon Riley, who guided me with his usual flawless judgement and attention to detail through the writing and revision process, and an outstanding agent, Derek Johns, without whose perspicacity and unflagging encouragement *The Dark Clue* would never have been conceived, let alone written.

I also want to acknowledge the help of my family, who all, in different ways, made an enormous contribution to the book – Paula by her inspiration and support; Tom, by taking an informed interest that went far beyond the call of duty; Kit, by gamely tolerating my eccentric hours and preoccupations; and my mother, by putting at my disposal her enclolpaedic knowledge of social history, and working indefatigably as a researcher (so saving me at least six month's work), critic and morale-booster.

And finally, of course – my thanks to Wilkie Collins and J. M. W. Turner.

A note on sources

This is, of course, a novel, not a work of non-fiction, and I do not intend to list all the many books I turned to in writing it. In view of the subject matter, however, I think I should point out that there have been (as far as I know) seven major biographies of Turner. I used of all of them to some extent, but am particularly indebted to the first, Walter Thornbury's much reviled but hugely entertaining (and often, I think, very perceptive) *Life and Correspondence of J. M. W. Turner*; to Jack Lindsay's *J. M. W. Turner: a Critical Biography*, whose psychological and political insights I found invaluable; and to James Hamilton's *Turner: A Life*, which is illuminated by a good deal of more recent scholarship. I also drew heavily on John Gage's virtuosic and inspiring *J. M. W. Turner: a Wonderful Range of Mind*, which – although not strictly a biography – is a superb introduction to the relationship between Turner's work and the cultural and intellectual world in which he lived.